> *"Oh, God, to have a woman like this!*
> *It would be worth giving up*
> *his freedom."*

Her sobs were lessening, though she still clung to him. Reaching up, he stroked her gleaming hair. His hand slid along the smooth, soft column of her throat, then tipped her chin back until her gaze met his.

Her eyes widened and she parted her lips as if she was about to say something. Then his mouth lowered to cover hers. His mouth still pressed to hers, Garrett lifted Eden and carried her to the bed. He laid her down tenderly, his blue eyes flaming with need and desire.

"Eden, sweet Eden," he murmured, "let me take away the pain."

She flinched, but she could not deny the joyous warmth coursing through her. She wanted him, needed him, with an urgency that drove all else from her mind.

Other Bantam Books by Lynn Lowery
Ask your bookseller for the titles you have missed

MOONFLOWER

Starflower

Lynn Lowery

BANTAM BOOKS
TORONTO · NEW YORK · LONDON · SYDNEY

For Dora Hardon

STARFLOWER
A Bantam Book / January 1984

All rights reserved.

ISBN 0-553-23798-5

Published simultaneously in the United States and Canada

Bantam Books are published by Bantam Books, Inc. Its trademark,
consisting of the words "Bantam Books" and the portrayal of a
rooster, is Registered in U.S. Patent and Trademark Office and in
other countries. Marca Registrada. Bantam Books, Inc., 666 Fifth
Avenue, New York, New York 10103.

PRINTED IN THE UNITED STATES OF AMERICA

O   0 9 8 7 6 5 4 3 2 1

The starflower is a delicate member of the primrose family, found in sparsely wooded areas of North America. Its thin stem is topped by a circle of five to nine leaves, from the center of which grow two threadlike stalks, each crowned by a fragile, white, star-shaped flower with six to seven divisions.

I

THE SEEDS

1812—1835

1
August 15, 1812

Cradling her baby daughter in her arms, seventeen-year-old Leanna Halsey shifted in the saddle and looked back at the straggling line of soldiers and settlers evacuating Fort Dearborn. They were scarcely a mile from the fort now. One mile in their hundred and forty-five mile trek from the southwestern shores of Lake Michigan to the safety of Fort Wayne in Indiana Territory.

Leanna's gaze shifted to her husband, twenty-one-year-old Sergeant Ephraim Halsey, stiff and smart in the uniform of the United States Army. His mouth was set in a grim line as he maneuvered his mount near hers. Catching Leanna's eye, he softened his gaze and glanced down at their two-month-old daughter.

"Eden's sleeping?"

Leanna nodded, forcing a smile. "Although I'm sure I don't know how she can, with your army band making such noise." A shiver raced down her spine as she realized the band was playing the dead march.

"Ephraim?" she whispered urgently, "we'll be—we'll be all right, won't we?"

Ephraim looked away, attempting to hide the uncertainty in his eyes. "Yes, of course," he replied huskily. He hesitated, then asked, "You have the pistol I gave you? You remember how to use it?"

"Yes." Her voice quivered, but she squared her shoulders in a show of fearlessness.

They rode on silently, south, along the shoreline of Lake Michigan. To their right, the wind had whipped the sand into a series of dunes, forming a natural boundary between the beach and the miles of prairie stretching to the west. The soldiers and settlers continued along the beach, while their escort of five hundred Potawatomis ranged across the prairies.

Leanna glanced nervously toward the Indian escort, trying

to convince herself she had nothing to fear. In the year since she had married Ephraim and come to Fort Dearborn from New York, she had learned to accept the Potawatomis as friends.

She knew today's evacuation was being caused by the British, not the Indians. Since the United States had declared war on England two months ago, the British had been advancing against the western outposts. Fort Michilimackinac, on the straits joining Lake Huron and Lake Michigan, had already fallen. Detroit, and then Fort Dearborn, would be Britain's next target.

Yes, Leanna assured herself, the British, not the Potawatomis, were the enemy. Still, everyone knew the British had for many years wooed the Indians of the Illinois and Indiana territories with lavish gifts. Once a year, representatives of the Winnebagoes, Potawatomis, and other area tribes trekked to Canada's Fort Malden for generous supplies of blankets, broadcloth, calicoes, guns, kettles, and trinkets. If forced to choose, the Indians would surely ally themselves with the British, rather than the Americans.

Only four months ago, a party of Winnebagoes had attacked the settlers in the small community of Chicago, outside Fort Dearborn. All but two settlers had escaped the Indian fury. Those two had been murdered and scalped.

Peace had reigned since then, but the memories still haunted the whites. Leanna could not help recalling the horror of those days as she reviewed the events of the last week.

When he announced the evacuation, Captain Heald, Fort Dearborn's commanding officer, had promised the Potawatomis he would distribute all of the fort's provisions among them in return for safe passage to Fort Wayne. Two days ago, he had doled out the fort's food, blankets, broadcloths, and paints, as promised. However, instead of distributing the ammunition and whiskey, he had ordered it dumped into the Chicago River, and had thrown all reserve arms into the fort's emergency well.

Shuddering now at the Potawatomis' anger when they discovered Heald's treachery, Leanna wondered, wouldn't they feel justified in some treachery of their own?

Leanna's horse snorted, prancing impatiently, as if sensing the tension in the air. The baby, Eden, stirred and whimpered as Leanna shifted her in her arms.

The band had stopped playing now, and the sticky stillness of the August morning enveloped them.

Suddenly, the stillness was broken by the urgent cry of a soldier riding furiously back from the lead guard. "They are about to attack us!" he yelled. "Form ranks and charge!"

For a moment, Ephraim Halsey's pained eyes locked on his young wife's fearful gaze. Then, he turned his mount toward the dunes, lifting his rifle in readiness. "The pistol!" he shouted over his shoulder. "Remember what I taught you!"

Leanna's shaking hand closed around the pistol jammed into her belt as a volley of shots cracked over the sand dunes.

A grizzled old soldier fell forward on his horse, clutching his chest in agony. Another, hardly more than a boy, screamed as a bullet ripped open his shoulder.

Wincing, Leanna watched her husband spur his mount up the dunes and disappear over the ridge. Shouts and screams of horror and agony rang around her. Terrified, Eden began to shriek.

Leanna's horse stumbled, then fell to its knees with a high-pitched whinny. A wave of nausea engulfed Leanna as she realized the animal had been shot. Blood spread across its smooth chestnut coat in a thick, dark blotch.

Clutching her screaming baby, Leanna managed to jump clear just as the dying beast rolled to its side. She flattened herself in the sand, shielding Eden beneath her, as shots whizzed overhead.

With one arm pressing Eden to her bosom, the other stretched forward, holding the heavy, awkward pistol, Leanna crawled slowly toward the shelter of the dunes.

Reaching a dune, she collapsed against it, fighting back the tears of panic that filled her eyes. She shuddered convulsively at the savage yelps of the Indians, trying in vain to close her ears to them as she cooed to her frantic baby.

For several minutes, Leanna lay against the dune, wondering what to do. Her mouth felt dry and her stomach churned. Eden could not be comforted. Her tiny face was red and puckered from the exertion of screaming.

Leanna's head jerked up at a sharp cry directly above her. A soldier toppled back over the sand dune, a tomahawk imbedded in his skull. As he rolled toward the beach, he grazed Leanna's shoulder, leaving a trail of blood on her calico gown.

Recognizing him as one of Ephraim's closest friends, she looked away, choking back the hot vomit that surged up her throat. But she could not avoid seeing his eyes, wide, glazed, and vacant with the horror of death.

She whirled at a shrill series of screams behind her, and saw that a young Indian had climbed into the baggage wagon, where several young children were riding. Wildly swinging a tomahawk, he chopped them down like tender saplings.

Overwhelmed by dizziness, Leanna squeezed her eyes shut in anguish. In her mind's eye, she saw again the young soldier toppling toward her. But this time his face was Ephraim's. With a gasp of fear, she crawled to the top of the steep dune, hoping frantically to find and save her husband.

Raising her head to scan the prairie, she shuddered in terror at the hopelessness of the battle. The area was littered with the corpses of soldiers, Indians, and horses. Outnumbering the soldiers by eight to one, the Potawatomis clearly held the upper hand.

Each soldier had carried only twenty-five rounds of ammunition. Now, hardly a man was left with a shot. The Indians, too, had exhausted their ammunition. Still, those who had managed to survive the first round fought on, soldiers matching fists, swords, and bayonets to the Potawatomi tomahawks and scalping knives.

Swallowing her revulsion, Leanna forced her eyes over the scene, searching for her husband.

At last she located him, still alive, but locked in hand-to-hand combat with a Potawatomi warrior. As the Indian raised his scalping knife over Ephraim's chest, she stifled a scream and struggled to aim the pistol.

Before she could squeeze the trigger, another Potawatomi kicked the gun out of her hand and lunged at her with a bloodcurdling scream of rage.

Looking up into dark eyes glazed with hatred, Leanna pressed her baby closer to her bosom. The Indian's hand whipped out to grab her long, blonde hair, jerking back her neck ferociously. Gritting her teeth, Leanna bit back a scream as she fleetingly wondered if the Indian meant to scalp her while she was still alive.

The Potawatomi held her for a moment, his knife poised menacingly above her. Then the weapon began a slow descent. With a cry of fear, Leanna summoned all her strength and twisted in his grasp. The knife, intended for her chest, plunged into her shoulder. She stared in frozen horror as blood gushed through her dress.

Suddenly, the Indian's grasp relaxed, and he sagged slowly to the ground. Strong arms encircled Leanna's waist, hoisting her upward to the back of a horse. She turned her head to thank her savior, then stopped in horrified amazement as she realized he was another Potawatomi.

Her right arm ached from holding Eden, but she tightened her grip and lashed out with her left, pummeling the man's chest and face as she struggled to slide to the ground. Her strength was short-lived as pain burned through her shoulder and arm. The Indian's knife was still imbedded to the hilt. Blood pulsed over her shoulder, but her arm seemed powerless to reach up and pull out the knife.

Panicked, Leanna kicked at the Indian's shins. Her efforts were useless against the strong, implacable Potawatomi. She could only scream frantically for help as her captor bore her away from the battle.

Grunting in disgust, the Indian reached forward to pluck the knife from her shoulder. Leanna's relief was only momentary, as blood continued to pour from the throbbing wound.

Twisting her head, she stared at the grotesquely painted face of her captor. A shock of recognition traveled through her. She had seen this middle-aged chief many times at Fort Dearborn, and had always considered him a friend of the whites.

"Black Eagle!" she gasped.

Smiling, the Potawatomi nodded. "Yes, Black Eagle. Black Eagle will not hurt you."

"Then why did you capture me?"

He frowned. "Pee-so-tum would have killed you. Not good to kill women and children. Black Eagle save you."

Wincing at his matter-of-fact talk of killing, Leanna struggled to keep her voice calm. "Yes. You're very kind. I must thank you." Encouraged by Black Eagle's half smile, she asked, "Where are you taking us?"

"To home of Black Eagle. You be safe there."

"But my husband—"

Black Eagle's brow wrinkled. "No more talk now," he insisted gruffly. "Take care of baby."

Obediently, Leanna turned her attention back to Eden, whose sobs had now quieted to an exhausted whimper. Rocking and cooing to the baby helped divert her mind from her own pain and fears. By the time they reached the Potawatomi encampment on the south branch of the Chicago River, a few miles west of the fort, both Leanna and Eden appeared calm.

Dismounting, Black Eagle swung Leanna to the ground and pulled her toward a wigwam. Weak with pain and the loss of blood, Leanna stumbled. She would have fallen if Black Eagle had not caught her around the waist.

Uncomfortably aware of someone staring at her, Leanna looked up to the dark scowl of a squaw standing nearby. With a curt command, Black Eagle waved the woman away. He lifted the flap of the wigwam and pushed Leanna inside.

After the brightness of the August day, Leanna's eyes could not adjust to the dim inner light. She stumbled again, now too weak and wracked with pain to recover her balance. Black Eagle eased her to a woven rush pallet.

"You rest now," he said. "I get squaw to fix shoulder."

Nodding through her fog of pain, Leanna lay back. Carefully, she laid Eden down beside her, relaxing her hold on the baby for the first time since the ordeal began.

As Black Eagle left the wigwam, she wondered dimly if she ought to try to escape. Black Eagle had promised not to hurt her, but dare she trust him? Dare she trust the squaw, who had scowled at her so jealously? Or the other Indians of the encampment, committed to war against the whites?

Pulling Eden back into her arms, Leanna struggled to her knees and began to crawl toward the wigwam flap. The pain was a blinding red haze now, coursing through her body, searing and stabbing.

Leanna was only a foot from the flap when she collapsed, pinning her screaming baby beneath her.

Leanna winced as she awoke, finding it hard to draw a deep breath. Her fingers slid cautiously over her left shoulder, where her gown had been cut away and someone had bandaged her wound. She flinched as her fingers found the hole left by the scalping knife. The horror of the massacre slowly flowed back into her consciousness.

Focusing slowly in the dim light of the wigwam, she saw someone sitting a few feet from her. It was the same squaw who had scowled at her so jealously when she arrived at the camp. Turning away from the squaw's stern gaze, she raised herself on her right elbow, searching the wigwam for Eden.

The baby was gone!

Suddenly alert, Leanna sat upright. "Where is my baby?" she demanded. "What have you done with her?"

Still scowling, the squaw rose silently and left the wigwam. Leanna was about to follow when the flap was pulled open and Black Eagle stepped inside. Without the garish war paint he had worn in battle, he looked younger, gentler.

"So," he said, smiling as he sat down opposite Leanna, "you feel stronger."

"I want my baby," she said steadily. "Where is she?"

Black Eagle's smile widened. "The child is well," he replied. "No one has harmed her. But," he shrugged, "she needed milk. You could not feed her."

Leanna sighed in relief. "Thank you for your care. How long was I—unable?"

"One day."

"I want my child now," she repeated.

"Of course. Little River will bring her soon." He hesitated. "What do you call the child?"

"Eden."

He nodded. "And you?"

"Leanna."

"Lee-Anna?" Black Eagle shook his head slowly. "I do not like Lee-Anna. I shall call you Hair-of-Sunshine."

Leanna caught her breath, unnerved by his implication. "How long do you intend to keep us here?" she asked with forced calmness.

Black Eagle looked away for a moment, pursing his lips in thought. Then he reached for her hand and pulled her toward the wigwam exit. "Come, there is something I must show you."

Outside, as Leanna squinted into the midmorning brightness, Black Eagle pointed northeast, across the Chicago River.

Black billows of smoke spread above the river, as red-orange flames consumed a sprawling log structure. Leanna gasped as she realized Fort Dearborn was ablaze.

She turned her gaze to Black Eagle, who nodded with a fierce look of pride. "That is the end of white settlement on the Chi-ca-gou River," he said clearly.

Leanna's head reeled and her throat constricted with fear. "Yesterday," she choked out, "when we left the battle—what happened to those who were still fighting?"

Black Eagle shrugged. "Some killed. Some captured. A few escaped."

"My—husband?" Her voice was barely a whisper.

Silently, Black Eagle reached into the deerskin pouch he wore at his waist. Leanna gasped and swayed at the sight of his upturned palm. He held the simple gold band, engraved with her initials, that she had given Ephraim at their marriage.

Did that mean Ephraim was dead, or only captured? Was he, perhaps, a captive in this very village?

Her eyes flew to Black Eagle's, seeking confirmation for her hopes.

Slowly, the chief shook his head, his expression soft with pain. "They did not scalp him," he assured her gently. "I would not allow it."

"Oh!" Leanna's grief seemed to choke her.

Black Eagle's arm swept out to draw her firmly against his chest. With one hand he cupped her chin, tipping back her head to gaze into her glassy eyes. "Do not weep, Hair-of-Sunshine," he commanded gently. "Your man died with honor. Now, I shall be your husband. You shall be my wife!"

2
1813–1820

Four years passed before United States troops returned to rebuild Fort Dearborn. Two years later, in 1818, Illinois entered the Union as a free state. By then, Leanna Halsey had long ago given up any thought of returning to white civilization.

At first, Leanna had lain awake nights, planning ways to escape with Eden. She had heard rumors that other white captives had been turned over to the British or ransomed to white traders. She begged Black Eagle to do the same with her and Eden.

The chief gently but stubbornly refused. Though he would not force himself upon her, he hoped that in time he could wear down her resistance and make her love him. To dull her memories of Fort Dearborn, he even moved the encampment far from the original site, to a spot near the junction of the Kankakee and Des Plaines rivers.

To Leanna, Black Eagle's marriage proposal seemed out of the question. How could she marry into the tribe that had massacred her husband and friends?

Still, passing time convinced her she could not blame Black Eagle for the path chosen by his people, any more than she would have blamed Ephraim if Captain Heald had ordered an attack against the Indians.

Leanna could not help feeling grateful for Black Eagle's kindness. She knew she and Eden owed him their lives, and she could never forget that.

Almost nightly, Black Eagle came to Leanna's wigwam to talk and to play with Eden before the child went to sleep. In his eyes, Leanna could see that he wanted more than talk. But he never pressed her. He always left within an hour or so.

Then one night, when Leanna had at last ceased to think of herself as a captive, Black Eagle made no move to leave, and she did not bid him do so.

Except for the thinly veiled jealousy of Black Eagle's first wife and her children, life among the Potawatomis was pleasant. Black Eagle worshipped his Hair-of-Sunshine, and insisted she be exempt from the hard labors usually assigned Potawatomi women.

Leanna did not fell trees, plant and hoe corn, or carry heavy burdens. But she learned to weave the rush mats that made up the walls and floor of her wigwam, to dry and smoke meats and vegetables for winter consumption, and to make clothing from the skins and furs Black Eagle provided.

Most of the children of the village were left in the care of the old women, while the younger, stronger women performed their tasks. But Black Eagle, though encouraging Eden to play with other children, would entrust her only to Leanna.

In their long hours together, Leanna taught her daughter to speak both English and the language of the Potawatomi. She taught her to count in both tongues and taught her the white man's alphabet. Too young to remember another life, or the horror of the massacre, Eden grew to be a cheerful, contented child.

Still, Eden realized very early that she was different. She knew that the other children did not understand the tongue her mother preferred to speak. She was vaguely aware of the resentful way Black Eagle's squaw and older children looked at her. And she knew that her mother was the only blonde woman in the encampment, and that she was the only child with chestnut hair.

When she was seven years old, Eden demanded of her mother, "Why are we so different from everyone else in the village?"

Leanna hesitated. "Because we are not Potawatomis."

"Did we come from another tribe?"

"In a way. But we are not Indians." She hesitated again, considering her daughter's puzzled frown. "We are white people, citizens of the United States of America."

"But, if we are not Indians, why do we live here? Why don't we live with people like us?"

Leanna sighed. "A long time ago, when you were just a tiny baby, Black Eagle saved you and me from a terrible battle. He brought us here to live, and he has taken care of us ever since."

Eden's eyes widened. "Did I have a different father, before Black Eagle?"

"Yes." Leanna's voice thickened, and she looked away. "But now Black Eagle is your father."

"And that is why I am different," Eden concluded. The explanation did not totally satisfy her, but she sensed her mother had already said more than she wished, so Eden did not ask more.

Sometimes at night, Eden would lie awake, wondering about her first father. What had he looked like? Was he as handsome and brave as Black Eagle? What had become of him? Had he died in the battle her mother had mentioned?

Sometimes, when they thought she was asleep, she would hear her mother and Black Eagle whispering in soft, loving tones. If she squinted into the firelight, she could see them lying side by side, stroking one another. Their love sounds seemed to reach out and caress her, surrounding her with warmth, filling her with contentment.

That fall, Black Eagle took Eden out on the prairie and along the wooded riverbanks to see the wildflowers. They had taken a similar trip that spring, and now Eden was eager to show Black Eagle how well she remembered the names he had taught her.

They passed a pleasant afternoon until, along the riverbank, Eden stopped and frowned. For several moments, she looked around, searching for her favorite, a fragile, white, star-shaped blossom.

Smiling indulgently, Black Eagle knelt beside her. "What is wrong, little one?"

"I can't find any starflowers," she mumbled in disappointment.

He smiled again, smoothing her hair. "No, little one. You will not find any starflowers today. The starflower is a flower of spring. It blooms for a month, perhaps two, and then it is gone. Like all things, it has a season to live, and a season to die."

Eden nodded seriously, though she wondered why anything so beautiful had to die. For some reason, the mention of death made her think of her first father. Looking innocently at Black Eagle as he lifted her onto his horse's back, she asked, "Did you know my first father, Black Eagle?"

The chief scowled. "Who told you you had other father? My son, Lone Buffalo? My daughter, Prairie Flower?"

Eden shook her head. "No, Mama told me." Then, seeing Black Eagle's scowl deepen, she quickly explained, "She didn't exactly tell me. I asked her. And then, I don't think she wanted to talk about him. If you don't want to either, it doesn't matter. I just wondered."

Her voice died away wistfully, and Black Eagle's frown softened. "I did not know this man, your father," he said slowly. "Many times, I saw him, but we never spoke. I do know he was a brave man."

"Is he dead?" Eden whispered.

Black Eagle's arms tightened around her as he held her before him on his horse. "Yes, little one, he is dead."

For a long moment, Eden was silent. Snuggling closer against Black Eagle's chest, she sighed, "Mama says you saved our lives. I'm glad you are my father now, Black Eagle."

He leaned forward to kiss her brow. "I, too, am glad, little one. And now, I will tell you a secret. There is a new baby growing inside your mama's tummy. By spring, we will have a new life to share. I will have a new son or daughter, and you will have a new brother or sister. Does that please you, little one?"

"Oh, yes!" Eden's blue-green eyes danced excitedly. "Then we shall truly be a family!"

On the first day of the second moon of the New Year, Eden's mama gave birth to a frail boy who cried with a thin voice that frightened Eden.

Three days later, Leanna Halsey, Hair-of-Sunshine, was dead of childbed fever. Her baby lived only two days longer.

After Leanna's death, Black Eagle assigned his second oldest daughter, Morning Star, to care for Eden. A gentle, graceful girl of sixteen, she took Eden to a new wigwam to live.

Morning Star's eyes never held the triumphant look that Eden read in the haughty gaze of Black Eagle's first wife. She felt genuine sympathy for the little girl, rocking her and stroking her hair as Eden sobbed out her grief and loneliness night after night.

A full week passed after the tragedy before Black Eagle could bear to visit Eden again. His dark eyes were shrouded with sorrow now, and he seemed older and weaker. He would not speak of Leanna, and he refused to talk to Eden in the tongue her mother had preferred.

Often, he seemed to be in a trance. He stared at Eden, nodding or shaking his head to her questions, without really hearing her. His visits were short and infrequent, and when he left, it was always as if he were escaping something distasteful.

Suddenly, the fact that she was different, which she had once regarded with only mild curiosity, became the center of Eden's consciousness. While Leanna lived, it had not mattered that she was different, because she and Leanna had shared that bond. Now she was alone.

Black Eagle's withdrawal puzzled and upset her. She wondered sometimes if he had ceased to love her. Did he, perhaps, blame her for her mother's death?

Morning Star was kind, but she could not really love her in the way Leanna had.

Besides, all the kindness in the world could not make Eden feel anymore that she belonged among the Potawatomis.

Brett McKinnon combed a hand through his curly red hair and stretched his weary muscles as he settled himself more comfortably in his saddle. His lips curved into a smile as he reviewed the last two years. His uncle had called him a fool when he left his comfortable, boring job as a clerk in a Middlebury, Connecticut, general store.

"You'll never make a decent living among those prairie Indians," Uncle Jordan had insisted. "Within a year, at most, you'll be back here, with your tail between your legs, begging me to reinstate you."

Brett laughed aloud now, thinking how wrong his uncle had been. Joining John Jacob Astor's American Fur Company had been the best decision of his life. He loved living in the wilds of Illinois, and, at nineteen, he was well on his way to making a sizable fortune.

Two years ago, Astor, spurred by a trade war with the Hudson's Bay Company, had begun sending out expeditions to found new trading posts in the undeveloped West. Brett, as an untried youth of seventeen, had joined a group leaving Mackinac in the autumn of 1818.

It had been a grueling initiation to the fur trader's life. Like the French voyageurs who had charted the area before them, the party of one hundred men had paddled Lake Michigan in long bateaux, the rhythm of their paddles keeping time with the hearty songs they sang.

Many of the employees were, in fact, French-Canadians, descendants of the first voyageurs. Still bitter that Britain had ousted France from Canada nearly sixty years earlier, they were more than happy to work for a company that rivaled the British firm.

At first, Brett had found it hard to become accustomed to their mixed French and English banter and their custom of measuring distance by the number of pipes of tobacco they stopped to smoke in a day. But, from the beginning, he had loved the camaraderie of the traders.

At Fort Dearborn, they had paused to exchange their bateaux for packhorses, laden with calicoes, blankets, broadcloths, kettles, silver jewelry, and trinkets with which to barter for the Indians' furs. Then they had broken into smaller groups and set off across the prairies to establish new trading posts.

Brett had teamed up with John H. Kinzie, a young man with whom he had struck up an almost instant friendship at Mackinac. Although only fifteen when they met, young Kinzie already had the advantage of an excellent rapport with most of the Indian tribes in Illinois. He had grown up with as

many Indian as white friends, and was as familiar with the
Indian way of life as he was with white civilization.

In fact, young Kinzie and his family had been among the
few families spared by the Potawatomis when they massacred
the residents of Fort Dearborn. His father, John Senior, had
been an Indian trader near the fort since 1804, and his
kindness and fairness had earned him the friendship and
respect of nearly every Indian in the region. The Indians
themselves had transported the Kinzie family to the safety of
Michigan after the massacre, and had welcomed them back
four years later, when the fort was rebuilt.

Young John quickly initiated Brett into the Indian way of
life, teaching him how to win the trust and respect of the
tribes who would supply them with furs. As they traveled
west of Fort Dearborn, they stopped at several Indian
encampments, where John was always greeted enthusiastically,
and Brett was accepted as his friend.

By the time they had selected a site for their trading post,
on the Illinois River, northeast of Fort Clark, scores of prairie
Potawatomis and Kickapoos had promised to bring them their
beaver, otter, marten, mink, fox, and bear furs.

Brett and John's post was thriving within its first season.
Indian trappers from miles away, some of them with camps
closer to other trading posts, brought their prize furs to the
young traders. In the spring, when the furs from all the
outposts were shipped east to Chicago, and then north to the
company headquarters at Mackinac, their post was commended
for taking in the most furs, and those of the best quality.

That fall, the company had recalled Kinzie to Mackinac to
fill a post there. By then, the prairie Potawatomis and Kickapoos
were as fond of Brett as of John, so the Illinois River outpost
had continued to thrive.

Now, followed by the packhorse train bearing the spring
shipment, Brett was on his way east for some time off to relax
in Chicago. John had written that he would be down from
Mackinac with the shipments of goods and supplies for the
Illinois outposts, and Brett was anxious for their reunion.

He was equally anxious for the pleasures of the growing
town of Chicago, especially for the company of women. In
the last year, he had often considered forming a liaison with
some comely Indian squaw, as so many of the other traders
and voyageurs had. So far, he had resisted that temptation.

Impatient to reach Chicago as quickly as possible, Brett

had ridden ahead, leaving the pack train in charge of his team of French-Canadian engagés. He felt perfectly safe riding alone, certain that the Indians were his friends.

After almost two years, he knew the prairies almost as intimately as they. Several times in the last months he had gone on trapping expeditions with Potawatomi friends, impressing them with his speed in learning their skills.

As Brett neared the junction of the Des Plaines and Kankakee rivers, thick rain clouds turned the brisk spring day dark. By the time he was crossing the Kankakee, lightning was crackling around him, and Brett knew he would be wise to seek shelter. Recalling that the encampment of Black Eagle was only a few miles upriver, he spurred his horse through the driving rain.

Brett had not been to Black Eagle's encampment in several months, and it occurred to him now that the chief had not brought him a spring shipment of furs. Riding into the encampment, he wondered if the aging chief had died. But he quickly dismissed the thought, sure he would have heard such important news.

As Brett swung from the saddle, Lone Buffalo, Black Eagle's oldest son, ran to greet him. "Red Hair!" the youth exclaimed in his native tongue. "It is good to see you! You have not visited us in too long. Shall I take you to my father?"

Brett nodded. "He is well, I hope?"

Shrugging, Lone Buffalo led him toward a wigwam. "Yes, he is well," he replied without conviction.

Frowning, Brett stooped to enter the wigwam as Lone Buffalo held open the flap. Inside, Black Eagle was seated opposite a young girl, whom Brett judged to be less than ten years old.

Instantly, he was struck by the girl's chestnut braids and luminous blue-green eyes. Though dressed in the Indian fashion of doeskin leggings and dress, she was obviously a white child. He remembered hearing something about Black Eagle having a white wife. Was this child the product of that union?

Black Eagle looked up, his pained expression brightening as he saw Brett. "Ah, good friend! It has been too long! Sit down and speak with me."

Brett hesitated, glancing at the girl. For the first time, he noticed a striking young Indian maiden sitting to her left. "I

did not mean to interrupt," he said. "I was on my way to
Chicago when the storm waylaid me—"

"And you would have passed by your friend, Black Eagle,
without even stopping to greet me?"

"I—I was rather anxious to get there. Besides," Brett added
lightly, "I did not know if you were still my friend. You did
not come to see me at my post this spring."

Black Eagle's face clouded. "No. I could not come this
year." He turned to the Indian maiden. "This is time for men
to talk. Take the child away."

"But Black Eagle—" the little girl protested.

"Perhaps tomorrow, little one," the chief said, gently patting her head. "If the rain has stopped, perhaps we will ride
together."

"You never ride with me anymore," the child pouted.

Sighing, Black Eagle turned again to the maiden. "Take
her," he commanded softly.

As the young woman ushered the girl from the wigwam,
Brett frowned over the sad hunch of the child's shoulders and
the pitifully dejected way her chin pressed into her chest. He
could not believe she was a captive in the village, since she
obviously felt great affection for Black Eagle. Still, he sensed
that her profound sadness was caused by something deeper
than Black Eagle's curt dismissal.

Turning his eyes back to the chief, he remarked, "She's a
pretty child."

Black Eagle sighed. "Yes. Pretty. Beautiful. Always, I have
loved her. Always, she has brought me great joy. But now,
even to look at her, it hurts me here." He touched his breast
in the region of his heart.

Brett's dark eyes narrowed as he considered the statement.
Finally, he asked simply, "Why?"

For several moments, the chief did not answer. He busied
himself filling a pipe with *kinnikinnick,* the red willow bark
scrapings that many Indians preferred to tobacco. Slowly, he
lit the pipe, took several deep pulls on it, then passed it to
Brett.

As Brett puffed the pipe, Black Eagle shook his head sadly.
"When I look at her, I see always my beloved Hair-of-Sunshine.
Then, sadness eats at my spirit, so I can hardly bear to have
her near."

Brett frowned. "Hair-of-Sunshine? Your white wife?"

Black Eagle nodded, reaching for the solace of the pipe.

"Has she left you?"

"Her spirit left me this winter, when she lay in her wigwam, giving birth to my son."

Suddenly understanding why the chief had not visited him that spring, Brett closed his eyes. "I'm sorry, Black Eagle," he said.

"Yes. Sorry."

They passed the pipe between them several times in silence, before Brett asked, "The son, did he live?"

"Only for a few days."

"And the girl? She is your daughter by Hair-of-Sunshine?"

The chief shook his head. "No. She is Hair-of-Sunshine's daughter. She was a baby when I brought her mother here. No Potawatomi blood flows in her. Still, I love her like a daughter. But now—" His voice faded to a whisper. "It hurts me to see her. And it hurts to see her so sad. Once, we made each other laugh. Now we share only tears. I cannot bear to be near her when I caused her mother to die. Hair-of-Sunshine bore my child. If not for that, she would still live."

"But surely the child doesn't blame you? She seems too young even to understand."

"Yes, she is very young. Only seven winters." Black Eagle paused pensively before squaring his shoulders in resolution. "No more talk about my sorrows. Tell me, have you news of our friend, John?"

For the rest of the day, they talked of other things, but Brett could not put the child out of his mind.

The rain continued through the evening, and Black Eagle insisted that Brett spend the night. With customary Indian hospitality, the chief sent his eldest daughter, Prairie Flower, to the wigwam Brett occupied. But the young trader felt strangely unmoved by her charms and gently told her to go away.

As Prairie Flower lifted the flap to leave the wigwam, Brett called after her impulsively, "What do you know of the daughter of Hair-of-Sunshine?"

Laughing contemptuously, Prairie Flower turned back to him. "You mean the child of my father's whore? She does not belong here! Someday, she will come to the same end as her mother!"

The words upset Brett, so that he was able to sleep very little that night. What would become of the girl, he wondered, if something happened to Black Eagle? Would the maiden he had seen her with today continue to care for the child, or would she succumb to the will of the other villagers?

It was natural, of course, for Black Eagle's first family to be jealous of the affection he gave the child. It happened even when a chief took a second Indian wife. But it could not be pleasant, or even safe, for this girl. Shuddering, Brett recalled an incident in another tribe, where a chief had taken a white wife. In a jealous rage, the Indian's first squaw had attacked the woman's child with a tomahawk.

Drifting near sleep, Brett considered adopting the girl himself. He quickly dismissed the thought as impractical. He was only nineteen, unmarried, living in the prairie wilds. His work would not allow him the time to raise a child, particularly a girl. Still, there ought to be something he could do. His concern consumed him for the rest of the night.

The next morning, as he approached Black Eagle before continuing his journey, Brett thought again that the chief seemed to have aged considerably during the last winter. For a moment, he hesitated even to mention the child again, afraid of upsetting his friend. Then he thought of the dejected droop of the little girl's shoulders and the derisive statements Prairie Flower had made last night.

Black Eagle advanced to meet him, the smile on his lips unable to erase the pain from his eyes. "Already you are leaving?" the chief asked. "Our hospitality does not suit you?"

Brett smiled. "You know it does, Black Eagle. But, John is expecting me."

"Of course. You will take him my greetings?"

"Yes." Brett hesitated. "Black Eagle, I wanted to talk to you about the girl. What is her name?"

The chief's smile vanished as he answered. "Eden."

"Eden," Brett repeated. Quickly, before his nerve failed him, he blurted, "I'd like to take Eden with me to Chicago."

Black Eagle's brow creased. "You? Take her? I do not understand."

"You are not happy, and I think she is not happy. Perhaps it is time for Eden to go back to her own people."

"But her people are here! She has no Potawatomi blood, it is true, but she has lived here since she was a baby. She knows no other life."

"Perhaps it is time she did. The others in the village, do they think of her as one of them?"

His eyes clouding, Black Eagle looked away. "No," he admitted. "The others have had their minds poisoned by my first wife. They think of her always as the white child. Perhaps I, too, am to blame. Always I kept her and her mother a little apart." He paused, shaking his head as if to clear his mind. "I do not know what to say. It hurts me to see her. But it would hurt me to send her away."

"Perhaps," Brett suggested, "you ought to try to think of what is best for her."

"I know," Black Eagle mumbled. "I know. Sometimes I worry. I am becoming old. Since the death of Hair-of-Sunshine, I feel very old. What if I should die before Eden becomes a woman?" Looking up, he searched Brett's eyes. "But you, what will you do with her?"

3
April 1820–March 1821

Brett glanced warily at the girl riding beside him. She had not spoken since early morning, when they left the encampment of Black Eagle. At least her tears had finally dried, though her cheeks remained streaked, and her nose was red and raw from sniffling.

Even with her tear-streaked face, she was a pretty child, with every promise of becoming a beautiful woman. Already, she was more willowy than most seven-year-olds, and she rode her pony with an inborn grace. It was easy to imagine her as a woman, her radiant chestnut hair swept up in some sophisticated style, presiding over Chicago society.

But, for now, she was only a very obviously unhappy child. Dammit! Brett thought with an angry shake of his head. Here I am doing her a favor, and she's acting as if I'd kidnapped her! Maybe I should have left her with the Potawatomis. Why should I care about her, anyway?

A glance toward the sun told Brett it was about four

o'clock. They would reach the Kinzie homestead in time for
dinner.

Turning his eyes back to Eden, he pointed across the
prairie. "See those cabins in the distance?" he asked. "That's
Chicago. We'll be there in an hour or so."

Eden shrugged, pursing her lips as she squinted toward
the scattered, distant buildings. All day, she had struggled to
control her fears. But now, as she looked toward Chicago, so
different from the Indian encampments where she had spent
her whole life, her lower lip began to quiver. Quickly, she
closed her eyes to hide their sudden glassiness.

Brett sighed. If she started crying again, he'd be tempted
to leave her right here. "Look," he said impatiently, "you'll
like living with the Kinzies. They're good people. And they
have children you can play with."

"I liked living with Black Eagle," Eden said petulantly. "I
liked playing with his children and the other children there."

Narrowing his eyes, Brett shot her a hard, accusing glare.
"Did you really, Eden?" he demanded. "You didn't seem so
happy when I first saw you yesterday."

Lowering her eyes, she murmured, "Well, maybe I didn't
like it so much since"— she paused, swallowing nervously—
"since Mama died." For a long moment, she was silent. Then
she blurted out her fears. "What if those people in Chicago
don't want me? What then?"

"They'll want you, Eden."

"How do you know? Black Eagle didn't want me anymore!"

"Yes, he did. But, more than that, he wanted what was
best for you."

"Did he still love me?"

"Did you see the tears in his eyes when he told you
good-bye?"

Slowly, Eden nodded. "But—" She broke off as tears washed
her eyes again.

Touched, despite his impatience, Brett edged his mount
closer to hers. He lifted Eden from her pony and settled her
before him in his saddle. Awkwardly, he brushed away her
tears as he hugged her to his chest.

"Trust me, Eden," he whispered. "Everything will be all
right. Someday you'll be the queen of Chicago society."

Twilight was falling when they reached the Kinzie homestead on the north bank of the Chicago River. Compared to

the rude assortment of shacks that made up Chicago, the sprawling white house with its wide front piazza looked like a mansion. Eden, who could not remember living in anything but a wigwam, could only stare in awe.

As Brett swung from the saddle, Eleanor Kinzie, his friend John's mother, bustled from the house, wiping her hands on her apron.

"Well, it's high time you got here, Brett McKinnon!" she chided good-naturedly. "John's been beside himself, wondering when you'd arrive. He's just stepped over to the fort with his father. Ought to be back—" She broke off as Brett turned to lift Eden from his horse. "What's this, a little Indian princess?" she asked gently.

"No, Eleanor. This is Eden. A white child. But she's lived in Black Eagle's village nearly all her life. I thought, that is I hoped, you might take her in for a while."

For an instant, Eleanor's eyes narrowed speculatively. Then, touched by Eden's hurt, frightened gaze, she broke into a smile. "Well of course we will, Brett. You know our house is always open to any traveler." She bent down and stretched out a hand to the little girl. "Come along, Eden. We'll just go inside, and my daughter, Maria Indiana, can help you get ready for dinner."

Exhausted from her long day, Eden fell asleep soon after dinner, and Eleanor Kinzie carried her off to Maria Indiana's room. After clearing the table and tucking her own youngsters into bed, Eleanor returned to the dining table, where Brett, John, and her husband sat talking over whiskey.

"Eden's a sweet little child," she said quietly. "Just what do you intend to do with her, Brett?"

"I—well—I—nothing."

Eleanor's eyebrows raised questioningly. "Doesn't she have any family?"

"No. That is, not that I know of."

"So, in other words, when you asked if she could stay with us 'for a while' what you really meant was, could she live with us?"

"Well, yes, I guess I did. But I didn't want to discuss it in front of her. I'd already seen about as many tears as I could stand for one day." Quickly, he related how he had found Eden at Black Eagle's and decided to take her away.

John Senior nodded. "Black Eagle must have taken her and

her mother during the massacre. I'd heard that he had a blonde wife, but he kept her pretty well hidden. There was speculation for a time about who the woman was, but no one really knew. So many people disappeared during the massacre. And then, when Black Eagle moved his camp southwest of here, no one talked about the woman much anymore."

"Margaret might know who Eden's parents were," the younger Kinzie suggested. Margaret was his half sister, whose husband had been second in command of Fort Dearborn at the time of the massacre.

"I don't see what difference that would make," Brett said. "We already know both her parents are dead."

"But if we knew Eden's full name, we might at least be able to trace her family," Eleanor explained. "If she has anyone—grandparents, an aunt or uncle, anyone—she ought to live with them."

Brett's eyes narrowed as they flicked over the three Kinzies. Shaking his head in disbelief, he said coldly, "I'm sorry. Maybe I shouldn't have brought Eden here. I never imagined she would be so unwelcome."

Sighing heavily, Eleanor insisted, "She's not unwelcome, Brett. You know that no one is ever unwelcome in this house. But, well"—she paused, glancing at her husband before she plunged ahead—"the simple truth is it's just not as easy to make a living in Chicago as when John and I first moved here sixteen years ago. And with our own little ones—"

"Enough, Eleanor," her husband interrupted softly. "The child is here. She needs a home. That's all we need to consider."

"Of course," Eleanor agreed. "But if she does have a family somewhere, she belongs with them. I have every intention of writing to Margaret to ask about her. We owe that much to Eden, and to whatever kin she might have. But, in the meantime," she added, her voice softening as she reached across the table to pat Brett's hand, "you needn't worry about her feeling welcome. John and I and the children will give her all the love and care we can, for our whole lives, if need be."

By the time Brett rode out of Chicago five days later, he felt convinced he had been right to bring Eden. Though she had at first been shy and withdrawn, Eden could not help responding to the Kinzies' warmth. Now, she even laughed as she played with Maria Indiana and the other children beneath the giant cottonwoods.

Still, Brett had seen the sad, slightly haunted look that remained in Eden's eyes when he said good-bye to her. It would take a long time for that look to fade.

Brett knew it would not be easy for Eden to adjust to white civilization, but the Kinzies' knowledge and understanding of Indian ways would lighten the burden. Chuckling to himself, Brett remembered how uncomfortable Eden had looked in the calico dress Eleanor had insisted she wear to breakfast the first morning. How she had observed Maria Indiana from the corner of her eye, awkwardly imitating the older girl as she used Eleanor's fine silver and china.

Turning his thoughts away from the little girl, Brett reviewed his own pleasures during his stay in Chicago. It had been good to be back with John. No matter how long they were separated, he would always feel as if John Kinzie were his brother. Most nights, they had sat up for hours, long after the rest of the family had retired, sharing their adventures and reliving their first year at the post.

Several times, when Eleanor was safely asleep, they had slipped out to sample the delights of the half-breed women who lived a mile upriver. Remembering those leisurely nights, which stretched until dawn, Brett shifted uncomfortably in his saddle, willing away the sudden ache in his groin. The one drawback to his life at the trading post was the lack of female companionship.

By evening, when he was nearing the junction of the Illinois and Kankakee rivers, Brett's thoughts suddenly returned to Eden. He could hear the little girl's mumbled words as he mounted his horse that morning. "When you see Black Eagle again, tell him—tell him I still love him." Abruptly, Brett pulled on the reins and turned toward Black Eagle's camp.

Lone Buffalo met Brett as he dismounted, and immediately led him to Black Eagle's wigwam. A few yards from the wigwam, Brett stopped, aware that someone was staring at him. Turning, he recognized the Indian maiden who had cared for Eden on his last visit.

The girl flushed under Brett's questioning gaze, then hurried toward him. Eyes downcast, she murmured, "The little girl—Eden—you have word of her?"

"Yes," Brett said quietly. He waited for her dark eyes to rise to his before continuing. "Eden is well. I left her only this morning. She is living with good, kind people. They will take good care of her."

The maiden sighed in obvious relief. "That is good. I worried. She was so small. So sad. These people—they are white people?"

Brett nodded.

Again, she sighed. "That is best, I suppose. Life was not good for her here. And if my father should die—" She stopped abruptly, unnerved by Lone Buffalo's angry scowl. "Like an old woman, I talk too much," she said quickly. "Excuse me." Turning, she hurried away.

In the wigwam, Black Eagle expressed relief similar to the young maiden's. "It is good," the old chief said. "Now, I do not need to worry about her. When I go to join Hair-of-Sunshine, I can go happily, knowing that Eden is in good hands."

"Yes," Brett agreed. "I'm glad you let me take the child. It was the best thing for both of you. A few days ago, I even heard her laugh."

Black Eagle smiled in gratitude, though his eyes glistened with tears of remembrance. "A beautiful sound, her laughter. How often it filled my days. But I think that here she might never have laughed again." Nodding reflectively, he said, "Yes, it is good that you took her. Already, the pain of separation is fading because I know she is well."

Looking up at Brett, Black Eagle smiled. "You are indeed a good friend, Red Hair. And a kind man to stop in your journey to tell me that Eden fares well. Such kindness must not go unrewarded."

"I didn't come for rewards, Black Eagle," Brett said quickly. "Friendship is its own reward."

"Perhaps," Black Eagle agreed. "But you have given that little one new life. And you have lightened the burden of my final years. For that you deserve something more than friendship."

The chief paused, pursing his lips in thought. Then he nodded, smiling broadly in satisfaction. "Yes, I will give you my daughter. Then you will be not only my friend, but my son."

"Black Eagle, I can't—"

The chief's smile widened. "Do not worry. I will not saddle

you with Prairie Flower. I know she did not please you the last time you visited here." Going to the wigwam entrance, he called to Lone Buffalo, "Fetch Morning Star, at once."

As the chief settled back on his heels, Brett ran a hand frantically through his hair. "Black Eagle, you must believe me, this is a great honor. But, I don't know what to say. I don't think I really deserve—I mean, the daughter of a chief—I'm only—"

He stopped abruptly at the sound of a musical voice. "You sent for me, Father?"

Recognizing that voice, Brett looked toward the wigwam entrance. It was the girl who had spoken to him earlier. The maiden who had cared for Eden. His eyes traveled slowly down her lithe young figure, and suddenly he could think of nothing but the loneliness of another winter at the post without a woman.

It wouldn't be a marriage, exactly. Not in the same binding sense as if he married a white woman. Plenty of traders and voyageurs lived with Indian women. Some for a lifetime. Others for only a few years.

Pleased by Brett's sudden silence, Black Eagle motioned his daughter to sit. "What do you say, Red Hair?" he asked. "You will not insult me, will you, by refusing my daughter?"

Brett's groin was throbbing again, and he could not shift his eyes from Morning Star. "No, Black Eagle," he said clearly, "I will not refuse her. I will be honored to become the husband of Morning Star."

Eden paused on her way from the bakehouse behind the Kinzie home, inhaling the delightful aroma of freshly baked croissants. Her eyes scanned the garden area, searching for the first spring wildflowers. Would there be starflowers here, she wondered, like the fragile blooms she had so loved at home?

Quickly, she reminded herself that Chicago was her home now. The Kinzies were her family. After nearly a year in their care, her longing for her old life had finally begun to fade.

Still, Eden could not stifle all her memories, especially when Uncle John's Indian friends came calling. Often, she found herself wishing Black Eagle were among them. Was he well? Did he ever even think of her?

"Eden! Where are you, darling?"

Startled by Aunt Eleanor's call, Eden looked down at the

flaky rolls in her arms. If she didn't hurry, they would be cold before she reached the house, and Aunt Eleanor would surely scold her.

Breaking into a run, Eden found Aunt Eleanor waiting on the piazza, a letter in her hands.

"I'm sorry I took so long," Eden gasped. "I think they're still warm, though."

Eleanor Kinzie smiled. "That's fine, darling. Just put them on the table and then come and sit down for a moment. I have some very exciting news for you!"

Unexplainable fear washed over Eden as she followed Eleanor's directions. Unaware of the child's apprehensions, Eleanor sat down beside her.

"Eden, I have some wonderful news for you! We've found some of your family! Your grandmother and grandfather— your father's parents—are living in New York. And they are so anxious to meet you that they want you to journey there immediately!"

4
1828–1831

"Papa! Papa!"

Brett looked down at his one and one-half-year-old son, tugging at his trouser leg. Smiling, he put aside the letter he was reading and bent to pick up the boy.

"What do you want, Ben?" he asked, swinging the laughing child high above his head. "A little attention? Is that what you want?"

The baby laughed again, reaching out to grab his father's ear as Brett lowered him. Joining him in laughter, Brett gazed fondly at the boy. Like his older brother, Thomas, Benjamin looked little like Brett. Both boys had the dark hair and skin coloring of their mother, Morning Star. Only Benjamin's gray-green eyes betrayed his white blood.

Morning Star stepped into the room, carrying three-year-old Thomas. "Benjamin," she scolded lightly, "you must not bother your father!" Shifting her eyes to Brett, she mumbled, "I'm sorry. The little one slipped away from me as I was getting him and Thomas ready for bed."

Brett frowned slightly. "Sorry? Why should you be sorry my son sought me out? Do I seem annoyed?"

"Of course not," she said quickly. "It's just that you've been away so long, and I supposed you would want some privacy to read your mail—especially the letter from your friend John."

"The letter will still be here tomorrow," he replied, rising with Benjamin in his arms. "Come now, I'll help you tuck the boys in."

Much later, when Morning Star lay sleeping soundly beside him and his own physical desires had been thoroughly slaked, Brett lay awake, reviewing the scene in the parlor.

Why would Morning Star feel the need to apologize that Benjamin had come to him? Was it simply her Indian training that a wife and children must always be subservient? Or had he somehow created the impression he did not want to be bothered with the children? Or, for that matter, with Morning Star?

No. Surely she couldn't think that. It was true that he had not really been ready for marriage when Black Eagle had offered Morning Star to him. But that had been nearly eight years ago. It had taken time to adjust to having a wife, but he had never actually mistreated Morning Star.

Of course, his work took him away from home a great deal. In the last year, the American Fur Company had put him in charge of all its posts in Illinois. Lately, he seemed to spend more and more time away, visiting the Indian trappers who supplied him with furs. Sometimes in the winter, he hiked away on snowshoes for days at a time, carrying an eighty-pound pack of goods to trade with the trappers.

In the beginning, Brett had often taken Morning Star with him. But, since the boys had been born, that had not been practical. Now, the only place Morning Star went was to Black Eagle's camp, where she and the boys spent two or three months of the year.

Sighing to himself, Brett tried to convince himself he was imagining problems where they did not exist. Morning Star was a perfect wife. Gentle, eager to please, a wizard with the ducks and quail, venison and prairie chickens he supplied for her kitchen. And no one could question that she was a perfect mother. Thomas and Benjamin adored her.

Suddenly, that fact seemed to blaze in Brett's mind. Thomas and Benjamin adored her. But they didn't adore him. The thing that had touched him so about Benjamin's visit was that it was so uncharacteristic. Ben rarely approached him without Morning Star's urging, and Thomas never did.

In a way, the boys were not his sons. They were Morning Star's sons. Black Eagle's grandsons. Their blood was equal parts white and Potawatomi, but they were far more Indian than white. Already, they spoke as much Potawatomi as English, and they seemed more at ease in Black Eagle's camp than here, at the trading post. Given a choice, the older boy much preferred his Indian name, Swift Elk, to his Christian name of Thomas.

Was it possible Morning Star was deliberately alienating the boys from him, to pay him back for neglecting her in recent years? No, Morning Star was too sweet. She didn't possess an ounce of guile. Besides, he didn't really neglect her. A man simply had to devote himself to his work.

Annoyed and unable to sleep, Brett tiptoed back to the parlor to finish reading John Kinzie's letter. He scanned the opening paragraphs until he found the place he had left off reading:

> And now, for the really important news. I've finally followed your example and gotten married! I met Juliette Magill at her grandparents' in Boston last July. From the first, we seemed destined for each other. We married in August.
>
> Juliette promises to be the ideal life partner. She is well-educated and well-versed in the art of genteel homemaking. Yet, she never balked for an instant at the prospect of making her home in the wilds of Wisconsin, where the company has now stationed me. Indeed, she has laughed at privations that might have made a lesser woman faint! She is indeed remarkable, and I look forward to sharing with her the kind of bliss you have found with your Morning Star.

Brett paused, smiling wryly as he silently wished his friend a greater measure of bliss than he had found. Of course,

Morning Star was in her own way remarkable, too. At twenty-four, she was as lithe and lovely as she had been at sixteen. In fact, Brett could not find any specific fault with her. Yet he could not help feeling that, had he chosen a wife, rather than having one thrust upon him, it would not have been Morning Star.

Still, she was his wife. The mother of his children. It was pointless to consider what might have been.

Picking up the letter, he continued:

> After our wedding, we traveled by Erie Canal—a marvelous waterway!—to Buffalo, on the shores of Lake Erie. At my sister, Maria Indiana's, urging, we stopped in Geneva, New York, to visit Eden Halsey. You remember Eden, don't you? The little orphan has blossomed into a stunning young woman! Sad to say, her grandparents, with whom she now lives, are not terribly well. However, Juliette and I both feel certain Eden will not be at loose ends when they pass on. She must have a score of suitors, eager to make her their wife. Is it not heartening to know how your kindness years ago has helped to shape— perhaps even to save—a young life?

Dropping the letter again, Brett closed his eyes and tried to imagine how Eden Halsey must have looked as she entertained John and his wife. Long, flowing, chestnut hair, held back by a simple satin ribbon. Blue-green eyes dancing as she spoke.

It was not hard to imagine how she looked. In fact, it was a fantasy he had indulged in many times in the last eight years. One he would indulge in many more times in the next three.

Gently closing her grandmother's bedroom door, Eden Halsey stepped into the hallway with the young doctor, Daniel Carter.

"I can't be too encouraging, Eden," the doctor said gently. "Pneumonia at her age, with a body that's already so weakened—"

Eden nodded. "I understand, Doctor Carter. I think Grandmother does, too. In a way, I think she's almost been waiting for something like this. Since Grandfather died last year, she's all but lost her will to live. I suppose she's clung to life for my sake more than anything. But, now that I'm nearly nineteen—"

"She wouldn't have to worry about you, Eden," the doctor interrupted. "She could pass on peacefully, knowing your future welfare is assured."

Sighing, Eden looked away from his earnest brown eyes. "I—I can't discuss that now, doctor. You know I'm flattered —honored—but—"

"Can't you at least call me Dan?"

At her continued silence, he sighed heavily. "All right. I won't press you. I realize it's not the proper time. But I'd like to take care of you, Eden. Whatever happens, you know I'll always be here."

She nodded. "Yes. I know. And I do appreciate that. Thank you—Dan."

After seeing the doctor out, Eden walked slowly back up the stairs to her own bedroom, the room that had been hers since she first came to Geneva, a frightened child, nearly ten years ago.

When Eleanor Kinzie's letter arrived in 1821, informing them that Eden, the child of their only son, had somehow managed to survive the Fort Dearborn massacre, Sarah and Jedediah Halsey had been overcome with joy. They had sent for Eden at once, certain she would be eager to join them. But instead of a child overjoyed to be united with her family, they had received a frightened, confused little girl, homesick for both the Kinzie homestead and Black Eagle's wigwam.

Several times, Eden had tried to explain to her grandparents how good Black Eagle had been to her and her mother. Gradually, she realized that they could never accept her Indian life. The Potawatomis had killed their son. That fact was proof enough of "Indian savagery."

Eden had only suspected that her father had been killed by the Indians. No one had ever told her, and since both her mother and Black Eagle seemed reluctant to speak of him, she had never asked.

She supposed that she should hate the people who had killed her father, her own flesh and blood. But, how could she hate the chief who had opened his heart and adopted her? How could she hate the man who had saved their lives?

As a confused nine-year-old, Eden had pondered those questions in secret, sensing she could never discuss them with her grandparents. In time, she had found peace in her own conclusions. Black Eagle's people had killed her father. Her father's people—her people—had killed relatives of Black Eagle. Neither fact diminished the goodness of either man.

Eden learned to love the man, reborn in her grandparents' recollections, who had been her father. Still, in secret, she continued to cherish Black Eagle and her memories of him.

Something else about her grandparents also upset Eden during her early months in Geneva. She sensed that they disapproved of her mother. When Eden innocently related how her mother had died after bearing Black Eagle's son, Sarah Halsey had clamped down her mouth and shot Jedediah a scandalized glare.

Still, for all their inflexibility, Sarah and Jedediah Halsey gave Eden a good home. Never did she doubt their love for her. They took the frightened, homesick child and transformed her into a well-educated, gracious, self-assured young woman.

By the time she completed finishing school in Albany at the age of eighteen, Eden was well-versed in literature, music, mathematics, and the French language, could dance more gracefully than most young women, excelled in needlework, and knew how to manage a genteel home.

But her grandparents' love and her fine education had never quite extinguished Eden's homesickness. As she matured, she had simply learned to hide it. Gradually, she had resigned herself to a future in Geneva. She could never hurt her grandparents by abandoning them. Certainly, she could not break their hearts by returning to Chicago, no matter how great a fascination the town still held for her.

At eighteen, Eden was seriously considering the proposal of Doctor Daniel Carter. Though she did not love him, she was genuinely fond of him.

Then, unexpectedly, her grandfather's heart had given out. Soon after, her grandmother's health had begun to fail.

Eden had put off accepting Dan's proposal then, explaining she was too involved in caring for her grandmother. In a way, that was true. She loved Sarah and certainly did not wish for anything to hasten the old woman's death. Still, she realized with an undeniable sense of excitement that Sarah Halsey's passing would free her from the future she had always imagined. Without Sarah, there would be nothing and no one to bind her to Geneva.

Getting up from her bed, Eden went to her desk and took

out her stack of letters from Maria Indiana Kinzie. For ten
years, the girls had corresponded, and Eden had eagerly read
and reread each letter, absorbing the color and excitement of
the growing frontier town that was Chicago. Often, Eden
imagined herself back there with her friend.

Sliding the most recent letter from the satin ribbon that
bound the packet, Eden read:

> You would scarcely believe how Chicago has grown
> recently! We must have fully one hundred residents
> and twenty houses now, not to mention Mr. Went-
> worth's tavern, the schoolhouse, and the Agency
> House. Mama is living at the Agency House now,
> finding the old homestead too difficult to endure
> since Papa passed on. Mr. Bailey, the postmaster, is
> occupying our old home.
>
> The talk of the town at the moment is Mark
> Beaubien's new hotel at Wolf Point. It is two stories
> high, with bright blue shutters at all the windows.
> Really quite a showplace! I can remember when
> Papa's house was the only "inn" in town. Now,
> having an establishment like Mark's just proves Chi-
> cago is becoming an important town. In a few years,
> I'm sure we will all be laughing at the city folk who
> had the temerity to call us "The Mudhole of the
> Prairie."
>
> How I wish, dear Eden, that you could be here
> with me.

Feeling a familiar rush of excitement, Eden closed her eyes
and whispered, "I *will* be with you, soon, Maria Indiana! I'll
never leave Grandmother, as long as she needs me. But,
when everything's over here, I'm coming back to Chicago.
It's my home."

5
April–July 1832

Eden stood on the deck of the ship *Lake Erie* as it maneuvered through Lake Michigan and into Chicago's harbor. The return trip to Chicago had been so much easier than her departure eleven years earlier. The Erie Canal had eliminated the long coach trip between Geneva and Buffalo, and even the voyage through the Great Lakes had seemed smoother than she remembered.

Of course, Eden realized that part of the ease stemmed from the fact she had wanted to make this trip, had dreamed about it for years. Leaving Chicago, she had been a frightened child, not at all certain where New York was, but quite certain she did not want to go there. Now she was a grown woman, almost twenty years old, coming home.

Looking out over the score of log buildings, Eden's heart soared as she realized she was, indeed, coming home. She had lived in the houses of white civilization too long now to yearn for the wigwams where she had spent the earliest years of her life. But, somehow she knew her yearning for Chicago would always be with her.

Beyond a range of sandhills and dwarf willows, Eden could see the Kinzie homestead, where she had spent one happy year. Behind the house still stood the two giant cottonwoods under which she and Maria Indiana had once played. Shifting her eyes to the front of the house, she saw a young woman—could it be Maria Indiana?—running through the row of Lombardy poplars that shaded the front yard.

No, she quickly told herself, it couldn't be her friend. The Kinzie family didn't live there anymore. And Maria Indiana was now married to Lieutenant David Hunter of the Fort Dearborn garrison.

Misty-eyed, Eden turned her attention to Fort Dearborn, directly opposite the Kinzie homestead, on the river's south

35

bank. Had the old fort, the one the Indians had burned, the one where her mother and father had lived, looked the same?

As the ship docked, Eden's eyes swept the pier. To her delighted surprise, she saw that the young woman she had glimpsed had indeed been Maria Indiana. Her friend waited impatiently beside Jacques, an aging voyageur who had joined the Kinzie household fifteen years earlier.

Eden nearly flew down the gangplank into Maria Indiana's arms. Laughing and hugging her, she asked, "How did you ever know I'd be aboard the *Lake Erie?*"

"I didn't," Maria Indiana giggled. "I've met nearly every ship since your letter arrived. I daresay, poor Jacques is heartily sick of being dragged to the harbor!"

The Frenchman grinned sheepishly as Eden turned to embrace him. "Bonjour, Mademoiselle Eden. I am glad you are here at last. Now, I find your bags. You go with Mademoiselle Marie."

Linking her arm through Eden's, Maria Indiana steered her along the riverbank. "You don't mind walking up to the house, do you? The wagon broke an axle this morning."

"Of course I don't mind," Eden assured her. "But don't tell me you're living in the house again?"

"Oh, yes! As soon as Mama found out you were coming, she insisted on moving back in. She didn't want to house an Eastern-bred lady in the Indian Agency House. Most of the time, David and I stay at the homestead, too. It's more comfortable than the fort."

"But I didn't want to inconvenience your mother! I'd thought perhaps I could stay in Monsieur Beaubien's inn until—"

"The inn!" Maria Indiana cut her off with a peal of laughter. "Oh, my dear, you don't know what you're saying! I'll admit Mark's place is rather elegant by Chicago standards, but it's no place for a woman—even a frontier woman. With all the people passing through Chicago, the inn is always overflowing with all sorts of men. And Mark never turns anyone away. When he runs out of beds, he just issues the traveler a blanket and tells him to sleep on the floor!"

Eden shrugged with feigned nonchalance. "Well, I spent nearly eight years sleeping on wigwam floors."

"But that's not all," her friend continued with dancing eyes. "Mark has only two or three extra blankets. So, as soon as one man falls asleep, Mark steals his blanket to give to the next lodger! He says that way he never runs out of rooms or blankets!"

Eden frowned. "Don't his lodgers become terribly upset?"

"Oh, no. Mark is so jolly, no one can stay angry with him. Besides, he has the only inn in town!"

Unable to hold back a laugh, Eden shrugged. "Well, the man's inventive, I must admit. Still, I think I'll prefer staying at the Kinzie home!"

Less than a month later, Eden and her hosts were moving out of the Kinzie homestead and into Fort Dearborn. Settlers and traders from all over Illinois and southern Wisconsin streamed into the fort as a new war with the Indians suddenly exploded.

Sixteen years earlier, a Sauk chief, without the consent of his people, had sold all his lands in Illinois and Wisconsin to the United States, in exchange for the life of a family member accused of murdering a white. For many years afterward, the Sauks and Foxes had complained bitterly when white settlers came to take over their lands. Little by little, they were forced west until, in 1831, the last of them had moved to the west bank of the Mississippi River.

Now, less than a year later, three hundred sixty-eight Sauk and Fox men, led by the Sauk chief Black Hawk, had recrossed the Mississippi to the contested lands.

At first, the Indian party gave no sign of attacking. But their numbers were so awesome the settlers were terrified, and the army responded in panic. A detachment led by General Stillman attacked Black Hawk's party, and the Black Hawk War began.

At Fort Dearborn, five or six families crowded into each room while the parade ground echoed with the tramp of boots and the crisp commands of officers drilling their troops.

Eden wondered if she had been foolish to return to Chicago after all. Her life had begun there with an Indian massacre. Would it end in the same manner?

The war spread eastward and north, into Wisconsin. Almost daily, runners reached the fort with reports of Indian massacres. But the fighting came no nearer Chicago than the Fox River, forty miles west of the town. In the end, a different, but equally horrifying, scourge swept the frightened masses jammed into Fort Dearborn.

Anxious to protect the settlers, in June the army rushed

troops west from Fortress Monroe in Virginia. Commanded
by General Winfield Scott, the reinforcements landed at Fort
Dearborn to the cheers of the frantic settlers. They brought
hope—and cholera.

Within thirty-six hours, the disease was rampant in the
fort, spreading quickly among the overcrowded families. The
settlers faced a terrible dilemma. They could remain at the
fort and risk succumbing to cholera, or they could move
outside the palisade, where they might fall prey to the Indians.

Most chose to stay. The mess hall was converted into a
hospital, and Eden and Maria Indiana joined the scores of
women nursing the ill.

The horror of the scene overwhelmed Eden. At least when
she had nursed her grandmother, she had been consoled that
Sarah was an old woman who had lived a full life. But most of
the soldiers and settlers were young people who, like her,
had come west in a burst of youthful enthusiasm, seeking the
life of their dreams.

Eden's stomach clenched spasmodically at the constant
vomiting. She gagged at the overwhelming stench of diarrhea.
Several times each day she had to turn away and blink back
tears at the sight of children, whose faces and bodies were
contorted in agonizing cramps.

By the second day, the ravages of the disease had aged
most of the patients several years in one stroke. Their cheeks
seemed to have sunken into their faces, and there was a faint
bluish cast around their lips and sunken eyes.

The first deaths, a young mother and an infant girl, occurred late that day. Eden and the others nursed the survivors.
They washed them, took away their soiled clothing and linens,
massaged cramped and aching muscles, pressed cold com-
presses to feverish brows, carried water to thirsting, dehy-
drated patients. Nothing they did could turn back the disease
in those already prostrated by it. Nothing could prevent its
spread to the other soldiers and settlers packed within the
fort.

By the third day, the makeshift hospital was overflowing
onto the parade ground. Deaths were becoming more frequent.
But, for every death, there were three or four new victims.

Scarcely sleeping, even in the few hours she snatched for
herself, Eden moved as if in a trance. Days and nights
merged in one endless chain of horror. Still, she pushed
herself on, doing what little she could to alleviate the agony,

thanking God that so far she and Maria Indiana and the other Kinzies had been spared, wondering when the cholera would reach out and grasp one or all of them in its death embrace.

Brett lay on the narrow army cot, cursing the illness that made every movement an effort. His throat burned from constant vomiting, and his legs and stomach tightened with miserable cramps. He felt no better than an infant, lying in his own puke and body wastes, unable either to control or clean himself.

He sensed someone moving over him, then felt a cool cloth wiping his face, washing away the partially dried spit and vomit. Opening his eyes, he stared upward, wanting at least to thank whoever was helping him.

Brett blinked, certain he must be delirious. It couldn't be her! Surely he had imagined her once too often, and now his fantasy had returned to haunt him. And of course, he had never seen her as an adult. Still, those eyes, the peculiar shade of blue-green. Could anyone else in the world look quite the same?

She began to turn away and, without realizing it, he called her name.

"Eden!" he croaked in a voice made husky by his illness.

She hesitated, then turned back to him, brushing a wisp of chestnut hair from her face. "Did you call me, sir?"

Too weak even to nod, he blinked in response.

Stepping closer, Eden looked down at him skeptically. "You called me Eden. Do you know me?"

"Br—" His lips went slack, defeated by the simple effort of saying his own name. Again he tried. "Bre—"

She frowned, absently reaching down to smooth his curly red hair. Her gaze moved down the long, muscled body, over the broad expanse of chest. Suddenly, her eyes widened in remembrance.

"You're Brett! John Kinzie's friend Brett!"

For the next several days, whenever she could spare a moment, Eden hovered over Brett McKinnon's cot. Though she hardly knew him, she felt a special bond to this man. He was her link with the past. He was the one man on earth who had known her both as an Indian and a white child. Somehow she must keep him from dying.

Whether through Eden's efforts or Brett's own innate

resilience, he did begin to recover. Within a week he was able to sit up in bed. A few days later, when the Kinzies decided to move back into their house, they insisted that Brett come with them to recuperate. The Black Hawk War had not ended, but the action had been limited to Wisconsin, so now the family no longer felt threatened.

Eden was delighted. She longed to ask him about the Potawatomis, about Black Eagle, about Morning Star, about his life as a trader.

But the thought of having Brett McKinnon in the house filled her with a rare excitement that was not entirely due to a desire to talk to him. Something about him attracted her more than Doctor Daniel Carter or any of the other genteel young men of Geneva ever could. To her, Brett McKinnon's rugged resilience, his unruly red hair, his lean, muscled body, his understanding of the Indians, seemed the very embodiment of the West.

Brett, too, was pleased. It was almost worth a bout with cholera to be thrown into the gentle, capable hands of Eden Halsey. Gracious, but unaffected, she looked so much like the girl he had fantasized about, that he could scarcely believe his eyes. And beyond her beauty was an inner strength. She faced the cholera crisis with none of the panic he might have expected from an Eastern-bred girl.

She seemed to be the woman of his dreams. And, if he could not carry her off to share the rest of his life, he was at least determined to prolong his convalescence at the Kinzie homestead for as long as possible.

He wanted to know more about this woman. Sitting in the Kinzie parlor on the first afternoon, Brett asked Eden how she came to be in Chicago again. "John wrote me a few years ago about visiting you in New York," he said. "He seemed to think you'd marry and spend the rest of your life there."

Eden sighed. "For a long time, I thought the same. I had a good life there, among good people. But there was always something pulling me back to Chicago. It was foolish, I suppose. Just some silly girlish dream. If I'd known I'd end up in another Indian war, I'm not certain I would have come back."

Brett's face clouded angrily. "You mustn't let what's happened these last weeks color your feelings. This war should never have happened. Black Hawk's group was not a war party! Any trader or agent with an ounce of sense could tell you that! Black Hawk's party had at least a hundred women and children in it. The Sauks don't take women and children into battle."

Frowning, Eden asked, "Then why did they cross the Mississippi?"

"Most likely, to visit relatives among the Winnebagoes and Potawatomis. You lived with the Indians long enough. You ought to know their love for family. And who are we to tell them they can't cross the river whenever they want?"

"Then our soldiers attacked without provocation?"

Brett nodded. "The only thing provoking them was panic. Theirs and the settlers'. But now, Black Hawk's warriors have to defend their honor. What choice do they have but to fight?"

Shaking her head, Eden buried her face in her hands. Here she was, facing the same conflicts she had thought to escape when she left Geneva. The settlers were no better than her grandparents and their friends, automatically assuming the Indians were bad. But they didn't know. They hadn't lived among the Indians for nearly eight years as she had.

As if reading her thoughts, Brett sighed softly. "I know," he muttered. "It's hard to know which side to take. White soldiers and settlers are being killed now. Their scalps are being taken. When you're white, you have to side with the whites. But when you're part Indian, like you and me—even if your blood isn't Indian—your sympathy lies with the Indians, too.

"I came here to see the commanding officer, hoping to talk some sense into him, to spare some lives. He listened, but I'm not sure my words ever really reached him. Then the cholera hit me, and I couldn't do anything. Now, I think it's too late to stop what's been started. The army won't settle for less than Black Hawk's life. But we'll pay with plenty of white lives."

Dropping her hands from her face, Eden looked at Brett earnestly. "What about Black Eagle?" she asked. "Will he be pulled into the war?"

Brett shook his head. "Black Eagle's been dead now nearly five years. The natural death of an old man," he added quickly, as Eden's eyes clouded with grief. "As for his camp, I don't think they'll be involved. They're too far south of the conflict, and I doubt they have any relatives among Black Hawk's party."

Maria Indiana, who had entered the room a moment earlier, quickly asked, "What about Morning Star? Is she safe? Do you want to send her a message?"

"She's safe," Brett answered curtly. "She's at her late father's camp."

Excited by the discovery of another link with her past, Eden did not notice Brett's discomfort. "You know Morning Star?" she asked anxiously. "She was sort of my Indian mother, though she was very young, after my own mother died."

Maria Indiana laughed. "Know her? She's Brett's—"

"Yes, I know her," Brett cut in, flashing Maria Indiana a dark scowl. "Black Eagle introduced us years ago, after I first brought you to Chicago."

"Oh!" Eden's eyes glowed with excitement. "Do you think perhaps, after this war is settled, you could take me to see her someday? If it wasn't for her kindness after Mama died, I don't know how I would have survived."

Frowning, Brett shook his head. "I don't get in to Chicago very often. And when I'm here, I can't take the time to travel back and forth to her encampment just to take you."

"I see," Eden murmured in disappointment.

"Well," Brett relented, "I'll take her a message if you wish. And someday perhaps I'll find the time to take you after all. But I can't make any promises."

Later, when Eden had gone out to the Kinzie bakehouse for some fresh bread, Maria Indiana demanded, "Why didn't you tell Eden that Morning Star is your wife?"

"Because she's not!" Brett replied sharply.

"What do you mean? She's borne you two sons!"

"But she's not really my wife! Not in the white sense. We were never married before a priest or reverend."

"What has that got to do with it? Half the marriages in the West are performed without benefit of clergy. If every couple had to wait for a circuit priest or reverend to ride through, no one would ever get married."

"Well, I didn't want to scandalize Eden."

"Scandalize her! Brett, you're talking nonsense! Her own mother had a marriage to Black Eagle that was no more sanctified than yours to Morning Star."

"But Eden was too young to understand that. Now, with her Eastern upbringing, she might see things a bit differently."

"Oh, pooh! I know Eden—"

"And I know about stuffy Eastern morals!" Brett cut her off

adamantly. "Sure I've been here fourteen years. But I spent the first seventeen years of my life in Connecticut. I know how they raise young ladies back East. Eden's no pioneer girl anymore. She's strong, she's hardworking, and it's obvious she loves Illinois. But she's Eastern-bred, and it will take more than a few months for her to get over that."

Maria Indiana stared at him petulantly. "I still don't see what any of that has to do with Morning Star being your wife."

Sighing, Brett averted his eyes from her piercing gaze. "Don't try to understand. And don't ask me to explain any more. And don't meddle in my affairs!"

6
August 1835

The long line of Indian warriors wound around the homes and stores of Chicago. Bloodcurdling war whoops filled the air as the Chippewas, Ottawas, and Potawatomis, eight hundred strong, danced and gyrated through the town.

Peeking from behind the Kinzies' parlor curtains, Eden shivered apprehensively. A group of warriors stopped in front of the house, not more than ten feet from where she stood, waving their tomahawks and clubs menacingly.

Dressed only in breechcloths, the braves had daubed their chests with vermilion. On their faces, hideous vermilion stripes, edged with black, gave the impression of ferocious grins. A few had even pierced their bodies with spears, mingling streaks of blood with their war paint. Their bodies glistened with sweat in the sultry morning, as they danced and shrieked in a frenzied passion.

Stepping back from the window, Eden stifled a scream of terror. There was nothing to fear, she told herself over and over. She recognized many of the Indians as friends she and Eleanor Kinzie had frequently traded with at the Indian Agency House. Besides, Brett McKinnon had stopped at the house last night to tell them what was happening.

"They'll look ferocious," he had warned, "and they'll do their best to scare the life out of you. But it will just be a show. One last attempt to regain their pride. And, by evening, they'll be gone for good."

Yes, by evening, they would be gone, banished to the far side of the Mississippi River. Ever since the Black Hawk War, the settlers had viewed all of their Indian neighbors with suspicion. A year after the war, the government had coaxed the tribes remaining in Illinois to sign a treaty relinquishing their lands.

Under the treaty, the tribes had been permitted to remain in Illinois two more years, receiving an annuity from the government. The annuity, in the form of blankets, kettles, and other merchandise, was distributed to the Indians each year in Chicago. Now, the final payment had been made. This evening was the deadline for the Indians to begin their westward trek.

Turning back to the window, Eden watched the Indians move on to the next house. Suddenly, tears filled her eyes as she realized the scene was more pathetic than frightening. With the passing of the Indians, an era would end for her as well as for them.

At twenty-three, Eden knew she could no longer avoid the question of what to do with the rest of her life. Since arriving in Chicago more than three years earlier, she had worked with Aunt Eleanor at the Indian Agency. That job would be ending now, and she knew she could not simply continue to impose upon Aunt Eleanor.

Maria Indiana and her husband had moved away more than two years ago when David had been assigned to a new army post. With the surplus of men in Chicago, Eden herself had suffered no lack of proposals. But she hesitated to marry anyone she simply liked but did not love. She could have done that in Geneva.

Sighing, Eden admitted to herself that she had resisted other men's advances because of her fascination with Brett McKinnon.

Three years had passed since she'd nursed him through cholera, and though he visited the Kinzie homestead several times a year, Brett had never so much as hinted at a marriage proposal.

His reticence puzzled Eden, since she was almost sure he came to Chicago primarily to be with her. Even Aunt Elea-

nor had mentioned several times, with a wry smile, that Brett
McKinnon seemed to have a great deal of business in Chicago
ever since Eden joined the Kinzie household.

During his visits, they talked until all hours of the night,
walked for miles along the lakefront, raced on horseback
across the prairie west of the city, always laughing with
delicious abandon.

At times, especially if Eden talked about Morning Star,
Brett withdrew into a sultry mood. She knew he had a
reputation among men for being quick to anger. But those
traits only made him seem more fascinating as she worked to
draw him out of his mood or tame his explosiveness.

She admired Brett for both his strength and his compassion.
He understood the Indians as few other men she had met,
neither sympathizing with their every action, nor blaming
them for every conflict with the whites.

Above all, Eden felt an undeniably strong physical attraction to Brett. Whenever Mark Beaubien held a dance at his
Sauganash Inn, and Brett took her in his arms for a waltz,
Eden could barely control her quivering. And she was sure
she saw a spark of tenderness, reserved for her, in his gray-
green eyes.

Yet, he never spoke of love. When they walked home from
a dance on a moonlit night, he never even tried to kiss her.

He must want me! Eden thought desperately, blushing at
the immodesty of her own thoughts. He's a man, after all. A
strong, virile man. Considering what his touch does to me,
surely he must feel something, too. So, why doesn't he say
something, do something? How long does he expect me to
wait?

Now, as she watched the whooping, gyrating Indians move
on, Eden could not help wondering if this change would force
Brett to reexamine his life. What would he do now that all his
Indian trapper friends were being pushed to a new home?
Would he finally consider a future with her?

In a small, but blessedly private room of the Sauganash
Inn, Brett stood facing Morning Star. Huddled on the bed,
holding nine-year-old Benjamin on her lap, she seemed to
Brett even more hauntingly lovely than usual. Their older
son, Thomas, or Swift Elk as he preferred to be called, was in
the streets, dancing with the other Potawatomi braves. At
eleven, he had insisted he was old enough to join the men.

"You don't have to go, you know," Brett said softly. "As my wife, the mother of my children, you can stay here with me. I'll have to look for a new position, of course. The fur company won't continue to support a trading post when there's no one to trade with. But Illinois has practically been trapped out for some time now. Anyway, we can build a house here in Chicago, or somewhere else if you'd rather. Maybe at the junction of the Des Plaines and the Kankakee rivers, where your father's old camp was."

He paused, suddenly aware Morning Star was not responding. Even her eyes showed not a flicker of emotion.

For a long moment, she stared at him expressionlessly. Then she slowly shook her head. "No. To go where my father once lived, where my people are no longer permitted, that I could not bear."

"Then we'll stay in Chicago. Or we'll go to Wisconsin."

"No!" She shook her head again. "I cannot stay where I know I do not belong! At the trading post, it was different. There were people of all races. But this is a town of white people. I do not belong here. I will go with my people."

"And the boys?"

"I will take them with me. They are young. They will learn to love this new Indian Territory the White Father in Washington has reserved for us."

"But they're my sons—"

For the first time, Brett saw a flicker of bitterness in Morning Star's eyes. "Are they your sons, Brett? Have you only now remembered that?"

Brett sighed. "I never neglected you or them. I had a job. If I didn't perform my duties, how would I have provided for all of you?"

"Indian fathers provide for their families," Morning Star said softly. "Yet they do not work for any far-off company."

"But I'm not Indian!" Brett exploded.

"But I am. And so are your sons."

"They're half white."

"Only their blood. Would a white child be dancing in the streets now as our son Thomas—Swift Elk—is?"

"That's only because he's used to the Indian ways. The war dance seems exciting to him. But he can get used to white ways, too." Dropping to his knees, Brett addressed the nine-year-old child on Morning Star's lap. "What do you want,

Ben? Do you want to go away with your mother? Do you want to leave me?"

The little boy's eyes glistened with unshed tears as he slowly shook his head.

"Don't, Brett," Morning Star chided, tightening her hold on her son. "Don't make it difficult for him. What can you expect him to say? Of course he loves you. I taught him to. But you must think of what is best for him. Here he would always be a 'half-breed.' You know that is true. Among my people, he will be respected as my son, the grandson of Black Eagle."

"But I want him to remember he is my son, too."

"Then come with us! My brothers respect you. They would not turn you away."

Brett stared at her, reading the challenge in her dark eyes. Closing his eyes, he shook his head. "I can't," he murmured hoarsely.

"No," Morning Star whispered, "of course you cannot. Your place is with your people, just as my place is with mine. For a little while, the two peoples mingled. Now, like the slender stalk of the starflower, we must divide and each bear our own blossoms."

Brett combed a hand distractedly through his hair. Her serenity unnerved him. His own sense of guilt grew. How could he let her take away his sons, his own flesh and blood? But what choice did he have?

Seeing the pain written on Brett's face, Morning Star set Benjamin on his feet and went to him. She touched his hand, and as he lifted his gaze to hers, Brett saw that her eyes were shining with tears.

"Ah, Brett," she murmured, sliding her arms around his waist and resting her head on his chest, "can't you understand I am trying to make things easy for you? It is not your fault you never loved me." Feeling him stiffen, she smiled slightly. "No, do not insult me by denying it. I've known from the first, and I've never held you responsible. You did not choose me for your wife. My father pressed me upon you, and you would not hurt him by refusing me."

She shrugged. "It is a common enough happening. One that occurs among white people as well as Indians. But you and I are fortunate. You and I can begin again. When I leave tonight with my people, you will be free—free to find a woman you can love."

Wrapping his arms around her, Brett choked back a sob.
"Can you at least believe this—" he said huskily, "can you at
least believe I always cared for you? I always respected you. I
always felt great tenderness for you."

"Yes," Morning Star murmured. "I believe that much. I
always knew it, and for me it would have been enough. But,
for you, Brett, I want much more."

"If you really intend to go, you must promise me one
thing. If you ever need anything, no matter where you are, if
there is ever anything I can do, for you, or Benjamin, or
Thomas, you must let me know."

"All right." Her voice broke, and Brett could feel her tears
through his thin linsey-woolsey shirt.

He pressed her to him, thinking for the first time in the
fifteen years they had shared that perhaps he really did love
her. For a moment, Morning Star, too, tightened her embrace.
Then she pulled away, averting her eyes.

"Please go now, Brett," she whispered. "Leave me before I
change my mind about the future and we all regret it."

A ghostly silence settled over Chicago as night fell and the
last of the Potawatomis, Chippewas, and Ottawas left Chicago
for the last time. The half-breed Sauganash, known to the
whites as Billy Caldwell, led the procession. Brett stood atop
the Fort Dearborn palisade, watching the exodus until the
Indians blended into the darkness of the western prairies.

Hours later, long after the last war cry had been smothered
in darkness, Brett crossed the river to the Kinzie homestead.
As he slipped silently through the row of Lombardy poplars
in front of the house, Eleanor Kinzie called to him from the
porch.

"Is that you, Brett McKinnon? Good heavens, what's gotten into you, calling at this hour?"

"I'm sorry, Eleanor," he said as he mounted the front
steps. "I'd hoped I wouldn't be disturbing anyone."

Eleanor smiled, "Ah, Brett, you know you're always
welcome here, at any hour. Anyway, I suspect tonight
you're feeling rather low. Did Morning Star leave with the
Potawatomis?"

"Yes. And the boys, too."

"Ah." Eleanor was silent for a long moment before asking,
"What will you do now, Brett?"

"I'm not sure. I have some ideas. I've saved a goodly sum

from my seventeen years with the company. But—well—it depends." Looking around the darkened porch, he asked as casually as he could, "Is Eden here?"

Eleanor hesitated, gazing at him intently. "She may be in bed already. It seems to me she said something about retiring early.. But, if you'd like to come in, I'll see if she's still awake."

"If it's all the same to you, I'll wait out here. The evening breeze feels mighty good after the heat."

"All right. Excuse me for just a moment."

Leaning against the porch rail, Brett wondered had he been wrong to come here tonight? Morning Star had been right, of course. He had never loved her, never even deceived himself that he had. And, these last years, since Eden had returned to Chicago, he had found it harder and harder to pretend. Perhaps Morning Star had already guessed that he had found another woman.

"Aunt Eleanor said you asked to see me?"

Brett turned to see Eden framed in the doorway, tying the sash on a calico wrapper. Her features softened by moonlight, she looked younger than her twenty-three years, too vulnerable for the rough frontier town that was still Chicago. Looking beyond her, he saw with relief that Eleanor had discreetly retreated.

"I—yes—I'd like to talk with you." Eyeing the thin wrapper, he asked, "Are you warm enough to walk a bit, or would you rather go inside?"

She laughed lightly. "Well, I'm not exactly dressed for a dance at the inn, but we can stroll if you wish. It *is* a very pleasant night."

Taking her elbow, Brett guided her down the steps and toward the backyard. With surprise, he realized he was trembling. For several minutes, he did not dare speak, for fear of betraying his nervousness. It was Eden who finally broke the silence.

"What an exciting day it's been!" she sighed. "Yet, how sad! I wonder if Chicago will be the better, or worse, for sending the Indians away."

"Who can say?" Brett murmured. "The only thing certain is that all of our lives will change because of what's happened today."

"I know. I was thinking today that I'll have to be seeking a new job. And there aren't a great many jobs open to women here. Chicago already has a teacher. I'm a good seamstress, but there aren't enough women in the town to require my skills." She shrugged, trying to make light of her problem. "What will you do, Brett?"

"Oh, I think I'll move to Chicago. I could ask the fur company to transfer me out of Illinois, but I've grown kind of attached to the area. Anyway, I'm getting too old for the trading and trapping life. It gave me a good start as a boy, but when a man gets to be thirty-four, he ought to start planning a more substantial future."

"Such as?"

"I've been thinking of starting a meat-packing business. Arch Clybourne's done well with his slaughterhouse on the north branch of the river. And with the way this state's going to grow, I think it can support another meat business. Travel on the Great Lakes is improving so much, I could even start shipping my products back East. I'm not completely inexperienced in the business.

"Back in 1829, during a lull in the fur trade, I agreed to drive four hundred hogs to market for the farmers near my trading post. I'll admit it was not the easiest trip. But, I got them here. Didn't lose a single one. Only problem was, the ship that was supposed to meet us couldn't get through the ice on Lake Michigan up at Mackinac. Well, I couldn't drive them all back to the farms, so I slaughtered them myself, piled the carcasses on the riverbank, and sold the meat."

Brett paused awkwardly, sniffing the air as they passed the Kinzie bakehouse. "But I didn't ask you out here to talk about hogs. What I wanted to say is—I'd like you to marry me."

"I'd like *you* to marry *me*," Eden replied, surprising even herself with the quickness of her response.

Brett laughed, feeling a great sense of relief as he slid an arm around her shoulders. "Then I guess your problem is solved. Your new employment will be filling the role of Mrs. Brett McKinnon!"

"Wife of the foremost meat-packer in Chicago!" Eden quickly added.

He took her in his arms then and kissed her, gently at first, then with greater passion, as the vision of Morning Star and the boys slowly faded from his mind. Leaning back in his arms, Eden looked up at him earnestly.

"Brett," she whispered, "I've often wondered, why is it you never married before?"

Quickly, he looked away, afraid she might read the truth in

his eyes. He couldn't tell her now. Later, perhaps, when their life together was well-established. But he couldn't bring himself to ruin this moment.

"Because," he murmured finally, "when I first met you, you were far too young. But later you were far too much a lady to become a trader's wife. In between, I never wanted anyone else. Now, at last, I think we can build a future together."

Sighing, Eden lay her head on his chest and inhaled his heady male scent. He had given her all the answer she had ever hoped for.

Eleven days later, Eden stood before her bedroom mirror, arranging her chestnut curls over the shoulders of her satin and lace wedding gown. Both she and Brett had been anxious to marry as soon as possible, so Eleanor Kinzie had kindly offered Eden her own wedding gown, and the two women had worked night and day to alter it.

Hearing the rustle of taffeta, Eden glanced over her shoulder and saw Eleanor entering in a gown of midnight blue.

"You look lovely, Aunt Eleanor."

"No, no, dear. The bride is the only truly lovely one on her wedding day. You do that gown more justice than I ever did."

Surprised at the catch in the older woman's voice, Eden turned to see tears in Eleanor's eyes. "Aunt Eleanor, what is it?"

Briskly, Eleanor shook her head. "Nothing, dear. I suppose I'm just being a sentimental old woman. Feeling like I'm losing another daughter."

Eden hugged her tightly. "Oh, Aunt Eleanor, you know I'll always love you as my mother. But, it's not as if we're moving far away. Brett's just rented the old Bailey house on Rush Street. I'll barely be two blocks from you. We'll probably see each other every day!"

Nodding, Eleanor pulled back and forced a smile. "Eden, darling, I—I can't help thinking I ought to tell you something before—" She paused awkwardly, searching Eden's concerned eyes. "I mean, has Brett ever explained to you about—"

"The carriage is ready, Madame Eleanor," Jacques called from the parlor.

Relieved by the interruption, Eleanor sighed. "We'd best be going. It would never do for you to be late for your own wedding!"

"But, what did you want to say, Aunt Eleanor?"

"Nothing, darling. It doesn't matter. Just the idle musings of an old woman. Now, hurry. There's bound to be a crowd waiting to see the bride."

As Eleanor predicted, more than two hundred people greeted Eden outside the First Presbyterian Church at the southwest corner of Lake and Clark streets.

The guests packed the pews of the church, spilling into the aisles and out of the doors. But Eden saw none of them as she advanced slowly up the aisle. Her glowing eyes were fixed on Brett McKinnon, who stood beside the altar, beaming with pride at the woman who would soon be his wife.

She did not tremble as she clasped his hand, and together they turned to face the minister. Even in the churchyard, every guest could clearly hear them speak their vows. No one had ever entered a marriage with more confidence than Eden Halsey and Brett McKinnon.

When the minister pronounced them man and wife and Brett pulled her into a tender embrace, Eden swelled with joy. Her arm linked through his, she felt as if she floated down the aisle and out to greet the swarm of well-wishers.

Afterward, Eleanor hosted a wedding celebration at the Kinzie homestead. Guests crowded the parlor, while children played hide-and-seek among the Lombardy poplars in the yard. On the veranda, someone produced a fiddle, dancing began, and every man clamored for a dance with the bride.

The sun was beginning to set before Brett managed to pull his wife aside. Grinning, he said, "It's a lovely party, Mrs. McKinnon, and I'm sure we don't want to disappoint any of these fine people, but don't you think it's time we went home?"

She smiled, thinking how fine "home" sounded when it meant the place she would share with Brett McKinnon. "I think," she whispered, "that I can't wait another moment!"

Laughing, they slipped away and almost ran the two blocks to the house Brett had rented on Rush Street. He carried her over the threshold, kicking the door shut behind him, then heaving his shoulders back against it, as if afraid the crowd might follow them inside.

He pressed his lips to hers in a lingering kiss before taking the stairs two at a time to their bedroom.

His gray-green eyes smoldering, he lay her gently on the bed. Taking her face in his hands, he searched her eyes. His heart soared with joyful anticipation as he read neither fear nor hesitancy in her gaze.

Burying his face in her chestnut curls, he murmured, "Oh, Eden, how I've longed for this moment. For years. For too many years!"

Her fingers twined in his hair as she brought his mouth to hers and murmured, "I, too, my darling. How I've longed for you!"

Carefully, he undressed her, barely controlling his impatience at the myriad tiny buttons at the back of her gown. Both were consumed by the pulsing need of the moment. When she lay naked before him in the last light of day, Eden felt no embarrassment, only the desire to become one with him.

Brett's fingers caressed her, fanning her desire, until he felt the time was right to slide between her parted thighs. His breath warm in her ear, he whispered, "It may hurt for a moment, but only a moment. Then, I swear, I'll never hurt you again."

She tensed at the first probing thrust, biting back an involuntary sob. Then she felt him fill her, and she sighed as the pain faded.

He kissed her again, teasing her mouth with his darting, probing tongue, and then he began to move within her.

The feelings came so quickly Eden cried out in astonishment. A tingling that built and built until it raced in tremors up her spine. A flush, a silky wetness, a soaring sensation as she pressed him to her, arching against him, and found a rhythm to match his.

Brett paused, stroking her, kissing her, murmuring endearments. And then he began again, and she thought she would burst with ecstasy.

Hours later, when they lay spent and content, Eden recalled the morning's conversation with Aunt Eleanor. Smiling sleepily, she wondered, was this what the older woman had seemed so concerned about? Of course. Dear Aunt Eleanor had wanted to prepare her for her wedding night.

With a man less sensitive than Brett, perhaps some preparation would have been necessary. But surely nothing Aunt Eleanor could have said could have prepared Eden for the incredible joy, the wonderful sense of being cherished, that suffused her as she cuddled against her husband.

II

THE SPROUTS

1836–1847

7
1836–1840

Stretching sleepily, Eden reached across the wide four-poster bed to caress Brett. Her hands found only wrinkled sheets, cool enough to tell her he had been gone for quite some time.

Opening her eyes, she smiled in the early morning light. Dear Brett. He worked so hard. She wondered what time he had slipped out of bed this morning to go to his packinghouse on the south branch of the Chicago River. How typical of him to be thoughtful enough not to wake her.

Her smile broadening, Eden thought of last night's ardent lovemaking. It was a joy of marriage that still amazed her. Even her dear friend Maria Indiana had never so much as hinted at the ecstasy a husband and wife could find in bed. Perhaps that was because Maria Indiana didn't truly know. Perhaps what she and Brett shared was simply more special than the bonds of most couples.

Brett had been right about Chicago. In the ten months since their marriage, the frontier town had nearly doubled in size.

Years earlier, Congress had authorized the building of a ship canal from Chicago to the Illinois River. The canal would link the nation's two great waterways, enabling vessels from the Great Lakes to sail into the Lake Michigan port, down the canal to the Illinois, then on to the Mississippi. Since 1835, land sales along the canal right-of-way had been booming. Now that canal construction had actually begun, even more immigrants were pouring in from the East.

Unfortunately, Chicago's rapid growth had not increased the gentility of its residents. Most of the immigrants were men, hard workers and hard drinkers, bent on making a fortune as quickly as possible. Gambling was their favorite pastime, and not a few gambling disputes ended in deaths.

Still, with Brett, Eden felt nothing but contentment. In

57

less than a year, McKinnon Meats had become a thriving business. Farmers from all over Illinois, many of whom had known Brett in his trading days, brought their hogs and cattle to him. The hotels, boardinghouses, and dormitories springing up all over Chicago knew they could trust the quality of McKinnon Meats.

Caught up in her reverie, Eden did not at first notice that Brett had tiptoed into the room. He stood gazing at her for a moment, then chuckled softly.

"You're looking very thoughtful this morning, chérie." Like the voyageurs he'd employed, Brett still mingled English and French.

Looking up at him with mock reproach, Eden nodded. "Yes, I'm wondering how you managed to slip out of bed without me again this morning! Brett, I've told you to wake me so I can prepare you a proper breakfast!"

"But you looked so charming asleep I couldn't bear to disturb you! Besides, I'm used to fending for myself."

"But you shouldn't have to now that you have a wife. You make me feel as if I'm really no use to you."

Sitting down beside her on the bed, Brett slid a hand casually beneath her nightgown. "I hardly give you reason to think that, ma chère."

Shivering pleasantly under his caress, Eden smiled. "Now, tell me, what required your attention so early this morning?"

His gray-green eyes dancing excitedly, Brett said, "I had to meet with the captain of the Lake steamer *Henry Clay*. He's agreed to carry twenty barrels of our beef and thirty of our pork to the cities on his eastward route. If they find ready markets—and I'm sure they will—this could be the beginning of a regular shipping network over the Great Lakes."

"Can we get enough hogs and cattle to handle that much additional business?"

Brett laughed confidently. "At the rate Illinois is growing, I've no doubt we can get enough to supply the whole world!"

With a mischievous smile, Eden whispered, "You know, Chicago's going to be growing, too."

Uncertain of her meaning, Brett frowned. "Of course it is. It's never stopped."

"I mean, the McKinnon family, in particular, is going to be growing. About seven months from now, as near as I can guess."

Brett's eyes widened. "You mean, you're going to have a baby?"

Eden nodded. "That's exactly what I mean, *Papa* Mc-Kinnon."

Abruptly, Brett pulled away his hand, which had strayed to her breast. "Well, if you're carrying our child, we'd better start being more careful about your condition."

Laughing lightly, Eden snuggled against him. Her hand pulled his beneath her nightgown again. "Careful, yes," she murmured, as she pressed her lips to his. "But, I don't think we need to be *that* careful."

Eden's pregnancy made Brett uneasy. He wanted the child and looked forward to sharing parenthood with Eden. But, more and more, he found himself thinking of his sons Morning Star had taken west with her.

He had never found the right moment to tell Eden about his other family. At first he had worried that Morning Star might contact him, but he had gradually convinced himself she never would. Morning Star had too much Indian pride. With that assurance, Brett had continued to hide his past, telling himself it hardly mattered if he put off telling Eden. Surely he could not now risk upsetting her.

Whenever Eden asked him why he was brooding, he snapped, "I'm not brooding! I'm just thinking!" Then, softening, he would add, "I worry about you, that's all. Chicago is still such a rough place to live, an uncivilized place to bear a child."

Eden laughed. "Darling, you're being foolish! Women have borne children in much cruder conditions than these—for centuries." Secretly, she supposed he was thinking of her own mother's death in childbirth. And she loved him all the more for his fears and his clumsy attempts to protect her from them.

In March of 1837, the state of Illinois granted Chicago a city charter. That same month, the first son of Brett and Eden McKinnon entered the world.

Brett and Eden had not discussed names, agreeing that when the child was born they would choose a name that seemed appropriate. Now, smoothing back the newborn's wispy reddish hair, Eden beamed up at her husband.

"Somehow, I imagine you must have looked just like him as an infant," she whispered. "I think we ought to call him

Brett. Wouldn't you like that, darling? To have your first son carry on your name?"

Stiffening, Brett looked away from her. What would she say if she ever learned he already had two other sons? Clearing his throat, Brett shook his head. "No. I—I don't believe in naming children for their parents. Every child ought to have a name that's wholly his own."

"All right, then. What if he just shares your first initial? I've always thought Benjamin is a lovely name."

Brett closed his eyes, paling as he imagined the second-born of Morning Star. Benjamin, if he still called himself that, would be eleven now.

"Brett?" Eden whispered worriedly, "is something wrong? I haven't seen you so pale since you had the cholera."

"I—no—I'm just overwhelmed. So glad you and he are all right."

She smiled, thinking of how he had brooded during the last months. "What about the name? Does Benjamin suit you?"

"No!" he almost shouted.

Seeing Eden's surprise at his vehemence, he hurriedly explained. "When I was a boy back in Middlebury, I was very close to a cousin, about my age, named Benjamin. One day we went swimming together, and he drowned. I don't know what happened, he just—" Brett's voice became husky, strained by the lie.

Convinced he was torn by painful remembrance, Eden cut in softly, "It's all right. Don't say any more. I'm sorry I reminded you."

For several moments they were both silent; Brett consumed with guilt for his lie, but thanking God he had no living relatives to dispute it, Eden searching for a better way to comfort him. A sudden whimpering drew their attention back to the tiny bundle in Eden's arms.

Brett smiled, extending a finger to stroke the infant's cheek. "I think he's getting impatient for a name," he said. "What would you say to Burton?"

"Burton McKinnon," Eden said slowly. "Yes, that has a nice strong sound. What do you think, Burton?" she whispered, gazing down at the infant now nuzzling contentedly at her breast.

Lifting her eyes to Brett's, Eden smiled happily. "I think he agrees!"

* * *

Two months after Burton's birth, a bank panic shocked New York. By summer the panic was spreading throughout the United States as hundreds of banks failed.

In Illinois, construction of the Illinois and Michigan Canal abruptly halted as funds for the project dwindled to nothing. Land values crashed, and Chicago's phenomenal growth suddenly slowed.

Brett and Eden were more fortunate than most Chicagoans during the crash. Instead of joining the scores who had made their fortunes in land speculation, Brett had poured most of his fortune into his meat-packing business. Just before the crash, he had begun a regular meat-shipping line over the Great Lakes. Business was not booming as it had in the beginning, but there was no danger of failure. Whatever else happened, people felt they needed meat, and McKinnon Meats supplied good quality at a reasonable price.

"Do you think we were all wrong about Chicago?" Eden asked Brett one evening, as they sat on the parlor floor, playing with their one-year-old son. "Do you think the town will ever recover its spirit, ever start to grow again?"

Brett nodded. "It will grow. When the nation begins to recover, we can't help but grow. When people start to move west again—to the Mississippi Valley and the great unsettled Northwest, they'll all come through Chicago. Some of them will like what they see and stay, others will go on. When those that go on send east for supplies, all their orders will come through Chicago. And when the supplies are sent west, they'll come through Chicago, too. We're the crossroads of the nation!"

As the nation entered the 1840s, it began to pull itself out of the long, painful economic panic, and Brett was proven right. Wool, cotton, cattle, sheep, hogs, wheat, corn, and barley were funneled through Chicago from Western settlers. More and more ships crowded Chicago's harbor, bringing Eastern manufactured goods in trade for the Western bounty.

McKinnon Meats flourished with the increased supply of livestock. Grain elevators rose to store the barley, corn, and wheat. And plow works, wagon works, foundries, and blacksmith shops sprang up to supply the needs of Western farmers.

By that time, three-year-old Burton McKinnon had a young-

er brother, Clinton, born in 1839. Once again Eden felt
thoroughly contented. Chicago was growing. McKinnon Meats
was growing. Her family was growing. The future looked
perfect in every way.

8
October 1841

From her perch behind the registry desk of the Bull and
Boar Inn, Eden looked out on Southwestern Plank Road, a
small smile curving her lips. The boys, now sturdy toddlers of
two and four, were napping in the adjoining apartment.
Through the open door connecting the lobby of the inn with
the McKinnon apartment, Eden could hear Michelle, their
hired girl, humming a French-Canadian folk tune as she went
about her chores.

Glancing around the small, clean lobby, Eden nodded in
satisfaction. She loved overseeing the inn, loved playing a
larger role in Brett's business than she had in the first few
years of their marriage. In fact, she had been the one who
suggested they build the inn.

Brett had come home from the packinghouse one night, his
brow creased in concern. When Eden had asked what was
troubling him, he had snapped, "Nothing! Can't a man think
about his work without you assuming there's something wrong!"

By now accustomed to his moods, Eden smiled serenely.
"Certainly. But thinking about McKinnon Meats usually makes
you smile. What's troubling you, Brett?"

"I said nothing. Nothing you or I can do anything about,
anyway. I'm just wondering if Chicago's going to end up with
more packers than she can accommodate. All of a sudden it's
not just Arch Clybourne, Gurdon Hubbard, and me anymore.
Three more men have set up packinghouses on the river, just
in the last few months."

Eden raised her brows. "That's to be expected, isn't it?
You're always saying how Chicago and Illinois can't stop
growing."

"Sure! But I can't have these newcomers taking away my business! We've got a prosperous shipping line over the Great Lakes now, but if too much of the livestock goes to the new packers, I won't have enough meat to fill my orders."

"That won't happen," Eden calmly assured him. "You've been dealing with some of those farmers for five years. They know you give them a fair price for their stock, so they're not going to turn to someone else."

"How do you know?" he demanded querulously. "People are fickle. If one of the newcomers will pay them more, what can I do about it?"

Eden gazed at him thoughtfully. "What do the farmers complain about the most when they bring their livestock to market?"

Brett laughed sardonically. "Having to bring it to market at all! I mean, most of them don't mind an occasional holiday in the city, but they'd rather not drive in a bunch of hogs or cattle." He shrugged. "I can understand that. It's not fun trying to keep a lot of pigs or cows from going crazy when you drive them into a town the size of Chicago. But I can't see what any of that has to do with my problem."

"I can," Eden said quietly. "If you want to be sure you don't lose your suppliers, you'd better offer them something no one else does."

Brett shook his head. "You don't know what you're talking about! We can't go out to the farms and pick up the stock. We can't afford the men or time to do that."

"Of course not. But you *can* make the job of bringing livestock to Chicago easier for the farmers. Suppose you moved the packinghouse to the western outskirts of the city, so the farmers wouldn't have to bring their stock all the way in to town?"

"Not practical!" he snapped. "We're better off staying right where we are on the river. We need that ready water source."

"All right, then. What if you just moved part of the business to the outskirts? Suppose we built an inn on the western edge of town? Only, it wouldn't be just an inn, it would be an inn with extensive stockpens. The farmers and drovers could bring in their stock, sell it to you right there, spend a night at the inn, and continue in to town for a carefree, unencumbered holiday. Of course, you'd still have to transport the stock to your packinghouse. But, you could move the animals a few at a time, so it wouldn't be such a problem. In return for the boost to business, I should think the extra work would be worth it."

For a long moment, Brett stared at her skeptically; then he threw back his head and laughed delightedly. "Chérie, it's a marvelous idea! It seems I should have asked your advice long ago. Of course," he added soberly, "opening an inn would mean a great deal of extra work. I'm not certain I should really consider it. As it is, I already spend far too little time with you and the boys."

"Well, of course, I'd help," Eden said quickly. "An inn needs a woman's touch. Mother Murphy proved that when she took over Mark Beaubien's inn over at Wolf Point. I could oversee the housekeeping and meal preparation, and even help you with the bookkeeping if you'd like. I want to be a part of your business, Brett! Please say you'll let me!"

And so, the Bull and Boar Inn had been born. As Eden predicted, it had quickly become a great success. Though just a bit more than two miles from the center of Chicago and just within the city limits, it was surrounded by prairie. Weary farmers and drovers coming from the West were glad to spend the night there and be rid of their livestock as well.

More importantly, the inn gave Eden a new closeness with Brett. They had always shared a physical closeness, much more so, she now realized, than many other couples. Now she was a part of his work, as well.

Even though Brett spent a large part of each day away from home at the packinghouse, Eden felt she shared more of his life now. Recognizing her business sense in planning the inn, Brett trusted her more and asked her advice more often. Many nights, when they lay side by side, relishing the warm afterglow of their lovemaking, they talked for an hour or more, solving current business problems, or delighting in their plans for the future.

Their lives were intertwined now in a way that was much more complete than simply sharing a home and children. That part, as always, was wonderful. But now it seemed to Eden as if they had truly become one person. It seemed there was nothing they did not share, nothing each did not know about the other. She worked harder now than she ever had in her life, often falling into bed exhausted. But it was worth it for the sense of well-being that suffused her life.

The jingle of the bell attached to the door jarred Eden from her thoughts. She looked up, smiling, expecting to greet one of the drovers or farmers she had met in the last several months. Instead, she saw an Indian youth, no more than fifteen years old.

As he came nearer, Eden realized that the young man was not a full-blooded Indian. His hair was black, but his eyes had the grayish-green coloring of a white man's. Eden felt puzzled. She thought she knew all the half-breeds in the area, but did not recognize this youth.

Lifting her eyebrows quizzically, she asked, "May I help you?"

The Indian nodded. "They told me in town I could find Brett McKinnon here."

"I'm sorry, but he's away at the moment. He spends most of his day at the McKinnon Meats packinghouse, on the south branch of the river."

Nodding impatiently, the young man said, "I've been there already, but they told me he's left for the day."

"Ah, then I suspect he stopped to visit his friend, John Kinzie." John and his wife Juliette had moved back to Chicago a few years earlier and had become the McKinnons' closest friends. "I can't say how long he'll be, but you're welcome to wait for him. Or, if you prefer, I can give him a message."

"No, I'll wait." The young man looked around the lobby uncomfortably, until Eden waved him into a chair. He sat tensely, as if he was not quite sure he ought to stay. Watching him, Eden remembered her own awkwardness when Brett first brought her to the Kinzie household from Black Eagle's camp. She sensed that, despite his mixed blood, the young man was more accustomed to Indian than white ways.

Smiling in an attempt to put him at ease, Eden said, "I'm Eden McKinnon, Brett's wife."

At the last words, a look of horror crossed the young man's face. His eyes widened in disbelief, then darted away from Eden's questioning gaze.

"Is something wrong?" Eden asked.

"No—I—That is—" The young man rose quickly and started toward the door. "Perhaps I shouldn't stay, after all. My mother warned me that—but I could not believe he would—it did not seem possible—"

Eden felt her heart constrict with sudden, unreasonable fear. But she forced her voice to remain steady. "I'm afraid I haven't any idea what you're trying to say. Please sit down and try to explain to me—"

"No! I must go!"

"Then at least let me give Brett a message for you. At least tell me your name."

"Benjamin," he whispered hoarsely.

"Benjamin? Is that all? Will he know you by just your Christian name?"

"I think so. I'm not sure. It doesn't matter now, anyway."

"But if you want to see Brett—if it's important—will he know where to find you?"

"No. It doesn't matter." He hesitated. "I don't think he'll want to find me."

"Nonsense!" Eden insisted. "My husband is not the sort of man to ignore a friend who's come looking for him."

"I'm not a friend!" the young man cried painfully.

Eden frowned. "I don't understand." For a long moment, she stared at him, waiting for him to explain his strange statement. When the young man remained silent, she forced a light laugh. "Oh, I see. *You're* not Brett's friend. You're too young. But perhaps your family—was your father a fur trader?"

He stared at her mutely, his eyes begging her not to ask more. Slowly, he nodded. "Yes. He was a trader."

"And he knew Brett?"

"He—" Benjamin paused, searching for some explanation. "I'm sorry. I think I had best go."

"Please don't." Eden hurried around the desk toward him. "I'm sure Brett will be disappointed he missed you. Are you uncomfortable sitting in a white man's inn, is that it?" Without waiting for an answer, Eden plunged on, "Don't be. I understand. I spent my first eight years living among the Potawatomis, and when Brett first brought me to Chicago, I didn't know how to act. Perhaps you and I even have mutual friends among the Potawatomis. Did you ever know an old chief named Black Eagle? Or a lovely woman, a few years older than me, called Morning Star?"

Biting his lower lip, Benjamin looked away, but not before Eden saw the brief flicker of remembrance in his eyes.

"You did know them!" she exclaimed triumphantly.

Benjamin stared at her steadily. "Black Eagle was my grandfather," he said quietly. "Morning Star is my mother."

"But what a wonderful coincidence! When I was a baby, Black Eagle adopted me as his daughter. And, when my mother died, Morning Star took care of me. So, you see Benjamin, you and I are related—in spirit if not in blood."

Pausing, she gazed at him searchingly. "But then, who was your father? A voyageur? One of Brett's engagés?"

Benjamin's eyes met hers with the tortured gaze of a wounded, trapped animal. "Brett McKinnon is my father," he whispered huskily.

Gasping, Eden stared at him in disbelief. "No!" She shook her head. "It's not pos—"

"I'm sorry. Why did you make me tell you?" Benjamin asked in an anguished tone. "I didn't want to! I didn't want to hurt you! I'd never have come if I'd known he had a wife."

Her voice drained of emotion, Eden asked, "Is your mother— Morning Star—is she still alive?"

Benjamin nodded, too overwrought to speak.

Sinking into a chair, Eden averted her eyes. "There must be some mistake," she insisted. "Perhaps you've confused Brett with someone else. How old were you when you last saw your father?"

"I was nine," Benjamin said hollowly. "It was six years ago. The day the government drove the Indians from Chicago."

Eden caught her breath. The same day Brett had proposed to her! But why would this youth lie to her? And how could he be mistaken? A nine-year-old boy would surely know his father's identity.

"I'm sorry," Benjamin repeated lamely. "I should have left. It is not right for you to suffer when you are innocent. My mother would be disappointed in me."

"No," Eden said steadily, "she shouldn't be. In Brett, perhaps, but not in you. You were not wrong to tell me the truth. Someone had to," she added bitterly.

Suddenly, she felt very tired, overburdened by Brett's lies. They flooded her memory now. The night he proposed and she had asked him why he never married before. The day Burton was born, when he had rejected the name Benjamin.

How else had Brett deceived her? She had thought she knew all there was to know about him. Now it seemed she knew nothing at all.

Forcing her thoughts back to the present, Eden looked sympathetically at Benjamin. "It must have been very hard for you," she said, "losing your father at the age of nine. For your mother, too."

Benjamin shrugged uneasily. "It was hard for me to

understand, but I accepted it. There were other half-breeds
in the same position as I. Mark Beaubien's son, Medore. Our
guide, Sauganash." Again, he shrugged. "It was a strange
time. But no more strange for me than for the other Indians."

"You've lived the last six years in Indian Territory?"

"Yes. It has been a good life."

"Then, why did you come back to Chicago?"

"I wanted to know my father. When I was a boy, he was
often away. But when he was home, I loved to play with him.
At first when we moved away, I thought he would still come
to play with me from time to time. But he never did. I love
my mother, and my brother, but there was an empty part in
my heart that wanted my father, too."

"Your brother?" Eden repeated. "Brett has another son?"

Benjamin nodded, cringing inwardly as he read the pain in
Eden's eyes. "Swift Elk is two years older than I."

Both were silent for a long moment. Then Benjamin sighed.
"Now that I know my father has a new life, I will not stay. I
do not belong here."

"No, Benjamin," Eden said clearly, "you're wrong. You do
belong here. You have as much right to know your father as
my own two sons do. Brett owes you that much, at least."

9

October 1841

All through dinner, Eden could hardly bear to look at
Brett. She had given Benjamin a room in the inn and assured
the youth she and Brett would call for him later. Overwrought,
Benjamin had seemed relieved to postpone the reunion with
his father.

Now, watching her own two young sons chattering excitedly with their father, Eden found herself blinking back tears
of sorrow and disappointment. Brett seemed like such a good
father, such a devoted husband. Had Morning Star thought
the same? Had young Benjamin once stared up at him with

the same blind hero worship she read in two-year-old Clinton's eyes?

When the boys had finally been tucked into bed and Brett and Eden were alone in the parlor, Brett looked at her worriedly. "You've been extraordinarily pensive tonight, ma petite. Is something troubling you? Some problem with the inn, perhaps?"

"No. There are no problems with the inn."

"You're not ill?"

"No." Her voice was unusually curt.

His brow creased in puzzlement, Brett went to her and slid his arms around her. "You're not, perhaps, expecting another child?"

"No!" She pulled away abruptly, turning and taking a few steps away from him. "I should think," she whispered bitterly, "that you already have enough children, Brett."

Brett frowned. "I don't understand, chérie. Of course I'm quite content with our two fine sons, but I would welcome more children. After all, two children make a rather small family, especially," he added, forcing a laugh, "when you think of the twenty-three Mark Beaubien has fathered!"

"But you have more than two children, don't you, Brett? In fact," she said, turning to glare at him accusingly, "you have four!"

Brett's eyes narrowed slightly, but his voice remained level. "Eden, I assure you, I have no idea what you are talking about."

"Don't you?" She paused, staring at him, trying to fathom his expressionless eyes. "Benjamin is here."

She saw the flicker of pain in his eyes before he blinked, saw his throat tremble as he gulped. "Benjamin?"

"Yes, Benjamin! You haven't forgotten your second son, have you?"

"Eden—I—" He turned away, too unnerved to look her in the eye. Sinking into a chair, he murmured, "There must be some mistake."

"That's what I said at first. But now I'm sure there is no mistake. Now I finally understand the real reason you could never take me to visit Morning Star, why you never even wanted to talk to me about her."

Suddenly, all the pain and disillusionment she had nursed since Benjamin's arrival overwhelmed her, and Eden burst into tears. "Oh Brett, Brett," she sobbed, "why did you do

this to me? Why did you deceive me? I loved you! I was
foolish enough to believe you loved me!"

"I do love you, chérie," Brett insisted. "I've loved you
since the day you stumbled on me in the cholera wards of
Fort Dearborn. Even before that, I used to think of the little
girl I brought to Chicago, and dream of the woman she must
have become."

"I suppose you told Morning Star you loved her, too."

"No, Eden. I swear to you, I never told her that."

"But you married her."

"Not really. Not in the Christian sense. After I delivered
you safely to Chicago, Black Eagle proposed that I take her
for my wife. It was sort of a reward for seeing to your future,
a token of our continuing friendship. I couldn't insult him by
refusing. And, of course, Morning Star was very lovely. One
could not help but be fond of her. But I was never in love
with her. She always knew that."

Eden stared at him, mentally calculating the time from her
childhood arrival in Chicago until the Potawatomis were sent
West. "Yet you lived with her for fifteen years."

"I—" He stopped abruptly, sighing in defeat. "Yes, I did."

"And she bore you two sons."

Again he sighed. "Yes."

"And you never told me." Her voice was flat, devoid now
even of pain.

"I always intended to tell you, chérie. You must believe
that I never meant to deceive you. But, at first, I wanted you
so desperately I couldn't bear even to think of my past. Then
later, when Burton was born, I felt it would be wrong to
upset you. Finally, I convinced myself you would never find
out, so it was pointless to hurt you by telling you."

"But I would never have been hurt at all if you had only
been honest with me from the start! You were thirty-four
years old when we married, Brett. I wasn't naive enough to
imagine you had never been with a woman. I probably wouldn't
even have been shocked to learn you lived with Morning
Star. By the time you proposed to me I'd lived in Chicago
long enough to realize that plenty of traders had liaisons with
Indian women. But to find out now, after we've been married
six years, after I've borne you two sons—"

Exploding under the weight of her accusations, Brett
demanded, "Dammit, what difference does it make? It all
happened long before you returned to Chicago. And I can see

now I was right to keep the truth from you. You never would
have understood."

"No, I wouldn't have understood," she shouted. "I'll never
understand. Oh, I can accept your liaison with Morning Star.
I can even believe you lived with her so long when you claim
you didn't love her. You wouldn't be the first couple, married
or otherwise, to remain together without love. But how could
you turn your back on your two sons—your own flesh and
blood?"

"I didn't turn my back on them! Morning Star took them
away. It was her choice. I asked her to stay, but she refused.
She said it was time we began separate lives."

"And you never even saw her, or your sons, again?"

"I told her to let me know if she ever needed me. She
knew I would always do whatever I could for her or the
boys."

Eden stared at him incredulously. "Do you really think
that excuses you, Brett? She must have known you didn't
want her, or your sons, when you let them go away. Knowing
that, do you really think she ever would have asked your
help, no matter how much she needed it?"

"Of course she would have! There was no bitterness at our
parting."

"No, Brett," Eden shook her head adamantly. "You knew
she would never come to you. If you had ever even thought
there was a chance she or one of your sons would return, you
would have told me about them. You wouldn't have let me
find out about them this way. Unless"— her voice wavered
and she turned away from him —"unless you don't really care
about me, either."

"Eden! How can you even think such a thing?" His hands
descended on her shoulders, and he tried to turn her to face
him.

Angrily, she shook him off. "I don't know what to think
right now," she mumbled. "I don't even know what I feel for
you at this moment—whether I'm more hurt because you
deceived me, or more disillusioned because the fine man I
thought I married is not so fine after all. What kind of man
pretends his sons don't even exist? Would you do that to
Burton and Clinton?"

"Eden, you know I wouldn't!"

"How do I know? All I know is there's a young man

upstairs in our inn trying to figure out why he hasn't heard
from his father in six years!"

For a moment, Brett was silent. In the heat of the discussion,
he had almost forgotten Benjamin was there.

"What room is the boy in?" he asked gruffly. "He wants to
see me? All right, I'll see him. If he needs money, food,
anything, I'll see that he gets it. But he can't stay here. I
won't have him disrupting our lives, upsetting you—"

"Upsetting me!" Eden whirled on him, her eyes snapping
with fury. "You don't seem to understand, Brett. You're the
one responsible for upsetting me—not that innocent young
man! You can't just send him away because it's not convenient to let him be part of your life! He told me he came
looking for you because something was missing from his life.
There was an emptiness inside him, meant for a father to fill.
If he wants to stay here—for however long—it would be
worse than heartless to turn him away."

"I was only thinking of you and our boys—"

"You should have thought of us before! But, don't worry,
we'll manage. You'd better go and see Benjamin now. He's in
the room at the end of the hall on the second floor."

Brett hesitated outside the door of Benjamin's room, trying
to bring his emotions under control. He could not deny he
was angry at the youth's sudden appearance, disrupting his
near-perfect relationship with Eden. Nor was he pleased by
the thought of having a half-breed son to explain to his
neighbors and business associates.

At forty, with a solid reputation as both a businessman and
leading citizen of Chicago, Brett did not relish having his past
dredged up. His life with Morning Star had been perfectly
acceptable among the traders, voyageurs, and frontiersmen
who populated Chicago twenty years ago. But in recent years
those rougher elements had been replaced more and more by
"respectable," Eastern-bred folks. In their eyes, Benjamin
would be a bastard, and his father would be little better.

Of course, Brett supposed he couldn't blame Benjamin for
the problems. Certainly the boy could not have anticipated
them. Still, it was damned inconvenient having him turn up
now.

Sighing, Brett raised a fist and rapped on the door.
"Benjamin? It's—it's your father."

In a moment, the youth was standing in the doorway, his

eyes moving warily over Brett. Brett noted that Benjamin was tall for his age, but his eyes still held the innocence and hurt of a young boy. Suddenly, he wondered how he could have closed his heart and mind to Benjamin's existence for so many years. This youth was his son, no less than Burton and Clinton were his sons.

Without thinking, Brett opened his arms, and Benjamin rushed to embrace him, choking back a sob of relief.

After a moment, the youth pulled back, smiling though his eyes glistened with tears.

"You look just as I remember you, Father."

Brett smiled. "And you look much, much different. You were a boy the last time we were together, Benjamin. Now you are a man."

The youth nodded. "That is what Mother said when I decided to look for you. She did not want me to come, but she said I was a man now, and she could not stop me." He paused, his eyes clouding with pain. "I suppose now I should have stayed away. Mother tried to warn me, but I did not believe you might have a new wife. Now I understand why you never visited us."

Seeing Brett about to speak, he shook his head. "Don't explain. I've had all evening to think about it. At first I felt shocked, hurt that you would turn to someone new. Then I remembered your conversation with Mother that last day. All these years I've carried her words in my heart. Then, I was too young to understand. But now I know what she meant when she said your lives were like the slender stalk of the starflower, dividing to bear separate blossoms."

Brett looked away, his heart torn by the memory of that afternoon. "Is Morning Star all right?" he asked hoarsely.

"Yes."

"And Thomas? Or is it Swift Elk?"

"Swift Elk. My brother is very happy—content to be an Indian, as I never could be. I did not dislike the life of an Indian, but I wanted to know the rest of my heritage as well. Still, I never thought to upset your life. Your wife has been very kind, but I think my presence has disturbed her. Tomorrow, I will return west."

"No! Eden—that is we—insist that you stay as long as you wish."

Benjamin gazed at him searchingly. "I would like to see

more of you. To see more of how you live, what you do at this meat-packing business. But I would not wish to be a burden."

"You won't be," Brett said with more confidence than he felt. "It's late, so, tonight, you can remain here in the inn. But tomorrow we'll move you into a room in the family apartment."

"Will your wife mind? I wouldn't wish to inconvenience her, or the children you share with her."

"I'm quite certain she would not approve of any other arrangement."

Brett looked around the room uncomfortably, wondering what else to say to this stranger who was his son. What was the youth thinking of him? How would he explain the young man's existence to Burton and Clinton and the men at McKinnon Meats? John Kinzie was the only man still in Chicago who already knew about Thomas and Benjamin, and he had always been too discreet to mention them.

Realizing suddenly that Benjamin was watching him anxiously, Brett cleared his throat. "No doubt you've had a long day, and you'll want to get some sleep now. We'll talk more in the days to come."

Benjamin nodded, smiling contentedly. "Yes. Thank you, Father, for everything."

At the door, Brett hesitated, then turned back to face his son. "It seems to me I've given you little enough to thank me for." He paused, considering his next words. "Perhaps it would be best if you didn't call me 'Father,' at least for the time being."

"All right." Benjamin choked back his disappointment. He wondered, as the door closed behind Brett, whether he had actually been accepted or rejected.

In their bedroom, Brett found Eden already in bed.

"It's settled," he said as he began to undress, "Benjamin is staying with us. He'll be moving in here tomorrow."

Eden said nothing.

Getting into bed, Brett asked, "Are you awake, chérie? Didn't you hear me?" He reached for her, sliding a hand down the length of her body, pausing between her thighs as he tugged at her nightdress. He felt her stiffen at his touch, her body becoming leaden as he tried to turn her toward him.

"If you insist on making love to me," she whispered through

gritted teeth, "I won't deny you. It's my obligation as a wife, and I, for one, do not take obligations lightly. But I hope you won't be fool enough to expect it to be the same as it's always been. Nothing can be the same between us, Brett, ever again!"

Swearing softly, Brett slid out of the bed and stormed from the room.

10
September 1842–January 1843

Garrett Martin smoothed his blond mustache as he strode confidently into the Bull and Boar Inn. At twenty-two, he had the inbred assurance of a man born and raised on the frontier. His parents had been among the first settlers in the state of Illinois, and he had grown up herding cattle on the prairie.

As a youth, Garrett had accompanied his father to the Chicago livestock markets. When Garrett was sixteen, the trips had ended abruptly because his father was killed in a gambling brawl.

His mother, Louisa Martin, had fallen ill soon after, and begged Garrett not to leave her. Knowing she feared he, too, would lose his life in the rough town, Garrett had not had the heart to ignore her pleas. Although he had taken over the management of his father's ranch in central Illinois, he had left the cattle sales to hired ranch hands and drovers.

Last month, after a lingering illness, Louisa Martin had died. Though he had loved and respected his mother, Garrett could not honestly say he regretted her passing. For the last six years, she had made him a prisoner of her fears. Now, at last, he felt free to live and take the chances that were part of frontier life. He relished his independence, and he had no intention of allowing any other woman to curtail it.

Glancing around the lobby of the Bull and Boar, Garrett nodded in satisfaction. The cattle drive had been exhilarating. But it would be good to sleep in a comfortable bed tonight and have a hot bath. For the last two years, his drovers had spoken enthusiastically of the Bull and Boar, and Garrett looked forward to its comforts.

As he approached the registry desk, Eden looked up from her ledgers. Garrett smiled slightly as he recalled the comment of one of his drovers: "Even if McKinnon didn't offer the best price in town, he'd have half the drovers in the West stopping at his Bull and Boar, just to get a look at his wife!"

She was lovely, Garrett thought, with her softly coiled chestnut hair, her high chiseled cheekbones, and her luminous blue-green eyes. Still, her soft smile of greeting did not quite reach her eyes. There was something almost dead about her gaze, as if life had hurt her too many times, and she had finally stopped caring.

"Would you like a room, sir?" she asked.

Garrett nodded. "Four rooms, to be exact. I have three drovers out back getting my cattle settled in your stockpens."

"Very well. If you'll just sign the register." She turned the inn register toward him, watching as he signed. "Mr. Martin, is it? You wouldn't be connected with the Martin ranch down near Decatur?"

"Yes. That's my ranch."

"Oh." Eden flushed slightly, annoyed at the obvious note of surprise in her voice. He seemed very young for a ranch owner, and she knew Brett had been doing business with the Martin ranch for years. But, why should she care about his age? Garrett Martin was no more important to her than the scores of other ranchers and drovers who stayed at the Bull and Boar and dealt with McKinnon Meats.

"Well, Mr. Martin," she said briskly, "we're very happy to have you at the Bull and Boar. Your drovers have stayed here many times, and we've always been pleased to serve them."

"Yes, they've brought back fine reports of your hospitality." Inwardly, Garrett cringed. What was the matter with him? He sounded so stilted. In all those years cooped up with his mother, had he forgotten how to talk to a lady?

"Mama, Clinton's knocked over the honey jar in the pantry, and it's running all over everything!"

Garrett saw Eden's eyes soften as she turned to face a five-year-old boy. "Oh, dear!" she murmured. "What's the matter with Michelle? She's supposed to be watching you."

The boy giggled, flipping his reddish hair off his forehead. "Michelle's fallen asleep in the parlor!"

"Oh, dear!" Eden repeated.

"I'm in no hurry, ma'am, if you'd like to attend to your domestic crisis," Garrett said.

"Well—" Eden glanced toward the door just as Charley Streeter, one of Garrett's drovers, came in. "Oh, there's Mr. Streeter! He's been here before. He can show you to your rooms." She pushed four room keys across the desk. "Excuse me, please."

As Eden disappeared into the McKinnon apartment, Charley burst into a laugh. "Some problem with the little ones?"

Garrett nodded. "Apparently someone named Clinton upset the honey crock."

"That's the younger boy. Cute little mite, but a regular little terror at times. Well, come on," he picked up their saddlebags and started toward the stairway, "I'll show you where we sleep."

On the way upstairs, Charley whispered, "That Mrs. McKinnon's a pretty woman, ain't she?"

"Closer to beautiful, I'd say. But she looks kind of—sad. What's the matter, don't she and McKinnon get along?"

Charley shrugged as he dropped the saddlebags and inserted a room key into a lock. "Can't say for sure, as I've never seen them together, but I've always heard they had one of those perfect marriages. McKinnon's a good deal older than her, of course, but—" he stopped abruptly, narrowing his eyes at Garrett. "You're not getting any ideas about Eden McKinnon, are you? There's plenty of women in town easier to come by, with no husbands to get in the way."

Garrett laughed shortly. "Don't worry, Charley. I'm just curious, that's all. Something in her eyes made me wonder."

The drover scratched his head. "Well, come to think of it, she has seemed a little less cheery since that Indian boy came to live here last year. A half-breed." His voice lowered to a whisper. "Some folks say he's Brett McKinnon's son."

"What do you say, Charley?"

"I don't get myself involved in no speculation. Brett McKinnon's a good man to do business with, and his wife runs a good inn. That's all I care about."

That's all I should care about, too, Garrett told himself as Charley went on to his own room.

Stepping back into the inn lobby, Eden sighed with relief. Garrett Martin was gone. Not, she insisted to herself quickly,

that she actually cared whether he was there or not. Still, she
had to admit something about his arrival had upset her.

With his tanned face, sharply angular features, and his
blond hair, bleached as light as cornsilk, Garrett was unusually attractive. Eden met her share of lean, rugged men in
the inn every day. Still, something about Garrett had touched
her as none of the other drovers and farmers ever had.
Something in his piercing blue eyes told her he was more
understanding, more tender than other men. She had read
sympathy in his gaze, though he surely could not know that
she had any problems.

Stop it! Eden told herself sharply. You're being foolish!
The only difference between Garrett Martin and the other
men who frequent the Bull and Boar is that he's younger, he
might be a touch more handsome, and you've never seen him
before. If things were right between you and Brett, you
wouldn't give Garrett Martin a second thought.

But things weren't right between them. They hadn't been
right since Benjamin arrived. For the sake of the children,
they pretended that nothing had changed. Young as they
were, Burton and Clinton had accepted without question the
addition of another member to the family. Neither realized
Benjamin's arrival had destroyed the intimacy Eden and Brett
had so treasured.

Keenly sensitive, Benjamin himself had immediately seen
the strain caused by his presence. At first, he had hoped the
problem would disappear after they all became better
acquainted. When months passed and the situation did not
improve, he had approached Eden and suggested he return
to Indian Territory. Eden had insisted that he stay.

"But I'm a burden here," Benjamin argued. "I cause pain
for you and my father."

"No, Benjamin. You're wrong. We all love you. And your
father is very proud of you."

That much was true. Brett *was* proud of Benjamin, proud
of how quickly he caught on to the meat-packing business,
proud of the confident, but not cocky, way he handled himself among older men. Still, Brett could not bring himself to
acknowledge Benjamin as his son. Gradually, he had allowed
people to believe he and Eden had adopted the half-breed.
But he would never reveal their true relationship.

In a way, Eden felt sorry for her husband. She knew he
loved Benjamin, but was afraid to show it. On the surface, he

appeared distant from the youth, blaming him for the rift in his marriage. But both Eden and Brett knew that neither Benjamin's presence nor even his existence had caused their problems. Brett's deception was to blame.

Even when she tried to convince herself that he had deceived her in the hopes of sparing her from hurt, Eden could not forgive Brett. He had done more than deceive her. He had betrayed Morning Star, Benjamin, and his other son, Swift Elk. He had turned away from his own flesh and blood. That she could neither condone nor comprehend.

Anyway, why should she even think about forgiving Brett, when he did nothing to seek or win forgiveness? Since that night almost a year ago when he had stormed from their bedroom, a cold, hard wall had developed between them. It seemed he had no interest in making her understand. He had accepted Benjamin into his home and business as she demanded, but he did not appear inclined to make amends in any other way.

He did not talk to her, except in the presence of family, friends, and servants. He never tried to make love to her. If, in the middle of the night, he accidentally rolled against her in their bed, he pulled away abruptly, cursing under his breath.

If only she could talk to someone. But who? Not Benjamin, who was already upset enough about the estrangement. Not Juliette Kinzie, her closest woman friend. As the wife of Brett's best friend, Juliette could not be expected to offer impartial advice. Besides, Eden felt too proud to discuss the problem with another woman. She could not bear to reveal her own foolish naiveté, or Brett's deception and callous indifference.

So, what could she do? Continue to live in a loveless marriage, finding solace only with her children and her work? Pretend she wasn't hurt, that she didn't care, because to admit otherwise would only make the pain more unbearable?

"Pardon me, ma'am."

Startled, Eden looked up into the piercing blue eyes of Garrett Martin. Engrossed in her thoughts, she had not heard him enter.

"I was wondering about meals?" he said casually.

"The dining room is to your left," she replied curtly. "We'll be serving supper at six o'clock. I should think your drovers could have told you that."

Garrett smiled lazily. "I suspect they could have. But you can't blame me, can you, if I'd rather talk to a pretty lady than a weatherbeaten drover?"

Averting her gaze, Eden asked, "You do know, don't you, Mr. Martin, that I'm married to Mr. McKinnon?"

"Yes, ma'am. But I don't recall there being any laws against complimenting a married woman."

Eden flushed. "No, I suppose there aren't. Forgive me, Mr. Martin. My boys have been rather rowdy this afternoon, and I'm afraid I'm not myself."

Garrett nodded sympathetically. "It can't be easy, managing a house, an inn, and a pair of energetic boys all at once."

She shrugged. "A woman does whatever she's called upon to do."

"I suppose." He paused, thinking of his own mother, who had been so fear-ridden in her final years she had hardly been able to manage her own life. Gazing at Eden, he said, "Some might say you do more than you're called upon to do. I've heard that building this inn was your idea."

"You hear quite a lot for a man who's never been here before. But yes, it's true."

"Your husband must be mighty proud of you." His keen eyes seemed to bore into hers.

Dropping her gaze, Eden wondered, what was he really saying? What did he suspect? Could her problems with Brett be so obvious, even to a total stranger? Turning her eyes to her ledger, she replied offhandedly, "My husband is proud, and justly so, of everything connected with McKinnon Meats. Now, if you'll excuse me, Mr. Martin, I really must bring my bookkeeping up to date."

She did not look up again. But she could not concentrate on her figures until long after Garrett Martin's footsteps had receded up the stairs.

Eden made it a point not to be in the lobby the next few days, while Garrett Martin was a guest of the inn. Feigning illness, she asked Benjamin to stay home from the plant and take charge of the registry desk. Still, she realized with annoyance that she was listening for the young rancher's voice as she played with her sons in the McKinnon apartment.

Even weeks after he had gone, Eden could not stop thinking of Garrett Martin. Sometimes at night, she would wake from dreams of a man with sun-bleached hair and penetrating blue eyes and realize she had been dreaming of him.

My God! she would think, I must be going mad! The man's a complete stranger! I'm a married woman! In all my life, I've never even been attracted to anyone but Brett.

Seeing her husband's dimly outlined body in the bed beside her, she would reach out to press his hand, willing to forgive him his deception, and all the months of agony that had followed its discovery, for the blessed solace of sharing their lives again. But he always pulled away with a grunt, rolling to the far edge of the bed.

The chasm between them seemed wider than ever. The wound began to throb again, as raw as the day Benjamin had appeared at the Bull and Boar. And Eden lay awake, berating her foolishness for even thinking there could be a reconciliation.

The next morning, Brett would seem as unapproachable as ever, and Eden would insist to herself that she did not want to approach him. He had wronged her, after all, her, and her sons, and Benjamin, and Morning Star, and his other son, Benjamin's brother. Let him at least show some regret for his actions. Let him come to her.

But, of course, he didn't. If he ever might have, the time was now long past. After fifteen months of estrangement, the future seemed to be carved in stone. The loneliness that enveloped Eden grew with each day, each week. It had become a part of her life, just as surely as her duties at the inn.

In January, Eden sat watching the snow swirling across Southwestern Plank Road. Her life had become as desolate as the scene outdoors. No, she told herself sternly, that's not true. You have two fine sons to live for. And Benjamin needs you, too. Still, she knew that none of them could fill the void in her life. She needed a man, and the need was even more potent because of the intimacy she and Brett had once shared.

With surprise, Eden suddenly noticed a tall figure emerging from the snow and heading toward the inn. She frowned. Though the Bull and Boar never closed officially, it rarely had guests in the winter. Who would drive livestock to market through five-foot drifts of prairie snow?

In winter, the packinghouse flourished, while the livestock-purchasing operations of McKinnon Meats waited for the return of warm weather. Since freezing temperatures prevented spoilage, winter was the only really safe time for slaughtering. Brett and Benjamin were gone now even longer hours than in the other months, when they dealt more with purchasing livestock and shipping preserved meats. And Eden, without the diversion of a bustling inn, felt her loneliness more keenly than at any other time.

The man had come through the door now and was dusting the snow off a heavy cowhide jacket and sweeping a snow-covered hat from his head. With shock, Eden recognized Garrett Martin.

Frowning slightly to cover the sudden flush that painted her cheeks, Eden asked, "Mr. Martin, what brings you to Chicago? I hope you didn't drive any cattle through this blizzard!"

Garrett grinned, showing two deep dimples in his cheeks. Eden's flush deepened as she realized she wanted to reach up and caress his wind-whipped face.

"No, I didn't bring any livestock on this trip," he replied evenly. "In fact, I rode here alone." His blue eyes danced, telling her he was quite aware of her nervousness. "Do you have a room for me?"

"Well, yes, I suppose we do. Of course, most of the men we do business with don't come here in the winter. In fact, we haven't had any guests in weeks, so I gave our cook an extended holiday. I suppose you could take your meals with the family, or I could send up a tray—"

"I'd be delighted to join your family for meals."

"Yes, well you may want to reconsider. The boys can be rather lively. In any case, you can take the first room on your left on the second floor. I'm afraid you'll find the fireplace cold, but there's wood in the box at the end of the hall."

"Thank you." He took the key she offered, his fingertips lingering against hers. "I'll go on up and start a fire. If it's not too much trouble, I'd appreciate something hot to drink."

"Tea?"

"Fine. Though I'd prefer strong coffee if you have it." He hesitated. "I'm sure you're not in the habit of playing chambermaid, but could you bring it up to the room?"

Eden swallowed. Did she detect a note of challenge in his voice? No, she must be imagining things. Those damned dreams were destroying her usual self-confidence. Garrett Martin was just another guest, and he deserved any service she could reasonably provide.

"Of course, Mr. Martin," she said crisply. "I'll bring up your coffee as soon as it's ready."

A quarter of an hour later, Eden knocked at the door of Garrett Martin's room.

"Come in!" he called.

She had intended to hand him the tray and hurry back downstairs. But when she opened the door, she saw that he was still on his knees before the fireplace, laying a fire.

"Could you just put that over on the table for me?" he said, glancing over his shoulder.

Shrugging, Eden carried the tray across the room. As she turned to leave, Garrett got up from the fireplace and walked toward her. His face was flushed from the nearness of the fire, and his hair was tousled like that of a small boy. He had shed his coat, and his woolen shirt was open at the neck. She could see the light brown hair on his chest.

He raised an eyebrow as his eyes moved past her to the tray, set with a coffeepot, a plate with a few biscuits left from breakfast, and a single cup and saucer. "Only one cup? I was hoping you would join me."

"I'm afraid that's impossible."

"Don't tell me your boys are in the honey crock again?"

Eden laughed, hoping to cover her tension. "What a good memory you have, Mr. Martin! But I suspect they're behaving themselves. Their nursemaid won't stand for too much foolishness."

"Really? I thought she was given to falling asleep at her job."

"You do have a good memory! But that was Michelle. She left us last month to get married. Our new woman, Marguerite, is a good deal more dependable." She stopped abruptly, aware she was saying too much, speaking too rapidly. Surely he didn't care at all about Michelle or Marguerite.

"Then, you see, you do have time to join me. You can't say your ledgers are waiting for you. With so little business, you can't have much bookkeeping at this time of year."

Averting her eyes, Eden started for the door. "I'd better go."

"You know," Garrett said softly, "it might help if you could just talk to someone."

She turned slowly and stared at him defiantly, damning herself for her unreasonable sense of panic. "I don't know what you mean."

"Of course you do. Something's bothering you. I could see it in your eyes the first time I came here, and I can still see it today."

Again, she turned away, afraid to look him in the eye. She was almost to the door when Garrett's words stopped her.

"It has to do with the half-breed. McKinnon's son."

Eden froze. "What makes you think Benjamin is Brett's son?"

"People talk. Anyone can figure things out. They've got the same eyes, for one thing."

Shrugging, she turned to face him again. "So, people know. What does it matter? I suppose I always knew they would guess."

"It's no reflection on you, you know. The boy is what, seventeen? You couldn't even have been old enough to be married to McKinnon when he was born. So, it's not as if McKinnon was unfaithful to you. Plenty of men your husband's age sowed their wild oats with Indian women. There are enough half-breeds in Illinois to testify to that."

"I know all that. And, as for Benjamin, I'm proud to have him here. He's honest, dependable, intelligent—everything a parent could want in a child."

"What's the problem then?"

He asked it so softly, with such tenderness and genuine concern that Eden felt all her defenses crumbling. How often had she longed for someone to talk to? When this man stood here, offering his compassion, could she really turn away? Wouldn't there be some blessed relief in letting everything out at last?

For a long moment, Eden looked into Garrett's penetrating blue eyes, and she knew instinctively that he wanted to help. She began telling him everything—all the deceptions, the pain, the disillusionment, the wound that continued to grow as month after month passed and Brett did nothing to repair the rift.

"Why can't he at least try to talk to me about it?" she demanded. "Why can't he at least acknowledge Benjamin as his son, at least try to make up for all the years he ignored the boy?"

In these last months of estrangement, Eden had thought she had finally become hardened to her pain. After that first night, she had never even wept. Now, as she talked, she was horrified to discover her face flooding with tears, her chest heaving with uncontrollable sobs. Dimly, she realized that Garrett had closed the door. Then his arms wrapped around her, and she felt the comforting warmth of his chest beneath her cheek.

"I loved him so much," she sobbed. "All I ever wanted was to be his wife. And he deceived me! Oh, maybe I could have learned to live with that. Maybe I could even have forgiven him in time. But when I think of what he did to those boys—six years without a father, without even any word from him! I don't know the older boy, but Benjamin is so sensitive. How terrible for him to keep hoping for a father who never came! And Morning Star—I knew her! She was like an older sister to me, almost a mother."

Garrett frowned; he could not understand the part about Morning Star. But his mind burned with righteous indignation toward Brett McKinnon. To be honest, at that moment he didn't care what Brett had done to Benjamin, or his other half-breed son, or Morning Star. But he cared very much what the man had done to Eden.

Here was a woman who was everything a wife should be. She was strong, capable, hardworking, imaginative. With her plans for the Bull and Boar Inn, she had made McKinnon Meats stand out among Chicago's meat-packers.

Eden McKinnon was the type of woman a man could lean on as much as she leaned on him. An equal partner. And Brett McKinnon had been foolish to hurt her.

Gazing down at her chestnut hair, feeling her tears through his shirt, Garrett felt a great wave of tenderness. Six years enslaved by his mother's fears had convinced him he didn't want to be tied to any woman. But, oh God, to have a woman like this! It would be worth giving up his freedom.

Her sobs were lessening now, though she still clung to him. Reaching up, he tentatively stroked her gleaming hair. His hand slid along the smooth, soft column of her throat, then tipped her chin back until her gaze met his.

Her eyes widened, and she parted her lips slightly as if she was about to say something. Then his mouth lowered to cover hers. A tremor sped through her body, unleashing a hunger she had not felt in months. Eden strained upward, pressing herself against his lean, hard form.

His mouth still pressed to hers, Garrett lifted Eden and carried her to the bed. He laid her down tenderly, his blue eyes flaming with need and desire. Her mouth opened in feeble protest, but in her eyes he read need that matched his own. Deftly unbuttoning the top of her dress, he pressed his mouth to the wildly throbbing hollow at the base of her throat.

"Eden, sweet Eden," he murmured, "let me take away the pain."

She flinched, but she could not deny the joyous warmth coursing through her. She wanted him, needed him, with an urgency that drove all else from her mind.

His fingers moved down the buttons of her bodice, his lips following as he bared inch after inch of flesh. His mouth found a swollen nipple and sucked tenderly while he lifted her slightly to loosen her petticoats and undergarments.

One by one, her garments fell to the floor, until she lay before him, naked, open, and so magnificently lovely he gasped in astonishment.

His hand stroked the silkiness between her thighs, testing her readiness, building her eagerness, as he tore away his own clothing with his free hand. She felt his hardness as he lay down beside her, but still he did not press into her.

He continued to stroke her, to kiss her, his mouth moving down to her navel and then lower, lower, until she squirmed and moaned with the intensity of her need.

Only then did he move his mouth back to hers, sliding atop her and into her in one smooth motion. She clung to him as they became one, her eyes widening as he brought her to one ecstatic peak, and then another, then another, until finally he unleashed his own pulsing climax.

For a long time afterward, they lay in silence, trying to collect their thoughts. Never, in all the months of anger, sadness, and disillusionment, had Eden considered being unfaithful. Brett was her husband. The father of her children. She wasn't even sure she had stopped loving him. But here she was, lying naked with a man she hardly knew!

"Mr. Martin—" she began nervously.

He chuckled. "Under the circumstances, I think Garrett might be more appropriate."

"All right. Garrett. I—I don't know what to say. I don't usually—"

"You don't usually make love with the guests of your inn? No, I'm sure you don't. I don't usually take married women to my bed. In fact, I'm rather surprised at myself. I came here wanting to know you better, but I never intended to seduce you."

"Can we—could we forget it ever happened?" Eden whispered hopefully.

Garrett frowned. "Could you? Really?"

"No, I suppose not. I—I'm not even certain I want to forget," she admitted.

Sighing, Garrett pulled her closer. "Eden, for you to let something like this happen, it's obvious you're not happy here. Why don't you come away with me?"

"I can't. My children."

"We'll take them with us."

"Benjamin. He needs me. Brett is so distant with him, and I'm the only one he can talk to who understands his feelings. I lived among the Indians until I was eight. I know how hard it is to adjust to white ways."

"You're not responsible for him. You don't owe him anything."

"Yes, I do," she stated quietly. "I'm the one who insisted he stay here. Besides," she mumbled, "I owe something to Brett. I made a commitment."

"He negated that commitment by his lying!" Sitting up, Garrett stared deep into her eyes. Shaking his head, he murmured, "You still love him, don't you? After all he did to you, you still love him!"

"I—I don't know. Honestly, I don't. But I can't say I love you, either, Garrett. My God, I hardly know you! I know you're kind, gentle. You've given me something I needed more than I ever imagined. But love?" She shook her head. "I'm not even sure I believe in it anymore."

Taking a deep breath, Garrett nodded. "All right. I understand. It's too soon. You don't really know me. I'd be wrong to press you. But I can't just walk out of your life. I can't just leave you like this, in a situation I know is so wrong for you. Will you at least give me a chance to prove myself? Will you at least give both of us a chance?"

Eden stared into his penetrating blue eyes. No, she thought. I can't agree to anything. It would be too easy to fall in love with this man. He's too compassionate, too handsome, too spirited. If I let him into my life, what will happen to me? What will happen to Clinton and Burton, to Benjamin, even to Brett? At least now we have some order to our existence. If

I open my life to Garrett Martin, the guilt and indecision will make a shambles of it.

His eyes held hers, mirroring his question. Slowly, despite her best intentions, Eden nodded.

11
1845–1846

Snuggling in the crook of Garrett's arm, Eden basked in the intoxicating afterglow of their lovemaking. After more than two years, she still found herself living for his visits to the Bull and Boar. She still felt a terrible emptiness each time he returned to his ranch.

At first, she had been determined never to repeat what happened that snowy day when he had come alone to the inn. But she had found it impossible to resist him. Though she cherished the hours they lay together, the attraction was more than physical. It was such a relief to be able to talk to someone again, to share her innermost feelings, to feel the support and sympathy of another human being.

Living so far from the center of town, occupied with her children and overseeing the inn, Eden had no close women friends. She got along well with most women, but there was no one in whom she could confide. Juliette Kinzie was probably her most intimate woman friend, but, as the wife of Brett's oldest and best friend, she hardly seemed the best confidante. Garrett had filled a void in Eden's life, becoming both best friend and lover.

Garrett had the gift of being strong and masterful without seeming overbearing. He never implied that Eden was inferior to him, as so many men did. Even Brett, who had always respected her intelligence and ingenuity, had never really let her forget that he was older, hence wiser, than she. Even in the first six years, when they had been closest, Eden had always been conscious that Brett was an adult leading a responsible adult life before she even reached her eighth birthday.

Of course, she and Brett were no longer close. They were business partners now, who happened to share a home, two sons, and opposite sides of a bed. Even in their business, they shared very little. Eden managed the inn, Brett managed the packing plant, and they rarely talked. If Brett noticed that Garrett Martin stayed at the Bull and Boar more often than any other rancher, he never mentioned the fact. Perhaps, Eden thought, he didn't even care.

If Brett had ever indicated, even by a look or casual comment, that he suspected something or felt jealous of Garrett, Eden might have found the strength to end the affair. But Brett's indifference propelled her into Garrett's arms time after time.

Eden had no problem arranging to be with Garrett. Brett and Benjamin were away at the packing plant from dawn until dusk. Marguerite could be trusted to supervise Clinton and Burton. Since, with the exception of the cook, Eden ran the inn entirely by herself, no one questioned her if she disappeared upstairs for hours at a time.

Still, Eden could not escape the guilt that haunted her. When Garrett was with her, six, perhaps eight times a year, as often as he could get away from his ranch, she felt only joy. But each time he left, she wept, as much with shame as with sorrow.

How could she justify their being together? How could she justify deceiving Brett when she had been so hurt by his deceiving her? Surely Brett's deception did not make hers any more honorable. Yet, she needed Garrett. He was her lifeline in a raging whirlpool of disillusionment and unhappiness.

As the months passed and Eden realized she and Garrett were falling in love, she felt guilty for what she was doing to him, too. He was young, attractive, he should be marrying and starting a family of his own. He shouldn't be devoting himself to a married woman, with two young sons.

Now, feeling him stir beside her, Eden told Garrett, as she had so many times already, that he ought to look for a woman who was free to give him her life. Garrett only shook his head. "I don't want anyone else," he murmured, caressing her cheek. "I want you. And when you're finally ready to leave Brett McKinnon, I want to be here to take you away with me."

"But I'm too old for you!" she protested with forced levity.

"I'm eight years younger than you," he replied. "What

difference does that make? Does anyone comment when a woman marries a man eight years *older*? Did you hesitate to marry Brett because he was eleven years older than you?"

"Garrett, you know that's different!"

"Of course I know. Brett and I are different. For one thing, I've never lied to you. I never will."

"But I'm ruining your life! Using up your strong, young years. I may never be able to leave Brett. You have to realize that, Garrett. I've never made you any promises. I can't."

"Eden," he asked impatiently, "do you love me?"

"I—" She looked away from him, wanting to lie, wishing she had the strength to hurt him, not because she didn't love him, but because she did. If only she could make him believe she didn't care, perhaps he would feel free to go out in search of his own future.

"You do love me, don't you?" Garrett pressed.

"Yes." She sighed. What was the point of lying? He knew the truth without asking.

"Then I'll stay," he murmured. "You're not ruining anything. I'm a grown man. I know what I'm doing."

"I hope so," she whispered. "Oh, God, Garrett, I hope so!"

In the weeks, sometimes months, when Garrett was away, Eden felt enveloped by loneliness. Though she herself insisted he would be better off seeking a life of his own, she agonized after each departure that he might never return. Then what would she do? How would she bear her life, without his visits?

Of course, she would always have the joy of her children. At nine, Burton was a bright, inquisitive boy, already talking proudly of the day he would join Brett in the business. Clinton, at seven, had little interest in the business, though he occasionally accompanied his brother to the plant, simply to please his father. Having outgrown the mischievousness of his toddler years, he was unusually serious for his age.

Benjamin, at twenty, had become Eden's closest friend next to Garrett. Not wishing to destroy whatever respect he had for his father, Eden would never share with Benjamin her most intimate thoughts about Brett. But, she enjoyed his company, was grateful for his never-failing gentleness with his young half brothers, and admired him for his industriousness and sensitivity.

Often, Eden was grateful for Benjamin's mere presence,

diverting her thoughts from her own problems. Remembering her own inner turmoil when she moved from the Indian to the white world, Eden tried to bridge the gap for Benjamin, to smooth his adjustment to a new life. Many nights, they sat up long after Brett had gone to bed, sharing their individual memories of Black Eagle, Morning Star, and life in a Potawatomi camp.

Through Benjamin, Eden kept abreast of happenings at McKinnon Meats. Since Brett seldom confided in her anymore, Benjamin told her when their Great Lakes shipping line almost doubled its sales. And Benjamin excitedly described to her the progress as McKinnon Meats built a new and larger plant on the South Branch of the Chicago River.

Eden treasured Benjamin's friendship. Yet she worried sometimes that she leaned on him too much. Instead of spending his evenings with her, he ought to be out enjoying himself with other young people. Six days a week he worked hard at the packing plant. His nights ought to be his, to enjoy as he wished.

"But I do enjoy myself," Benjamin protested when Eden mentioned her thoughts to him. "After a day of hard work, there's nothing more precious than a relaxing night at home."

"Benjamin, you're letting the joys of youth pass you by! Wasn't there a dance in town at the Tremont House last Saturday night? You should have gone."

He shrugged. "I'm not interested in dancing."

"I can't believe that. Every young person loves to dance! Besides," she added teasingly, "how do you ever expect to find a wife if you never go out among young women?"

Grimacing, Benjamin did not reply for a long moment. Finally, he spoke softly. "I'm not likely to find a wife in Chicago, anyway."

Eden stared at him, flinching at the undertone of pain in his voice. "Well, of course you're not if you refuse to go out in society," she said with forced levity.

"Eden, be realistic! Society isn't ready for me. I'm an Indian, remember? A half-breed! Just because you've taken me into your family, and my father's given me a position at the plant, and John Kinzie and his wife receive me in their home doesn't change what I am!"

Stunned, Eden looked away from him. Had she been so caught up, first in her pain, then in the mixed joy and guilt of her affair with Garrett, that she had failed to see the obvious?

Too many Chicagoans still saw Indians as the villains of the Black Hawk War, the evil menace that had been banished to the far side of the Mississippi River. They treated any Indians who returned with wariness, if not outright hostility.

"Has it—have these years in Chicago been so hard on you?" she asked softly.

"No!" Benjamin answered with a sharpness that belied his denial. "No," he repeated more gently. "I knew there would be problems. Mother warned me."

"At the plant, or in town, do people treat you so badly?"

"At the plant, never. In town," he shrugged, "they could be worse. Sometimes they insult me. Mostly, they just stare for a few moments, and then they turn away and pretend I don't exist. But, I can tell most of the matrons wouldn't be too pleased to have me touch their daughters, even at a dance."

"I'm sorry," Eden said lamely. "I guess when I urged you to stay I never considered how cruel people might be. I suppose I thought it would be enough just to welcome you into the family."

"It has been enough," Benjamin assured her. "Only, sometimes I wish—" He broke off, shaking his head.

"What?" she pressed. "What do you wish?"

"It doesn't matter."

"What, Benjamin? Tell me."

"I wish, just once, Father would recognize me as his son. Is that asking so much of him? I think most of the men at the plant suspect our relationship, anyway. That's probably part of why they treat me decently. They don't want to hurt their chances with Father." He sighed. "I don't know. It's a petty thing to want, I guess. I share his home and his work. I ought to be content."

Touched, Eden looked away from him. "No, Ben," she whispered, "it's not a petty thing to want. You know Brett's proud of you. Perhaps in time his pride will make him tell the world who you are. But, I don't know. I'm afraid to think I know anything about Brett McKinnon anymore."

For weeks afterward, Benjamin brooded over Eden's words. It pained him to think he had caused the rift between Eden and Brett, but he had long ago realized he could not remedy it by going away. His father and stepmother were estranged not because he was there, but because Brett had never told

Eden he existed. If he had never come to Chicago, Eden might never have learned of the deception. But, he had come, and leaving could never change anything.

From the first, Benjamin had loved Eden for her compassion and sensitivity. He felt devoted to her, and he sympathized with her pain over Brett's deception.

Still, he loved Brett, too. He saw his father's pain over Eden's rejection, and felt that pain almost as deeply as Brett himself. He had hoped in time Eden, too, would see his father's hurt and would open her heart to him again. But, after nearly five years, his hopes had still not been realized. Perhaps, he thought, Eden's pain had blinded her to Brett's misery. Perhaps it was easier to forgive people one did not love quite so much. Perhaps the perfection of their early marriage had made Eden expect too much of Brett.

Unlike his older brother, Swift Elk, Benjamin felt no bitterness toward his father. While Swift Elk insisted that Brett had abandoned them, Benjamin had always remembered that last day, in the Sauganash Inn, when his father had asked his mother to stay with him. He remembered the hurt in both Brett and Morning Star's eyes when they finally separated.

He knew his father had not loved his mother, but he did not blame Brett any more than Morning Star had. Above all else, Morning Star had succeeded in teaching Benjamin compassion. He had not come to Chicago to punish Brett, and it pained him to see Brett and Eden continue punishing themselves.

More than anything else, he wanted to see his father and stepmother reconciled. Unable to discuss the matter with Brett, Benjamin finally decided he must discuss it with Eden.

Leaning back in his chair one evening, after Brett and the boys had gone to bed, Benjamin observed his stepmother through partially closed eyes. Her head bent over her mending, her auburn hair glistening in the firelight, she looked far younger than her thirty-four years.

No wonder his father hurt so over their estrangement! She was a phenomenal woman, not only beautiful, but hardworking, imaginative, independent. Strangely enough, Benjamin felt no bitterness or jealousy of this woman his father cared for far more than his own mother. He loved Eden. How could any man not love her?

Benjamin cleared his throat, and Eden lifted her gaze to his. For a moment, a lump rose in his throat, and he thought he could not say what he wished. He coughed self-consciously. Then, gazing straight into her blue-green eyes, he said, "Have you any idea how much my father misses you?"

Eden's brows drew together. "I don't understand what you mean, Benjamin."

"You must understand. He misses being with you, sharing things with you, feeling your interest in his work—loving you." He barely whispered the last words.

Frowning, Eden whispered, "He told you that?"

"He didn't have to! It's so obvious. Surely you can see it for yourself. He's dying inside because he craves the closeness you had before I came here."

Eden shook her head. "No, Benjamin. You're wishing for something that can never be. And your wishing has made you see things that don't exist."

"Like the kind of love that helped the two of you build McKinnon Meats out of nothing?" he demanded. "Eden, wake up! My father loves you, and the thought that he's failed you is destroying him!"

"You're wrong, Benjamin. If he cared about me, he'd try to make amends. He'd take an interest in the inn, like he used to. He'd ask me out to see the new plant. He'd talk to me!"

"Like you talk to him?" Benjamin whispered accusingly. "How can you expect him to talk to you when you turn away whenever he enters a room? I know he hurt you, Eden. I can't give you any excuses for the way he deceived you. I can't even blame you for rejecting him when you first found out. But how long are you going to go on rejecting him? How long are you going to go on blaming him for being less perfect than you once thought?"

Spots of red flamed in Eden's cheeks. "Benjamin, you have no right to talk to me that way!"

"For God's sake, someone has to! The problem with both of you—you and my father—is that you're too damned proud! If someone doesn't shake some sense into you, you'll both just go on building a wall you'll never be able to pull down."

"Benjamin, that's enough!"

"No, it's not!" He was pacing now. "Don't you care about him at all anymore, Eden? Didn't you ever in your life make a mistake, do something you couldn't be proud of, deceive someone, even a little?"

Eden stared down at her lap, thinking of Garrett. How many times had she been unfaithful to her husband? How many times had she lied to Brett, by the simple act of not telling him? But she never would have deceived him if he hadn't deceived her first!

"Benjamin, please!" she murmured, the words catching in her throat.

His tone softening, Benjamin knelt beside her chair. "Oh, Eden," he sighed, "you're such a wonderful person. So kind. So sensitive. So giving. Can't you find it in your heart to reach out to my father again?"

"I—I don't know," she sobbed.

"You might think about what you're doing to your boys."

. Her eyes widening, she looked up. "What do you mean? Surely they haven't said anything to you?"

"No, but your playacting has worn a bit thin. It's only a matter of time before they realize something between you and my father isn't right. Oh, maybe Burton won't notice for quite a while. He's too engrossed in himself. But little Clinton's perceptive. What are you going to say when he asks you? What do you want me to say if he asks me?"

Her eyes fell to her lap again. "I'm not sure. I'll have to think about it."

"Think about our whole discussion tonight," Benjamin said quietly. "Then maybe you'll never have to explain anything to Clinton at all."

12
1846–1847

My darling Garrett—

Writing this letter is undoubtedly the hardest thing I have ever done, or ever anticipate doing, in my life. But it would be so much worse to see you face to face. Perhaps I am a coward to handle the situation in this way. I prefer to think I am simply sparing both of us unnecessary pain.

By now, I suppose you have guessed what I am about to say. I cannot see you again, and I hope you

will be understanding enough not to come to the
Bull and Boar in the future. Of course, I hope you
will continue to do business with McKinnon Meats,
but perhaps you could send your drovers without
you, or perhaps you could arrange to stay at a different inn.

I won't insult your intelligence by saying I've
stopped loving you. You must know that can never
happen. I only wish I could have loved you unself-
ishly enough to break with you long ago. Underneath,
I suppose I always knew we could not have any real
future together. We *both* knew, didn't we, darling?
I'm not the sort of woman who can turn her back on
commitments and responsibilities, and I can't believe you would really want me to be. For a while,
you and I were swept along in a delicious dream.
Now I've finally awakened, and I find I can't step
back into that dreamworld.

I suspect your first reaction to all this will be to
jump on your horse, ride to Chicago, and try to
convince me to change my mind. Darling Garrett,
please don't! I assure you it would be an exercise in
futility, causing untold pain for both of us.

Frowning, Eden reread the last paragraph. Would Garrett
really believe that, or would he know she was simply afraid
her resolve would crumble if she even saw him again?

The fact was she had not even talked to Brett yet. Despite
all that Benjamin had said, she was not even sure she could
reconcile with Brett. But she knew she had to try. And it
would be easier to try if there was no chance of ever going
back to Garrett. Writing to Garrett now, she hoped, would
help to exorcise some of her guilt before she faced her husband.
Besides, if she ever hoped to rebuild any of her relationship
with Brett, she had to be sure Garrett would not be near to
tempt her.

Sighing, Eden dipped her pen into the inkwell and
continued:

You must know, my darling, that my decision to
end our liaison was not brought about by anything
you did or anything I could ever conceive of you
doing. You are the most decent man I have ever

known, more deserving of love than any other man on this earth.

However, I have finally realized that Brett, though he hurt me with his deception, is inherently decent, too. I've committed enough deception of my own in the past four years to know we all have our frailties. If I ever had a right to judge him—and I wonder now if I ever did—I most certainly forfeited that right with my infidelity. It's time I started facing my problems with Brett as an adult, instead of as a spoiled child who, for the first time, did not get her own way.

I hope you will not feel any guilt, my darling. You are not to blame. If anything, my own stubborn pride caused this problem. I will always cherish the time we shared, and hope you will be able to as well.

But Garrett, please, go beyond cherishing our past! Find yourself a woman deserving of all the wonderful things you have to give.

If you require more reasons for my decision, consider my sons. Soon they will be old enough to sense the tension between me and Brett—if indeed they have not already. It is important to me to mend my marriage before that happens. Never having known my natural father, and having lost my mother at a very young age, I want to be certain my boys grow up with both their parents, without feeling the need to side with either one against the other.

There is so much more to say, and yet there is nothing more to say. Only, thank you, darling Garrett, for all you have given me, but most of all for your understanding. I pray to God you will not disappoint me by being any less understanding now than you have been in the past.

> With love for all time,
> Eden

As she folded the letter, Eden's vision blurred with tears. I haven't lost him yet, she thought. I can still crumple this letter, throw it in the fireplace. No one, least of all Garrett, will ever know I wrote it.

But, I must not destroy it. I can't disappoint Benjamin by not even trying to make things right with Brett. I can't risk hurting my sons. And no, I can't even bring myself to hurt Brett anymore.

In the past two weeks, ever since her discussion with Benjamin, she had forced herself to look, really look, at Brett for the first time in years. At forty-five, his hair was still as red and unruly as ever, but he walked with a slump, and his gray-green eyes had lost their sheen.

Eden knew Brett was still considered a first-rate businessman. But, away from the business, he seemed dull, listless, easily tired, often retiring even before Burton and Clinton at night. The impulsive, impatient man who had seemed to Eden to embody the spirit of the prairie no longer existed. The temper, which had once flared so easily, and had as quickly been replaced by a laugh or a tender word, had disappeared.

With a jolt, Eden realized she had robbed Brett of his vigor. Oh, it was easy enough to explain away her guilt—to say he had caused the whole problem. But, if Benjamin had forgiven him, why couldn't she? He was her husband. The father of her children. The man to whom she had pledged her life eleven years ago.

She would always regret hurting Garrett, always regret that she had not had the foresight to end their romance long ago, or, better still, never to have begun it. But Garrett was younger, still only twenty-six. He would recover—far more quickly than she, no doubt.

Resolutely, Eden sealed the letter and went out herself to post it.

At dinner that night, Eden could not take her eyes from her husband. I have to do it now, she thought. I have to reach out to him now, tonight. If Garrett disregards my wishes and returns here anyway, I must already have begun to reconcile with Brett. That's the only way I'll be able to resist Garrett, the only way I'll be able to save all of us from a continuation of this foolishness.

She was aware of Benjamin watching her, could almost hear his thoughts, wondering if she was ever going to do anything about their discussion.

As the meal ended, Brett pushed his chair away from the table. "I'm going to bed," he said dully. "It's been a long day."

Scraping back her chair, Eden stretched sleepily. "I think I'd like to turn in, too," she said. Looking directly at Benjamin, she asked, "Would you mind helping Marguerite with the dishes, and then seeing that the boys get to bed?"

Benjamin grinned and his eyes sparkled. "No, ma'am," he said. "I wouldn't mind at all!"

In their bedroom, Brett looked up in surprise. He honestly could not remember the last time Eden had retired at the same hour as he. Most nights she sat up long after him, creeping into bed when she thought he was sound asleep. But, whether she realized it or not, he rarely was asleep. Sleeping came hard for him these days.

With McKinnon Meats the top meat-packer in Chicago, this should have been a marvelous time of his life. But every time he thought about spending the rest of his life—thirty years, perhaps more—with a woman who despised him, Brett felt sick.

Not that he wanted to end their marriage. He still loved Eden and felt glad for her presence, however reproachful. Of course, he visited the brothels along the levee from time to time now. But that was only for the physical relief a man sometimes needed. He didn't even enjoy the sessions, since he always ended up thinking of Eden. If only he knew how to break through her iciness! If only he wasn't so afraid she would hurt him more if he tried!

Eden began to undress, and Brett turned away awkwardly. He couldn't bear to see her when he couldn't even touch her. "You sick?" he asked gruffly.

"Sick? No, why do you ask?" With surprise, Brett noticed her voice was quivering.

"You don't usually come to bed this early, so I thought perhaps you were feeling ill."

"No, I'm not si—" She broke off abruptly and went to face him. "Oh, why should I lie? Yes, Brett, I am sick. I'm very sick. I'm sick inside over what's happened between us. I don't want to live this way anymore."

Brett stared at her, his gray-green eyes widening in dismay. Oh, God, here was the terrible moment he'd been dreading all these years! She was going to ask to divorce him! What could he say? How could he stop her now, after he'd let their marriage deteriorate for the last five years?

When he remained silent, Eden pressed frantically. "Aren't

you weary of this too, Brett? Can you honestly say you want to go on this way?"

When he finally spoke, it was not with the strong, sure voice of Brett McKinnon, but with the hoarse, strained voice of a stranger. "You're saying—you mean—you want a—a divorce?"

Eden leaned toward him, her eyes round with shock. "Is that what *you* want, Brett?" she whispered.

He looked away, biting his lips, unable to answer. For her sake, he should say yes. If he really loved her, he'd agree, wouldn't he? He'd free her from the hell of living with a man she neither loved nor respected. Wasn't it time he accepted her feelings toward him? Wasn't it time he let her go?

No, he couldn't do it. Not without at least one desperate try to hold her. Perhaps it was too late, but he had to try.

"No," Brett said softly. "I don't want a divorce."

To his amazement, he heard her expel a long sigh of relief. "Oh, Brett, darling," she blurted, "I don't either! All I want is a marriage! The kind we used to have—full of sharing, and caring about each other, and laughing, and—and touching."

His eyes flew to hers as he blinked back unaccustomed tears. "You mean, you've forgiven me?"

Eden laughed as delicious relief washed over her. "Oh, my darling, I'm not even sure anymore that there's anything to forgive! You were wrong, of course, not to tell me about Benjamin and his brother. But I was so unbearably self-righteous I don't know why you didn't walk out on me long ago."

"Because I love you," he said simply.

She hesitated. "I haven't been perfect myself. In fact, I've done a few things that might make you change your mind about loving me."

Drawing her into his arms, Brett whispered, "I don't want to hear about them. We're starting fresh now. The past doesn't matter."

"But—" She paused, then nodded. "You're right. We must forget the past—at least the bad parts, the last five years." For an instant, a vision of Garrett loomed in her mind. How could she ever forget him?

Brett gazed down at her thoughtfully. "Eden? Do you think we'll be able to do it? To rebuild what we had together?"

"I—" She wavered, trying to dispel her vision of Garrett. Then, looking Brett in the eye, she shook her head. "No. It won't be the same. I hope it will be better. This time I won't be so childish. I won't expect the impossible—from either of us. I've had enough blame and anger, hurt and unhappiness to last me a lifetime."

Brett smiled tenderly and, for the first time in years, Eden thought how handsome he was. Reaching up, her fingertips gently traced the dark circles beneath his eyes, as if she could erase them by her mere touch.

For a moment, he held her very close. Then he lifted her in his arms and carried her to their bed. He blew out the lamp and lay down beside her. As he took her into his arms again, Eden was glad for the darkness that hid the tears in her eyes. For even she was not certain if they were tears of joy or of regret.

Garrett Martin sat at his kitchen table, reading Eden's letter over and over. Outside, his drovers were loading camp supplies for a cattle drive to Chicago. If they left tomorrow morning, as planned, they should reach the Bull and Boar inside of two weeks.

Until this morning, Garrett had intended to go with them. He hadn't been to Chicago in almost two months, and his hunger for Eden was more than he could bear. Until now, his main problem had been figuring out how he could stand the slow pace of the cattle drive when, alone, he could cover the distance in three days. Now he didn't even know if he should go.

Damn Eden! What was the matter with her, anyway? How could she do this to him after he'd given her four years of his life?

Angrily scraping his chair away from the table, Garrett went to the stove and poured himself a mug of strong coffee. He searched in the cupboard for the whiskey bottle and added a liberal dose to his mug. Gulping the hot, bitter liquid, he turned to look out the window at the wagons being loaded.

Why shouldn't I go? he thought defiantly. If Eden wants to be fool enough to make up with her husband, that's her affair. But, she can't tell me what to do! I stopped letting any woman direct my life when Mother died.

Or did I? Hasn't my whole life these last years been geared toward Eden? Even when I'm here on the ranch, all I can think about is getting back to her. Maybe I ought to thank her for freeing me from the kind of life I never really wanted.

Oh, hell, who am I kidding? I wanted a life with that woman more than anything in the world.

So, what am I going to do about it? Ride to Chicago and try to shake some sense into her? Make her feel rotten for deciding to uphold her commitments and responsibilities? Beg her to keep seeing me in secret, even while she tries to rebuild her marriage?

It wouldn't be any good. Even if she agreed to take up with me again, and I doubt that she would agree, I couldn't stand it. It was different before. At least then I could delude myself that she'd eventually leave McKinnon. I knew I wasn't sharing her with him, because the two of them were so alienated. But, now that she's made up her mind, she's not likely to change it.

The hell of it is, I really respect her for what she's doing. I've never felt anything but contempt for women who walk out on their husbands, causing their children all sorts of pain and confusion. She's right to stand by McKinnon. I've had enough dealings with him to know he's a decent man. Maybe I'm the one who's not so decent, carrying on with his wife all these years.

Garrett turned back to the stove abruptly, concentrating on refilling his coffee mug, as Charley Streeter, his foreman, stepped into the kitchen.

"Well," Charley said briskly, "we're just about all loaded up. Should be ready for a good and early start tomorrow." He took down a mug from the cupboard and poured himself some coffee as Garrett moved away from the stove.

"What time you figure on heading out tomorrow?" Charley asked.

Garrett shrugged, keeping his back to his foreman. "You're the foreman. You decide."

"I would, if it was just going to be me and the boys, but since you're—"

"I'm not going, Charley," Garrett cut him off sharply. There, he'd said it. Staying away was the least he could do for Eden. He'd appealed to her when she'd been most vulnerable.

Charley was silent for several moments, his eyes moving between the letter on the table and the whiskey bottle on the cupboard. "Well, suit yourself. I suppose you've been to Chicago enough this year."

Garrett turned slowly to face the older man, wondering

just how much Charley suspected. "Perhaps I've been there too much," he said softly.

Coughing in embarrassment, Charley turned away. "I'd better see if there's anything more for me to take care of outside."

"Charley?" Garrett's voice stopped his foreman at the door.

"Huh?" Charley turned to face him.

"How many men are you planning to take with you?"

"Three. Maybe four now that you're not going."

"You'll leave Jed Hemmings to keep an eye on things while you're away?"

"If that's what you want. But I was thinking of asking him along, now that you've changed your plans. You can manage the place yourself as well as Jed can."

"I—I may not be here the whole time you're in Chicago."

"Oh?"

"Last time I was in Decatur, Bill Hawkins was telling me about some good grazing country over in Iowa."

"Iowa?"

"Yes. I thought maybe I'd ride over and have a look."

Shaking his head, Charley glanced at the letter again. "Well, it sure would put you a little further from Chicago," he mumbled.

It sure would, Garrett thought.

Eden sat alone in her parlor, waiting for her boys to come home from school. It was springtime, which, for Chicago, meant the frozen ground had become a sea of mud. The city might be growing in population and bursting with new buildings, but it was still the "mudhole of the prairie."

Eight months ago, she had approached Brett with the hope of saving their marriage. Since then, he had been even more tender than in their first years together. Of course, she thought, patting her bulging abdomen, he had good reason now. Who would have thought that, at thirty-five, with her youngest son eight years old, she would be expecting another child?

She was glad, though, hoping the miracle of motherhood would help her forget Garrett. Her memories of him were the one flaw in the new love she and Brett shared. At least he had been kind enough not to come to the inn again.

Hearing the door slam, Eden got up, expecting to greet her boys. Instead, Brett strode into the parlor and hugged her warmly.

"You're home early," she said. "I was expecting the boys."

"And you're disappointed it's me?" he teased.

"Of course not." She kissed his cheek.

"Well, I thought I could leave Benjamin to attend to matters at the plant. I wanted to check on the mother-to-be."

Eden smiled. "If you keep that up, you'll be missing a lot of work. The baby's not due for another month."

"That's all right. I haven't any boss to report to. By the way, do you remember that rancher Garrett Martin, owned a place down near Decatur?"

Looking away, Eden pretended to search her memory, hoping her husband would not realize her discomfort. "Mr. Martin? Yes, I believe I remember him. Why?"

"He was in to the plant this afternoon. Said he's starting up a new ranch way out west, around Des Moines. He'll still be bringing us his beef, though. Anyway, he said to give you his greetings. Guess he decided to stay someplace closer in to town since he didn't bring any cattle this trip."

"How kind of him—to send his greetings, I mean."

"Yes. I told him we're expecting a little one within the month. For a minute there, he seemed kind of shocked. Guess he thought I was a little old to be a papa again. He can't be out of his twenties yet, himself. Anyway, then he recovered and offered his congratulations."

Paling slightly, Eden said, "Brett, darling, I'm suddenly feeling very weary. Would you mind awfully if I lay down?"

Frowning, Brett lifted her into his arms and carried her to their bedroom. "You're all right, aren't you? Should I go for the doctor?"

"No, I'm just tired. I'll be fine after a little rest."

"You're sure?" Brett looked at her doubtfully.

"Quite sure."

Twelve hours later, Eden gave birth to a small but healthy girl. They named her Paige Halsey McKinnon.

III

THE BLOSSOMS

1850–1857

13
April 1850

"Come on, Burton," Clinton pleaded. "It'll be dark soon, and Mama will be worried about us. She'll be mad anyway that we didn't come right home from school like we promised."

Thirteen-year-old Burton McKinnon cast a disdainful look at his eleven-year-old brother. "Go on home yourself, if you're so worried," he said. "I don't know why I brought you, anyway."

"Aw, come on, Burt. You know I was just as curious as you. But it won't do us no good just to stand around here staring all day. We ain't going west. Papa says the only people running out to California are those that couldn't make it in their own towns."

Burton snorted. "That just goes to show you how old Papa's getting! From what I hear, he was getting along all right back in Connecticut before he decided to come to Illinois as a trader. He just wanted something better, something more exciting than he had back East. Now, he's all settled in with his big successful business, and Mama, and our baby sister, and he's forgotten what it's like to want a little adventure."

Clinton jammed his hands in his pockets and pursed his lips. His blue-gray eyes scanned the field south of the old, deserted Fort Dearborn, where a wagon train headed west was making camp for the night. Scrawled across the canvas of one prairie schooner was the message, "We'll Get Thar." Another had the more chilling slogan, "Reach It or Die!"

"Well, maybe you're right," Clinton said slowly. "But I can't see where going west would do either of us any good. You'd have to be pretty lucky to find anything to make you richer or more successful than Papa."

"Oh yeah?" Burton retorted. "What do you think of that sign over there?" He pointed toward another wagon, bearing the long message, "Plenty of Gold in the World, I'm Told—On the Banks of the Sacramento."

107

"Aw, Burton, that's just a line from a dance hall song! I don't really think you're supposed to believe it."

"Why not? I bet the people in that wagon believe it."

Clinton frowned and turned away. "You coming home or not?"

"Yeah, I guess I might as well. I'm getting hungry, anyway."

As Burton had suspected, their mother was too occupied with their three-year-old sister Paige to give him and Clinton more than a light reprimand when they finally arrived home. She was always occupied with Paige. That, or decorating the new house Papa had just had built on Wabash Avenue, a few blocks south of the river.

The house was nice, or at least Mama seemed to think so. But Burton missed living at the Bull and Boar Inn. He missed talking to the drovers, hearing their tales of the western prairies. Once in a while, one of the ranchers came to the new house for dinner, but they all seemed too genteel in the new setting of damask draperies, fine china, and rosewood furniture. To Burton, they seemed to lose all their rough, adventurous appeal.

Lying awake that night, Burton tried to sort out his feelings. Why was he so restless lately? Maybe it wasn't just the change in houses. Maybe it was just that Chicago was changing. It wasn't the frontier town that it had been when he was younger.

Of course, anyone coming from the East still said the city was rather rough. Even Mama, who always said she loved Chicago, said it was a different kind of society than she'd grown up with in New York. But Chicago *was* changing.

It had a telegraph link with the East now. The Illinois and Michigan Canal, begun even before Burton was born, was finally in full operation. There was even a railroad, though it did only extend five miles out of the city. All these things made Chicago seem a little less wild and a little more boring to Burton.

Still, he supposed he shouldn't feel bored. Papa was always talking about the railroad as the best thing that ever happened to Chicago. Within a few years, Papa said, Chicago would have a lot more railroads, linking it with all the important cities of the nation. Then Chicago, and the meat-packing business, would really start to grow.

Of course, Burton thought, sighing to himself, Papa was

looking at things from a businessman's viewpoint. No wonder Papa was so excited.

There was a time when Burton would have shared that excitement, a time when he had looked forward to growing up and joining his father in the business. Once, he had dreamed of taking his place at the head of McKinnon Meats. When had he stopped dreaming of that?

Benjamin! he thought suddenly. In the last year or so, he had gradually begun to sense that Benjamin was usurping his place in the family. Benjamin, whom he had always accepted as a brother.

Was Benjamin, in fact, his brother? Shifting uneasily in his bed, Burton recalled a few times when he had entered a room at McKinnon Meats and the conversation had abruptly halted. What had the men been talking about? What words had his ears picked up when he hadn't even really been listening? Half-breed? Inheritance?

It's foolish even to think of it, Burton insisted to himself. Benjamin uses the name McKinnon, but that's only because he lives with us and Mama and Papa have sort of adopted him, isn't it? Besides, everyone knows Indians don't have last names of their own. Anyway, what if Benjamin is my half brother. Papa wouldn't cheat me out of my inheritance for a— a bastard, would he?

Still, Papa does seem to place a lot of trust in Benjamin. Sometimes he even puts Ben in charge, when he leaves the plant.

It isn't fair, really, that Benjamin is so much older than me. He's already had nine years at McKinnon Meats to worm his way into Papa's good graces. By the time I'm old enough to work full time at the plant, there won't even be a place for me.

The thing is, I think I'm old enough now, but Mama would never hear of me leaving school. She's got some idea that I should go to school till I'm seventeen or eighteen—maybe even longer. The other day I even heard her mention something to Papa about sending me and Clinton east to college. Clinton probably wouldn't care. Anything to please Mama. But I'm not going to go east for four years and let Benjamin push me out of the business completely.

What am I going to do? Wait around here, going to school every day, while he pushes me out anyway? No! I've got to find a way to make Papa notice me. I've got to prove to him that I'm smarter, more resourceful, more worthy than Ben.

Suddenly, a plan that had been fermenting in the back of Burton's head all day took shape. I'll do it, he thought, sitting up decisively. I'll go to California! I'll find a heap of gold, and get rich, and then they'll all see how clever I am!

He swung his legs over the side of the bed, ready to slip out of the house and find a hiding place in one of the wagons waiting south of Fort Dearborn. Then, pausing to reconsider, he frowned and shook his head.

It wouldn't work. There was little chance he could sneak into the wagon train undetected. One of his friends had tried that with another train a couple of weeks ago and had been caught. The town crier made it a habit to check any wagon trains several times a night for adventure-seeking youngsters bent on leaving home without their parents' permission.

Besides, once Papa and Mama realized he was gone, the wagon train would be the first place they'd look. Clinton would be sure to tell them he'd been looking it over. Even if the train left at dawn, the cumbersome wagons were so slow-moving Papa could easily catch up in an hour or so.

Burton smiled. Perhaps the slow pace of the wagons could help him get to California after all. Papa would check the wagon train that was in town now. But would he think to ride ahead to check the one that had passed through Chicago three days ago?

That was the answer, Burton thought confidently. Before dawn, before anyone else in the house was up, he'd slip out to the stable, saddle a horse, and head west, following the wagon ruts that had worn into the prairie in the last few years. With any luck, he would catch up with the wagon train before the day was over, and his future would really begin.

"Brett?" Eden was breathless when she reached the foot of the stairs. "Burton's not here! I just went to his room to wake him for school, and he's not there!"

Looking up from his coffee, Brett smiled mildly. "He probably just thought he'd give you a shock by getting up before you called him. You know how you're always after him to get ready for school on time."

Eden shook her head. "I don't think so. I asked Clinton and Benjamin if they'd seen him, and neither had."

"Well, why don't you just sit down and drink your coffee?" Brett said, pouring a cup and pushing it toward her. "He'll probably come strolling in here any minute."

Sitting down reluctantly, Eden picked up the coffee cup.

Frowning, Brett asked, "Look, you don't have any reason to think anything's really wrong, do you? I mean, you and Burton haven't had any real arguments lately, have you?"

"No, but—"

"I'm sure our Burton is too sensible to run away from home," Brett went on evenly.

"I suppose—"

Clinton galloped down the stairs and joined them in the dining room. "Hi," he said cheerily, brushing his sandy hair off his forehead. "Did Burton show up yet?"

"No, he didn't," Eden replied shortly. Pursing her lips, she asked, "Clint, would there be any reason why your brother wouldn't want to go to school today?"

Clinton grinned. "You mean, why he wouldn't want to go any more than on any other day? Well, he was supposed to have kind of a big spelling test today, and you know how he almost flunked the last one!"

Brett laughed, reaching across the table to pat Eden's hand. "There now, you see," he said. "I told you there was nothing to worry about. The boy obviously decided he didn't want to go to school today, and took off before you could force him." Chuckling, he added, "I can't say that I blame him! But I'll give him a good thrashing when he comes home tonight and a lecture about worrying his mama, and I doubt that it will happen again."

Eden smiled weakly. "Well, I guess I was being a bit foolish to worry, anyway."

The fact that a horse was missing from the stable seemed to confirm Brett's theory. But when evening fell, the family sat down to dinner, and the boy still had not returned. Eden began to worry again.

"Do you suppose he could have ridden too far and gotten lost?" she asked anxiously. "Or, what if his horse went lame, or he was hurt somehow?"

Brett sighed. "In all likelihood, he did ride too far, and didn't allow himself enough time to get home for dinner. But he's a strong lad. I wager he'll be here before long."

Clinton glanced uneasily between his parents. He had an idea of his own where Burton might be. On the way to school, he had noticed that the wagon train he and Burton had looked at yesterday was gone. But, there was no sense in saying anything yet. Maybe Burton would turn up in an hour or two. If he did, he'd be angry with Clinton for even mentioning the wagon train.

By half past eight, Clinton felt certain his brother was not coming home. "I think I know where Burton is," he said hesitantly.

Eden's eyes flew to her younger son, and Brett raised his brows quizzically.

"He's been talking about the wagon trains a lot, and going over to see where they camp, south of the fort. Well, there was one there yesterday, and it was gone this morning—"

"Of course!" Brett exclaimed. "I should have suspected that!"

"Well, we'll have to go after him at once!" Eden said.

Brett shook his head. "Tomorrow morning will be soon enough. I'm not going to disturb a whole wagon train in the middle of the night. Anyway, they're probably not more than ten miles from here. Ben and I can catch them easily tomorrow. Besides," he added grimly, "a night away might teach our son to appreciate his home a bit more."

14
April–August 1850

Burton sighed in relief as he finally sighted the wagon train, making camp for the night. The trail out of Chicago had not been as easy to follow as he had expected. Since the wide-open prairie provided few barriers to travel, none of the wagon trains took exactly the same route. At least half-a-dozen times, Burton had followed the wrong trail, only to discover, when he inquired at nearby towns, that no wagon train had passed in the last few days.

Now, he was hungry, dirty, and anxious for rest. But, as he drew near to the wagons, pulled into their tight evening circle, he also began to feel a bit apprehensive. What if the people on the wagon train would not agree to let him join them? He just couldn't go back home. But the day's travels had made him quite certain he wasn't experienced enough to find his way to California all by himself.

"Hey there, young fellow!" a voice out of the twilight hailed him.

Dismounting, Burton led his horse toward a middle-aged man standing at the outer edge of the circle of wagons. "Good evening, sir," the boy said tremulously.

The man squinted at him in the fading light. "You ain't one of our boys, are you?"

"No, sir. I mean, yes. That is—I'd like to be."

The man laughed. "Well, you ain't alone, sonny. Half the boys we've passed so far want to join us. 'Course, we can't let 'em." He paused and chuckled. "If we did, we'd have half the parents from Pennsylvania to here running after us to get their sons back! You see," he added more seriously, "we can't accept just any boy who's got a mind to run away from home."

"Oh, I'm not running away, sir," Burton said quickly. "I mean, not from my parents or anything. You see, I'm—I'm an orphan."

"An orphan, eh?" The man looked him over dubiously, eyeing his obviously well-bred horse. "Ain't you got no kin to stay with?"

"Well," Burton paused, searching for a logical way to embellish the lie, "yes and no. I've got an aunt back in— Philadelphia—who wants me to come live with her. But I don't want to go east. I'm a Western boy, and I just know I'd be awfully unhappy back there."

"A Western boy, eh? Where you from?"

"Chicago, sir. Born and raised there."

"Well, I don't know." The man scratched his chin. "I sympathize with you, boy. I really do. But I don't know what to say. Anyone who joins this here wagon train has to do his part. What can a little lad like you do?"

Sensing the man was beginning to weaken, Burton said eagerly, "I can shoot! Really, I'm a pretty good hunter. My pa taught me—before he died, that is. And he was one of the best hunters and fur traders in Illinois!"

The man's eyes widened. "Was he now? In that case, I probably knew him. I was a trader myself before Illinois got trapped out and they sent all the Indians west of the Mississippi. Then I moved out to the Rockies to do my own trapping, which is how I ended up being a guide for this here wagon train. Anyway, that's all neither here nor there. What was your pa's name, boy?"

Burton gulped. He should have thought more before mentioning Papa. Now what was he going to say? He didn't know the names of any other traders, except John Kinzie, and he was afraid the man would know if he made up a name. Well, he'd just have to tell the truth and hope the man hadn't had any contact with Papa in recent years.

"Well, speak up, boy! What was his name?"

"McKinnon, sir. Brett McKinnon."

The man expelled a low whistle. "Brett McKinnon's dead? How'd it happen, boy? When?"

"Uh—cholera—last year."

"And your mama, too?"

Burton nodded, wondering how God would punish him for lying about his parents. He really wasn't hurting anyone, was he?

The man shook his head. "So, old Brett McKinnon's gone! I remember the times, before he started living with Morning Star—" He broke off, narrowing his eyes at Burton. "You don't look much like a half-breed, boy."

Burton felt sick. So, it was true! Benjamin was his half brother. No wonder Papa thought so much of him. Maybe Papa was even thinking of making Ben his heir. Well, that was all the more reason why he, Burton, had to get to California and prove himself.

"I'm not a half-breed, sir," Burton said steadily. "My mother is—was—a white woman. Papa married her after he quit trading."

"Hmmm," the guide grunted. "Well, I suppose that makes sense. Indian wives are all right for traders, but if a man lives in a city, I guess he needs a more respectable mate. Myself, I've got a Shoshone girl out in the Rockies—well, never mind—" His voice trailed away as he extended his hand. "Name's Gabe Norton, boy. Now, I reckon if you're going to be riding with me, I'd better be able to call you something besides boy."

Burton's eyes glowed as he shook the man's hand. "I'm Burton McKinnon, Mr. Norton. Do you mean I can join the wagon train?"

"I reckon so," Gabe replied, squeezing Burton's hand. "If I say it's all right, no one is going to object. And any son of Brett McKinnon is more than good enough to ride with me."

*   *   *

Brett and Benjamin's horses picked their way back east, toward Chicago, across the darkening prairie. Sighing, Benjamin said, "What are we going to tell Eden? She'll go mad when she hears we didn't find him."

Brett frowned. "I know it! All we can hope is that he's turned up home while we've been away. If I could lay my hands on that boy now, I'd thrash him so hard he wouldn't be able to sit down for a week!"

Benjamin forced a laugh. "You wouldn't, really. You'd be so relieved to see him safe and sound you'd probably kiss him!"

"Well, maybe I would, but only because I'd be so relieved that Eden could stop worrying. The thing is, I really can't believe that he's not safe and sound, somewhere. Burton's no Indian, but he knows how to take care of himself on the prairie. It's hard for me to think he could have gotten hurt, or lost, or that anything else happened to him."

"So, where is he?" Benjamin asked quietly.

Brett shook his head. "Damned if I know! There's thousands of square miles in this state. He could be anywhere. We don't even know for certain that he came west. He could have gone into Indiana. Or, maybe he stowed away on one of the ships going back east over the lakes. You know how boys that age are—they get an idea into their heads, and they never stop to think how they might be affecting anyone else."

Benjamin nodded, recalling how, when he was only a few years older than Burton, he had disrupted the lives of the entire McKinnon family. "Yes, I know. And I tend to agree with you that Burton is all right—somewhere. The problem is going to be convincing Eden. And, if we do convince her, I hope to God we're right. It would be too cruel to keep her hopes alive, only to have them dashed months from now."

Riding ahead of the wagon train, accompanying Gabe Norton on his scouting, Burton felt a heady sense of importance. He'd been with the wagon train more than a week now, and any lingering fears that his parents might find him had finally vanished.

He'd also begun to relax more with the guide. Though Gabe often regaled his young friend with wild tales of his and Brett's youth, he no longer asked probing questions, assum-

ing Burton was still too overcome with grief to talk much
about life with his father.

The outdoor life, with no school or parents to direct him,
appealed to Burton. Of course, Gabe issued a few orders,
which Burton would never think of questioning. Still, the
older man seemed more a friend than a father, even insisting
that Burton call him Gabe, rather than Mr. Norton. Anyway,
anything Gabe did or said was all right with Burton, as long
as the guide got him to California.

Now, as they neared the Illinois-Iowa border, Burton asked,
"About when do you figure we'll be hitting California, Gabe?"

"Well, if we're lucky, we'll get to Fort Laramie, in Wyoming Territory, by June. Then I suspect we'll make it across
the Rockies by the beginning of July. So, I suspect we'll be in
California's gold country by October. Maybe September."

"October!" Burton exclaimed in disappointment.

Gabe eyed him in amusement. "Anxious to stake your
claim on that California gold, are you?"

"Well—I—"

"Don't worry. From what I hear, there's more than enough
to go around—if you know the right place to look."

Burton's face fell. "How am I going to know the right
place?"

"I couldn't say." Gabe shrugged. "Seems to me it's more a
matter of luck than anything else." His eyes narrowed. "You
ain't worried, are you, Burt? I mean, your pa left you a little
something to tide you over, didn't he? Seems to me I heard
something about him going into meat packing after he gave
up trading. Rumor had it he was pretty successful at it, too."

"Yes, yes he was," Burton said quickly. "No, I ain't worried,
Gabe. Just curious, that's all. Curious about what's out there,
and anxious to get there and see for myself."

Laughing, Gabe clapped him on the shoulder. "Well, I
can't blame you for either of those feelings, boy! All I can say
is, you're going to have to have a little patience. We'll get
there when we get there—not before!"

For Burton, a little patience was too large an order. Sitting
in camp that night, he mentioned his anxiety to another
youth, Philip Armour. Five years older than Burton, young
Philip had already traveled well over one thousand miles
from his home in upstate New York. Leaving his family
behind, he had gone by lake schooner to Milwaukee before

traveling south to join the wagon train. Now he earned his way by tending the oxen that many people used to pull their wagons.

Squinting into the firelight, Philip nodded at his young friend. "I know how you feel. Worse maybe, since I've already come so far. If I had my own horse, like you do, I would have ridden on ahead of the train long ago."

Burton frowned. "How would you know where to go? I can tell you, it's not easy finding your own trail."

"Maybe not. But it's not easy moving along at a snail's pace, either. I've got a little money, and I'll tell you, the next town we hit I'm buying myself a horse or mule and starting out on my own. I've already tried to buy one from everyone on this wagon train, but no one wants to sell."

For several moments, Burton was silent, arguing within himself. It was foolish to travel alone. He knew that from his experience the first day out from Chicago. Still, Gabe had taught him a great deal in the last week about following a trail and spotting trouble. And he wouldn't be alone if he left with Philip. Philip was eighteen—almost a man. Surely he'd had some experience that would prove helpful.

"Would you—would you consider taking a traveling partner?" Burton asked hesitantly.

The older boy grinned. "I don't see why not. What have you seen on your scouting missions? When will we reach the next town?"

"The day after tomorrow, I think."

"Good. With any luck we'll be able to strike out on our own by the day after that. And, with a little more luck, we ought to reach California in a couple of months."

Eden sighed and forced a smile as three-year-old Paige babbled excitedly about the six-foot-tall sunflowers waving in seemingly endless fields across the Illinois prairie. In past years, Eden had always loved these rides out to the prairie with Brett and the children. Watching the wildflowers change from white in early spring, to blue in late spring, to golden yellow in summer, and browns and burnt oranges in fall, she had always thought back to her own youthful excursions with Black Eagle. But today she could think only of her missing son.

Ten years ago, red-haired Burton had babbled as excitedly as little Paige. Now, despite all Brett's assurances, Eden was

118   *Starflower*

not even certain that her firstborn was alive. He had left in
April. It was almost September now. And they had never
received a word from him.

It was useless even to discuss the situation with Brett
anymore. He would tell her the same things he had been
saying since April—that Burton was an intelligent, resourceful young man; that if the boy had gone west they could
hardly expect a letter within a few months' time; that he and
John Kinzie had managed to survive in the wilderness when
they were nearly as young as Burton.

Everything Brett said made sense, but Eden couldn't help
feeling something terrible had happened. And there was
nothing anyone could do or say to ease her mind. No one
could go out looking for Buton, because there seemed to be
no logical way to organize a search. He could be anywhere—or
nowhere.

Brett's voice intruded on her thoughts. "I think we'd better
head home now, Paige. Your mama seems to be tired."

"Are you ill, Mama?" Clinton asked.

Smiling weakly, Eden turned her gaze to her middle child.
So often he seemed the most sensitive of her children. "No,
darling," she said, reaching out to rumple his sandy hair, "I
was just kind of lost in thought."

Clinton nodded and whispered, "Don't be sad, Mama.
Burton's all right. I know he never meant to hurt you."

"No, of course he didn't."

Brett cleared his throat loudly and shot Eden a disapprov-
ing look. "We'll go home, all right?"

"It's really not necessary, Brett. If you and the children
want to stay—"

"I think I ought to stop back at the plant," Brett said
curtly. "I left Ben with too much work this afternoon."

On the ride home, Clinton entertained Paige in the back of
the wagon, while Eden and Brett remained silent. As they
stepped into the house, Brett directed Clinton to take his
sister upstairs. Then he turned to Eden and spoke sternly.

"You've got to stop it, Eden! You've got to stop acting as if
you're in mourning for Burton!"

"It might be easier if I really were in mourning!" she
replied quietly. "If I at least knew for sure that he's—" she
faltered, unable to say the word "dead." Looking away from
Brett, she murmured, "I just can't live with this uncertainty."

"Well, you'd better learn," he said harshly. "Before long,

you'll be wrecking Clint and Paige's lives with your damned misery."

Hurt by his seeming insensitivity, for a moment she stared at him openmouthed. "What do you expect me to do?" she demanded. "Forget about Burton?" Before he could answer, she rushed on, "Yes, I suppose that's exactly what you expect! After all, you forgot your two oldest sons for six years!"

Brett's eyes widened as if she'd slapped him, and Eden immediately felt sorry for her words. "Oh, Brett!" she sobbed, "I didn't mean to say that! I don't want to hurt you. I swore to myself four years ago that I'd never hurt you about Ben and his brother again. I don't even know what I'm saying anymore. I just feel so helpless!"

"I know, I know," Brett soothed, taking her into his arms and cradling her against his chest. "But you've got to try a little harder, for the sake of the other children. Now, come sit down in the parlor, and I'll get you some brandy to calm your nerves."

Sitting stiffly while she waited for Brett to pour her brandy, Eden glanced at the small octagonal table, where the maid had laid out the day's mail. Recognizing the handwriting on the top letter, she leaned closer and picked it up with a trembling hand.

Still afraid to believe her eyes, she tore open the envelope and looked for the signature. "Brett!" she exclaimed in a voice filled with disbelief, "we've a letter from Burton!"

Brett set down the brandy and rushed across the room to put an arm around her. Together they read the brief message:

> Fort Bridger, Wyoming Territory
> May 26, 1850
>
> Dearest Mama and Papa—
> By the time this reaches you, I expect to be in California, staking my gold claim on the banks of the Sacramento. I had not intended to write to you until after I'd made a success of myself, however, my traveling companion, Philip Armour, convinced me that you might be worried. So, I am just writing to let you know that I am perfectly well. I hope my absence has not caused you too much concern. I'm sure you can understand why I did not ask your permission to make this trip, since you doubtless

would not have given it. I hope that you and everyone else in the family are well. I'll write to you
again from California, after I've made my fortune.
                                    Your devoted son,
                                             Burton

Sighing in relief, Eden looked up at Brett. "At least we
know he's alive," she said. "And if he has a traveling companion,
I suppose they can look after one another. This Philip Armour
must have some sense if he convinced Burton to write to us."

Brett nodded. "I always knew the boy was all right. But, if
I could get my hands on him right now, I'd wallop the living
daylights out of him! The nerve of that boy—worrying you for
four months, and then tossing it off so lightly!"

Feeling giddy with relief, Eden laughed. "Brett McKinnon,
I'd forbid you to lay a hand on him! Besides, just where do
you think Burton could have gotten such ideas? If there'd
been a gold rush when you were a boy, I wager you would
have been the first one out to California!"

Throwing back his head, Brett laughed heartily. "My darling Eden, I fear you know me entirely too well!"

"Perhaps," she replied soberly. "But it seems I don't know
my children well enough, at all."

15
September 1850–January 1851

Burton sighed wearily as he trudged along the rugged mountain trail. In the two months since he and Philip Armour had
stumbled on their first mining camp, California had yielded
one disappointment after another. In July, his horse, exhausted from the push across the continent, had stumbled in
the Sierra Nevada Mountains and broken a leg. Since then,
nothing had gone right.

Life along the trail had been rugged and exhausting, but
life in the California mining camp of Jackass Gulch had proved
to be a thousand times worse. On the trail, there had always

been hope. In the camp, hope quickly turned to disillusionment. The camps held too many men desperate for riches, too many thieves, swindlers, and even murderers, ready to prey on the unsuspecting.

Burton and Philip had panned for gold until their fingers were numb from the cold mountain streams and their hands were scraped raw from shoveling dirt and gravel into their pans, hoping with every handful that they would finally see something glitter among the filth. Between them, they had found less than one hundred dollars worth of the precious metal.

Finally, this morning, Burton had convinced Philip they should move on to another camp, where their luck might improve. Now, he was sorry. His feet ached, and his waterlogged shoes had begun to split. Philip's horse had gone lame, so they were both reduced to walking.

A lone man, riding a mule, picked his way toward them on the narrow trail. As they passed him, the man tipped his hat, and Burton asked, "Would you know how far it is to the next camp?"

The man hesitated, eyeing Burton shrewdly as the boy shifted painfully from one foot to the other. "Gomorrah?" he asked. "Oh, I'd say she's about five—ten miles from here. Course I can't really say I've kept track. A man doesn't much notice the miles when he's riding along in comfort."

Burton nodded. "That's a fine mule you've got there, sir."

"Yep, she is," the man agreed. "Fine and strong. The best friend I've had since I got to Californey."

Glancing at Philip, Burton asked, "You wouldn't know where we could buy one like her, would you?"

"Like my Sukey?" The man shook his head. "I don't reckon there *is* another mule quite like Sukey." His eyes narrowed as he studied the two boys. "You boys been out here in Californey long?"

"A few months," Philip replied.

"Well, now, I'll tell you, being that you're such fine young men, and being that I always believe in the Golden Rule, I might just consider selling Sukey to you."

Philip frowned skeptically. "Why would you want to do that?"

"Like I said, I believe in the Golden Rule. Besides, it seems to me that, between you, you two boys need her twice as much as I do."

Shifting eagerly on his swollen feet, Burton asked, "How much would you want for her?"

"Oh," the man closed his eyes in thought, "seein' as how she's such a good mule, I don't think I could sell her for less than a hundred dollars."

"Oh." Burton's spirits fell. He should have known the price would be outrageous in this land where flour sold for four hundred dollars a barrel.

Not to be put off, Philip said coolly, "Back where I come from, she wouldn't fetch more than fifty dollars."

The man shrugged. "Maybe so. But you ain't back where you come from now. Sorry I can't be of service to you boys." He started to move on.

"Would you take sixty dollars?" Burton asked desperately.

The man paused, then shook his head. "Sorry, much as I'd like to, I can't be that charitable. Maybe I could go down as far as eighty, but, even then, you'd be making a fool of me."

The two boys looked at each other for a moment before Philip reluctantly nodded. "All right," he said. "We'll give you eighty dollars."

By the time they reached the mining camp called Gomorrah, Philip and Burton's spirits had improved tremendously. They had taken turns riding the mule for the last several miles, and felt sure they had gotten a bargain.

But, as they entered the camp, a tall, dark-haired man ducked out of a tent, pointed an accusing finger at them, and yelled, "Thieves!"

Within moments, they were surrounded by men, glaring angrily as they closed around the boys. One of the group, a burly man with a bushy beard, weighed a pistol in his hand as he demanded, "What's the problem here, Jake? What'd they steal from you?"

"Why, my mule!" the dark-haired man spluttered. "If that ain't my Sukey, I'm a slant-eyed Chinaman! It's Sukey, all right, look at the notch on her ear, where a wildcat attacked her once!"

The other men nodded agreement, and Burton shuddered in terror at their muttered comments.

"That's Jake's mule, all right."

"Thievin' little bastards! I say we string 'em both up, right now!"

"Me too! Can't be too easy on horse thieves—or on mule thieves, either!"

"We didn't steal her!" Burton burst out. "We bought her from a man a few miles down the trail."

"Lyin' won't make us treat you any easier!" the dark-haired man threatened. "Sukey was tied up by my tent when I went to sleep last night, and when I got up this morning she was gone. You two snuck into camp last night and took her. Might as well own up to that fact."

Speaking carefully, Philip asked, "If we'd really stolen your mule, wouldn't we be rather foolish to ride her right back into your camp? As my partner said, we bought her. If anyone stole her, perhaps the man we bought her from did."

Jake pursed his lips, eyeing Philip and Burton shrewdly. "Just assuming there really was another man that you bought her from, what'd he look like?"

"Oh, about your size," Philip replied. "Brownish hair. Kind of a longish mustache. Wearing one of those slouch hats."

The men in the surrounding group began to mumble among themselves. "Hey, Jake," one of them said, "don't that sound like your partner, Hal? Where is he today, anyhow?"

"He's—well—he's—" Jake scratched his head. "To tell you the truth, I ain't seen him all day! He said something last night about going further upstream a bit. Guess I figured that's what he'd done."

"If you ask me," the man said, "what he's done is gone off and deserted you! If I was you, I'd check and see if your gold dust is still in your tent. Any man who'd steal his own partner's mule—well, no tellin' what he might do!"

Guffawing loudly, the men started to drift away, leaving Jake to scratch his head in consternation. "I can't believe it," he muttered. "How could Hal—Hal of all people—Listen, boys," he said kindly, "I guess I owe you an apology. But you can't blame me for jumpin' to conclusions. I mean, these camps are full of thieves, and Sukey *is* my mule. Still, I can't believe Hal would—"

"I suppose you'll want your mule back," Philip sighed.

"Well, sure I want her back! But it hardly seems fair takin' her from you after you paid for her. How much did you give him, anyway?"

"Eighty dollars."

Jake whistled. "Well, lemme just see if I've got enough

money to strike some kind of bargain with you." He ducked
into his tent, but came back out a few minutes later, shaking
his head. "That varmint actually cleaned me out! Look," he
added after a long pause, "I can't take that mule away from
you after you paid eighty dollars for her. That just wouldn't
be right. What would you say to the three of us becomin'
partners? We'll share the mule and whatever we make out
here."

Looking to Philip, Burton shrugged. "It's all right with me.
We haven't been doing so well by ourselves, anyway."

Philip nodded. "Might as well give it a try."

"Good." The man beamed, extending his hand. "Name's
Jake Fenton, boys. Now, why don't I just see if I can rustle
up some grub to make up for all the trouble that scheming
Hal caused you?"

The next morning, Philip and Burton were on the trail
again, following Jake Fenton to the next mining camp, Devil's
Retreat. "No sense stayin' on in Gomorrah," Jake said. "I
been here two months already, and the place is just about
panned out. Too many men there—each one more shiftless
than the next. Wouldn't surprise me none if one or two of
'em was in on Hal's stealing Sukey and my gold. That's the
trouble out here. A man can't trust no one. You boys are darn
lucky you hitched up with me. Plenty of men would take
advantage of you bein' so young and inexperienced—just the
way Hal did when he sold you my mule."

When they were alone, Philip whispered to Burton, "Just
between you and me, I wouldn't trust old Jake any more than
any of the other miners. He seems all right, but, I don't
know, something about him makes me wonder."

Burton shrugged. "Well, he treated us all right about the
mule. I mean, he didn't have to believe us."

"Umm, no, I suppose he didn't. But—I don't know—that
whole situation seemed kind of—funny. I can't seem to put
my finger on it. Maybe I'm just jumpy from these mines. All
I'm saying is, we'd better keep our eyes open, that's all."

Burton supposed Philip was right. After all, they really
didn't know Jake Fenton, and the man volunteered very little
information about himself. It was wise to be wary of partners,
anyway. Back in Jackass Gulch, they'd seen a man whose
partner had sliced off his ear in a fight over gold profits.

Still, Jake was so likable it was hard not to trust him. He

told the funniest stories, and laughing helped Burton forget, at least for a few moments at a time, that they still hadn't struck it rich. Besides, Jake was a better cook than either Burton or Philip. If teaming up with him hadn't made them rich, at least it had made the constant failure more bearable.

By the end of October, when most of the mining camps were closing down for the winter, the three adventurers had barely made enough to support them until spring.

"Well," Jake said as they finished their salt pork and beans one night, "what do you boys want to do about this partnership? Should we give it another try in the spring, or should we just call it quits right now?"

Shaking his head ruefully, Philip said, "I don't know about you and Burt, but I think I've done just about all the prospecting I want to do. Some people are just lucky, I guess, and I don't seem to be one of them."

Burton stared at him in alarm. "You aren't planning on going home, are you?"

Philip laughed. "Not yet. I'm sure not going back east across the mountains and prairies with winter coming on. And I doubt that I've got enough money to buy ship's passage around the Cape. But, I think I've figured out a better way to make some money. If we dug ditches out from the Sacramento River, I'll bet we could find plenty of prospectors willing to pay for the water rights. What we'd do is rent out sections of our ditches to them."

Frowning, Jake shook his head. "Digging ditches is hard work, boy."

"At least I'd get paid for it," Philip countered.

"Well, that kind of work just isn't for me," Jake said, rising and stretching. "So, I guess we'll just have to call it quits between us." Nodding to Philip and Burton, he ambled off toward another campfire.

"What do you think, Burt?" Philip asked. "You want to try the ditch-digging business with me?"

"I don't know. It's not exactly what I thought I'd be doing when I came out here."

Philip shrugged. "Well, think about it. I'm turning in for the night." He crawled into their tent, leaving Burton alone by the campfire.

Dang it! Burton thought miserably. Why couldn't things have worked out right? I thought by now I'd be rolling in riches. But, here I am with hardly enough to scrape through the winter. It's just not fair that some men have made so much out here, and I haven't.

Now, I'm really stuck. Even if I could get home, I couldn't go now. I wrote Mama and Papa that I was going to make my fortune out here, and I absolutely can't go home until I do.

I can just imagine old Clinton saying, "I told you so." And Benjamin. Benjamin probably wouldn't say anything, but underneath he'd be gloating that I turned out to be such a fool.

Mama'd make a big fuss over me, and act like I was still a little kid. And Papa'd smile indulgently and say, "Well, that must have been quite an adventure, son. I hope it taught you a thing or two about life." And then he'd go right on relying on Benjamin as his number one assistant at the plant. Only, it'd probably be worse than ever now, 'cause Benjamin's had all those months since I've been gone to prove how great he is, while I couldn't even do a simple thing like find some lumps of gold.

Nobody'd understand what it's really like out here, even if I told them. And, of course, I can't tell them, 'cause that would be like admitting I was wrong to come out here.

"What's the matter, boy? You look like you just found out our last side of bacon was rancid!"

Forcing a smile, Burton looked up at Jake. "Nah. I'm just trying to decide what to do."

Jake squatted beside him. "It seems to me, you don't much care for your friend's ditch-digging plan."

Burton shrugged. "It's all right, I guess."

"But not the sort of thing you really want to get involved in, right?" Without waiting for an answer, Jake plunged on. "Yeah, I could tell from when I first met you that you've got a lot more ambition than young Phil. Now, don't get me wrong, he can probably make some money with his ditches. But, you're like me, you don't want to just make some money. You want to get rich, right?"

"Well, sure I do! But there doesn't seem to be much chance of it by prospecting."

"True. True." Jake nodded. "But I've got another idea. Come spring, I'm gonna make my way by selling meat to the prospectors."

"Meat!" Burton repeated unbelievingly. "Where are you gonna get it? A scrawny little chicken costs four dollars around here. Beef is almost unheard of."

"Oh, I have my sources," Jake proclaimed loftily. "Acquaintances around San Francisco. Of course, being a former miner myself, I won't overcharge people the way most dealers do around here. Not that I'd *give* it away. After all, a man's entitled to a handsome profit. I don't think anyone would begrudge me whatever I charged, as long as I kept the price below all the other dealers. I'd be providing a service, after all. A man's got to have meat."

He paused, studying Burton in the firelight. "Say, didn't you tell me your pa was in the meat business back east?"

Burton nodded.

"Wouldn't he just be proud enough to burst if he knew his son was starting up his own meat business in California?" Jake mused. "Course, I don't suppose you'd be interested in joining me. You probably wouldn't want to leave your friend, Phil."

"Couldn't—couldn't Phil be in on it, too?" Burton ventured.

Jake shook his head. "Nah. My—uh—friends in San Francisco say we can only use one more man. And, to be honest, I don't think Phil's quite cut out for the work like you are. What do you say? Does it sound good to you?"

Good! Burton thought. It sounds perfect! All I ever dreamed about was helping Papa run McKinnon Meats. I never would have come to California if I hadn't felt Benjamin was pushing me out of the business. But this will really make Papa sit back and notice me! I'm not even fourteen yet. I'm younger than Ben when he started at McKinnon Meats. But Jake called me a man. He said I'm cut out for this work. And he's right. Phil won't mind. He's got his own plans. He doesn't need me.

"Yes," Burton said, eagerly shaking Jake's hand. "The more I think about it, the more I like your plan!"

By January, sitting in his San Francisco hotel room, Burton burned with anxiety to begin working in the meat business. His funds were running low, and he was tired of sitting around with nothing to do.

Jake spent most of his time in the saloon downstairs, drinking whiskey, flirting with the women, and gambling at cards. He seemed to be remarkably lucky, winning large sums six out of seven nights every week. Often, when he'd had an especially good night, he'd treat Burton to dinner at Delmonico's, the best restaurant in town, where even the cheapest meal cost at least five dollars.

Those outings helped break the monotony of one dollar dinners at San Francisco's many Chinese restaurants. But they hardly made up for the hundreds of boring hours spent in the hotel room, or wandering around the muddy streets of the rapidly growing city.

Several times, Burton asked Jake when they would meet with the friends who had promised to help them get started in the business. Jake only grinned and said, "Never you mind, we'll get together with them when the time is right. In the meantime, just relax. Once we get started, you won't have much time for that. I've got great plans for you, boy."

For lack of anything better to do, Burton finally decided to write to his parents again. Anyway, he reasoned, once his business started, he'd probably be too busy to write.

For a long time, he stared at the paper, wondering exactly what to tell them. Finally, with a broad smile, he began:

Dearest Mama and Papa—
Forgive me for taking so long to write to you, but I've been terribly busy. Philip and I did very well in prospecting, but we've since decided to part company.

You must know I've always been more interested in the meat business than anything else. So, I've decided to invest my gold profits in a thriving partnership, which sells meat to the miners. By this time next year, I will probably be writing to you about the West Coast branch of McKinnon Meats . . .

16
March–June 1851

Burton whistled happily as he rode beside Jake. They were twenty miles from San Francisco now, riding into the twilight, on the way to meet Jake's friends and begin their business venture.

"Riding all afternoon has made me hungry," Burton mused aloud. "I sure hope your friends have plenty of food waiting for us."

Jake flashed him a wry smile. "Oh, there'll be plenty of food on hand. Of course, whether or not we eat will depend on you."

Burton frowned. "I hope you didn't tell them I'd cook. You know what a disaster that would be."

Chuckling, Jake shook his head. "Nope. You don't have to cook. All you have to do is pay attention and do exactly as I tell you."

Perplexed, Burton shrugged, but stifled any more questions. He'd been with Jake long enough to know the man only explained what he wanted, when he wanted. Besides, he could contain his curiosity a little longer. Within a few hours, at most, he'd finally be getting started in their business.

It was dark when three men rode out of a grove of trees to meet them.

"Say there Sonny, Jay, Raoul," Jake called out. "This here's the boy, Burton, I told you about."

The three men eyed Burton, and the tallest, the one Jake had called Sonny, spat at the ground. "You don't think he's a little young, Jake? Ain't he gonna be squeamish about this work?"

"I'll be all right," Burton said quickly. "My pa's a meat-packer, so I'm used to all the blood and guts and smells of slaughtering."

"Huh," Sonny grunted. "We'll see." He maneuvered his horse next to Jake's, and jerked his head toward the right of the road. "Well, everything's ready. They're just waitin' for us down there."

Jake nodded. "Then, let's not keep 'em waiting all night."

With Jake and Sonny in the lead, the group started down into a valley. Puzzled, Burton asked Jay, who was riding beside him, "Is this a shortcut to your ranch?"

Guffawing, Jay replied, "You might say. Yeah, that's a good way to think of it. A shortcut to 'my ranch'!"

Ahead of them, Sonny sighed. "You sure it was a good idea, bringin' that kid, Jake?"

"Don't worry," Jake said. "He'll be fine. I told you, he's small and fast, and he knows something about butchering. We can use someone like that. Besides, he's just like you and me. All he wants is a fast buck."

"Yeah, well you better be right."

At the bottom of the incline, Burton could vaguely make out dark shapes. Sniffing the pungent air, he realized they were grazing cattle.

Turning back to look at him, Jake whispered, "Ain't they pretty? That's our herd."

Burton nodded, his heart pounding with excitement as they rode closer to the peacefully grazing animals.

"Where are the wagons?" Jake asked Sonny.

"Over in that brush. Two of 'em. Ought to be able to handle three or four carcasses each."

"All right. You ready, Raoul?" Jake asked the Mexican, who was riding at the rear of the group.

Burton saw the glint of steel as the Mexican brandished a long knife and grinned.

"Good." Jake turned back to Burton. "Now. Here's what's gonna happen. Raoul will sneak up on some of them critters and slit their throats. Then Sonny and Jay will skin 'em. Your job is gonna be finding the brands and cutting 'em out. We don't want any markings showing on the hides we sell, or even when we carry them away."

"But why—" Burton stopped abruptly as he realized all the men were watching him with sly, menacing grins. Suddenly, he understood why Jake had refused to tell him anything until now. "These cattle don't—they don't belong to any of you, do they?" he whispered.

Jake laughed. "Sure they do! Or, at least, they will in right short time."

Swallowing nervously, Burton squared his shoulders. "I don't think I want to be a part of this business, after all."

"Ah, shit!" Sonny spat. "I told you the kid'd be trouble, Jake."

With a scowl, Jake raised his rifle. "I don't think you have any choice in the matter, Burt. Now, let's quit wasting time and get to work."

Burton eyed the rifle uneasily. "What's your job gonna be, Jake?"

"Mine?" Jake smiled unpleasantly. "I've got two jobs. One is keepin' this rifle ready, in case any of those brutes gets a notion to charge you boys. The other is keepin' this rifle ready in case you should change your mind about doing your job."

"Enough talk," Raoul growled. "Let's get to work."

Swiftly, silently, the Mexican crept up on a steer and slit its throat. The animal fell without a cry, its vocal cords slashed. The blood was still spurting from its neck arteries when Sonny and Jay began skinning it.

Choking with revulsion, Burton watched Raoul move on to another steer. He weighed his own Bowie knife in his hand, wondering if he could plunge it into Sonny or Jay's back before Jake shot him. Would it be worth it to die?

No, of course not. Maybe he could just grab one of the others from behind and put the knife to his throat. Would Jake lower his rifle and let him ride away, to save his friend's life?

No. He couldn't trust Jake to do anything in the name of friendship. All these months he'd thought Jake was his friend, but now Jake was sitting there with a rifle trained on his heart.

The first hide, still warm from the slaughtered steer, landed at Burton's feet. "All right, kid," Sonny snarled. "Get to work."

Glancing up at the menacing rifle, Burton did as ordered.

Within two hours, they had slaughtered and skinned eight steers and loaded their carcasses into the wagons.

Burton felt filthy, drenched with blood and perspiration, and horrified by the thought that he had become part of an outlaw band. How could he get out of it now? They'd never just let him walk away, a living witness to their crimes. Perhaps his only hope was to play along, to pretend he had really become one of them. Then perhaps, one day, they'd let down their guard, and he could escape.

Riding beside him, Jake clapped Burton on the shoulder. "Sorry I had to threaten you back there, boy, but I couldn't afford to have you mess up that chance. If I were you, I wouldn't feel too soft about takin' anything from these ranchers. They're thieves themselves! Look at what they were charging us for meat up in the gold fields last year!"

"I suppose you're right," Burton mumbled. "Anyway, I guess they're all so rich they won't miss eight or ten head."

"Hell no! Anyway, we got a right to steal from them. Most of these ranchers out here aren't even real Americans. They're Spanish—Mexicans." Jake practically spat out the nationality. Prejudice ran high among the miners against Mexicans, Chinese, and Indians.

"Raoul's a Mexican, isn't he?"

"Yeah, but Raoul's a special case. Ain't many men can handle a knife like him."

There was a wicked glint in Jake's eye again that made Burton shudder.

"Anyway, boy," Jake said, "all you got to remember is to do your job, like tonight, and we won't have any problems. In fact, between all of us, we stand to make a heap of money this year. And that's what we all want, right?"

"Right!" Burton hoped he sounded more confident than he felt.

"Just don't start worrying about it being wrong to make your fortune from stealing. When you get right down to it, there ain't a business in the world, not even your pa's, that don't make out by stealing from someone."

Burton pressed his lips together, knowing it was best not to argue. But, he couldn't believe McKinnon Meats stole from anyone. Papa was too honest. Still, in a way, he supposed the firm was stealing from him, the way Benjamin seemed to be moving into the spot that ought to be his.

Of course, that wasn't really stealing. But, as the oldest *real* McKinnon son, he should have certain rights. And if he hadn't felt his rights were being threatened, he wouldn't have come to California, anyway. Well, maybe he would have, just to see what it was like. But, by now he would have gone home and never gotten involved in this mess.

The outlaws rode until dawn, when they finally stopped to make camp. Exhausted, Burton wanted to curl up in his bedroll after a hasty meal of jerky and coffee. But Sonny had other ideas. "All right, kid," he said gruffly, "Jake tells me you got all kinds of experience in butchering, so let's see what you can do with these carcasses."

Burton had no choice but to attack the pungent meat, choking back his vomit as he tried to remember how the butchers at McKinnon Meats worked. One thing he remembered clearly. They didn't butcher in spring or summer, when the meat could rapidly spoil. But he didn't dare mention that fact to Sonny and the others.

Finally, at midday, the butchering was done, and he was allowed to sleep. He had been asleep less than two hours when he awoke to angry voices. He lay still, hoping they would think him still asleep. Gradually, he realized Jake and Sonny were arguing about him.

"I still say the kid was a bad idea, Jake. He's squeamish—and not just about the blood."

"Aw, Sonny, you don't know what you're talking about. I had a talk with him after the slaughter last night. It was just first time jitters, you'll see. Anyway, he did a good enough job with the butchering, didn't he? With no complaints, either."

"Yeah," Sonny admitted grudgingly, "he did all right. But I still think we could've done just as well ourselves. I don't care if he is a meat-packer's son, I don't like no greenhorns working with me. Whatever happened to that guy you used to work with? The one you had the mule scheme going with."

Jake chuckled. "Hal? Oh, we decided to split up for a while. We'd worked so many camps and sold and recovered that damn mule so many times we were afraid guys were gettin' a little suspicious of us. It was a good trick while it lasted, though."

"Yeah, well I wish you'd brought Hal with you instead of the kid."

"I tell you, Sonny, the kid'll work out better than Hal. He's a good worker when we need him, and, when it comes time to divvy up the profits, it'll be a whole lot easier to get rid of a greenhorn than it would be to get rid of Hal. That means more for the rest of us."

"Well, you're right about that." Sonny sighed. "Okay, we'll keep the kid on—for a while."

The whole next day, while Sonny and Jay went up to the gold fields to sell the meat, and Jake rode into Stockton to sell the hides, Burton kept thinking about that conversation.

They planned to kill him! Not right away, unless he stopped being useful to them, but soon enough. Probably before the summer was over.

Philip had been right about everything, even his vague feeling of something being wrong about that mule sale. No wonder Jake had been so willing to accept their story, to forgive them for having his "stolen" mule. It had all been a trick!

Where's Philip now? Burton wondered. What I wouldn't give to be digging ditches from the Sacramento River beside him!

He looked up at Raoul, who was sharpening his knife. The Mexican flashed him a proud smile as he slashed the air with the glistening blade.

"A beautiful weapon, do you not think?" Raoul said. "Much better than a gun. Quiet, quick, light, no need for bullets."

Burton nodded. "You're very good with it."

"I am the best," Raoul proclaimed with a grin. "You were impressed last night? You should see me fight a man. You should see me slit his throat, before he can even scream."

Perhaps I will, Burton thought grimly. Perhaps I'll see you slit my throat.

For two months, the outlaw band roamed the San Joaquin Valley, rustling wherever they could, selling the meat to prospectors, the hides to local leather merchants. To Burton's surprise, none of their customers ever professed any curiosity about the source of their goods. No one cared where the beef came from, as long as the price was lower than the next merchant's. No one cared if the hides were stolen, as long as they bore no brands to prove it.

Perhaps Jake was right. Perhaps the whole world was made up of thieves and liars. Perhaps it was true that no man should trust another, that any man who tried to be too honest was a fool. At fourteen, Burton had seen enough to doubt that he would ever again trust any man.

Childish selfishness had possessed him when he ran away from Chicago to find his fortune in California. Now, experience had hardened him and embittered him, giving birth to a much more vindictive selfishness.

Every day required that, in the simple interest of survival, he think first of himself. And Burton swore to himself that if he ever managed to escape, he would not forget that lesson. He would live for himself, grasp what he wanted in life, and damn anyone who got in his way.

Early one morning in June, Burton awoke abruptly as a boot nudged his ribs.

"C'mon, kid, get up," Jake said gruffly. "You're going up to the hills with me to sell the meat from yesterday's raid."

Rubbing his eyes, Burton sat up in surprise. He had never been invited to take part in any of the selling trips. Why today?

Suddenly, a chilling certainty swept over him. Today he would go into the hills with Jake. Tomorrow, only Jake would return.

Lately, the other members of the gang had begun to express uneasiness. They had robbed every rancher in the area. Jake had deposited a considerable fortune under a false name in a bank in Nevada City. Perhaps it was time to divide the profits and move on to some other scheme. And everyone would be happier with a four-way, rather than a five-way, split of profits.

If Burton had any doubts about the plans, they quickly dissolved when he saw Sonny's sly smile.

"Okay, Jake," Sonny called after them as they rode out of the camp. "We'll be waitin' for you, outside of Nevada City."

Jake did not speak as they rode north, their wagon heavily laden with meat.

When will it be? Burton wondered. Somewhere along this trail? Or tonight, after we've sold all our beef in some mining camp?

Maybe he won't really kill me. Maybe he'll just sneak off at night and abandon me.

He glanced at the hard line of Jake's jaw. No, he'll try to kill me. Jake Fenton doesn't do things halfway. I wonder how many men he's killed already in his life.

The wagon lurched on the mountain trail, and a miniature landslide skittered down the mountainside as the right rear wheel slid off the embankment.

"Shit!" Jake spat, looking back over his shoulder. "Jump down and see if you can give her a shove back onto the trail, Burt."

Burton inched along the edge of the trail toward the back of the wagon, his mind working furiously. This might be his chance, if only he could keep his wits about him.

Bending down to examine the wheel, he called, "I can't do it, Jake! There's a boulder big as a horse's hind end wedged between the wheel and the trail." Grunting, he pretended to strain against the imaginary boulder. "Nope, I can't budge it by myself, and if you try to drive over it, you'll bust the axle for sure."

"Shit!" Jake jumped down to examine the problem himself. "What are you talking about, boy? There's no boulder—"

Bent toward the wheel, Jake didn't see Burton's foot shoot out to trip him. He didn't notice Burton's hands reaching out to shove him. He was already slipping over the side of the mountain when he started to yell, "What the hell—!"

Burton didn't wait to see if Jake managed to catch hold of any scraggly brush to break his fall. He raced to the front of the wagon, jumped onto the seat, and flicked the reins across the backs of the nervous horses.

They snorted and bolted, and for a moment Burton thought

the entire wagon might go crashing down the mountain. But the wheel jerked back onto the trail, and they took off at breakneck speed, leaving Jake Fenton's screams far behind.

Hours after dark, Burton arrived at the ranch of Juan Cabrillo, the cattle rancher they had robbed only two nights earlier. He had abandoned the wagon in the hills, unhitching one of the horses to ride. By the time he knocked at the door of the adobe ranch house, he looked bedraggled enough for his story to be believed. He claimed his older brother had been killed by thieves in the gold fields and he had barely managed to escape with his own life.

The next morning, prompted by his wife's desire to help the "poor orphan," Juan Cabrillo offered Burton a job feeding livestock. Burton accepted without a second thought.

The hard work did not please him, but the comforts and security of the ranch did. Not knowing if Jake had survived, he could hardly have risked staying in the gold fields. Nor could he wander anywhere that Sonny and his band might find him.

His stay on the ranch would only be temporary, until he could convince his father of his rightful position at McKinnon Meats.

Now, more than ever, Burton was determined that he, not Benjamin, must become the heir apparent of the firm. Because of Ben, he had come out to California to prove himself. Because of Ben, he had almost gotten killed. He would not abandon his goals now. One thing he had learned from Jake Fenton was to find a means to get whatever he wanted, no matter who stood in the way.

Within a month, Burton had figured out how to use his time on the Cabrillo ranch to impress his father. He recalled that Brett had often mentioned the possibility of establishing his own ranches to supply beef for the firm. In fact, Brett had been quite excited about the idea, though Benjamin had seemed quite skeptical.

Now Burton knew he had a chance to use both his father's dreams and his half brother's lack of enthusiasm to his own advantage. He could show Brett he had the foresight to recognize the merits of ranch owning, while at the same time discrediting Benjamin's ability to plan for the future. And, if he exaggerated, how would any of the family, thousands of miles away, ever know?

Taking pen and paper, Burton quickly wrote:

Dearest Mama and Papa—
I am so busy I haven't time for more than a quick
note. However, I just want to let you know that my
meat dealership proved so profitable I've been able
to go into another area of the meat business. I've
just purchased part interest in a thriving cattle ranch
here . . .

17
1852–1855

Shaking her head, Eden looked up from Burton's latest glow-
ing letter from California. "It's still hard to imagine our
Burton running a thirty-thousand-acre cattle ranch," she sighed.
"Why, he's still only a boy!"

Brett smiled indulgently. "He's hardly a boy anymore,
Eden. He's fifteen. And living in the wilderness makes a man
grow up fast. I've told you how independent John Kinzie was
at fifteen."

"Yes. But those were different times. I can't help wishing
Burton were still here in school, where he belongs."

"No one belongs in school any longer than he feels right
about being there. Burton knows what he wants from life,
and his ranching will help him get it a good deal faster than
hours and years poring over books. Look at our Clinton—an
excellent student, but he hasn't the faintest idea what he
wants to make of his life."

"Brett, that's unfair! Clinton is only thirteen! I suppose
next you'll be saying that Paige ought to be planning her
future, even though she's only five."

"Paige is different. As a girl, all she needs to do is learn to
run a household and snare a promising man."

Eden stared at her husband in outrage. Since the birth of
their youngest child, when they'd moved away from the Bull
and Boar, she had not been as active in the business. But,
after all she had done to help build McKinnon Meats. . . .

Misinterpreting Eden's expression, Brett said quickly, "Well,

all right, maybe I am being a little hard on Clinton. I guess
I'm just disappointed he hasn't shown much of an interest in
meat packing yet. You're right, he is young. But, at his age,
Burton was already on his way to California."

Eden sighed. "I wish he'd never gone. Sometimes, when I
read his letters, I feel as if I don't even know him anymore."

Smiling, Brett took her hand. "That's only natural. He's
growing up, and it's hard for you to accept that because
you're not beside him to watch him grow. He is changing.
He's becoming a man. But, he'll always be our son."

Forcing a return smile, Eden stifled the urge to say that
she wasn't at all certain Burton was their son anymore. Brett
was so proud of him, so pleased with his ingenuity, that she
felt she should be, too. But she could not shake the conviction that her firstborn was not developing into quite the man
she might have hoped.

Every three or four months, another letter arrived from
Burton, brimming with all the optimism of his earlier messages.
Brett glowed with enthusiasm for his son's future in the meat
business, but Eden grew more and more apprehensive. There
was something too ecstatic about Burton's tone. His success
seemed too unrelenting to be real.

Knowing Brett would not discuss the letters objectively,
Eden turned to Benjamin. "What do you think of Burton's
letters?" she asked pointedly.

Her stepson shrugged. "I think he's been extraordinarily
lucky. Men twice his age have come back from California
with barely more than the shirts on their backs."

Eden hesitated. "Do you—do you think he's telling the
truth?"

Pursing his lips, Benjamin looked away. "It's possible.
Burton's always seemed very ambitious. I've no doubt he
could accomplish anything he set out to do."

"But it's also possible that he's—exaggerating—isn't it?"

"Eden, don't put me in the position of criticizing my half
brother! Sure he could be exaggerating—a lot of men do it to
save face when they get in a tight position." He paused,
rubbing his jaw thoughtfully. "For my father's sake, I hope to
God he isn't."

Nodding, Eden said quietly, "I know. Brett's making some
pretty grandiose plans, isn't he?"

"The plans themselves aren't really so grandiose if you

think about them. He wants to start a ranch of his own to
provide top-quality beef, and that in itself makes sense. A lot
of other packers are talking about doing the same thing. They
say there's plenty of good grazing territory down in Texas,
and once the railroads really start .expanding, there won't be
any problem getting the cattle to market. The only part of the
plan I question is putting Burton in charge of the new ranch.
But I hate to say anything to Father and have him think I
question the abilities of my brother. There's never been any
feeling of rivalry between me and my little brothers, and I
don't want anything to start now. Still, Burton's awfully young,
and I'd hate to see him disappoint Father."

"So would I," Eden sighed. "But I guess there's no sense
worrying about it. Brett's too stubborn to listen to anyone
once he's made up his mind about something."

"Well, it's a bit early to worry, anyway," Benjamin assured
her. "The plans are still rough. It'll be years before the
railroads have expanded enough to put Father's ideas into
operation. By then, I hope Burton will have gained enough
experience to justify Father's trust. I'd like nothing better
than to have our misgivings proved wrong."

As Benjamin had predicted, the railroads expanded slowly.
Still, propelled by the success of the Illinois and Michigan
Canal, which linked the Great Lakes with the Mississippi
River, and with the first railroads entering Chicago from the
East, Chicago's livestock market and meat-packing industry
continued to grow. By the middle of the 1850s, railroads
were crisscrossing Illinois, bringing agricultural products from
Missouri and Iowa, and carrying finished goods back to the
farmers.

Burton's periodic letters continued to keep the ranch idea
alive in the back of Brett's head, but he knew the idea was
not yet practical. Meanwhile, McKinnon Meats expanded in
other directions.

Early in the decade, the firm had begun experimenting
with the canning of beef, even shipping some of the canned
goods to England. Now McKinnon Meats had become one of
the few packers offering canned goods on a regular basis to a
market eager for the new products.

With the surge in business, the plant had also been forced
to expand its stockyards. The Bull and Boar yards were no
longer able to accommodate all of the livestock, so Brett had

built new stockyards and moved his entire operation to Twelfth and State streets. Near the Michigan, Southern, and Northern Indiana Railroad line, the new McKinnon yards had pens for five thousand cattle and thirty thousand hogs.

While McKinnon Meats expanded, the city of Chicago, too, was changing its face. Determined to rid their city of the derisive title "Mudhole of the Prairie," the city fathers began a massive project to raise the level of the streets above the Chicago River. In some areas, street levels were raised as much as twelve feet. As a result, shoppers walking along the wooden sidewalks that lined the streets often found themselves level with the second floor windows of shops and hotels. At the end of a block, walkers frequently discovered that the cross street had not yet been raised. So, it was necessary to descend a wooden staircase, cross the lower, muddier street, then climb another set of stairs before continuing along the raised street.

Eden found the process tedious, but somewhat amusing. On many shopping excursions, she had to restrain a smile as older women warned of ill-mannered "sidewalk oglers," who stood beneath the staircases, straining for a glimpse of ivory limbs as women climbed or descended the stairs.

Raising the streets, and then raising the buildings that lined them, was a project that would extend into the next decade. But Eden was resigned to the inconvenience—in return for the promised luxury of dry, mud-free feet, and the assurance that her wagon or carriage would not become mired in mud.

She was out shopping one afternoon in the fall of 1855 when Brett sent home a message that he would be bringing a guest home for dinner. Entranced by the large selection of Parisian hats in Potter Palmer's Lake Street store, she lost track of time and arrived home much later than usual. To her surprise, she found the kitchen in an uproar, as Louise, their cook, bustled about preparing the accompaniments for a fragrant roast ham.

"Do you want the children to eat early tonight, ma'am?" Louise asked.

"Of course not," Eden replied. "You know Clinton and Paige always have dinner with Mr. McKinnon and me."

"Yes, ma'am, but Mr. McKinnon's message said he was bringing someone important to dinner, so I just thought perhaps he wouldn't want the distraction of children at the meal. Of course, I realize your son is nearly a man, but little Paige being hardly eight years old, I thought—"

Frowning, Eden interrupted, "Did you say my husband is bringing a guest?"

"Yes, ma'am. The messenger said it was someone important."

"But he didn't say whom?"

"No, ma'am." Louise shook her head.

Eden's frown deepened. The message was so unlike Brett. Occasionally, he brought a rancher or other businessman to dinner, but he always identified the guest in advance, and he usually gave her more notice. Since most ranchers who made the trip to Chicago stayed for a few days, Brett usually issued an invitation and informed Eden of his plans a day or two in advance. Who could be so important that Brett would bring him on the spur of the moment—unless—

Suddenly, Eden's frown changed to a smile. Burton! It had to be Burton! He must have gone directly to the packing plant. No doubt he and Brett had decided to surprise her at dinner.

"What about the children, ma'am?" Louise's voice interrupted her thoughts.

"The children?"

The cook sighed. "Do you want them to eat early or—"

"No, no. Clinton and Paige will eat with us. I'm quite sure that's what my husband intended."

In her bedroom, Eden hummed brightly to herself as she laid out a green, watered-silk dress. A part of her wanted to rush over to McKinnon Meats immediately, but she was determined not to spoil Brett and Burton's surprise. Bursting with excitement, she almost ran to tell Clinton her suspicions, then decided to let him be surprised, too.

Half an hour later, dressed in her green gown with the becoming off-the-shoulder bodice, her auburn hair arranged in a sleek series of sausage curls, Eden let herself out of her room. She was at the head of the stairs when the front door opened and Brett stepped into the house, followed by a tall, blond man.

Eden froze, staring in disbelief at the visitor's sharply angular features, his penetrating blue eyes. It was unthinkable that he would be here, in her house, after nearly ten years.

"Darling," Brett said smoothly, "you remember Garrett Martin, don't you?"

Shocked, Eden still stood frozen, searching Garrett's eyes for some clue as to why he had come. "Where's Burton?" she asked without thinking.

"Burton?" Brett laughed uneasily. "I suspect he's in California, tending his ranch. But, if my plans work out, he may be much closer to us within a few months' time."

When Eden did not respond, Brett galloped up the stairs toward her. "For God's sakes, Eden," he whispered through clenched teeth, "what's the matter with you? Can't you at least make some effort to welcome our guest?"

Forcing a smile, Eden started down the stairs toward Garrett. "You must forgive me, Mr. Martin. When my husband sent word that he was bringing a guest to dinner, I somehow got the notion it was my eldest son, Burton. He's been away so long and—well, I'm sure you can understand if you have children of your own."

Garrett smiled, showing the boyish dimples Eden had always loved. At thirty-five, he still possessed a beguiling youthfulness. "I haven't any children," he said simply. "I never married. Still, I think I can understand how you feel."

Eden flinched, reading the message in his eyes. Garrett Martin knew exactly how it felt to be cut off from a loved one. He knew because she had cut him off nine years ago. Suddenly, she wondered if Brett also knew about her long-buried affair. Was that why he had brought Garrett home?

Glancing uneasily at Brett, she saw that he was frowning over her unusual behavior. If he hadn't been suspicious of her and Garrett before, she was surely giving him reason to be now. Turning back to Garrett, she said with forced brightness, "I do appreciate your understanding, Mr. Martin. Brett tells me I worry far too much about our son. I suspect he's right, but it's in a mother's nature to worry. Burton left for California when he was only thirteen, you know. Still, he's done extraordinarily well out there, and now that he's eighteen I suppose I ought to stop worrying."

"Yes." Garrett nodded. "Your husband has told me a bit about your son's success. I must congratulate both of you. Surely you've both had a hand in making him the man he is."

Seeking an escape, Eden inclined her head toward the parlor. "Perhaps you'd like to sit down and have a drink before dinner, Mr. Martin? I'll leave you with my husband while I go to check Louise's progress in the kitchen."

Throughout the meal, Eden managed to maintain a light,

friendly tone, but the effort left her with a pounding headache. As Louise cleared away the remnants of her flaky cherry tart and Brett invited Garrett into his study for brandy, Eden smiled thankfully.

"I'll leave you gentlemen to your business," she said, "while I put our Paige to bed. It's been a pleasure seeing you again, Mr. Martin."

"I wish you'd join us again after you've tucked Paige in," Brett said. "I think you'll be quite interested in the proposal I wish to discuss with Mr. Martin." Turning to Garrett, he added, "I've always valued my wife's participation in McKinnon Meats. I hope you won't mind her joining us."

"Not at all," Garrett replied smoothly. "In fact, I'll be delighted. You're a smart man, McKinnon, to appreciate her worth. Too many men in your position forget their wives helped them achieve success."

Tightly grasping Paige's hand, Eden hurried from the dining room. She felt a flush painting her neck. She had thought she was over Garrett years ago, when she and Brett had managed to patch up their marriage. Not seeing him, she had gradually stopped longing for him. But now, having him in her home, the pain, the guilt, and, yes, the desire were almost too much for her to bear. How could Garrett do this to her? Was he paying her back, at last, for the way she had hurt him?

By the time she had tucked Paige in and returned downstairs to knock at Brett's study door, Eden was quivering inwardly. How could she face the two of them? What in the world did Brett intend to discuss?

Brett opened the door, smiling as he slid an arm around her waist. "Oh, there you are, darling! I was just about to pour us another brandy. Will you join us?"

"I—yes." Why not? Perhaps the brandy could help her to relax.

After serving the brandy, Brett led Eden to a settee, where they sat down opposite Garrett. He waited for her to take a sip of the amber liquid, before he began.

"You know I've been talking for some time about setting up a ranch," Brett said to her.

"Yes." Eden began to relax. Perhaps Brett simply wanted Garrett's advice about ranching. She'd heard over the years that Garrett had one of the most successful ranches in Iowa.

"But I thought you'd decided to put off the idea until the railroads had expanded a bit more."

"I had." Brett nodded. "But lately I've been thinking I might be wiser to move now. In the last ten years, since the United States annexed Texas, cattle raising there has really grown. They've got excellent grazing lands, and the actual cost of running a Texas ranch is negligible. They say the cattle multiply so rapidly there a man can increase his herd by thirty percent in a single year. With that sort of recommendation, before long every meatman in the country will be wanting a Texas ranch. If I wait too long, all the best land will be taken."

Eden shrugged. "That makes sense, I suppose. But it won't do you a great deal of good to have all that cattle if you can't get them to your packing plant."

"But I can! All we have to do is drive them to New Orleans or to some other port along the Mississippi. The cattle can be sent up the river and then on across Illinois on the canal. It may not be an ideal plan, but it could hold us over till the railroads work further west."

"I see. How soon do you think you could begin the ranch?"

"Next spring, I hope. But that depends on Burton. And on Mr. Martin."

Garrett frowned. "I'm afraid I don't quite see how I'm involved."

"Of course not. I haven't given you my proposition yet." Brett smiled broadly, pausing for emphasis. "Mr. Martin, I'd like you to share management of the Double M ranch with my son, Burton."

Eden gasped, and Garrett's brow wrinkled in perplexity. "Why me?" he asked quietly.

"Because you've got the most successful ranch in Iowa. I trust your judgment. I don't know you particularly well as a person, but I know you're a businessman of the first order. I know you could make my ranch succeed."

Garrett smiled lazily. "So could a lot of other men, I suspect. From what you've told me of your son, I would guess he could manage your ranch well enough on his own."

"I'm inclined to agree with you, Mr. Martin. But Burton's young. He hasn't got your experience. And he's not accustomed to running a ranch anywhere near as large as what I have in mind. He could probably get along without any major mishaps, but I'd feel a good deal more relaxed if I knew he could turn to someone with your experience and insight." Patting Eden's hand, he added, "I'm sure his mother would, too. She's already told you how she worries about the boy."

Garrett nodded. "I'm flattered by your confidence, Mr. McKinnon. But I can't say I relish the idea of giving up my own ranch to work for another man."

"Texas offers a lot more opportunities than Iowa," Brett prodded. "There's a lot more range land, the chance to manage a much bigger ranch."

"I understand that. But independence is worth a great deal. A man in your position ought to realize that."

Brett sighed. "I thought you might feel that way. So, I'm prepared to offer you half interest in the ranch. You'll realize a far greater profit than you ever would in Iowa, and I'll still have the advantage of my own beef supply. What do you say, Mr. Martin?"

Garrett's eyes moved slowly between Brett and Eden, seeking an answer in Eden's gaze. Had she asked her husband to give him this offer? And, if she had, why? Did she want to begin again with him? Or did she simply want to have some power over him? Her confusion when he first arrived, and her gasp when Brett made the proposition, indicated she had had no idea what her husband intended. But, she might have been acting. After nine years, he didn't really know her, did he?

What was that look in her eyes now? Was it pleading? Pleading for what—that he accept the proposal or reject it?

Rising stiffly, Garrett extended his hand to Brett. "The offer is tempting," he said. "But it's asking a lot to expect a man to change his life, to give up everything he's built for himself. I'll have to think about it."

Later, as they prepared for bed, Eden looked at Brett questioningly. "What will you do if Mr. Martin does not accept your proposal?" she asked quietly. "Will you put off founding the ranch for a bit longer?"

Brett shook his head emphatically. "No. The time is right now. If Martin isn't interested, I'll have Burton manage the ranch alone."

For most of the night, Eden lay awake, worrying about Brett's plans. What if Garrett did not accept the proposal? Why should he? She ought to hope Garrett would reject the proposition. As a part of McKinnon Meats, Garrett Martin would become an irrefutable part of her life again, dredging up all the pain, guilt, desire, and bittersweet memories of their past.

Still, Eden could not bear to think what would happen if Garrett did not join the firm. Try as she might, she could not shake the conviction that Burton could never manage the ranch alone.

Brett accepted Burton's supposed success in California as only natural. Burton could not help but succeed, simply because he was the son of Brett McKinnon. But, somehow, Burton's letters had never convinced Eden that he was doing as well as he claimed.

Eden had long ago given up discussing the point with Brett, and she knew that anything she said now would fall on deaf ears. But, if Brett allowed Burton to manage the ranch on his own, she feared the project would be doomed to failure.

That would crush Brett, who had always worked hard and been rewarded by success. If Burton failed, Brett might even turn against him. The one thing Brett could never forgive or understand was failure, especially if it touched his own business.

By morning, Eden had thought of nothing to allay her concern. Knowing she could not discuss the situation with Brett, she wished she could at least confide in Benjamin. But Benjamin had left for the Kansas Territory three days ago to visit his mother and brother. He would not return for at least ten days. By then, Garrett Martin would have made his decision and returned to his Iowa ranch. And Eden felt fairly certain of what that decision would be.

Early in the afternoon, Eden finally accepted what she must do. For Brett's sake, for Burton's sake, she seemed to have only one choice.

Stepping into the lobby of the Tremont House Hotel, Eden pulled her hooded cloak more tightly around her face. She had sent a servant ahead to find out Garrett's room number so she need not stop at the hotel desk. Still, she worried that someone might notice and recognize her. Gossip still traveled through the city as quickly as through a small town.

Finding room 424, Eden knocked hesitantly. What if her servant had made an error? Or, if this was the right room, what if Garrett was out? She couldn't wait for him. But she couldn't leave a message for him to call at the house, where

Brett might discover them. She felt a mixture of relief and apprehension as a muffled, but familiar, voice called, "Just a moment."

Garrett opened the door and stared at her for a long moment. His eyes narrowed to blue slits and his lips pursed in thought.

"Mrs. McKinnon," he said sardonically, "I don't think you ought to be here. Should I invite you in?"

Eden's heart sank as she swept past him into the room. Last night he had played the role of the perfect gentleman. But there was no mistaking the bitterness in his tone today. Perhaps he was still too bitter even to consider anything she might ask.

Glancing at the bed, she saw his packed saddlebags. "Are you leaving so soon, Mr. Martin?"

"Yes. My business in Chicago is completed, so I'm anxious to get back to Iowa."

"Have you considered my husband's proposal?"

He nodded. "I'll stop at the plant on my way out of the city and give him my answer."

"Which is?" She tried to sound disinterested.

Garrett frowned. "Can't you guess? At one time, I thought you knew me well enough to know how I would react to such a proposal. I'm happy where I am. I don't need the extra money a partnership with McKinnon Meats would give me." Looking away, he added in a barely audible whisper, "I don't need the heartache, either."

"I wish you'd reconsider, Garrett."

His eyes snapped back to hers. "What are you saying? That you're finally ready to leave McKinnon for me? I think we could find a less heartless way to break the news than by me becoming his business partner."

Eden shook her head. "You know that's not what I mean, Garrett. I married Brett for better or for worse—and most of these last years have been for better."

"Then what *are* you saying? You can't expect me to enter a partnership with the man who's kept me from the only woman I ever loved!"

Catching her breath, Eden asked softly, "Do you still love me, Garrett?"

"What does it matter if I do or not?"

"Do you still care enough to do something for me?"

"If you mean, will I give up my independence to become

part of the McKinnon empire, the answer is no, I won't! I can't. The price is too high, and I wouldn't get a damn thing in return."

"The money—"

"I've already told you, I don't care about money."

"Well then, would my gratitude mean anything to you?"

Turning away, he ran a hand haphazardly through his sun-bleached hair. "Your gratitude can't keep me warm when I'm lying alone on the prairie," he said bitterly.

"Garrett, please, don't make this so hard!"

Whirling on her, he demanded, "Why in hell shouldn't I make it hard? Do you think you made things easy for me when you wrote your self-righteous little letter?"

"I tried to warn you time and time again—"

He snorted derisively. "Yes, you tried! You tried so hard you crawled into bed with me every time I put up at the Bull and Boar!"

For a moment, Eden stared at him, her jaw dropping open in outrage. Starting toward the door, she said crisply, "Forgive me. I shouldn't have come. I can see you're not the gentle, sympathetic man I once loved."

She was already opening the door when she felt his hands on her shoulders. Turning her gently toward him, he probed her tear-clouded eyes with his clear blue gaze.

"Why did you come, Eden?" he asked softly.

"Because if you don't help manage that ranch, I'm afraid it will be doomed from the start! That would crush Brett. Maybe Burton, too."

At his frown, she quickly described all her fears and misgivings from the time Burton had left for California. She outlined Burton's letters, Brett's soaring pride, and her own increasing skepticism, ending with her fears that Burton was not yet ready to manage a ranch.

Garrett raised his brows, smiling slightly. "It seems to me you haven't much faith in your firstborn."

"It's not that. Burton's a very capable boy. But I'm afraid he's been exaggerating. He wants so badly for us to believe he was right in going to California that I'm afraid he may be getting carried away in describing his success."

Garrett shrugged. "On the other hand, he may just be incredibly successful. After all, I started managing my father's ranch when I was only sixteen."

"But you'd been raised on the ranch, it was practically in your blood."

"Well, if your son is exaggerating about his abilities and experience, a little failure might be just what he needs to get his feet back on the ground."

"But, don't you see, it wouldn't be just 'a little failure.' Brett's not talking about a little ranch."

"So, in other words, you're asking me to step in to save your son from embarrassment and your husband from a major financial setback. Doesn't that seem a bit much to ask when your husband and your children were your reasons for breaking off our relationship?"

Gazing at him steadily, Eden shook her head. "It would be too much to ask of almost any other man. But I don't think it's too much to ask a man of your caliber."

Returning her gaze, Garrett chewed on his lower lip. His hands, still on her shoulders, could feel her quivering beneath his touch. "I'll think about my decision," he said huskily. "Now, I think you'd better go."

Looking up at him, Eden drew a long, unsteady breath. "I'm not sure I want to go," she whispered.

Brett was late coming home from the plant that night, but when he stepped into the hallway, his face was aglow with triumph. "It's settled," he announced. "Garrett Martin's going to join us in the Double M ranch!"

"That's wonderful, darling," Eden said in feigned surprise.

"Yes. From his attitude when he left last night, I'd have sworn he wouldn't agree. Not that Burton couldn't manage on his own, but Martin's experience in ranching can't hurt us any. Anyway, he's gone back to Iowa to make arrangements to sell his ranch. By spring, he should be ready to ride for Texas with me."

"Then he's left Chicago already?"

"Yes. I asked him home to dinner to celebrate our new partnership, but he was anxious to start back for his place. Never mind, darling, we'll have our own celebration, won't we?"

"Indeed we will," Eden replied, hoping she sounded more enthusiastic than she felt.

18
May–August 1856

Benjamin McKinnon looked up in surprise as his seventeen-year-old half brother, Clinton, burst into the office of McKinnon Meats.

"Did you hear what's happened in Kansas?" Clinton demanded. "The proslavers have sacked Lawrence! Destroyed both newspaper offices! Threw the presses and type into the Kaw River! Shelled the Free State Hotel with cannon!"

Grimacing, Benjamin mentally calculated the distance from Lawrence to the Potawatomi reservation, where his mother, Morning Star, lived. It was a mere thirty miles, hardly a safe distance in a territory gone mad in the fight between men who favored slavery and those who opposed it. Ever since the Kansas-Nebraska Act created the territory of Kansas two years ago, the area had been a hotbed of controversy. The act had decreed that the settlers themselves would decide whether Kansas would be slave or free, touching off a violent confrontation between the two factions.

Knowing that his seventeen-year-old half brother was a strong supporter of the Free-State movement, Benjamin tried to hide the depth of his own concern. "What's going to happen now?" he asked with forced calmness.

"It's already happened! John Brown and his men massacred a bunch of proslavers along Mosquito Creek. It looks like there's going to be a major war this time!"

Benjamin sighed. At thirty, he was a good deal less hot-blooded than his young brother. "Let's hope not," he said quietly. "There's already been enough killing in that territory. People are beginning to call it 'Bleeding Kansas.'"

Instantly subdued, Clinton nodded. "I know. There ought to be a better way to solve the slavery question." He paused uneasily, looking away from Benjamin. "Are you worried about your mother and Swift Elk?"

"I wish I could say I wasn't. Mother should be safe, I

150

suppose. There's no reason for either side to attack the reservation. But then, there was no reason for all the killing that's already gone on. As for Swift Elk—yes, I'm damned worried. When I visited there last year, he was talking about joining the Free Staters. He sees a kinship between the Indian and the Negro, since both have been oppressed by whites. What could I say? Both Swift Elk and I are half white, but our separate lives these last fifteen years have made me more white, him more Indian."

He paused, shaking his head. "When I first came here, I didn't feel very white. Even now, I think very few proper Chicagoans would want me, with my Indian blood, marrying their daughters. Still, overall, the white world has been good to me. I feel at home here. But I see, as my brother does, the evil in some white men. I agree with him that slavery and subjugation must not be encouraged. In my heart, I would like nothing better than to see the end of the kind of thinking that elevates whites above Indians, or Negroes, or any other race."

Clinton nodded. "Will you go to Kansas then, to help Swift Elk in the fight and to protect your mother?"

"No." Benjamin shook his head. "How can I go now, when Father is away establishing his Texas ranch? He entrusted the business to me, expects me to look after your mother. I cannot turn my back on my responsibilities." Sighing, he admitted, "It is true I feel torn. To whom do I owe the most? Father, Mother, Swift Elk—they are all my flesh and blood. But, as I said, I think—I hope—Mother is fairly safe. As for Swift Elk, he is a grown man, older than I. Nothing I do or say can shield him from harm."

For a long moment, Clinton stared at Benjamin, his blue-gray eyes clear and unblinking. He had scarcely heard Benjamin's last words, as an earlier statement reverberated in his head: "Father, Mother, Swift Elk—they are all my flesh and blood." Benjamin had called Brett "Father" for several years now, but Clinton had taken that as a sign of affectionate respect for the older man who had taken him in. Now he realized there was much more significance in the name.

"So it's true," Clinton said softly. "You are Papa's son. You are my brother!"

Benjamin flushed slightly, hesitating before he nodded. "I'm sorry. I didn't mean to tell you. It's not my place to do so. I must have been more upset than I realized. But, now that you know the truth, I think you're old enough to realize the fact in no way reflects on our father or on your mother. Father married my mother, in the Indian fashion, when Eden was only a small child. After Father and Mother decided to part, he fell in love with Eden and married her—"

"You don't need to explain," Clinton interrupted. "I think I understand. Inside, I think I've known for a long time that you are my brother, and it's never bothered me. I'm proud to share your blood."

With a relieved smile, Benjamin stood to embrace his half brother. "I am proud to be your brother, too," he said. "In a way, I'm glad you finally know. Secrets between brothers are not good. Someday we will tell Burton, too."

Clinton nodded distractedly. "Benjamin," he said, "you can't go to Kansas, but perhaps I should."

Benjamin frowned. "Don't be ridiculous, Clint! I know you favor the Free Staters, but you haven't any place in Kansas. Your place, for now, is in school, where your mother wants you. You'd break her heart if you ran off to Kansas."

"If you are my brother, then Swift Elk is my flesh and blood, too," Clinton protested. "Don't I have a place supporting him in his struggles?"

Averting his eyes, Benjamin shook his head, "Not at the risk of hurting your own mother and father." Forcing a laugh, he added, "We're probably getting worked up over nothing. You know how often reports from the West are exaggerated. In all likelihood, the incident in Lawrence was just a small skirmish. In a few days, we'll hear the real story, and we'll see there's nothing to worry about."

"I think we can expect to hear the real story tomorrow evening. There's a rally scheduled at the Lake House Hotel, and General Lane is going to speak."

Benjamin grimaced. General Jim Lane was a prominent leader of the Free-State movement, so skilled in frontier oratory he could easily incite a mob to riot. Though Lane had lived in Lawrence more than a year, Benjamin doubted that he would present a completely honest picture. More likely, he would exaggerate whatever had happened at Lawrence, using the incident to fuel the antislavery fire.

"I hope you don't plan to attend that rally," Benjamin said blandly.

Clinton blinked in surprise. "Of course I plan to go! In fact, I thought you'd want to go with me."

* * *

Convinced Clinton would attend without him, and afraid General Lane might induce his brother to do something rash, Benjamin finally agreed to attend the rally.

As he expected, General Lane's impassioned plea for aid to the Free Staters incited the crowd nearly to hysteria. Three thousand people, crammed shoulder to shoulder into the Lake House ballroom, shouted their support of a free Kansas. Hearing that the persecuted Free Staters needed financial as well as moral support, one excited man immediately donated five hundred dollars. That act prompted others to donate, and by midnight twelve thousand dollars had been given.

Tugging Clinton's arm, Benjamin whispered, "Come on, it's late. If we don't go home, we'll never be able to get up for church in the morning."

Clinton shook his head. "Go on, if you want. I want to stay till the end."

"It's almost over anyway," Ben pressed. "There's someone up in front calling for adjournment right now."

But the crowd was too inflamed to adjourn. Donations poured in for another hour, reaching the fifteen thousand mark by one A.M. Then, General Lane stood at the front of the crowd and shouted, "Brothers in the fight for freedom, we thank you for every dollar and every cent you have given to ensure free speech, a free press, a free society in Kansas. But, we need more than your money. We need men. Men willing to put their lives on the line. Men ready to leave tomorrow for Kansas, to settle the territory and make certain the proslavers do not gain a majority. How many among you are man enough to leave behind your comfortable city homes and join our fight for freedom?"

The crowd surged forward as men rushed to declare their support. Clinton pushed toward the front of the meeting, but Benjamin caught both his arms and held him back.

"Don't be a fool, Clint!" Benjamin urged. "Lane and his kind are fanatics! If you sign up with him, you'll be walking straight into the jaws of death!"

"I don't care!" Clinton declared, struggling to break Benjamin's grasp. "This is something I believe in. I have to do it."

"Even if it means breaking your mother's heart?"

"She'll understand. She'll be proud of me. Anyway, I can't

always do what she wants. Burton didn't worry about her feelings when he ran off to California!"

Benjamin sighed. "No. But I'll tell you something. Even when you were small boys, I never thought Burton would be half the man you would."

"Don't, Benjamin," Clinton said softly. "Don't try to make me feel guilty for doing something I believe in."

"I'm not. I'm simply trying to make you be sensible. If, in the end, you decide you must go to Kansas, there's nothing I can do about it. I was younger than you when I made up my mind to come to Chicago. But I won't let you be carried away by a raving mob."

In the end, Clinton admitted it was just as well he hadn't joined the first group of recruits. Those sixty-six men, who left Chicago less than three weeks after the rally, entered Kansas under an armed guard of proslavers who had captured their boat on the Missouri River. After a brief imprisonment at Fort Leavenworth, during which most of their provisions and supplies were confiscated, the Free Staters were returned to Illinois with a warning not to attempt any similar schemes.

Not to be defeated, the Free Staters devised a new route to Kansas, through Iowa and Nebraska, then south to the embattled territory. All through July, Clinton read with increasing excitement the newspaper stories about the "Lane Trail," and "General Lane's Army of the North."

By the end of the month, Clinton could no longer bear to be an outsider to the movement. Thankful his father was still in Texas and could not stop him, he left brief notes for his mother and Benjamin and took the train to Iowa City. There he purchased a horse and set off after Lane and his "army."

Thinking of how his mother had mourned Burton's departure, Clinton felt a few pangs of conscience. But he consoled himself that at least he had left a message. Besides, he had left home for a more noble purpose than Burton. His brother had left in quest of personal gain, while he rode in defense of a principle.

Catching up to "General Lane's Army" shortly before it crossed into Nebraska, Clinton quickly discovered it bore little resemblance to a real army. Although four hundred strong, almost half the "army" was made up of women and young children.

Overall, they seemed poorly equipped for battle. In fact, they were not even very well equipped for emigration. Clinton felt a chill of apprehension as he attached himself to the motley, undisciplined group.

Two days' journey into Nebraska, they met a band of Free Staters, led by the legendary John Brown, who had ridden north from Kansas. After a brief consultation, General Lane announced he would leave the larger group of emigrants to settle on their own, while he led an army of thirty south. As one of the few emigrants with his own riding horse, Clinton was quickly chosen for the new, smaller "army."

Riding south, Clinton surveyed his fellow Free Staters with interest. At seventeen, he was by far the youngest of the party. Most of the others were young men in their twenties or early thirties, who looked up to the forty-two-year-old Lane.

Tall and thin, Lane had a gaunt face that was usually fixed in a scowl. It was easy to understand how he had earned the name "The Grim Chieftain of Kansas." His flamboyant dress—knee boots, a red sash, a flowing cloak, and a military cap—provided a stark contrast to his harsh features.

Beside the general rode John Brown, "Old Brown" as most of the men called him, since he was well into his fifties. With his wild, flowing gray hair, Brown looked every inch the radical. People whispered that there had been insanity in his family, and one look at the man's slate-blue, diabolical eyes made Clinton begin to believe the stories.

Brown was already a fiery folk hero, so Clinton was glad to observe him at close range. Still, he felt slightly regretful that "Old Brown" had joined the contingent. He had heard a great deal about the man's vengeful raids, and he was not sure he entirely approved of them. Defense of a principle was one thing, but the mere thought of cold-blooded murder and revenge turned Clinton's stomach.

Tearing his eyes away from the leaders, Clinton looked more closely at the other riders. One, riding slightly apart from the others, was an Indian, barechested, wearing only leather leggings and moccasins. While the other men talked and joked among themselves, the Indian rode with a quiet, cold confidence that set him apart from the rest.

Edging his horse nearer, Clinton studied the Indian. Was he a Potawatomi? he wondered. Had he known Benjamin? Did he know Swift Elk? Was it even possible he *was* Swift

Elk? Clinton stared openly, searching the Indian's face for some family resemblance.

With a disdainful smile, the man turned his gaze to Clinton's. "Why do you stare, white boy?" he asked, his tone softly mocking. "Have you never seen an Indian before?"

"Of course I have," Clinton replied. "Lots of them. I'm not some Eastern city boy. I'm from Chicago!"

Snorting, the Indian looked him up and down. "Then, I think you have not seen many Indians. Your white fathers drove them out of Illinois long before you were ever born."

Conscious of the jab at his youth, Clinton drew himself up more erectly. "Not all of them," he insisted. "Some stayed. And others came back. My brother—half brother—Benjamin is Potawatomi, and he's lived with us fifteen years."

At the name Benjamin, the man quickly looked away. Noting the reaction, Clinton pressed, "Did you know him perhaps? Benjamin McKinnon?"

"McKinnon is not an Indian name!" the man said shortly.

"No, of course not. It's his father's—my father's—name. I'm Clinton McKinnon."

Keeping his eyes averted, the Indian did not reply.

Uncomfortable in the silence, Clinton went on quickly. "I've been hoping that while I'm in Kansas I might meet my other brother, Swift Elk. He lived in the Potawatomi settlement north of Lawrence, but Benjamin thought he may have joined the Free Staters by now. Do you know him, perhaps?"

The silence hung between them as the Indian kept his eyes averted, and suddenly Clinton felt afraid. Why couldn't the Indian give him a simple yes or no? Could it be because he did know Swift Elk, and Swift Elk had already perished in Bleeding Kansas?

"You do know him, don't you?" Clinton pressed in a quavering voice. "Can't you please answer me! Is it because—did something happen—"

Slowly, the Indian turned his gaze to meet Clinton's frightened, blue-gray eyes. "*I* am Swift Elk," he said quietly.

Stunned, Clinton stared for a moment before his face split in a grin and he extended his hand to the older man. "Then we're brothers!"

"No!" Swift Elk shook his head sharply.

"Of course we are! We share the same father."

"I have no father!"

Clinton faltered. "I don't understand. Aren't you and Benjamin—Isn't Brett McKinnon—"

"In my eyes," Swift Elk said coldly, "my father died when I was eleven years old—when he sent us away from Chicago without him, when he never even contacted us again."

Now it was Clinton's turn to avert his gaze, as his stomach contracted with uncertainty. He had never heard anyone criticize his father. Benjamin had been a part of the family for so long that he had naively supposed there were no problems between Brett and his first family. But, of course, that could not be true.

Why had Brett never openly acknowledged Benjamin as his son? Why had it taken a slip on Benjamin's part for Clinton to learn they were half brothers? Why had Brett never sent for Swift Elk?

"You could have come back to Chicago," Clinton said lamely. "I'm sure Papa would have welcomed you, as he did Benjamin."

"Why should I have gone to a man who would never come to me?" Swift Elk demanded. "I did not want Chicago. I wanted a father, a father who would live with my mother when I was a child. By the time Benjamin went to Chicago, I did not need a father. I was a man then. Still, there were times—" He broke off abruptly. "I have only one brother, Little Deer—the one you call Benjamin. He, at least, gladdens my mother's heart with a visit from time to time."

Turning his gaze forward again, Swift Elk said evenly, "I prefer to ride alone. Leave me."

Hurt and confused by Swift Elk's rejection, Clinton did not approach him again. For four days, they rode in the same party, camped in the same camps, often no more than a few paces from one another, but they never spoke.

Clinton consoled himself that Swift Elk seldom spoke to anyone. The conversation they had had on the day they left Nebraska was the longest he had seen the Indian engage in. Still, they were brothers. They ought to be closer than the other men of the party.

On the evening of the fourth day, as Clinton spread his bedroll, Swift Elk approached and beckoned to him.

When they were several paces from the campsite, the Indian turned to his half brother with sorrowful eyes. Sighing, he said, "I have not been fair to you, and I am sorry. You are innocent of whatever passed between your father and my mother, and it is unjust to blame you."

Clinton, nodded, reading in Swift Elk's eyes the difficulty of the apology. "I've been trying to understand," he said slowly. "But I can't because I know so little. Benjamin has told me about your mother—about her beauty, her gentleness, her sweetness. But no one has ever told me what happened between my father and Morning Star. Do you know?"

For a long moment, Swift Elk was silent. "I know what my mother has told me," he replied quietly. "But I am not sure that is the complete truth. She told me it was her decision to come west with the other Potawatomis instead of remaining with your father. She told me it was not possible to reconcile an Indian life with the white ways. Little Deer—Benjamin— was there when she told your father. He says your father begged her to stay—"

"Then it wasn't Papa's fault!" Clinton exclaimed in relief.

"Perhaps not. But there is more to the story than what she said, or what Little Deer, who was only a boy of nine, can recall. My mother is a sweet, devoted woman. She would not leave her husband unless he had hurt her—unless she felt in her heart he did not want her."

"But surely my father never—"

Swift Elk shrugged. "He was away a great deal. And even when he was home, he did not show her much affection. But she loved him. Even after we settled in Kansas, she still pined for him. She thought I did not know. But, sometimes, late at night, I heard her weeping."

"She never married again?"

"No. There were men in the settlement who would have been proud to take her as their wife. But she rejected so many that in time they ceased to ask. Now, if anyting should happen to me, she will be alone."

Clinton stared at him in alarm. "What do you mean? What is likely to happen to you?"

Swift Elk smiled ruefully. "You are young, but can you really be so naive? Tomorrow we will reach Franklin, Kansas, a stronghold of the proslavers. Blood will be shed, on both sides. Our band is called 'General Lane's Army.' Is it not usual for an army to wage war?"

Nodding, Clinton looked away. He had always known, in the back of his mind, that they would eventually engage in battle. Benjamin had taken pains to impress upon him that if he went to Kansas he might be killed, and he had accepted that fact without fear.

Still, he had not joined the Free Staters for the raw excitement of warfare. He had fooled himself into believing their major purpose was simply to build up a Free-State majority in Kansas.

Swift Elk's pensive voice broke the silence. "I haven't the charity of Benjamin. I do not think I can ever forgive your father. But, I will not be unjust enough to carry the blame to you. If we go into battle tomorrow, let us do so as brothers. Let us declare our kinship now, before it is too late."

He grasped Clinton's wrist, then drew him into a brief, hard embrace.

There were tears in Swift Elk's eyes as he stepped back. "And, if I should perish tomorrow, or in some future battle, I will charge you to comfort my mother. And, if anything should happen to you, I will swallow my pride at least enough to send word to your family."

On August 12, as Swift Elk had predicted, General Lane and his army of thirty rode into the southern Kansas town of Franklin. The settlers were ready for them, barricaded in their log blockhouse, and the moment the army was sighted, they opened fire.

Seeking refuge behind the scattered houses outside the blockhouse, the Free Staters returned the fire. For over an hour, proslavers and Free Staters traded shots. A few men were injured on each side, but neither side appeared to be weakening. The fight could well go on indefinitely with no victor.

Looking around, Clinton saw John Brown staring at a wagon sitting empty outside an open barn. Suddenly, Old Brown's eyes lit with a savage intent, and he hurried to confer with General Lane.

A moment later, Brown scurried to the shed that sheltered Clinton and Swift Elk. "You two," he barked, "pull that wagon into that barn and load it up with straw."

Clinton stared at him in perplexity. "But why?"

"Don't ask questions! Just do as you're told." Brown waved his pistol in a menacing way that left no doubt of what would happen if they hesitated too long.

As he and Swift Elk followed the order, Clinton whispered to his half brother, "Do you know why he told us to do this?"

Swift Elk nodded grimly. "I have an idea. And if I'm right, I don't approve. I suspect there are women and children in that blockhouse."

As Brown stalked in to check their progress, Swift Elk looked at him defiantly. "If you intend what I think, Brown, you're more of a barbarian than I already thought. It's a vicious plan, not worthy of the Free-State movement."

Brown snorted derisively. "This is war, boy! War ain't sweet-tempered and kind! Even the Good Book says 'without the shedding of blood there is no remission of sins'! So, don't preach to me, boy. I know what I'm about, and it's God's work!"

A few minutes later, Brown was ordering some other members of the army to pull the straw-filled wagon out of the barn. Then, using the wagon as a shield between themselves and the blockhouse, the men backed the wagon up to the palisade and set it afire.

Within minutes, the entire load of straw was ablaze and the flames were leaping to the dry timbers of the blockhouse. Clinton watched in horror as the blaze spread, and he heard the high-pitched screams of women and the terrified cries of small children.

Suddenly, men began streaming from the fort and shots exploded from all directions.

Clinton raised his shotgun, but found he could not fire. It had been different before, firing at faceless enemies within the blockhouse. But, how could he know that the men rushing at him now were really enemies?

Was every man in this town a proslaver? What about those who, in the fury of the fire, had lost their weapons? Surely he couldn't shoot them in cold blood.

The noise of battle was so deafening he did not hear Swift Elk fall beside him. Turning toward his half brother, he recoiled in horror as he saw him lying motionless, a dark red stain spreading across his chest.

Crying out with his own inner pain, Clinton dropped to his knees and cradled Swift Elk's head in his lap. With an effort, the Indian opened his eyes.

Wincing in agony, Swift Elk whispered, "Tell Mother I am sorry to leave her alone."

Blinking back tears, Clinton murmured, "She won't be alone, Swift Elk. I promise you that."

Swift Elk forced a slight smile as his heavy lids shaded his eyes again. "Thank you, brother. Thank—you—"

While Clinton knelt beside Swift Elk, vainly willing him to continue breathing, the battle around him came to a swift end. The Free Staters captured fourteen prisoners.

Above him, John Brown was exulting that the Free-State toll was only six wounded and only one dead. Clinton alone seemed to understand the painful fact that "only" could never apply to any death.

At that moment, Clinton wondered if he even wanted to continue as a member of General Lane's Army.

19
September 1856–October 1857

Riding east, toward Chicago, Clinton slid a sidelong glance at the Indian woman riding beside him. At fifty-two, Morning Star was still an uncommonly attractive woman.

Her hair was beginning to whiten, and her face was creased from years of worries and squinting into the sun. But she was still slender, she still carried herself with an erect grace, and her dark eyes still held a quiet, unpretentious beauty.

She had not wanted to come with him. Clinton had had to talk her into making the trip. He hoped that he had been right.

Clinton had remained with General Lane's Army only long enough to see Swift Elk buried. Then, he had ridden north, knowing he must keep his promise to his brother to seek out and console Morning Star.

During the two-day ride, Clinton had decided he would not rejoin Lane's forces. He had come to Kansas to defend a principle. But it seemed the other Free Staters had no more principles than the proslavers they fought against.

As long as Clinton lived, he would never forget the smell of burning flesh, or the terrified shrieks of the women and children trapped in the Franklin blockhouse.

He had also decided during the ride that he would take

Morning Star away from Kansas, back to Chicago with him. It was the least he could do for Swift Elk, and for Benjamin.

However, arriving at the Potawatomi reservation, he had found Morning Star less eager to leave than he had expected. When he introduced himself, her eyes had flickered slightly at the name McKinnon, and then they had widened in fear.

"Have you come because of Benjamin?" she asked urgently. "Has something happened to him?"

Clinton shook his head. "Benjamin is well—or at least he was when I left Chicago two weeks ago." Seeing Morning Star relax, he felt a stab of pain as he continued, "I've just come from the south of Kansas Territory, where I rode with General Lane's Army and had the honor of meeting your son, my brother, Swift Elk."

Morning Star's chin lifted a bit, and her eyes shone with pride at the mention of her older son. "Did he send a message?"

"Yes—no—he—" Clinton hesitated, miserable with the message he carried.

He saw the brief flash of pain in her eyes before she looked away. She said softly, "He will not be coming back, will he?"

"No," Clinton whispered. "He told me to—to tell you he is sorry to leave you alone."

There was a pause, and then Morning Star turned her gaze back to Clinton's. Though glassy with unshed tears, her eyes held a quiet inner strength. "But I am not alone," she said clearly. "I have still brothers and sisters, nieces and nephews living on this reservation. And, always, I will have memories."

"You have more than that," Clinton replied. "You have a son in Chicago. I will take you to him."

"No!" Morning Star shook her head adamantly and lowered her eyes.

"Because of my father?"

"Because of your father—and because of your mother."

Clinton flushed. "I'm sorry. You must think me very insensitive. Of course it would be hard for you to meet my mother after you and Papa were once—"

"No. It would not be so difficult for me. I chose to come here—to leave your father. But for her, perhaps. For Eden, it might be difficult. And I have no wish to cause her pain. She suffered enough as a small child."

"Did you—did you once know my mother?"

Morning Star nodded. "I knew her. I knew her well. She

was part of my family long before your father ever met her. And, without knowing it, as a small child, she was the person that brought your father and me together."

As Clinton listened in spellbound silence, Morning Star told the whole story of Eden's early life in Black Eagle's encampment, her own marriage to Brett McKinnon, and their subsequent parting.

Although Eden had told Clinton she had survived the Fort Dearborn massacre and had lived several years among the Indians, she had always been rather vague about the details.

Assuming it hurt her to recall that part of her life, Clinton, though curious, had never pressed her. Now he began to understand why his mother had never talked more openly, especially after Benjamin had joined the family.

When Morning Star finished her story, Clinton said quickly, "Surely Mama would be glad to see you again! I'm certain she would open her home to you in your time of need, just as you cared for her when she was small."

"But I am not in need," Morning Star said firmly.

"I think you are. Kansas is not a safe place to live. There are some high-principled men in the fight—men like Swift Elk. But for every man like him, there are ten others who won't be satisfied until every square mile of the territory bleeds."

"Surely you exaggerate. Here, I am safe."

"I would like to think so, but I can't be certain. Even two months ago, Benjamin, who knows Kansas far better than I, was worried about you. He would have come for you then, except that Papa was away in Texas and had left him in charge of the business. Besides, he trusted Swift Elk to look after you. Now, if I left you behind, I think he would never forgive me."

In the end, Morning Star had agreed to accompany Clinton to Chicago, but only for Benjamin's sake.

Eden toyed with her coffee cup as she gazed at Brett across the breakfast table. "The news from Kansas frightens me," she whispered. "Every day I hear of more killings, massacres worse than the one my mother and I survived at Fort Dearborn. When I think of Clinton there—"

Brett sighed heavily. He had returned from Texas only last night, puffed with pride over his new ranch, but Eden had hardly seemed to hear his glowing descriptions. All she spoke of was Clinton, and her worries about him.

"Maybe you shouldn't think about Clinton!" Brett said gruffly. "Thinking and worrying won't do anyone a mite of good. What you should have done was kept him from going there in the first place!"

"Like you kept Burton from running off to California?" she retorted angrily.

Stung, Brett reached across the table, taking her hand in a conciliatory gesture. "All right, I shouldn't have said that. It seems both our boys are too headstrong for anyone to stop them doing something they really believe in. But it *is* pointless to worry. Anyway, Burton came through his adventures in one piece. In all likelihood Clinton will do the same."

"Burton didn't go riding into a small-scale war. Anyway, I'm not the only one worried. Benjamin's been in agony over his mother and brother. I think he would have gone to them long ago if you had been home." She paused, searching Brett's eyes, "Aren't you concerned about them?"

Biting his lower lip, Brett averted his gaze. "I—I try not to think about them," he whispered.

Of course he was worried. Riding north through Missouri, he had been shaken more than he would have expected by the reports of increased hostilities in Kansas.

In all the years Benjamin had lived with them, Brett had never so much as sent a message to Morning Star and Swift Elk. It had always seemed too awkward. Still, he had never really stopped caring about them. It pained him to think he could have prevented them ever being in Kansas. If only he had not let them go on that day more than twenty years ago. But then, of course, he would not have Eden.

Watching the worries ride across Brett's face, Eden suddenly felt sorry for him. "You've hardly told me anything about the ranch!" she exclaimed with forced brightness. "Or about Burton! How is he?"

"Burton? Oh, he's fine, fine."

He couldn't tell her how painfully obvious it had been that his son knew very little about ranching. Garrett, of course, had seen Burton's lack of expertise. But Garrett had been kind enough to say nothing. Brett depended on him to teach Burton, to make the Double M a success.

Another thing Brett could not tell Eden was about the change he had sensed in their elder son. He had expected Burton to have matured and put aside his childhood naiveté. But he had never expected the hardness he saw in Burton's eyes, or the wall of coldness the young man had built around himself.

"How does Burton look?" Eden asked eagerly. "Is he healthy enough? Is he as tall as you yet?"

"Maybe an inch or two shorter. About Clint's size, I guess."

"Oh, I wish I could see him! Do you realize it's been almost six years?"

"I know. As soon as everything's running smoothly, I'll take you down there. I would have taken you this time if I thought—"

Brett stopped abruptly at a flurry of activity in the hallway. They both looked up to see Clinton framed in the dining room doorway.

"Clinton!" Eden shrieked, rushing from the table to fling herself into his arms.

Brett rose stiffly and extended his hand. "It's mighty good to have you home, son. You've had your mama in quite a state."

"Yes, sir," Clinton nodded, still hugging his mother. "I'm sorry about the worry. It's good to see you safely home, too."

"Now, come and sit down and tell us everything. Are you all right? Have you had breakfast yet?" Eden tugged him toward the table.

Laughing, Clinton said, "I'll answer all your questions in a moment. But first, is Benjamin home?"

"No. He left early for the plant."

"In that case, I guess you'll have to welcome our guest for him." Clinton stepped back to pull someone in from the hall.

For a moment, Eden stared. Thirty-six years had passed, and she had only been a child of seven when last she saw her, but with one glance at Brett, she knew.

Stepping to the Indian woman, Eden lightly kissed her cheek. "Welcome to our home, Morning Star," she said.

Neither Brett nor Eden begrudged Morning Star their hospitality, especially when they learned of Swift Elk's death. When Benjamin, sensitive as always, suggested it might be best if he and his mother sought different living quarters, both Brett and Eden flatly vetoed the idea. Still, though they would not admit it, even between themselves, the situation was awkward.

Eden soon found that she loved Morning Star as much as she had long ago in Black Eagle's encampment. Indeed, it would be difficult not to love her.

Often, the two women passed entire afternoons in shared

remembrance of the idyllic days with Black Eagle. For Eden, the time had special sweetness, since Morning Star was the only person she knew who had also known her mother. And, though Leanna Halsey had replaced her own mother in Black Eagle's affections, Morning Star confirmed Eden's memories of her as a good and beautiful woman.

Yet, despite their kinship, a wall remained between Eden and Morning Star—a wall caused by their shared love for Brett. From the first, Eden saw in Morning Star's eyes that years had not dulled her deep love for Brett. Eden's heart ached with Morning Star's pain.

Try as she might, Eden could never quite convince herself that she was not responsible for Morning Star's unhappiness. She hadn't taken Brett away from Morning Star. He had turned to her only after Morning Star had left Chicago with his sons. And yet, wasn't it possible that if Brett had not already known her, he would have prevailed upon Morning Star to stay with him? If she had not agreed so readily to marry him, wasn't it possible Brett would have followed Morning Star and reconciled their differences?

Eden felt no jealousy of Morning Star. She knew Brett did not love the Indian woman, though he cared about her more than she once might have imagined. But she wondered if Morning Star felt jealous of her, and Eden knew that if their situations were reversed, she could not help but feel both jealous and bitter.

The situation took its toll on Brett, too. Conscious of the hungry glances Morning Star tried so hard to hide, and wishing to spare her more pain, he became less and less demonstrative with Eden.

The casual kisses and passing caresses they used to share many times each day, regardless of the presence of children or servants, were quickly curtailed. Now, Brett rarely even touched his wife, except in the privacy of their own bedroom. Even there, he found his passions greatly lessened by the knowledge that Morning Star, the mother of his first two sons, now shared his house.

Any number of times, Brett considered talking with Eden. Knowing he could never be at peace while Morning Star lived with them, he thought it might be best to accept Benjamin's suggestion that he and his mother move into another house. But, afraid Eden would accuse him of being cold and uncaring, afraid she might turn away from him again, as she had when Benjamin first came to them, Brett said nothing.

That silence soon spread through their relationship. Brett found it harder and harder to talk to Eden about anything.

For the first few months, Morning Star's grief over Swift Elk dulled her awareness of the tension surrounding her. But, she gradually realized her presence was causing a strain in the McKinnon household. Several times, she spoke of returning to Kansas. But Eden always insisted her return was out of the question while hostilities still raged.

Finally, in October of 1857, Morning Star made up her mind. "I'm going home to Kansas. I've spoken to Benjamin, and he will take me. We leave tomorrow."

Eden stared down at her teacup, guilty over the relief she felt at the announcement. "You don't have to go anywhere, Morning Star," she said quietly. "This is your home."

"No." The Indian woman shook her head. "My home is with my own people. Now things are quieter in Kansas, so there is no reason why I should not go. You have been good to me here. You will always have my gratitude. More than that, I am grateful for the good and loving home you have given my son. He, it seems, belongs here. I do not."

"Morning Star—"

"Please, say no more. It is not your fault. It is no one's fault. It is simply the way things are. When Brett comes home, we will tell him."

In his office at McKinnon Meats, Brett tried to vain to concentrate on the papers spread before him. This year would be the most successful yet for the firm. For the first time, it had been able to engage in summer slaughtering, almost doubling the output over previous years.

In the past, responsible meat-packers had not dared to slaughter cattle and hogs anytime except in winter. But, last winter, Brett and Benjamin had conceived the idea of cutting ice from frozen lakes and streams and storing it in icehouses for year-round cooling. Their scheme had revolutionized the industry.

With the results of his first summer's slaughtering, plus encouraging reports from the Double M ranch, Brett should have felt exhilarated. Instead, he felt depressed and listless.

If only he could resolve the problems at home!

If he could at least find some physical relief, perhaps some other solutions would present themselves. Abruptly, Brett got up from his desk and went to find Benjamin, who was drawing up plans for another icehouse.

"I'm going out for the rest of the afternoon," Brett said sharply.

Frowning, slightly, Benjamin nodded. He had been intending all day to tell Brett that he was leaving tomorrow with his mother. Now, he supposed the news could wait until evening. "All right," he replied. "I'll see you at dinner."

Brett hesitated, then nodded. "Yes, at dinner."

Alone at his desk once again, Benjamin frowned to himself. With all the work the firm had, his father rarely left his desk before five o'clock, and often worked even later. When he did go out, it was always on business, and he always told Benjamin where he was going.

Of course, Benjamin did not begrudge his father some time away from the plant. He knew the last year, since Clinton had brought Morning Star home, had been especially difficult for Brett. If his father wanted some time to himself, he certainly deserved it.

Still, Benjamin could not shake the vague sense of foreboding that tinged his curiosity. Without quite understanding why, he shoved the icehouse plans into a drawer of his desk and hurried outside.

On State Street, about two blocks away, Benjamin could see Brett walking north. Maybe he had simply decided to go home early. That, however, seemed unlikely, since Brett had been avoiding home as much as possible.

Keeping his eye on the tall figure just crossing Ninth Street, Benjamin began strolling north.

At Eighth Street, Brett hailed a hansom cab, climbed in, and continued north. Now thoroughly baffled, Benjamin hailed another cab and directed the driver to follow his father. Finally, at Randolph Street, Brett's cab turned right.

Ah, Benjamin thought, I should have guessed, the wholesale dry goods district! He's probably just going to order some cheesecloth for the plant. The cabs continued east on Randolph Street. Ben's cab reached the corner of Michigan and Randolph just in time for Ben to see his father get out and disappear into a building.

To Benjamin's shock, the building was not Potter Palmer's wholesale firm. It was a neat, unmarked frame structure that Benjamin recognized as Annie Malone's sporting house.

For a moment, Benjamin sat frozen, sick to his stomach. How could his father come to a place like this when he had a beautiful woman like Eden at home?

Of course, Ben knew the home situation was complicated by his own mother's presence, and that Brett had not really been himself since Morning Star joined the household. Still, how could his father demean the McKinnon name by frequenting a place like Annie Malone's?

Seized by righteous indignation, Benjamin started to climb out of his cab and pursue his father. Abruptly, he stopped. It was, after all, none of his business. If an afternoon with one of Annie Malone's girls could help his father face his problems, who was he to question it?

Dismissing the cab, Benjamin began the long walk back to the plant. His stomach churned, and he did not unclench his fists until he was sitting behind his desk again.

On the third floor of Annie Malone's, Brett lay watching a golden-haired girl. In the parlor below, she had seemed the most attractive of the girls—young and fresh enough to be unhardened to life in a brothel, the kind of girl who could make a man forget anything.

Now, watching her undress, he regretted his choice. She was so young, just a few years older than his own daughter, younger than Morning Star when Black Eagle had given her to him.

Smiling nervously, the girl sat on the edge of the bed and began to unbutton his shirt. "What's the matter?" she asked in a pouting tone. "Don't you like me? You picked me."

Turning away from her, Brett said thickly, "You're very lovely. Too lovely for this sort of place. How old are you?"

"I'm fourteen."

Oh, God! Fourteen! If he'd married earlier, he could easily have a granddaughter her age! His lunch suddenly soured in his stomach, and he pushed the girl's hands away as she tried to continue undressing him.

"Don't you want me anymore, Mr. McKinnon?"

Brett looked at her sharply, and she laughed. "Are you surprised I know your name? Madam Annie whispered it to me before we came upstairs. She said you're one of the most important men in Chicago. I suppose she'll be pretty put out if she figures I didn't please you."

"It's not your fault," Brett sighed. "I've just—I've kind of changed my mind." Touched by her sad blue eyes, he added quickly, without thinking, "Look, it must be hard on you, worrying all the time about pleasing Annie. How would you like to come home with me?"

The girl's eyes widened. "You mean, be your mistress? You'd take me just like that? Without even trying me out?"

Brett grimaced. "That wasn't exactly what I meant. You'd be more like my daughter."

Frowning, the girl asked, "What would your wife think of that?"

Indeed, what would Eden think? Brett wondered with a wry smile. She'd already taken in his half-breed son and his Indian wife—Indian mistress, most people would probably say. How would she react to his bringing home a girl from a whorehouse?

He'd come here seeking relief, and instead he was letting himself in for more problems. How could he even explain meeting the girl? Well, at least Eden couldn't accuse him of being insensitive!

"She wouldn't like it, would she?" the girl pressed.

"Well, let's just say she'd be—surprised. Do you want to come with me?"

"I—I guess so."

"Then go and get your things together. I'll wait here, and then we'll go down together and tell Annie."

Lying on the bed, waiting for the girl, Brett shook his head in disbelief. What in God's name was he doing? How much more could he expect Eden to endure? The girl—he didn't even know her name—certainly wouldn't solve the problems at home. The most she would do is divert the family's attention to the new problem—her.

Why didn't he just tell the girl he'd changed his mind, give her a few dollars, and leave? He'd never been a do-gooder reformer, and, at fifty-six, it was too late to start.

Buttoning his shirt, he got up from the bed and began to pace. Where the hell was the girl, anyway? What was taking her so long?

Brett paused in his pacing, wrinkling his nose at a strong smell of smoke. Did Annie's patrons have to smoke such ghastly cheap cigars? He paced some more, then stopped again. Were those screams coming from below? Maybe it wasn't cigar smoke he smelled!

Opening the door, Brett went to the landing. The smoke was thicker in the hall, and it definitely was not from cigars.

He ran down to the second floor, and saw that the entire first floor was ablaze. Already, the flames were beginning to lick up the rickety staircase. The bannister was hot under his hand.

Brett stared at the flames, weighing his chances of plunging down the stairs and out the front door.

He'd be badly burned, but he could make it. But, he'd have to do it now, before the entire staircase collapsed.

"Mr. McKinnon!" Brett heard a plaintive wail from the floor above. "Mr. McKinnon! Oh, I knew he wouldn't wait!"

His heart contracting at the sad cry, Brett turned and galloped back up the stairs. His lungs were burning from the smoke and heat. Grabbing the girl's hand, he rasped, "Come on!"

She stumbled after him, but froze at the second floor, paralyzed by fear.

"Oh, no!" the girl shrieked.

The flames were almost to the landing, and the smoke was getting thicker by the moment.

"Come on!" Brett pulled her forward.

"I can't!"

Muttering an oath, he swung her into his arms and raced down the stairs.

He could feel the flames searing his back, could smell his own flesh burning.

Three steps from the bottom, the stair gave way with a deafening crack.

Brett's foot plunged through. Trying frantically to pull it out, he tripped.

Brett McKinnon fell, face forward, cracking his forehead on the tile entry hall, pinning the screaming girl beneath him.

20
October–December 1857

The clock struck half past nine as Eden stepped into the parlor after tucking Paige into bed. Benjamin and Clinton looked up from the chessboard. Neither had moved a piece in the last fifteen minutes. Morning Star stared silently into the fire.

"Ben, you're sure your father didn't say he was going anywhere this evening?" Eden asked anxiously.

"No. He was just working late. No doubt he got involved revising my plans for the new icehouse and completely lost track of time. You know how he is when he starts working on something."

"Yes. But, well, he's never been this late. I'm beginning to wonder if—"

"Look, Mama," Clinton said, getting up from the chessboard, "Why don't I just run down to the plant and bring him home?"

"No!" Benjamin blurted. "I'll go!"

Clinton shook his head. "You ought to be turning in soon if you're planning to start for Kansas tomorrow. I'll just tell Papa he should be getting home to get some rest, and that McKinnon Meats will still be there in the morning."

"All right, we'll both go," Benjamin insisted. "You know how stubborn he can be. Besides, I'll want to see him before leaving anyway."

On the way to the stable, Clinton eyed his half brother keenly. "Why did you really want to come?" he asked. "Isn't Papa at the plant?"

Benjamin hesitated. "I'm not sure. I hope he is." Refusing to say more, he saddled his horse, mounted, and rode toward State Street. Father has to be at the plant, he told himself. He couldn't have stayed at Annie Malone's this long.

McKinnon Meats was dark, with no sign that Brett had returned since his early departure that afternoon.

"Well?" Clinton stared at Benjamin.

Shrugging, Benjamin replied dully, "I might know where he is. Come on."

On Michigan Avenue, about a block from Randolph, they began to smell smoke and charred wood.

Sniffing the air, Clinton remarked, "Mama mentioned that she heard an awful lot of fire wagons this afternoon. I wonder what burned."

As they rounded the corner at Michigan and Randolph, they had their answer. The entire section of Randolph Street, from Michigan Avenue to the lake, lay in smoldering ruins.

Benjamin froze, his horrified eyes moving to the charred remnants of Annie Malone's sporting house.

"Papa was here?" Clinton whispered.

Benjamin nodded. "He was at one time today. I hope to God he got out before—" He stopped, unable to finish the thought, much less speak it.

As if in a trance, the brothers dismounted and stumbled down the fire-ravaged street. Firemen still roamed the block, putting out the last of the blaze. At least a score of bodies lay in the center of the street, guarded by a grim-faced policeman.

When Benjamin and Clinton approached, the policeman drew himself up sternly. "Here now," he said, "get away. We don't want no folks pawing over the bodies, desecrating the dead."

Benjamin stared at the officer distastefully. "Believe me, sir, we have no intention of doing anything of the sort. We'd simply like to assure ourselves our father is not among the victims." He was quivering inside, wondering how his voice could be so calm.

The policeman shrugged. "Well, I can't say whether you'll have much luck. Most of 'em are burned beyond recognition, poor souls, may they rest in peace."

Slowly, Benjamin and Clinton moved down the line of bodies. The policeman was right. It was impossible to identify any of them. One looked about the size of Brett McKinnon, but his clothing had been destroyed, and the flames had eaten away at his flesh, leaving only a charred, faceless form.

For a long time, both sons stared at the body, searching for some clue to convince them beyond a doubt it was not their father.

Finally, Benjamin turned back to the policeman. "What happened?" he whispered.

The officer shrugged. "Fire started about two o'clock. By the time the first wagon got here, it was spreading through the block."

Two o'clock, Benjamin thought. That was just about the time he had been returning to his desk at McKinnon Meats.

The officer peered at Benjamin and Clinton more closely. "Say, aren't you McKinnon's boys?"

They nodded.

Frowning, the policeman asked, "What kind of business would a meat-packer have had in this neighborhood?"

"He said something about coming up this afternoon to order some cheesecloth for the plant," Benjamin replied.

"Oh." The policeman nodded. "Then I suspect he would have gotten out safely. They say the blaze started at Annie Malone's. He probably would have had time to get out if he was at Palmer's or one of the other wholesalers."

"I see." Benjamin nodded quickly. "Thank you very much."

He started toward Michigan Avenue, with Clinton hurrying after him.

Benjamin's eyes flicked back toward the bodies.

"You don't think— You heard what the officer said— The fire started at Annie Malone's. And you said yourself he was—"

Turning to his brother, Benjamin nodded slowly, "That's right. And that's exactly what I'm going to tell Eden."

Comprehension slowly spread across Clinton's face. "He wasn't buying cheesecloth, was he?"

Sighing, Benjamin turned away. "What does it matter now? The important thing is to make your mother believe he was. There's no sense in letting her suffer more than necessary."

"Benjamin?"

"Hmm?"

"You're certain Papa was there?"

"Yes. I wish I weren't." Briefly, he told Clinton what had happened that afternoon.

At the end of the story, Clinton shook his head. "Why did he do it? How could he do such a thing to Mama?"

For a moment, Benjamin was silent, remembering that he had wondered the same thing earlier that day.

Finally, he said quietly, "I don't really think he was doing it *to* Eden. He loved your mother, even when things weren't quite right between them. But, you're old enough to know that sometimes a man has a need that can't be denied. I don't suppose he thought that your mother would ever know."

They were silent the rest of the way home, each battling with his own grief, each struggling to compose himself before facing Eden.

Seeing their grim, pale faces as they entered the house, Eden immediately knew something was wrong.

"What happened?" she whispered. Then, more urgently, as Ben and Clinton exchanged uneasy glances, she demanded, "Tell me!"

"We're not sure," Benjamin began, taking her elbow and leading her back to the settee in the parlor. "He wasn't at the plant but—there were some notes on his desk about—about needing cheesecloth—for handling and wrapping the meats."

Her brow furrowing, Eden stared at him wide-eyed. "Benjamin! Where *is* he?"

"He—he must have gone to the wholesale dry goods district to order the cheesecloth."

"But, that's only a few blocks away. He should have been home long ago."

"Eden—" He hesitated, taking her hand, wishing there were a better way to tell her. "Eden—there was a fire—the entire block was destroyed. We saw—we saw at least twenty bodies—"

Behind him, Benjamin heard a gasp, and realized his mother was still in the room. He felt torn, wondering whom he should be comforting. From the corner of his eye, he saw Clinton go to Morning Star, and he turned his own attention back to Eden.

She was staring at him in disbelief, her face pale, her hand trembling in his.

"Eden," he whispered, "it's possible he got out safely. We couldn't identify any of the bodies."

"No." She shook her head. "If he escaped, he'd be here."

"It's even possible he didn't go—"

Benjamin stopped, unable to look at her as tears coursed silently down her cheeks. "Oh, Eden," he murmured, pulling her into his arms.

For a moment, she clung to him, drawing strength from his body. Then, she stiffened and pulled away. "I'm going up to bed," she said quietly. "I'd like to be alone."

As Eden left the room, Morning Star, too, rose. She was not weeping, but her eyes glistened with unshed tears. Going to Benjamin, she murmured, "We will not leave tomorrow. I think perhaps Eden will need our presence. Besides," she added, "we've caused enough pain in this family. It is only right that we should stay to share this time of sorrow."

"Mother," Benjamin said quickly, "you had nothing to do with the tragedy. As I told Eden—"

"Yes, yes," Morning Star cut him off. "I heard it all. But, perhaps if I had not been here, Brett would never have gone there tonight. Perhaps he would have come home and left the errand for another day."

She shrugged, then stood on tiptoe to kiss her son's cheek. "Good night, my son. At least Eden and I have you here to lean on."

A moment later, Clinton excused himself, leaving Benjamin alone in the parlor. He banked the fire, then poured himself some brandy from the decanter on the central table.

Taking the glass of amber liquid, he went to the window and stared out at Wabash Avenue.

"Ben?"

Eden's voice startled him. He turned to see her standing in the doorway, looking very young and fragile in her blue flannel wrapper. Her eyes were dry now as she gazed at him questioningly.

"Suppose you tell me what really happened to Brett," she whispered.

Benjamin frowned. "I have told you, Eden. God knows, I wish I could have told you something different."

She shook her head as she went to pour some brandy for herself. "Didn't you say at dinner that he was working late at the plant?"

"I—well, yes," Benjamin admitted, cursing himself for his own shortsightedness. If he hadn't tried to cover for Brett earlier, Eden wouldn't be questioning him now.

"And he never said anything then about needing cheesecloth?"

"Well, the fact is, I think he did mention something. But I was so wound up in my icehouse plans I didn't pay much attention."

Eden stared at him disbelievingly. "But why would he have gone tonight? Wouldn't all the dry goods establishments have been closed?"

Benjamin shrugged. "I don't know. I've heard Potter Palmer puts in almost as many hours as Father. I suppose Father knew he could find him in."

"I don't think so, Ben. I saw Mr. Palmer over at his retail store this morning, and he told me he was having dinner at Mayor Wentworth's tonight."

Benjamin was silent, concentrating on his brandy.

"I thought of that," Eden went on, "and then I thought of how I hadn't heard any fire wagons all evening. But, I did hear them this afternoon, and I wondered—"

"Eden, what's the point of this?" Benjamin cut her off irritably. "I told you what I know—or the best I could surmise. I can't help it if it doesn't all make sense! From what I've observed, death seldom does."

"Benjamin," she pressed, "I'm sorry. I know you're upset, too. Brett was your father, after all, though, Lord knows, he wasn't always the best. But, I can't help feeling you're hiding something from me. If you're trying to protect me, please believe me, I don't want to be protected. He was my husband,

Benjamin. For twenty-two years, for better or for worse. I deserve to know the truth!"

"Eden, please!" Benjamin turned to her with beseeching eyes.

"If you won't tell me," she declared stubbornly, "I'll just assume the worst. I know there was a—a house of ill repute in that block—" She broke off abruptly, reading the truth in Benjamin's pained eyes.

There was a strained silence between them, and then she whispered, "Oh, my God, that's where he was, wasn't he?"

"Eden, I told you—"

Oblivious to her stepson, Eden sank down on the settee, dropping her brandy on the rich Oriental carpet. "I killed him," she murmured. "It's my fault. If I would have been a better wife, he never would have been there. Oh, God, to think he had to turn to a—a whore—and that doing so cost him his life!" She buried her face in her hands, sobbing and shaking.

"Eden, you mustn't do this to yourself! It's not your fault. Father wouldn't blame you. He loved you too much."

Eden snorted sardonically. "And, what did he get in return for his love? A self-righteous wife, and the memories of her reproachfulness!"

"You know that's not true!" Benjamin said sharply. "The trouble between the two of you ended long ago, before Paige was born. Each of you had wronged the other, but those wrongs were buried beneath all the good years you've shared since."

"Then, why did he go there, Benjamin? What made him seek solace in a place like that?"

"I—I don't know. How can I answer that? All I can say with certainty is, it wasn't your fault. Perhaps it wasn't really his fault, either."

Eden shook her head. "Of course it wasn't his fault. But you'll never convince me it wasn't mine. If I'd shown a bit more understanding years ago, when you first came here, perhaps he wouldn't have felt so tense about having your mother here now."

"And perhaps he would! I know my father made mistakes, Eden, but I also know he was more sensitive than a lot of people might have supposed. He was perfectly capable of feeling guilt where my mother was concerned, without you forcing him to feel it. And if you're going to start assigning

blame, maybe you ought to blame Mother for coming here,
or Clinton for bringing her, or me for disrupting your lives
sixteen years ago, or even my grandfather, Black Eagle, for
throwing Mother and Father together when they weren't in
love."

"Stop it!" Eden shrieked, clapping her hands over her ears.
"You're not making any sense!"

"Of course I'm not, but neither are you! There *is* no sense
in what happened, Eden. Father is dead, and we'll all miss
him and grieve for him, and remember him with love. But
it's not going to do anyone a damn bit of good for you to start
blaming yourself!"

"But it's so unfair!" Eden wailed. "Brett had his failings,
but he was a better man than most. If he hadn't had the
kindness and sensitivity to bring me to Chicago when I was a
child, Lord knows what might have happened to me. And
now, because of one ill-timed infidelity—"

She broke off abruptly, thinking of her own years of infidelity with Garrett. Why had she never been punished for that?
Or, was she being punished now?

"Eden," Benjamin said gently, "I don't think anyone needs
to know the circumstances of Father's death—for your sake,
for Paige's, for the sake of his memory. If we say he was there
ordering cheesecloth, I doubt that anyone will question us."

Eden nodded. "Of course. Whatever you think best." She
paused to swallow the lump in her throat. "Benjamin, I know
you planned to leave tomorrow, but would you mind staying
on for a bit? It's going to be difficult telling Paige, getting
through the next few days, and I'd very much appreciate your
support."

"Certainly, I'll stay. Mother and I have already discussed
that."

Gasping, Eden exclaimed, "Your mother! I've been so
involved in my own concerns, I haven't even thought of her!
Is she all right?"

"Yes."

Eden's blue-green eyes filled with tenderness as she gazed
at Benjamin. "Your mother loved Brett very much, you know."

Benjamin nodded. "We all did."

In all, twenty-one persons perished in the fire. Since it was
impossible to identify any of the bodies, a mass memorial
service was held in City Hall Square.

At Eden's urging, Benjamin also arranged for a private memorial service for Brett in the Second Presbyterian Church, at Wabash and Washington. All of Brett's friends and business associates came to pay their respects, and none questioned the explanation of his death.

A month later, the McKinnon family faced another funeral. During the night, Morning Star's soul slipped quietly from her body.

For twenty-two years, she had borne the pain of separation from her beloved. Finally, the tragic death of her older son, coupled with the death of the one man she had always loved, had proved too much.

At the age of fifty-three, Morning Star, daughter of Black Eagle, went to join Swift Elk and Brett, Black Eagle and Leanna Halsey, leaving behind her younger son and a grieving family that would always remember her as one of them.

IV

THE FRUITS

1861–1872

21
January–July 1861

Eden hummed softly to herself as she bent over her desk at McKinnon Meats. It was hard sometimes to realize the firm was more than a quarter of a century old. Since the day in 1835 when Brett had founded it, McKinnon Meats had never stopped growing.

In fact, Chicago meat-packers were fast claiming a place at the head of the United States meat industry. At the current rate of growth, Chicago would soon outstrip Cincinnati, which had long been known as "Porkopolis," the meat-packing queen of the nation.

Through the open door, Eden could see Benjamin, hard at work at his own desk in the adjoining office. How much she owed to him! If it weren't for him, she would not be sitting at this desk right now.

Smiling slightly, Eden recalled the day, more than three years ago, when she had asked Benjamin to stay on as head of McKinnon Meats. They had only begun to recover from Brett's death when Morning Star had passed away. Confident that hard work could help him overcome the loss of both parents, Eden had urged Benjamin to take over the reins of the firm.

"I'm certain it's what Brett would have intended," Eden had said. "He often said how well you managed things while he was in Texas, establishing the ranch."

"Perhaps," Benjamin agreed, "but I don't want to take anything away from Burton or Clinton."

"You wouldn't be. Burton is quite content running the ranch, and you know as well as I, Clinton has never had much interest in meat packing. Besides, they're both still so young and inexperienced. In the future, you may want to consider establishing a partnership. But, at the moment, you are the logical choice to head the firm. After all, you've worked there sixteen years. No one has more experience."

Benjamin smiled. "I can think of one person who's given more years to McKinnon Meats."

Frowning, Eden said, "If you're thinking of one of the workers, I'm sure you'll agree it would hardly be appropriate for one of them to preside over the firm. While I, of course, wish to see every man justly rewarded for his work, I do think Brett intended both the ownership and management of McKinnon Meats to remain—"

"I wasn't thinking of one of the workers," Benjamin cut her off gently.

Her frown deepening, Eden asked, "Then who?"

"You, of course."

"Me? Benjamin don't be ridiculous! I don't know the first thing about meat packing!"

"That's not quite true, you know. I seem to recall that you had quite a lot to do with the birth and early growth of McKinnon Meats. Every packer in Chicago respects you for your foresight in establishing the Bull and Boar Inn."

"But, that was years and years ago! McKinnon Meats was just a tiny business compared to what it is today. I haven't kept up. I don't know anything about icehouses and modern packing methods."

"Of course you do! You discussed the business with Father and me every day."

"That wasn't the same as being there, taking part, making decisions."

"What you don't know, I can teach you," Benjamin said firmly. "Within a few months, you'll be running McKinnon Meats as if you've done it all your life."

Eden stared at him speculatively. "Benjamin, why are you so anxious for me to do this?"

"Because I'm convinced it's right for you! I know why you want me to take over the firm. Besides the fact that you know I'd do a good job, you figure that hard work is a darn good way to bury my grief. Well, I challenge you to convince me the same medicine wouldn't work for you!"

"I suppose it would, but—"

"There's another reason," Benjamin went on, ignoring her reticence. "I'm convinced that Father would have wanted you at the head of the firm. You say he talked to you about *my* capabilities. Well, he also told me plenty about yours. He said you helped build McKinnon Meats, that without you, there wouldn't have been a McKinnon Meats."

Eden flushed, pleased despite herself. "Well, I'm sure that was a slight exaggeration! After all—"

"McKinnon Meats is my father's legacy to you, Eden. You owe it to him to preserve and expand the firm he gave so much of his life to building. You owe it to your sons too, to preserve the firm for them."

"Ben, I have every intention of preserving McKinnon Meats for Burton and Clinton. With you at its head—"

"But I won't be at its head," Benjamin insisted. "And, if you try to force me, I'll simply pack up and go back to my uncles and aunts in Kansas. I don't belong at the head of McKinnon Meats, Eden. You do."

Seeing that her stepson could not be moved, Eden had reluctantly agreed.

Now, from the vantage point of more than three years, she could admit that Benjamin had been right. Standing at the helm of a thriving, growing business had saved her from years of brooding and grieving.

There were still aspects of the business she avoided. After one session, she had quickly decided she could not stomach being present at slaughterings. She let Benjamin, or Clinton, who now worked full time for the firm, handle any problems or innovations in the slaughterhouses, while she sat at her desk and concentrated on clean, fresh figures.

Eden enjoyed the daily pattern of hard work. She found that she thrived on making decisions and directing workers. Her blood raced with the excitement of competition with other meat-packers. Her brain whirled with ideas for using the packing wastes. At her urging, the plant had installed its own tanks and boilers for converting fat and tallow into soap, lard, and candles. They sold the bones to button makers, the hides to leather merchants, the pig bristles to brush manufacturers.

In many ways, Eden supposed that her work at McKinnon Meats had saved her life. It filled her days while Paige, now a winsome girl of fourteen, was away at school. It left her neither time nor energy to brood over the unfortunate circumstances of Brett's death.

In short, McKinnon Meats had saved Eden from becoming a bored, self-pitying widow at forty-nine.

Still, there were times when she felt less than contented. At night, after Paige and Benjamin had retired, while Clinton was out working for the Underground Railroad, helping fugi-

tive slaves escape to Canada, Eden often sat alone, pondering
her future. What could she expect of the next twenty or
thirty years—the rest of her life?

Certainly, there was a kind of fulfillment in running a
prosperous, powerful business. And she could not deny a
certain pleasure in reaping the admiration and even awe of
other packers, who admitted she ran McKinnon Meats as
well as any man could, and better than some.

Yet, there remained, at the very core of her existence, an
emptiness. Eden wanted something more, though, even in
her most private moments, she tried to deny it.

After the first shocked weeks, she had reconciled herself to
Brett's death. Even in the strain of their last months together,
she had never stopped loving him, and she supposed a part of
her would always miss him. But she was grateful for the
twenty-two years they had shared, for the three children they
had produced, and she was determined not to tarnish the
memories of their good times with senseless mourning.

But loving memories could not fill her need for a man. She
was still young enough to despair at the emptiness of the big
four-poster bed, still alive enough to ache at the memories of
shared passions. And, she was still human enough to think of
the one man, besides Brett, who had stirred her passions.

At first, Eden had tried to put Garrett Martin out of her
mind. While Brett lived, she had rarely thought of him. She
had convinced herself that their one stolen afternoon in 1855
had been as much for Brett and Burton and the Double M
ranch as for herself. But now she ached for Garrett, ached for
the solace only he could offer.

Over and over she told herself it was wrong even to think
of Garrett. Brett had died in a whorehouse fire, a fate from
which she might have saved him, had she been more
understanding. How could she now even think of turning to
the man with whom she had cuckolded Brett, however long
ago?

Still, Eden waited, wondering when Garrett would come
to her.

On learning of Brett's death, he sent a short, exceedingly
proper note of condolence. She told herself it was too soon to
expect more, that Garrett was too sensitive to fly to her
immediately, to risk harming her in the eyes of society.
Besides, he could not desert his responsibilities at the ranch.

Indeed, Burton himself had not deemed it possible to come north to console her.

And so, Eden continued to wait. Every time she received a report from the Double M ranch, she scanned it anxiously, searching for some hint that Garrett would soon be coming north. She was always disappointed.

She considered going to Texas herself, but worried that she might be making a fool of herself. What if she was wrong in feeling Garrett had joined the ranch out of love for her? Or, what if his feelings had changed since he went to Texas?

She had just convinced herself it would be perfectly reasonable for her to go to Texas to visit her oldest son and look over the ranch when South Carolina announced it was seceding from the Union.

Abraham Lincoln, the newly elected President, insisted that no state had the right to secede. As more Southern states prepared to follow South Carolina, war clearly loomed on the horizon. Eden knew, without even discussing the matter with Benjamin or Clinton, that it would be foolish to travel south.

For the moment, she would have to be content to remain in Chicago. Benjamin assured her that, even if war did break out, Burton should not face any immediate danger in Texas. In the meantime, Eden had Paige, Clinton, Benjamin, and McKinnon Meats to fill her life. When so many women had less, she could not ask for more.

Garrett Martin wiped the dust from his face as he walked from the stable to the ranch house of the Double M. It was February 1. He wondered how many inches of snow were covering the prairie west of Chicago now. He wished he had stayed in Illinois, or at least in Iowa, especially since he'd heard the news at Fort Belknap, Texas, that afternoon.

Stepping into the ranch house kitchen, Garrett frowned. Burton was standing by the stove, his arms around the slim Mexican cook, playfully cupping her breasts as she tried to stir the stew.

Garrett cleared his throat, and Burton looked up, smiling cockily.

"I thought you were going to ride out to the Brazos River to check on better watering areas," Garrett said curtly.

Burton shrugged. "I was. But I decided that could wait. We don't have any longhorns dying of thirst."

"Forget it, I'll go myself tomorrow." Garrett turned away.

"Well, you're certainly in a fine mood! What was the problem at Belknap?"

"No problem. Telegraph message came in while I was there, though. The Texas legislature's voted to secede from the Union."

Burton whistled. "You don't say! Of course, I guess we've been expecting that. Might not be too great for business though. If war breaks out, we'll have one hell of a time getting any cattle to the Mississippi and shipping them north."

Garrett shook his head irritably. "Can't you ever see beyond your own selfish interests? Forget about what war will do to the business! I'm sure McKinnon Meats has enough money right now to support you, your mother, your brothers, and any children you might have, for the rest of your lives. But think of what war will do to the country! Just think for a moment how many lives will be lost—and for what?"

"Not a very pleasant thought, is it?" Burton agreed idly. "But there's not a great deal we can do about it, so there's no point in brooding about it too much."

"You might at least think of your mother," Garrett said quietly.

"My mother?" Burton stared at him incredulously.

"In case you haven't noticed, if there is a war, you and your family will be on opposing sides. Maybe you should think of going back to Chicago while you can still get there."

Burton snorted. "I doubt that my mother will waste much worry on me. She seems quite content with her beloved Benjamin and Clinton. After all, she hasn't exactly written to me, begging me to come home."

"Maybe that's because she knows her pleas would be wasted. From what I understand, you didn't give much consideration to how much she wanted you home when you ran off to California."

Scowling, Burton said, "Listen, Martin, I hope you're not going to start lecturing me on my responsibilities as a son. You and I are supposed to be partners on this ranch. You're not my boss, or my father."

Garrett's brows arched quizzically. "Partners, are we? Well, for a partner, it seems to me you do damn little work around here!"

"I don't have to work! That's what we hired the Mexican *vaqueros* for. If you get a thrill out of riding the range and playing at cowboy, that's your business. But don't tell me how to live!"

Garrett nodded, his face a stony mask. "All right. What you do is up to you. I'm staying on the ranch—not because I favor secession, but because I want to protect what belongs to me and your moth—uh, McKinnon Meats. I'm forty-one years old, so I don't stand much chance of being drafted into the army—at least at the beginning. But you're only twenty-three. What are you going to do when they try to press you into service?"

"I'll worry about that when the time comes. They say money can buy a man out of anything. Anyway, I stand a damn better chance of escaping a draft down here, than up North, under that war-hungry Lincoln. Besides," he turned to swat the trim rump of the cook, Conchita, "I can have more fun here than I'd ever have in Chicago, in my mother's house."

"And Eden ought to be glad to be rid of you," Garrett muttered under his breath as he turned away in disgust.

On April 12, all speculation about a coming war ceased. Confederate troops under General P. T. Beauregard fired on Union forces stationed at Fort Sumter in Charleston Harbor. Two days later, the fort surrendered.

The following day, President Lincoln called for seventy-five thousand volunteers to serve three months and put down the "insurrection."

While Burton played in Texas, Clinton agonized in Chicago. He did not want to go to war, not because he was afraid, but because he had seen enough killing during his brief stay in Kansas.

Chicago was quick to mobilize. There were meetings in Bryan Hall that overflowed into Courthouse Square. Men crowded Metropolitan Hall, churches, street corners. They jammed the Wigwam, the giant building erected at Lake and Market streets only a year earlier for the Republican Convention that had nominated Abraham Lincoln.

All over the city, men pledged their loyalty to the Union, their willingness to fight to defend it. Eden, like many other business leaders, agreed to continue paying any workers who enlisted in the army, so their families need not starve while they were away at war. The work force at McKinnon Meats quickly dwindled.

As men his own age, and thousands even younger, rushed to enlist, Clinton questioned his own reticence. But they were rushing to the glory and excitement of war. Clinton already knew war was not glorious.

It was killing other men. It was disillusionment. It was witnessing atrocities on both sides and wondering how either side could be considered noble.

Since returning from Kansas, Clinton had turned his energies to the Underground Railroad. Night after night, he had gathered with others at Allan Pinkerton's home on West Adams, planning ways to spirit fugitive slaves north to Canada, where they could be assured freedom.

The job had not been particularly difficult, since Chicago authorities, sympathetic to abolitionism, had been extremely lax in enforcing the Fugitive Slave Laws. Often, Clinton and Pinkerton had put as many as twenty or thirty slaves on one Canadian-bound lake steamer. Occasionally, they had to deal with irate slave owners, who had tracked their slaves to Chicago. But, for the most part, the Southerners were easy to avoid or overpower.

Now, as war began, Clinton could look back with pride on what he had accomplished. Together with others working at Underground Railroad stations throughout the North, he had guided more than seventy-five thousand fugitives to freedom. Surely he had already done his part.

Or had he?

The first call for volunteers was quickly filled. But in May the President asked for forty-two thousand more. Now Lincoln was no longer calling the conflict an "insurrection." It was war, and the men who volunteered were pledging three years, not three months, service.

Chicago newspapers joined with Chicago churches in proclaiming the righteousness of the Northern cause. Once again, Clinton began to question his reluctance to enlist.

The war, which had begun over the question of whether or not a state had the right to secede, was now turning into something much more complicated. Abolitionists saw it as a way to further their cause. Press and preachers insisted the Union had a moral duty to defeat the slave-holding states and abolish the sin of slavery.

Suddenly, Clinton found himself wondering if he had, indeed, done enough. What was the point of helping seventy-five thousand slaves to escape, if hundreds of thousands more continued to suffer the misery and indignity of slavery?

Benjamin, now thirty-five, had joined the Home Guard in Chicago, made up of men twenty-eight to forty-five. Too old to be among the early recruits, they were nevertheless training for the time they might be needed. Eden organized Chicago's business leaders to give vast sums to the Union cause. Even fourteen-year-old Paige diligently joined the ladies sewing circle at the Second Presbyterian Church, preparing bandages for the wounded.

Observing all of them, Clinton felt quite useless. Chicago had easily filled the first calls for volunteers, and he knew his mother was relieved he was not among them. Still, he could not escape the feeling he should be contributing more.

In July, the Union forces were routed by Beauregard's troops at Bull Run. Clinton made his decision.

At dinner that night, he looked calmly from Eden, to Benjamin, to Paige. His eyes moved back to his mother, and he announced, "I enlisted today in the 42nd Infantry. Within the month, I'll be leaving Chicago."

22
October–November 1861

Benjamin strode swiftly up Michigan Avenue, on his way to pick up Eden at her sewing circle. He smiled wryly to himself, knowing how she would protest that she was perfectly capable of getting home alone.

He supposed she was. In their years together at McKinnon Meats, and even before, at the Bull and Boar and at her home on Wabash Avenue, Eden had proven herself one of the most capable women alive.

Still, Chicago was changing. With the war raging, it was no longer as safe as it used to be. More and more of the honorable men were leaving town in Union uniforms. And the streets were filling with more and more gamblers and

profligates, who had moved to the North as the war put a
stop to their riverboat lives in the South.

It wasn't wise for any woman to be out alone after dark.
Especially a woman as lovely as Eden.

Crossing Randolph Street, Benjamin paused and glanced at
the wooden storage house where Annie Malone's sporting
house had once stood.

Last week had marked the fourth anniversary of the disastrous fire. His father had been dead four years. For four
years, Eden had been without a husband.

Benjamin pursed his lips as he continued north and on
across the river. Four years. Had he waited long enough?

Deep in thought, his eyes downcast, Benjamin did not
notice the two women approaching him.

"On your way to meet your lady-love?" a voice asked
teasingly.

Flushing, Benjamin looked up at Eden, walking with Juliette
Kinzie. "You know I was coming to meet you," he said
quietly. "I wish you wouldn't go out unescorted after dark."

"I'm not alone," Eden replied cheerily. "Juliette and I are
escorting each other. And you, Benjamin, ought not to re-
prove your stepmother in public."

Her blue-green eyes twinkled as she spoke, but Benjamin
winced at her words. Did she really still think of him as a
stepson?

"I'm not reproving you," he assured her. "I just worry
about you."

"It's always nice to know someone worries about you, isn't
it, Eden?" Juliette said kindly. "Well, I'll say good night
here."

She turned off at her own house, and Eden and Benjamin
walked on alone.

"I don't know why you have to go to those sewing circles
anyway," Benjamin said. "You do enough war work through
McKinnon Meats. We must be supplying half the troops
mustered out of Illinois."

"And the government's paying us quite handsomely for it,"
Eden responded quietly.

Frowning, Benjamin asked, "You're not feeling guilty about
that, are you? We're certainly not cheating anyone, and we
make sizable donations of money and provisions, not to mention the workers we've lost."

Eden shook her head. "No. I'm not feeling guilty. I just want to do all I can, especially now, with Clinton gone."

"I understand. But I wish you wouldn't overtax yourself."

Eden laughed. "Oh, Benjamin! How can I overtax myself just sitting among a bunch of gossipy women sewing? You do worry too much! I'm really not *that* old, you know!"

"You're not old at all," he said quickly. "I don't think you'll ever really seem old."

Something in his tone embarrassed her, and she quickly asked, "Did you leave Paige home alone?"

"No, not alone. Louise is still bustling around in the kitchen." He sighed. "Listen, Eden, I've been thinking. Maybe I ought not to live with you and Paige anymore."

She stopped and stared at him. "I'm afraid you're not making sense, Benjamin. First you talk about how unsafe it is for a woman to be alone, and then you suggest leaving me and Paige to live alone with our doddering old cook! What kind of nonsense is that? You're part of the family!"

"Not in the way I want to be."

Eden's eyes widened. "Benjamin, I don't understand. Have we done something? Do you honestly feel mistreated? I know it was hard for you the first few months, but that was twenty years ago, and I've always tried to give you the same consideration as the other children—"

"But I'm not one of your children, Eden," Benjamin cut her off quietly. "I'm almost as near your age as I am to Clinton's. I'm much nearer your age than I am to Paige's. I'm a grown man, Eden!"

She stiffened, suddenly realizing his implications. "Benjamin," she whispered, "what are you trying to say?"

"That I love you! That I want to take care of you! That you've lived without a man long enough! That I want to marry you!"

Stunned, Eden looked away. Why hadn't she sensed this coming? Why had it never occurred to her when she wondered why Benjamin had not married that she might have been the reason? She had always assumed that his time would come. After all, Brett had been thirty-four when he married her. Benjamin was only a year older now.

Now Eden felt forced to examine her feelings for Benjamin. She had always felt special affection for him. In the last four years, working so closely with him, she had been drawn to him more than ever.

She had cherished him as a special confidante. She valued his opinions. There had been times, even when Brett was still alive, when she had felt Benjamin was the one person to whom she could turn.

From the beginning, she had never really thought of him as a son. He had been more of a younger brother, a younger brother who had sometimes proved himself wiser than she.

She admired his strength of character, respected his business acumen, allowed herself to depend on him in so many ways. Yes, she even loved him. But, not in the way he was professing to love her.

Hurt by her silence, Benjamin muttered, "I'm sorry. I guess I shouldn't have said all that. I didn't mean to offend you."

"You haven't offended me. I'm touched—flattered. But, Benjamin, you must know it's an impossible proposal. You're my husband's son—"

"Your late husband's son," he corrected. "And of course I don't mean any disrespect to Father. While he was alive, I didn't even allow myself to think of you in this way. But he's been dead four years now, Eden. We have to pick up our own lives."

"I know, but—"

"If you only knew what hell I've been through. Living in your house. Working with you every day. Wanting you as a woman. But, all the time afraid to say anything for fear you'd pull away from me. And then tonight, it finally hit me—I can't go on living this way!"

As she turned her face to his, he saw her eyes glistening with unshed tears. "Benjamin, I don't know what to say. I'd give anything in the world not to hurt you—"

"But you don't love me." His tone was flat, and his eyes widened as he tried to hold back his own tears.

"Of course I love you! But I've never thought about you in quite that way. When Brett was alive, there was no room in my thoughts for another man." She paused awkwardly, thinking of Garrett, and how he still dominated her thoughts. Aware of Benjamin's intent gaze, she plunged on, "And, these last years, I've been so involved in the business. I guess I haven't seen what's been happening around me. I guess I haven't really looked at you."

"Then, look at me now! Tell me you like what you see! Tell me you'll marry me!"

"Oh, Benjamin! I do like what I see. I'm so proud of the man you've become. So grateful for all you've always done for me. But—I don't know. I'm afraid Brett's ghost would always be between us."

"Why should it be? We wouldn't be doing anything to hurt him. We never have."

They were standing in front of the house now, gazing at each other earnestly. Both were thinking of the day, twenty year ago, when Benjamin had turned up at the Bull and Boar Inn.

From the beginning, Benjamin had adored Eden. But even he had never suspected their relationship would come to this.

Looking up at the house, he mumbled, "I'm sorry if I upset you, Eden. I guess I was kind of foolish and thoughtless to let everything pour out at once. It's just that, all of a sudden, I just couldn't seem to keep it in any longer."

She nodded. "I understand. I think we could both benefit now from a good night's sleep."

Benjamin shook his head. "You go ahead in. I don't think I could sleep just yet. I'll see you tomorrow."

Eden's heart ached as she stood on the stoop, watching him walk back toward the lake. For an instant, she wanted to run after him. But, what could she say? She didn't know. Perhaps by morning it would all seem clearer.

Eden was still awake near dawn when she heard Benjamin come in. She had lain in bed for hours without sleeping, but she still did not know what to say to him.

Of course, she couldn't agree to marry him. It wouldn't be fair to him, when the only living man she wanted was Garrett Martin.

But Garrett, obviously, did not want her. Garrett had had four years to ask her to marry him, or at least to declare his desire for her. But he had not so much as indicated that he ever thought of her.

It was time, Eden insisted to herself, that she stop dreaming of Garrett. But surely it would not be fair to turn to Benjamin. Much as she loved Benjamin, she was not at all sure she could ever love him as a wife should.

The fact that he was fourteen years younger than she bothered her less than it would most women. Her affair with Garrett had taught her that age was relative and a woman could find great joy with a younger man. But, she doubted that she could ever give herself to Benjamin as completely as a wife should. The fact that he was Brett's son would always stand between them.

Benjamin deserved more than the type of love she could promise him. He deserved a woman who would devote herself to him wholeheartedly, with no memories of past loves. He ought to marry a woman who could give him children, not someone who was nearly fifty years old.

In short, Benjamin should not marry her.

Still, how could she tell him without hurting him? How could she make him understand? When she told him her decision, would he insist on moving out? Would they lose the closeness they had cherished for so many years? Even knowing she would not marry him, would he ever seek solace with another woman?

In most things, Eden knew, Benjamin combined remarkable sensitivity with extraordinarily rational thinking. But, she sensed that his feelings for her might obscure his usual rationality.

Did she owe him something for all his years of devotion to her? Certainly. But how much? And how much could she give without hurting both of them more than if she didn't give at all?

Thinking back to a conversation fifteen years earlier, Eden wondered if her meddling had already robbed Benjamin of all chances for happiness. Then, as a young man of twenty, Benjamin had confessed his feeling of rejection from most whites. The subject had never come up again, but neither had he mixed any more freely with Chicago society as he grew older.

If only she had been farsighted enough to foresee the problems when, as a youth, he had first appeared at the Bull and Boar Inn! If she had not insisted he stay, Brett might have sent Benjamin back to his mother. Among the Potawatomis, he would have been accepted. He would have married and found happiness.

Of course, Benjamin had never seemed particularly unhappy in Chicago. And, since the start of the war, the attitude of Chicago society had changed considerably. As a respected member of the business community, a major contributor to Union causes, Benjamin McKinnon was suddenly considered one of Chicago's most eligible bachelors.

Hadn't he noticed the way young women, under their

mothers' approving gazes, flirted with him at charity balls? Or, was he too scarred by his early years to take note of the change? Was he turning to her because he still believed she was the only woman in this white society to accept a half-breed?

Within the hour, Eden heard Benjamin leave again. At the plant, she found a message on her desk, informing her he would be busy with problems in the slaughterhouse all day. He did not come home to dinner, and she was not sure whether he came home at all that night.

For three days, they did not see one another. Benjamin managed to be conveniently absent from his office whenever Eden was in hers. Evenings, he occupied himself drilling with the Home Guard, or in fund-raising activities for the Union cause.

Finally, on the fourth night, Eden was lying awake when she heard him come in. Slipping into a wrapper, she hurried from her room and stopped him as he tiptoed up the stairs.

"I'd begun to wonder if you still lived here," she said, the quiver in her voice belying her casual words.

Benjamin forced a weary smile, and Eden had all she could do not to take him in her arms as she noted his haggard, gray face.

"I made a fool of myself the other night," he whispered. "I've been afraid to face you since."

She sighed in relief. "Then, you do realize how impossible your proposal would be."

He shook his head. "No. It's not a question of possibility. I just realize you don't want to consider marrying me. I was foolish to ask. Before, I could deceive myself that you might be pleased with my proposal. Now, I can't even do that."

Eden stared at him, her heart nearly bursting at the defeated look in his eyes. "Benjamin," she said softly, "we must talk. Please—" She motioned him into the small sitting room adjoining her bedroom.

Shrugging, he followed her into the room. "I don't think there's a great deal more to say," he murmured. "Except, perhaps, that I'll be moving out as soon as I can find suitable quarters."

"Benjamin, I wish you wouldn't do that."

His gray-green eyes were sorrowful as they met hers. "I wish I didn't have to."

"Benjamin, please try to understand! I'm more than flattered by your proposal. You're a fine, fine person, and I *do* love you. But that's not enough. I'm too old for you. I can't give you half of what a younger woman could. I can't even give you children. Surely you must realize at least a dozen girls in Chicago would jump at the chance to marry you tomorrow."

He grimaced. "I don't love anyone else. If you won't marry me, I won't marry at all."

But think of the scandal if we married! For all its size, Chicago is still a small town where gossip is concerned. We'd both be branded as incestuous, and God knows what else!"

"But we wouldn't be committing any sins. We don't share a single drop of blood. The fact that you were married to my father has nothing to do with us."

"That's not quite true, you know."

"All right. I suppose it isn't. The truth is, Father loved you so much he would have been glad to see you marry me—knowing that I'd love you, and cherish you, and always take care of you."

"Do you really think so?"

"Of course. Don't you? Anyway, the question is not what anyone else would do or say, but whether you really want to marry me. I hardly think it matters whether society gives us its blessing. I've lived on the fringes of society all my life. And, I think you're strong enough to withstand any barbs society might throw your way—if you want to."

Those last words were added almost as a desperate plea, tearing at Eden's heart, crumbling her resolution. Looking into Benjamin's clear, gray-green eyes, Eden could see all the best qualities of Brett—the sensitivity, the compassion, the passionate devotion, the calm inner strength.

Slowly, she nodded. Swept away by the tenderness she felt for him, before she could think more, she whispered, "I do want to, Benjamin. Yes, I'll marry you!"

He sighed, his eyes searching hers. "Don't do it just because you feel sorry for me," he murmured.

"No," Eden shook her head. "It's not that. I'm lonely. And—I do love you."

He smiled then, his face suffused with tenderness. Crossing to her, he took her into his arms. His voice muffled against her chestnut hair, he murmured, "I'll make you happy, Eden. I swear I will! I'll never let you regret this decision."

*   *   *

With a coarse laugh, Burton dropped the letter from his mother
into his lap. "Well, it seems that my half brother has really
outdone himself this time! I always knew he wanted to beat
me out of full control of McKinnon Meats, but I never
dreamed he'd try anything like this!"

Frowning, Garrett looked up from the desk, where he was
working on the ranch budget. Since the start of the war seven
months ago, the Double M had been cut off from its usual
Northern markets, and it was becoming difficult to balance
the books. Burton had urged that they begin seeking markets
among the Confederate troops, but Garrett had so far refused.

"What are you talking about, Burton?" Garrett asked
irritably. "If Benjamin had wanted full control of the firm, he
could have stepped in four years ago, when your father died,
instead of turning over the reins to your mother."

"Maybe. Or maybe he just wanted to lull us all into thinking he didn't want to take over. But, now that Clinton's away
at war, and I'm stuck down here in Texas, he's decided to
make his move."

Garrett waited, his brows raised quizzically.

"He's married my mother!"

"What?" Garrett felt his face pale as he got up. "What kind
of nonsense is that?"

"See for yourself." Burton waved the letter and Garrett
snatched it from his hand.

Turning away, so Burton could not see the pages trembling
in his hand, Garrett read:

> I suppose this will come as a shock to you, but
> Benjamin and I have just been married. I've been
> so lonely since your father died, and, as you know,
> there is no finer man alive than Benjamin. I hope
> you will understand, my darling, and wish us your
> very best.
>
> In peacetime, we would of course have waited for
> all the family to share the occasion with us. However,
> with times as uncertain as they are, we thought it
> best to marry as quickly, and with as little fanfare,
> as possible. Paige was here to share the moment
> with us. She is quite pleased, as I trust you and
> Clinton will be.

Of course, we've had no thoughts of a honeymoon. With orders pouring in from the government, and half our workers away in the Union Army, we can hardly snatch a few hours of sleep each night . . .

"Amazing, isn't it?" Burton's voice intruded on Garrett's thoughts.

With an effort, Garrett managed to keep his voice cool. "Not particularly. After all, your half brother is a handsome man. Your mother is an extremely attractive woman. They've been working together all hours of the day and night. I'd say it's only natural—"

"Oh, crap! Sure my mother's good-looking, but she's about fifteen years too old for Benjamin! All he wants is her money and position."

Garrett shook his head. "I think you're wrong. Your mother's too good a judge of character to marry someone like that."

"How would you know? You've only met her once or twice, haven't you?"

Inwardly cringing, Garrett shook his head. "No. I—I talked to her a number of times when she was still managing the Bull and Boar. You were just a young boy then. You wouldn't remember."

"Well, I'd still guess I know her better than you do! And Benjamin, too! He's been scheming to take over McKinnon Meats ever since he joined the family."

Garrett shrugged. "So, what do you intend to do about it?"

"For the moment, nothing. I'll just sit back and wait out the war." With a half smile, Burton added, "If I'm lucky, maybe Benjamin will join the Union forces and get himself killed! That would sure save me a lot of trouble."

Grimacing, Garrett started for the door. "I'm going out on the range for a few days. I've a feeling the Rebs are rustling our cattle."

Burton frowned. "Aren't you going to finish the budget?"

"It'll keep 'til I get back."

Without waiting for an answer, Garrett left and strode toward the stable, all the while cursing himself for ever getting involved with the McKinnon family again.

23
1862–1863

Her arm linked through Benjamin's, her head held high, Eden smiled to herself at the loudly whispered remarks of the passing matrons on Michigan Avenue.

"My dear, can you believe she would be so brazen as to marry her own stepson? Why, compared to her, he's no more than a boy!"

"And, to think they've actually been living under the same roof all these years! One wonders exactly what's been going on between them since Brett McKinnon died—or even before!"

The first woman clucked loudly. "It's a pity, really, with her young, impressionable daughter living with them. The girl can't be more than fifteen. Whatever can the poor child think?"

Her friend shrugged. "Lord knows! But then, that Eden McKinnon always was a strange one. Imagine a woman taking over a slaughterhouse! It's just not proper! Things were different thirty years ago, when Chicago was just a frontier town. But a woman today ought to have a bit of gentility!"

Patting her hand, Benjamin smiled down at his wife. "Do you mind terribly what they say?"

Eden shook her head. "Why should I mind? Their remarks are a small enough price to pay for the happiness you've given me. Anyway, I think they're just jealous. No doubt they had their eyes on you for their own daughters."

Benjamin's gray-green eyes widened in mock horror. "A half-breed?"

"A half-breed with money, darling. To some people, that makes all the difference."

He laughed then, sliding an arm around her shoulders. "Ah, Eden, you always were an astute judge of character! Seriously, though, do you think we're setting a bad example for Paige?"

"How could we be? We're simply showing her that love

201

can happen at any age, between people of any ages. Surely there's nothing shameful or immoral about that! Besides, you know she heartily approves of our marriage."

Eden turned her gaze from Benjamin, pretending to study the lake, as she wished all of her children had been so understanding. Clinton had immediately sent his hearty congratulations. But Burton had so far chosen to ignore their marriage.

What, she wondered, was her elder son thinking? After twelve years separation, she hardly knew him, or what to expect from him.

"Well," Benjamin said, "I suspect all the gossip will be over soon. With a war going on, people have better things to talk about. In the meantime, I hope you're not sorry I talked you into this marriage."

Eden smiled. "I'd be a fool to be sorry."

She meant what she said. In the three months since their marriage, Eden had found serenity and contentment with Benjamin. They had already been sharing so much of their lives, it seemed only natural that they should wholly belong to one another.

Even the physical aspect of their relationship, which she had approached a bit fearfully, brought her more joy than she had imagined possible. Their first night together, she had felt awkward and unsure of herself. But Benjamin had quickly dissolved her uncertainties.

"You're beautiful," he had whispered, as he gently helped her undress.

Then, he had carried her to their bed and made love to her so slowly, so skillfully, with such exquisite tenderness, that she could not help but respond. He carefully nurtured her long-dormant passions, until she felt like a woman again, in the most intimate way.

Throughout most of their marriage, Eden and Brett had shared a casual but intense intimacy that expressed itself in scores of ways every day. Now, Eden was rediscovering the same joys with Benjamin.

It was not quite the same as it had been with Brett, or with Garrett. However, as she neared her fiftieth birthday, Eden felt profoundly grateful for each moment she shared with her new husband.

She loved snuggling against him as she fell asleep each night. She loved waking beside him. She felt rejuvenated when, in the middle of a wearying afternoon, she looked up from her desk and felt his eyes upon her.

Still, she had not stopped thinking of Garrett. In all honesty, she doubted that her longing for him would ever completely vanish. But Garrett was in Texas, where he apparently gave no thought to her. Benjamin was in Chicago, devoting his life to her.

Benjamin had done so much for her, over the years, Eden felt she owed him equal devotion. And, he was so fine and loving, she did not find the debt difficult to pay. With each day, she surprised herself by the added depth of her love for him.

Besides, with the bleak news of war swirling constantly around them, they both deserved whatever happiness they could grab.

As Benjamin had predicted, the gossip soon died out. Patriotism was the watchword in Chicago, and McKinnon Meats contributed so much to the Union armies that no one could find fault with the firm's ruling family.

Hurrying to the plant early one morning, Eden reflected that it would hardly have mattered if society had ostracized them. With ever larger orders, and ever fewer workers, she and Benjamin had little time for socializing.

They also had little time to spend with Paige, a fact that worried Eden a great deal. Her daughter seemed happy enough, and insisted she understood the pressing needs of the war. But Eden wished she could be home more, to oversee her development.

She consoled herself that Paige spent several hours each day preparing bandages with the Ladies War Committee, a group that could hardly lead the girl astray.

Late on the night of July 17, Eden was in the warehouse, organizing a shipment to the Union forces in Missouri. As she picked up a heavy crate of canned beef, Benjamin, who had just entered the warehouse, hurried to take it away from her.

"You shouldn't be lifting anything this heavy," he chided. "Why didn't you call one of the men to do it?"

Eden smiled wearily. "As I'm sure you've noticed, all the men are already overworked. We're so shorthanded I don't know where to turn."

Benjamin sighed. "I'm afraid we'll be a good deal more shorthanded soon. I just picked up the *Tribune*. Congress has authorized the President to call out all able-bodied men between eighteen and forty-five."

Groaning, Eden said, "If he does that, we'll hardly have enough men to keep the plant open. How can we continue to supply the Union troops if we haven't enough men to do the slaughtering, butchering, packing, and shipping?"

Shrugging, Benjamin looked away. "I don't know," he replied quietly.

Suddenly, the full impact of the news struck Eden. Reaching for Benjamin's hand, she stammered, "They won't—the President—you won't have to go, too, will you?"

He smiled sadly. "Last time I looked I was still under forty-five."

"Benjamin, be serious!"

He sighed. "No, I don't suppose I would have to go. No doubt I could buy my way out. Plenty of other men in positions similar to mine have done just that."

He stopped himself, on the verge of naming Burton as an example. That was different, of course. Burton had bought himself out of a position in the Confederate Army. None of the McKinnons would have wanted him fighting for the enemy.

"But, you won't even consider that option, will you?" Eden whispered in resignation.

Benjamin shook his head as he drew her into his arms. "No. It wouldn't be right. There's not a family in Chicago without at least one member fighting in this war—"

"Including ours! We've already sent Clinton—"

"I know, and it's for his sake as much as anyone else's that I've got to do my part. You know how I feel about war, Eden. That's why I never got involved in the mess in Kansas. But this is different. There's no avoiding it."

"But I need you here!"

He smiled tenderly. "I know. I need you, too. But we can't be selfish enough to think we need each other any more than any of the other couples who've been torn apart by this war. As for the business, you're as capable of managing without me as with me."

She buried her face against his chest, knowing it would be useless to argue anymore.

"Try not to worry," he whispered. "I won't be going immediately. And the order is only for a nine-month period of service. It may all be over sooner than you think."

But, somehow, they both knew that was a false hope.

* * *

Benjamin did not leave until early September. By then, the Confederacy had trounced Union forces in Virginia at the Second Battle of Bull Run, and General Lee's army was crossing the Potomac into Maryland.

Eden scarcely had time to read the war reports in the daily papers. At the plant, she felt as if she had to be in a dozen places at one time. Putting aside her squeamishness, she supervised the slaughterers, butchers, packers, canners, shippers. She rode through the yards when the drovers brought in new livestock, choosing the cattle and hogs to be slaughtered, rejecting the lumpy-jawed, diseased animals.

The Southern livestock sources were completely cut off from Chicago now, and at times even the Northern drovers could not get through the battle lines. Eden reflected that was just as well, for McKinnon Meats was so shorthanded it could hardly handle more stock.

Although she still needed more men to handle the heavy, grueling jobs, Eden began to enlist women for as many other jobs as possible. Poor mothers, whose husbands were away at war, were glad to supplement the meager army pay. But the well-to-do turned up their noses at the idea of "slaughterhouse" work, preferring to do their part in genteel, gossipy sewing circles.

Fifteen-year-old Paige volunteered to take over much of her mother's office work. She arrived at the plant soon after school ended each afternoon and often stayed until nearly midnight, when Eden was ready to go home. Several times, Eden found her daughter asleep over her desk, her auburn curls spread across shipping orders and Army requisitions.

Eden's heart ached for the girl. By the time the war was over, her youth would have been wasted on barrels of beef and the stench of stockyards.

But, at least at the plant she could be sure of where to find Paige and what her daughter was doing. Since the war began, there were too many temptations on Chicago's streets, too many suave gentlemen with less than honorable intentions.

The war had put an end to the carefree Southern tradition of riverboats and gambling houses frequented by debonair gamblers and men-of-the-world. Few Southerners could afford the time or money for an idle afternoon in a gambling parlor, and Mississippi River pleasure boats had given way to military transports. Anxious to preserve their easy way of living, professional gamblers had moved in a steady stream up the Mississippi, across the Illinois and Michigan Canal, and into the prosperous city of Chicago.

Eden did not entirely disapprove of gambling, as a casual sport a man might enjoy from time to time. But, she was concerned over the type of man who would devote his life to cards and dice, particularly when his country was engaged in a horrible war.

The never-failing prosperity of most of the professional gamblers made her wonder just how honest they were. And the fact that most of them chose Chicago madams as their steady companions confirmed her suspicions that they were somewhat lacking in morals.

Still, Eden had always considered herself fairly tolerant, and the mere presence of gamblers did not upset her. What worried her was the way young women, including Paige, idealized and romanticized the men.

With so many of their own young men away at war, she supposed it was only natural that the girls should turn their thoughts to the handsome, elegantly dressed gamblers. But, she worried where such fascination might lead, and she warned Paige a number of times to stay away from Randolph Street, between State and Dearborn, where most of the gambling dens were located.

Eden was fairly confident her daughter had heeded her warnings, until a late spring night, when they were on their way home from the plant.

It had been raining most of the day, but the rain had now tapered off to a fine mist. Since the street grading, begun in the 1850s, had still not been completed, spring rains often transformed Chicago streets into miles of muddy ruts in which carriages could easily become mired. Anticipating the problem, Eden had driven a sturdy old farm wagon, instead of her usual more fragile carriage, to work that morning.

Now, at the intersection of State and Washington streets, it seemed her foresight was not to be rewarded. As they turned east onto Washington, the wagon's rear axle cracked, nearly tipping them over into the mud.

"Oh, drat!" Eden muttered wearily. "Well, I guess there's nothing to do but get out, unhitch the horses, and lead them home. Thank goodness we're only a block from the house."

Paige, who had been asleep before they left the plant, and

had nearly dozed off again in the wagon, looked down at the muddy street distastefully. But she said nothing as she slipped from her seat to help her mother loosen the harness.

Bent over the harness, neither woman saw a solitary rider approach.

"Good evening, ladies," a cultured Southern voice startled them. "Did you have an accident? Might I be of some assistance?"

As they looked up, the rider, a slender, dark-haired young man in a dark suit and blue brocaded waistcoat, pulled back in surprise. "Why, Paige! What's happened here?"

Paige flushed, aware that her mother was staring at her strangely. "Oh, Jeff! I'm so glad to see you! Our axle's broken, and now we've got to lead the horses home on foot."

The young man frowned. "In this mud, your shoes will be ruined before you walk half a block. Why not let me offer you a ride? And I'll be glad to lead the horses home, too."

Hesitating, Paige glanced at her mother. "That's very kind of you, Jeff. But you can't mean to carry both me and Mama."

He smiled. "One at a time, of course!" Turning to Eden, he dismounted and made a sweeping bow. "My apologies for not introducing myself at once, Mrs. McKinnon. Jefferson Montgomery, at your service. I've heard a great deal about you, ma'am, and admire you very much."

Eden smiled thinly. "Thank you, Mr. Montgomery. But, I don't think we'll require your assistance. We've only a short distance to go."

"I know," he replied, casually beginning to unharness the other horse. "But surely I can make the trip go more smoothly. No use punishing your feet after a long day of work."

"If necessary," Eden said coolly, "I can simply ride one of these animals bareback."

He grinned. "I'm sure you could, having grown up with this city. No doubt you've faced worse crises in your day. But, I think Paige might be a bit too inexperienced to follow your example. If you want to ride one of your own horses, be my guest. I'll take Paige on mine, and lead your other horse."

With that, the young man mounted his own horse, swung Paige up before him, and picked up the trailing harness of one of their team. Too tired to argue, Eden glared at him a moment before struggling on to the back of the other horse.

At the house, Eden quickly dismounted and led her horse

toward the stable. Silently, she bedded him down, while Jefferson Montgomery did the same for their other horse.

As they left the stable, Paige spoke to the young man. "Mama's so tired I'm sure it just slipped her mind. But I know she would want you to come in for some refreshments in return for your kindness."

Glancing at Eden's reproving frown, Jefferson Montgomery shook his head. "I think your mama is far too tired to entertain anyone. Perhaps another time." He touched Paige's cheek before returning to his own horse and riding away.

Inside the house, Eden turned to her daughter angrily. "You seemed rather well acquainted with him. Where did you meet him?"

Paige tossed her auburn curls defiantly. "On State Street, a few weeks ago." She paused a moment before accusing, "You were very rude to him, Mama."

"Paige, he's a gambler!"

"So what if he is? That doesn't make him the Devil Incarnate! What does it matter what he does? I don't suppose Papa's position as a fur trader was considered very genteel when you married him!"

"No. But what your father did was good, hard, honest work. People respected him—"

"People respect the gamblers, too!" Paige insisted. "If you ever spent any time outside that meat-packing plant, you'd know that scores of men in Chicago are trying to dress and act just like Jefferson Montgomery and the other gamblers. Everyone talks about them all the time. And, what's wrong with trying to bring some color and gallantry into this drab, war-weary city?"

Sinking wearily into a chair, Eden shook her head. "Nothing's wrong with that. But—oh, Paige, you're just so young, so inexperienced! I just don't want you to be hurt!"

Paige rolled her gold-flecked green eyes disdainfully. "What's going to happen to me? If you're worried about me going into one of the gambling halls, you needn't be. I asked Jeff, just to see what they were like, and he flatly refused to take me. He said they've begun to call that part of Randolph Street 'Hairtrigger Block,' because of all the shootings there connected with gambling disputes."

"You see! That's exactly the type of thing I'm trying to protect you from! What kind of a man engages in a so-called profession where violence smolders so near the surface? Gamblers just aren't decent, dependable men! Look at the company most of them keep."

"Such as people like me?" Paige retorted hotly. "Honestly, Mama, I've never known you to be so narrow-minded. After all, you married a half-breed, and think of all the things people say against Indians!"

Paling, Eden rose and slapped her daughter across the mouth.

For a moment, Paige stood quite still, rubbing the back of her hand across her mouth, her eyes still flashing defiantly. "I didn't mean that as an insult," she said quietly. "You know I love both you and Benjamin. I was just trying to make you think, Mama. You know that everything people say isn't true. Can you honestly say Jeff did anything wrong tonight?"

Eden hesitated. "No. For the most part, he was very— gallant. But I did think he took unnecessary liberties in lifting you onto his horse, and the way he caressed your cheek before he left."

Paige sighed. "Oh, Mama! In case you haven't noticed, I am a woman."

"Not really, darling. You've only just turned sixteen. I know you've been doing a woman's work in my office, and I appreciate that more than I can say. But, I'm afraid you still have a great deal to learn about being a woman."

"Jeff doesn't seem to think so!"

Hiding her dismay, Eden asked cautiously, "You've been seeing him often?"

Paige nodded. "Nearly every day. The gamb—uh, Jeff and his friends like to stroll on State Steeet in the late afternoon. I usually join him for a bit after school, before I come to the plant."

"And that's the only time you see him?"

"Practically. He's taken me for tea at the coffee shop of the Tremont House, over at Lake and Dearborn."

"And—" Eden hesitated, almost afraid to ask, "two nights ago, when you said you were going to the War Committee sewing circle, instead of coming to the plant?"

"I did go to the sewing circle. But first Jeff took me to dinner at the Sherman House, on Randolph and Clark."

"I see," Eden said softly. "And, don't you think perhaps you should have told me about those plans before the dinner?"

"I—I considered telling you, but I was afraid you would forbid me to go, and I didn't want to be forced to disobey

you. Please try to understand, Mama. It's not that I care any
less about the war than you do. I think about and pray for
Clinton and Benjamin every day. But, is it so very wrong for
me to want to have a little fun, once in a while?"

"Of course not, darling. It's just that—you hardly know this
man."

"Please give me credit for being a halfway decent judge of
character! And, you might have enough faith in me to know
I'm not going to do anything to disgrace you."

"I know you wouldn't—not intentionally. But, sometimes a
man—well, it's very late. We both need some sleep. We'll
talk more about this tomorrow."

Eden started for the stairs, but Paige's voice stopped her
when she had taken only a few steps.

"Mama?"

Eden turned. "Yes?"

"You're not going to forbid me to see Jeff, are you?"

"And if I did?"

"I wouldn't like to disobey you. But I would."

Smiling sadly, Eden nodded. "I thought as much." She
sighed. "No, Paige, I won't forbid you to see him. I suppose
as long as you limit it to strolls, and tea, and perhaps an
occasional dinner, the whole relationship is rather harmless. I
just hope you have the good sense not to expect anything
more from Mr. Jefferson Montgomery."

And, not to give him anything more, she thought, as she
trudged wearily to bed.

24
May–August 1863

Riding slowly among the grazing longhorns, Garrett Martin listened to the low-toned, soothing songs of the Mexican
vaqueros. As sons, grandsons, and great grandsons of cowboys,
they knew how to keep the cattle content, mesmerized by
their singing.

Some crooned folk tunes. Others sang hymns. Most sang

whatever words came to mind, set to any convenient tune. Garrett chuckled as he heard one vaquero cursing the longhorns, his words set to a soothing religious melody.

For the men, it was a kind of game to see how many names, masked by sweet, mellow inflections, they could call their charges. The longhorns didn't mind. And the game relieved the monotony of a long night on the range.

On a night like this, with the air warm, the spring breezes gentle, and a full moon overhead, the longhorns might graze all night.

No matter how beautiful the midnight sky, or how restful the endless plains, no one could blame a man for feeling bored. Or lonely. Cowboy comrades and lowing cattle were small comfort when one wanted a woman.

Sighing irritably, Garrett rode back to the campfire, dismounted, and squatted to pour himself a mug of bitter coffee. A shadow fell over him, and he looked up into the grizzled face of Charley Streeter, his old ranch foreman, who had accompanied him when he moved to Texas from Iowa.

"You ought to try to get some sleep," Charley muttered. "There's enough men keeping an eye on the cattle. Besides, those critters ain't goin' nowhere."

"They sure aren't!" Garrett snorted. "They haven't gone anywhere in two years! By the time this damn war is over and we can start driving them to market again, half of them will be too old and tough to be worth the trip."

Charley shrugged. "Well, I could say you wouldn't be in this fix if you'd stayed in Iowa. Never did understand why you pulled up stakes there so sudden-like."

Pressing his lips firmly together, Garrett stared silently into the fire.

"Course, I always kind of figured it was none of my business. Don't much matter to me if I'm punching cows in Iowa or Texas. Still, I'd a whole lot rather be in the United States than in the Confederacy."

"You talk too much, Charley."

"Huh?" The old cowboy blinked at his boss.

"You must be getting old. You used to know when to shut up."

"Hmph!" Wounded, Charley turned away.

A moment later, the old man turned back on Garrett, his eyes flashing angrily. "What the hell's gotten into you, Garrett Martin? Don't an old friend mean anything to you anymore? If you can't take the monotony out here on the range, maybe you'd better go back to the ranch house for a few days."

Garrett shook his head. "I don't think that's the answer."

"No, I suppose not. I couldn't stand being around the McKinnon kid too long, either. Never thought he'd turn out so bad."

Garrett did not respond.

"Well then, why don't you ride into Fort Belknap for a change? I've heard they've got some pretty women there. Pretty and willing!"

"I don't want a woman."

"The hell you don't! You just can't have the one you want, and it's eatin' you alive!"

Garrett looked up sharply, and Charley nodded at the confirmation in the younger man's eyes.

"You been mopin' around this ranch ever since you found out Eden McKinnon got married again. Why don't you just forget about her, already? One woman's as good as the next."

"That's not true."

"Well, maybe not. But there ain't no sense in wrecking your life for a woman who don't care about you. And it's plain to me she don't care about you if she married someone else."

"You don't know what you're talking about, Charley."

The old man sighed in exasperation, but this time he did not take offense.

For several minutes, Garrett and Charley squatted, staring into the fire. Garrett took a sip of his now-cold coffee. Grimacing, he poured it out on the ground. He stood and stretched slowly as he thought.

"Charley, what would you say if I said I was thinking about organizing a cattle drive?"

"I'd say you're plumb crazy! Where you going to drive any cattle with a war going on?"

"Through the Ozark Mountains. Up northeast to the Missouri River."

"Let me get this straight. You're forty-three years old. I'm damn near sixty-five. And you think we—"

"I didn't say you'd have to come."

Charley spluttered. "Well, dammit, you know I wouldn't let you do a damn fool thing like that by yourself! But, what's the point?"

"There are Union troops along the Missouri. No doubt

they could use some fresh meat. I'd like to be the one to take it to them."

"Well, that's a real noble idea. But you won't be much of a hero if you get yourself killed along the way."

"I don't care about being a hero. I'm just sick and tired of sitting down here in a confederacy I don't even want to be a part of."

The old man peered at him closely in the firelight. "You're really serious about this idea, ain't you?"

"I'm dead serious, Charley. I'm going to do it!"

As Garrett had expected, Burton received his plan with more enthusiasm.

"What an excellent idea!" Burton exclaimed. "No doubt General Schofield and his Army of Missouri will be eternally grateful to you. I only wish there were some way I could arrange to accompany you."

Garrett smiled wryly. "You've suddenly become a patriot?"

"I've always been one! It's not my fault this war has cut me off from my country. Anyway, much as I'd like to participate in this venture, I'm sure you will agree at least one of us ought to remain behind to manage the ranch. If we both left, the Confederates might be suspicious. And I'm certain they wouldn't hesitate to step in and help themselves to our stock."

"You're right about that. But, somehow, I think your decision has more to do with our cook, Conchita."

Burton grinned lewdly.

"I ought to warn you that her brother, Rafael, is not overly pleased about your relationship with her."

Shrugging, Burton remarked, "I don't see why not. Being the mistress of the boss practically assures her and him continued employment."

"Does it? You're not planning to marry Conchita, are you?"

"Are you kidding?" Burton laughed harshly. "Why would I marry a Mexican?"

"I don't know. But don't forget that Mexican men seldom forgive anyone who uses one of their women and doesn't marry her."

"So? What's Rafael going to do? Stick a knife in my ribs?"

"He might."

Burton laughed nervously. "You'd like that, wouldn't you Garrett?"

"No. Because I'd be the one who'd have to tell your mother."

Eyeing Garrett seriously, Burton said, "Then, in the interests of sparing both of us, suppose you just take big brother along on your cattle drive?"

"I intend to ask him. He's one of the best vaqueros we have, and I'd value his help. But, I won't take anyone who doesn't want to go. The venture's far too risky. I don't want any man's death on my conscience."

Nodding, Burton extended his hand. "You're a brave man, Garrett Martin. I wish you good luck."

But Garrett saw a peculiar glint in the younger man's eye, and knew there was a hollow ring to his words.

For the first three weeks, the trip went smoothly. Driven over familiar Texas rangelands, the longhorns contentedly plodded along at the rate of ten to fifteen miles per day.

Along the trail, the animals picked at grass. After dark, when the cowboys had made camp, the longhorns lay down and slept for a few hours, before rising and feeding, sometimes for most of the night.

Anticipating the problems lying ahead of them, crossing the Ozarks and evading Confederate raiders, Garrett had chosen to take only six hundred head. A usual drive to market might include two or three thousand.

But this was no ordinary drive, and Garrett knew that the six hundred longhorns would cause problems enough for him and the six cowboys accompanying him.

Rafael, brother of Conchita, had elected to join the drive. Charley Streeter had, after several hours of heated discussion, agreed to stay behind.

Garrett would have liked Charley's company. But, the man was admittedly too old for such a trip. Besides, Garrett needed to leave someone dependable at the ranch, to care for the livestock and direct the remaining vaqueros.

He might easily be gone three or four months—if he got through at all. During that time, he strongly suspected that Burton and Conchita would rarely roll out of bed. Bringing Charley along would have meant leaving the ranch virtually without management.

At the beginning of the fourth week on the trail, they crossed the Arkansas River and started into the Ozark Mountains. The going became rougher as they drove the longhorns out of the prairies and into the wooded foothills, and on into the Boston Mountains, the most treacherous stretch of the Ozarks.

Disoriented by the trees and mountains, the animals grunted nervously, and their eyes darted from side to side. Now Garrett and his men had to be constantly on guard for the sudden rolling of a steer's tail that signaled the start of a stampede.

Riding over rough, unfamiliar terrain, the herd made little progress each day. Often they had to stop by early or midafternoon, as soon as the men could find adequate campgrounds. Grazing space, for even so small a herd, was severely limited in the mountains. If they passed up one spot, they might not reach another until after dark. And it would be suicide to try driving a herd of longhorns any distance through mountains in the dark.

In camp, while the other men alternated sleeping and the night herd duties of crooning to the cattle, Garrett rarely slept. Each day he became more convinced Charley had been right. He had been crazy even to imagine making this drive. Surely there were easier ways to commit suicide.

The herd had not stampeded today, but what was to keep them from doing so tomorrow? How could he be sure the crazed beasts would not crush him, and all the vaqueros, in a mad rush to get out of the mountains?

Even at night, when the cattle seemed to be peacefully grazing, the danger of stampede always hung over them. No one knew when a real or imagined movement or sound might startle a longhorn and send him charging out of the herd, scaring all the other animals into frenzied movement. Here, in the strange mountain surroundings, where even men shivered at unfamiliar sounds, the cattle seemed especially jumpy.

Somehow, they managed to control the drive through Oklahoma, and across the northwestern corner of Arkansas. The cattle were far from content. But they had so far behaved better than Garrett had dared to expect. By the time they settled down for the first night in the Missouri portion of the mountains, the men were beginning to consider a mountain drive almost routine.

Crouching around the campfire to fill their plates, the vaqueros talked easily with Garrett.

"Hey, boss," one joked, "where's all the trouble you said

we'd be having? You sure you going to pay us extra for this nice vacation?"

"That's why he said there would be trouble," another chuckled. "If our amigos back at the ranch knew how easy this would be, they would all have wanted to come. Then the boss would have had to pay out too much!"

Garrett smiled good naturedly. "I hope the whole drive goes this easily. And I'll be glad to pay even a bigger bonus than I promised. But, we haven't made it out of the mountains and down to the river yet."

Rafael, who was acting as assistant foreman, or *segundo*, on the drive, frowned. "What are you expecting?"

"I'm not sure." Garrett shrugged. "But it's been too easy. I'm surprised we haven't met any Confederate raiding parties yet."

"But we are out of the Confederacy now, are we not?"

"Yes. But the rebel guerrillas have raided as far north as Topeka, Kansas. I wouldn't be surprised if they tried to 'requisition' a few head from us. I've heard the Confederate Army's been getting mighty hungry."

Rafael laughed. "I'd like to see any rebel soldier handle a longhorn! He might change his mind in a hurry!"

The others chuckled in agreement before drifting off to open their bedrolls or take the first watch of night herding.

Exhausted from the weeks on the trail, Garrett managed to fall asleep despite his worries. He had been asleep more than an hour when angry voices woke him.

"I tell you," Rafael insisted, "you cannot take our cattle!"

"We'll take whatever we want," a harsh voice drawled. "Quantrill is not in the habit of being refused!"

Recognizing the name Quantrill, Garrett sat up quickly. William Clarke Quantrill was one of the most notoriously brutal rebel raiders. There was no sense getting anyone killed over a few head of cattle.

In the dim light of the campfire, he could see Rafael, mounted for night herding, gesturing angrily at a group of about ten rebel raiders. One raider slowly raised his rifle and aimed at Rafael's head.

Springing to his feet, Garrett called urgently, "I wouldn't shoot, if I were you."

With a coarse laugh, the raider demanded, "Why not? I wouldn't go to hell for killing a dirty Mexican, would I?" Deliberately, he cocked the rifle.

"If you shoot, you'll probably start a stampede," Garrett warned. "These cattle are already as jumpy as a pony with burrs in its saddle blanket. One strange sound and they might kill all of us."

The raider laughed again. "You think the men of William Clarke Quantrill are afraid of a bunch of cows? We'll shoot who we want, when we want, and damn the consequences!"

"Yeah! You shut up, mister! Don't try telling us what to do!" another raider sneered.

Shrugging, Garrett walked slowly toward them. "If you choose to ignore the advice of a man with more than twenty years experience in cattle ranching, that's your affair. But, I'll tell you this," he continued, his hand raising slowly to reveal a revolver, "I'll kill any man who shoots Rafael or any of my other men, and I'll leave your body on the ground for the stampeding cattle to trample!"

"Oh, no you won't!" the raider said, training his rifle on Garrett. " 'Cause you'll already be dead, you damn Yankee!"

Behind him, Garrett could hear the cattle grunting nervously. The night herders were singing more loudly than usual, attempting to divert the longhorns from the disturbance. But the tension in the air had already transmitted itself to the jumpy beasts. It might already be too late to avoid a stampede.

"Listen," Garrett said as calmly as possible, "we'll give you however many head you need. Just tell us what you want."

"You won't give us nothin'! We'll take what we want!" the rebel leader said. "Adam, Joel, go on over there and pick us out some good-looking beef."

"You'd better let my men help you," Garrett persisted. "These cattle aren't used to strangers."

"I said, we'll take what we want!" the leader snarled.

The rebels rode into the nervous herd, looking for the choicest longhorns. Finding a prize specimen, the rebel named Joel prodded it with his rifle.

"This here one ought to be real—" His words were drowned by the enraged bellow of the longhorn. It raised its head toward the sky, rolled its tail, and charged away from the offender.

In the next instant, the night air reverberated with the snorts and bellows of frantic cattle. Longhorns began charging in all directions, colliding with one another and with the horsemen in a panic-stricken rush.

At the risk of being trampled, Garrett looked around wildly

for his mount. Rafael reached down a helping hand, and
Garrett jumped up behind his *segundo*, barely escaping the
horns of a charging longhorn.

Quantrill's raiders were forgotten as every man scrambled
to bring the stampeding herd under control.

Garrett's horse galloped by, and he flung himself onto its
bare back. He struggled out of his woolen vest and began
waving it over his head as he urged his horse forward to cut
off the lead longhorns.

Around him, the vaqueros were wildly waving blankets,
vests, and bits of brush, screaming obscenities and shooting off
their pistols as they frantically attempted to surround and
head in the herd.

For the first half hour it was impossible to tell if their
efforts would be successful.

The snorts and bellows of the longhorns drowned out even
the sharp report of the pistols. The animals, which lumbered
along so slowly all day, now seemed to be moving at breakneck speed.

Garrett's horse plunged down a hillside after the largest
number of beasts, whinnying and shying as Garrett urged it
through to the front of the herd.

Ahead, he saw one of the vaqueros thrown into the air as
his horse stumbled, snapped a leg, and hurtled to the ground,
to be trampled by the maddened longhorns. The bloodcurdling death scream of a dying horse rose above the noise
of the herd. Garrett felt a shiver race down his spine as his
own horse trembled and whinnied in fright.

A moment later, he saw with relief that the rider had been
thrown clear of the herd and was crawling to safety.

A sudden searing pain snapped Garrett's eyes down to his
own leg. He felt a rush of wetness, and saw the blood pulse
through his pants where a passing steer had gored him.
Awakened so suddenly, he had not had time to slip on his
boots.

Thanking God his horse was still unhurt, he gritted his
teeth and kneed the animal forward. As long as he was
mounted on an uninjured horse, he would be all right. The
wound could be attended to later.

An hour later, the vaqueros had managed to surround most
of the herd and press them together. Then the longhorns
began the characteristic milling that came at the end of every
stampede.

Still grunting and bellowing, they rushed around in a frenzied pinwheel, choking the riders in a cloud of unbreathable dust. They milled for another hour until, exhausted at last, they slowed and returned to peaceful grazing as if nothing unusual had happened.

Stiff and sore, his leg coated with drying blood, Garrett called his men together as the dawn began to lighten the mountains.

Rafael and three other vaqueros answered the call. The chuck wagon cook had already ridden back to camp, to prepare coffee and breakfast. Two of the vaqueros were missing.

"All right," Garrett sighed, "I saw Carlos go down, so I'm pretty sure where we can find him. Rafael, you come with me. Chico, you stay with the herd, though I think they're too tired to try anything now. Does anyone have any idea what happened to Juan?"

The men shook their heads, then one pointed to the base of the hillside, where a solitary figure was limping toward them. The man waved feebly, and the group rode down to meet the vaquero named Juan.

"My horse, he went over the mountainside!" Juan exclaimed. "I was lucky to get off in time!"

That left only Carlos, the vaquero Garrett had seen thrown, to account for. Sending the others back to camp, Garrett took Rafael and rode toward the rock outcrop where he had last seen the vaquero.

They found Carlos lying on his chest, his arms stretched forward in a final attempt to crawl, his lifeless head at an awkward angle, his neck broken.

Looking away, Garrett muttered hoarsely. "That should have been me. What a fool I was to start this drive!"

"No," Rafael insisted softly. "You were not a fool. This could have happened anywhere. Even on normal drives a man can die in a stampede, or even be crushed to death as the cattle rush to a watering spot." He paused and shrugged philosophically. "It is a risk a vaquero chooses to take."

"But in this case it was so unnecessary!"

"You warned us of the dangers, and we chose to come."

Garrett sighed, knowing there was no more to say. Carlos was not the first man he had lost in ranching. Nor would he be the last. Still, Garrett would always feel more responsible for him than for the others.

"Well, we'd better take him back and bury him."

Garrett slid off his horse and took a step toward the dead man. His injured leg throbbed with sudden white-hot pain, and he fell to his knees with a muttered curse.

Frowning, Rafael dismounted and looked at the wound. "You should have stayed in camp," he said matter-of-factly.

"No." Garrett shook his head. "It's only a superficial wound. I'll be all right once it's cleaned up and bandaged." But he did not protest when Rafael alone lifted the body of Carlos onto a horse and helped Garrett to mount again.

At the camp, as they buried Carlos, each man sank into private reverie. As Rafael had pointed out, death was an accepted part of any cattle drive, and, though all grieved for their comrade, none but Garrett brooded for any length of time.

They spent the rest of the day in camp, recovering from the stampede, then started out again early the next morning. By then, Garrett's leg, though stiff and sore, could support his weight.

A count of the herd showed only three head missing.

"Well," Chico said cheerily as they resumed the drive, "at least we did not have to give any steers to that damned Quantrill! That stampede sure cleared out his men in a hurry!"

The other vaqueros laughed agreement. Only Garrett rode a little apart, brooding over the drive, the stampede, and the loss of a man's life.

Three weeks later, they made their way out of the northern edge of the Ozarks. Along the way, another half-dozen head had dropped from exhaustion. The remaining longhorns had lost a great deal of weight from the rigors of the mountain trail.

Garrett had expected to lose far more of the herd. If only Carlos were still alive, he could have considered the drive an overwhelming success.

Leaving Rafael in charge of the herd, Garrett rode ahead to Jefferson City, the capital of Missouri, to confer with General John Schofield.

As expected, the young leader of the Union forces in Missouri was greatly pleased by the gift of fresh beef. Within a week, the longhorns had been safely transferred to the U.S. Army.

It was only then, when the vaqueros began discussing their return to the Double M ranch, that Garrett realized he was not ready to return.

For the last two months, he had been obsessed with the single-minded goal of driving the herd to the Union forces. Over five hundred miles of treacherous trails, he had thought of little else.

Now, suddenly, he realized his journey was only a little less than two thirds over. He was only three hundred miles from Chicago, three hundred miles from Eden.

Had it not been for Eden and the torment she had caused him, he would never even have conceived of this drive. They would all still be in Texas. Carlos would still be alive.

Could he really turn back now, when he was this close?

The night before they were to begin their return journey, Garrett paid off each of the men, dividing among them the bonus that was to have gone to Carlos. He had carried the money, his own, all the way from Texas, so the men would be assured of being paid, even if something happened to him.

Turning to Rafael, he handed him an additional sum. "You'll be in charge on the way back," he said. "Without the cattle, it shouldn't be too difficult. I've a few more things to do up North before I go back to the Double M."

25
September 1863

Sitting at her desk at McKinnon Meats, her head in her hands, Eden wearily rubbed her eyes. The window was open, but there was no breeze blowing in from the lake. The mid-September humidity felt stifling.

Eden yawned and shook her head. It seemed she never got enough sleep anymore. There were never enough hours in the days or nights. And there were never enough men to keep the business running smoothly.

She supposed she should be happy to be overworked. The problems of running an undermanned business left her little time to worry about Clinton and Benjamin.

Still, they were in her thoughts every night before she fell asleep. Benjamin had been with Grant when the Union took

Vicksburg, Mississippi, that summer. Clinton was in Chickamauga, Georgia, now, where the Union reports were far less
promising.

At home, there was Paige to worry about. The girl was still
seeing that gambler, Jefferson Montgomery, and seemed more
enamored of him than ever.

Eden supposed she could solve that problem by insisting
Paige spend all her free time at the plant. But, Chicago held
so little gaiety for a sixteen-year-old these days that Eden
hadn't the heart to deny her daughter an occasional dinner or
tea.

Besides, she consoled herself, between school, studies,
sewing circles, and voluntary work at the plant, Paige really
had very little time. When the war was over, Jefferson Montgomery would go back to the riverboats, and Paige would
find a more suitable partner among the young men returning
to Chicago.

Yawning, Eden rubbed her eyes again and told herself she
really ought to get back to work. But she was so weary of it
all! If only there was something to look forward to at the end
of each day!

"Not sleeping on the job, are you?"

At the sound of the mellow, male voice, Eden froze, her
hands still covering her eyes. A shiver raced down her spine.
She was afraid to look toward the office door and see that she
had imagined the voice.

She heard the door close and the soft, long-legged stride
come toward her. Then she felt his hands on her shoulders
and heard the voice again.

"Eden? You're all right, aren't you?"

Her eyes flew open, and she turned in her chair to look
up into the sympathetic, penetrating blue eyes. She reached
up and traced her fingers lightly, lovingly over the sharply
angular features, the cheeks that dimpled slightly as he smiled
down at her, the blond hair, still as light as cornsilk from
his years on the range.

"Oh, Garrett," she sobbed, almost overturning her chair as
she jumped up to embrace him.

His arms held her tight, and it felt so good to feel the solid
warmth of a man. It felt so right to have him hold her. She
trembled slightly, her weariness swept away on a wave of
delicious memories.

Garrett chuckled softly as his lips brushed her chestnut

hair. "I must say, this is a more enthusiastic greeting than I'd dared hope for."

Stiffening, Eden pulled back and stared up into his beloved blue eyes. There was mild reproach in her voice when she asked, "Did you ever doubt that I would be glad to see you?"

He hesitated. "No. But after I heard you'd remarried—"

She turned her face away and broke out of his embrace.

After a moment, Garrett asked, "Are you happy with him?"

Eden nodded, still not looking at him. "Yes. Of course. You know Benjamin. He has all of Brett's best qualities—and—and more."

"I'm glad."

She turned back to him, her blue-green eyes almost pleading. "Are you Garrett? Really?"

"No." He smiled slightly. "I mean, I'm glad you have someone who's worthy of you. But I'm not glad you're married to another man."

"I wouldn't have thought you cared. I was a widow for four years."

He sighed. "I know. And for the last two years, ever since I found out you'd remarried, I've called myself every kind of fool."

Eden was silent, waiting for him to elaborate.

"At first, it just seemed too soon to ask. I knew you'd loved Brett, and I didn't want to seem like some vulture, swooping down as soon as he died. Then there was the ranch to think of. I couldn't just leave Burton in charge. He was too—inexperienced."

"You could have written."

"Maybe. But I was just so damned afraid you might not want me anymore."

"How could you have thought that, after that afternoon at the Tremont Hotel, when you agreed to join the ranch?"

"I don't know. I guess when I looked back on it I just couldn't feel sure you hadn't done it all for your husband and son."

"Oh, Garrett!"

"I know, I know. It sounds stupid now. I guess I just kept figuring that one day either you'd come down to Texas to check out the ranch, or I'd get up to Chicago on ranch business, and when we saw each other I'd know how things were between us. But then you wrote to Burton and said you were married, and all my dreams blew sky-high."

Averting her teary eyes, Eden was silent, groping for words.

Garrett sighed. "Well, I guess I was just stupid all the way around. I'd never have imagined you'd marry Benjamin. But I should have figured if I waited too long, *someone* would marry you. I swear, you look even more lovely than when I met you, twenty years ago."

Eden forced a smile. "Your eyes must be going bad on you! Lately, I've been feeling every one of my fifty-one years."

"It's not easy, doing everything, without a man, is it?" he said softly.

"No, it's not easy. But then, this war hasn't been easy on anyone."

There was an uncomfortable silence before he asked, "Eden, if I'd asked you, would you have married me?"

She hesitated. "What difference does it make now?"

"I didn't come to break up your marriage to Benjamin. I'd just like to know."

She drew a long breath. "Yes, I would have married you. Is that what you came all this way to find out?"

"Not really. I came just because I felt I had to see you. I had to know you were all right. And—I don't know, I guess I just needed you."

"And I need you," she whispered. "Oh, God, how I need you! But—oh, Garrett, why couldn't you have come sooner?"

Sighing, he enfolded her in his arms again.

"It's not the same as before," Eden sobbed. "I'm not as young and impulsive as I was then. And—Benjamin's never done anything to hurt me. I can't be unfaithful to him."

"I'm not asking you to be. But—you do still love me, don't you?"

"I've never stopped loving you."

Garrett smiled wryly. "Funny, isn't it, seventeen years ago, when I asked you to marry me, Benjamin was one of your reasons for refusing me. You said he needed you. And now you're married to him."

"Oh, darling, I wish you would have married in all those years."

"So do I. I wish I would have married you."

"Be serious!"

"I am." He hesitated. "Do you want me to go away again now?"

"Yes. No. Not yet. I don't know. It's so painful having you here. But, in a strange way, it's so comforting, too."

"I know. I feel the same way. If we've loved each other from a distance all these years—if we've loved each other without being able to be lovers—maybe it's not too much to hope we can love each other when we're together, without climbing into bed with one another."

Garrett paused, shaking his head. "I guess I've put it very badly. Does it make any sense to you at all?"

Eden nodded. "Yes. I don't know if it will work, but I'd like to try. I don't want to lose you again."

He smiled. "I'll have to leave again eventually, you know. I can't stay away from the ranch forever. And, no matter how pure and noble we manage to keep our love, it might get a little uncomfortable for both of us when Benjamin comes back."

"I know. Maybe it's foolish even to—" She broke off at a knock at the door.

"Mama? May I come in?"

Breaking away from Garrett, Eden whispered, "That's Paige." Then, louder, she called, "Of course, darling, come in!"

Paige opened the door, her green and gold eyes serious. "You're all right, aren't you? I was worried when I saw your door closed." The girl stopped abruptly, her eyes shifting to Garrett.

Laughing self-consciously, Eden said, "Of course I'm all right! You remember Mr. Martin, don't you? Our partner in the Double M ranch? We were just discussing some important business, and I didn't want to be disturbed. It's all right, though, I think we've just about finished now."

Smiling, Paige said, "Mr. Martin, I'm sorry I didn't recognize you right away. But, of course, I was only about eight or nine the last time we met."

Garrett smiled. "Yes, I'd venture to say you've changed a good deal more in the last few years than I have. Still, I think I would have known you. You look so like your mama."

Flushing, Paige murmured, "That's a great compliment, sir." Then she frowned. "But, if you're here about the ranch, I hope it's nothing—my brother's all right, isn't he?"

"When I left him, three months ago, Burton was in perfect health."

"Then, what brought you to Chicago? You haven't had trouble with the rebels?"

"No. At least not on the ranch. I led a cattle drive up to the Missouri River, to take some fresh meat to the Union troops stationed there. Then, since it was only a few hundred miles further, I decided to continue to Chicago. General Schofield was kind enough to give me safe conduct from Missouri."

Stifling a gasp, Eden busied herself with some papers on her desk. It would never do for Paige to realize she didn't even know about the cattle drive.

Paige, however, was far too excited and impressed even to notice her mother's reaction. "You mean, you drove a herd of cattle right through the war?"

Grinning, Garrett shook his head. "Well, now, it wasn't quite like that. There's not much fighting going on in Texas, and you won't find many battles in the middle of the Ozark Mountains. Of course, we did meet up with a few guerrillas—"

"You came through the mountains with a herd of cattle?" Paige's eyes were wide with admiration.

"Well, the Ozarks aren't exactly what you'd call full-scale mountains. Most of them aren't even half-a-mile high."

"Still, it's incredible even to conceive of doing something like that! Isn't it incredible, Mama?"

"Indeed," Eden nodded. "But Mr. Martin is an incredible man, which is precisely why your papa chose him to manage the Double M."

Paige shook her head. "Well, I still think it's really amazing! Did you lose many head on a drive like that?"

"Only nine out of the six hundred we started with." Garrett's voice softened. "Unfortunately, we did lose one of our vaqueros in a stampede."

Seeing the sudden pain in Garrett's eyes, Eden cut in. "Paige, darling, I'm sure Mr. Martin is exhausted from his trip. He was good enough to come directly here, to tell me the details of the drive. But now, I really think we should let him get some rest. Perhaps you can talk to him another time, before he leaves Chicago."

"Oh, certainly." Paige flushed. "I guess I just got carried away. Well, you'll be staying at our house, anyway, won't you, Mr. Martin?"

"No, actually, I thought I'd take rooms at the Tremont."

"Oh, no! Mama, you can't let your business partner stay at some stuffy old hotel, can you? What kind of hero's welcome is that, when we have so much space at home? After all, there's only you and me and Louise in that big house! If we went to Texas, we'd certainly stay at the ranch."

"Perhaps Mr. Martin feels more comfortable in a hotel," Eden said evenly.

"Oh, Mama, how can you even say such a thing! Wouldn't you feel more comfortable in a real home, Mr. Martin?"

"Well, I—" Garrett's eyes slid to Eden's.

"You're more than welcome to stay with us," Eden said noncommitally. "It's true, we do have plenty of room."

Garrett looked from Eden to Paige, then shrugged. "If you're really sure, then I'll be happy to accept the invitation."

"Wonderful!" Paige exclaimed. "Then you'll have plenty of time to tell us all about Burton, and the ranch, and your daring drive over the Ozarks!"

Eden quickly found she was glad for Garrett's presence, both at home and at the plant. With his intimate knowledge of cattle, and his quick grasp of the essentials of meat packing, Garrett was able to take over much of Eden's work. She trusted him to make decisions within the plant, and appreciated having someone to turn to when she needed to discuss a problem.

In a way, having Garrett at the plant was almost like having Benjamin there again. He lightened Eden's load, and his very presence brought a measure of joy and excitement back to her work.

But, Garrett was not Benjamin. Every night, Eden was painfully aware of that fact when, after an hour or two of relaxing conversation in the parlor, she and Garrett retired to separate bedrooms.

Since moving into the house, he had not touched her again. It was almost as if he was afraid to, as if he knew neither of them could maintain control if he did.

Still, despite all the pain of suppressed desire, she treasured his nearness and the depth of love that still burned between them.

To Eden's relief, Garrett's presence produced an added, unforeseen benefit. Thoroughly captivated by the handsome, world-wise, but unassuming rancher, Paige seemed to be losing interest in her young gambler. She rarely spoke of Jefferson Montgomery now, and Eden felt sure that she saw him only infrequently, much preferring to hear Garrett talk about ranching and droving.

They were at dinner, about a week after Garrett's arrival, discussing a letter that had just arrived from Clinton, when

Paige surprised both Garrett and Eden with her pointed question, "How is it, Mr. Martin, that you aren't serving in the army?"

Garrett looked questioningly at Eden, who quickly explained, "Paige has a young friend who chose not to serve, and I think she's anxious to use your case to defend him."

Flushing, Paige shook her head. "No. Jeff has nothing to do with this. I'm sorry. I certainly didn't mean to be impertinent, or to cast any aspersions on your courage, Mr. Martin. What I meant was, it would seem that a man daring enough to drive six hundred longhorns through the Ozarks would have enlisted at the first opportunity."

Smiling indulgently, Garrett said, "Well, some might say I'm a bit old for the army. I was forty-one when the war started. I'm forty-three now."

"Well, you don't seem any older than twenty-three! Anyway, they're drafting men up to forty-five now."

"That's true. But, until a few months ago, I was living in the Confederacy. Certainly you're not suggesting I should have enlisted there?"

"Of course not! I was just wondering if you ever thought of coming north and enlisting in the Union forces."

"Several times. But I hesitated to leave the ranch. Your brother was not too experienced, and I was afraid he might have trouble if the rebels tried to take over our cattle."

"But, you left now."

"Yes, I thought the circumstances warranted it—that I'd be more help to the Union by supplying fresh meat than I would have been as a solitary soldier toting a gun."

Paige sighed. "Well, I suppose I really have no right to cross-examine you this way when my own brother has chosen to remain on the ranch for the entire war. But, I really don't know Burton. I was only three when he left for California. And I feel, even after these few days, that I know you very well, and—oh, I don't even know the point of this discussion anymore! It's obvious, as you say, that you've more than done your part. I really do admire your ingenuity. Burton is lucky to have a partner like you to turn to."

Garrett smiled wryly. "I'll be sure to tell him you said so."

Later, when Paige had retired to her room to study, and Eden and Garrett had moved to the parlor, Eden said, "I hope Paige didn't upset you with her questions. She's young and impulsive, and I think her thoughts get a bit scrambled when she's around you." Smiling, she added, "In case you haven't noticed, my daughter seems to be a little in love with you!"

Laughing self-consciously, Garrett said, "I don't really think she is. Her youthful imagination has just blown me up to some kind of hero—when you and I know I'm just a very ordinary man!"

"Not ordinary, darling. And there's no reason to deny your effect on Paige. I'm certainly not jealous! If anything, I'm grateful. I couldn't have chosen a finer man for her to fall in love with. And I'm relieved to see the way you've taken her mind off her young gambler, Jefferson Montgomery."

Garrett frowned. "Eden, you're making me uncomfortable! I mean, I hope neither you nor Paige is waiting for me to propose to her!"

"Of course not! Paige knows you're too old for her. It's just a healthy, youthful infatuation that happens to come at a very opportune time. There are so few decent men in Chicago now, and you've given her a much-needed basis of comparison. I daresay, beside you, her gambler's self-centered exploits must pale."

"Umm. Well, she's a fine, sweet young woman, and I just wouldn't want to see her hurt in any way."

"I don't think there's much danger of that. You know," Eden mused, "Paige did say one thing tonight—about not knowing Burton—that's very true. I really don't even know him myself. His letters are all so terse and businesslike, and you've barely mentioned him since you've been here."

Without comment, Garrett got up to pour himself some brandy.

"Garrett?" Eden probed, "am I wrong in thinking you don't much like my eldest son?"

He concentrated on pouring his brandy. "It's not up to me to pass judgment on him."

"No. But I'd value your opinion."

Sighing, Garrett stared out at Wabash Avenue as he carefully formed an answer. "He's a bright boy, Eden. There's no question about that. He could probably do anything if he really put his mind to it."

"But?"

"Well, I think you were right when you came to me before

the ranch was started. He's given to exaggeration, and he thinks a great deal of himself."

"Are you trying to tell me he never owned a ranch in California?"

"Yes."

"Well, I've always suspected as much. To be honest, that lie doesn't even annoy me. He was only a boy then, and he wanted so badly for Brett and me to believe he was right in going to California."

Garrett was silent.

After a long moment, Eden asked, "What else?"

He ran his hands through his sun-bleached hair, weighing his thoughts before he turned to her. "Oh, hell, you might as well know! It may even save you some pain further down the road. Burton wants McKinnon Meats!"

Eden blinked. "What do you mean?"

"I mean that he considers himself the rightful heir to his father's fortune, and he's mad as hell that you took over and that Benjamin married you."

"But no one's trying to deny Burton anything that should be his! In time, the firm will pass to him, to Benjamin, and to Clinton, in equal shares. Although Brett had never made a will, I'm sure that's what he intended."

"No doubt you're right. But, your firstborn doesn't agree. He thinks Benjamin has no right to McKinnon Meats, and that everything ought to pass to him."

"Oh, Garrett, I'm certain you must be mistaken! If Burton is so displeased, why hasn't he communicated it to me?" Her voice faltered as she realized he had. Never had he written to congratulate her and Benjamin on their marriage or to wish them well.

Garrett shrugged. "I hate to say it, but I think he's just biding his time. He's hoping the war will eliminate his competition."

Paling, Eden whispered, "You can't mean that! He wouldn't wish for Benjamin or Clinton to be killed!"

"Well, maybe not Clinton. He's never said much about him. Maybe he figures Clint's not too interested in meat packing, anyway."

"But, Benjamin?" Her question was barely audible.

Gazing into her tortured eyes, Garrett slowly nodded.

She gave a short gasp of horror and dismay, and he hurried to enfold her in his arms. "I'm sorry, Eden," he murmured, stroking her chestnut hair. "Perhaps I shouldn't have told you. Still, I think it's best you know."

"I just don't understand it," Eden sobbed. "How can Burton hate his own brother enough to wish him dead?"

"I don't think it's really Benjamin he hates. It's just the thought of someone usurping his place at McKinnon Meats."

"But I thought he was happy at the Double M."

"He is, for the moment. He's happy playing the role of the cattle baron—having scores of men and thousands of longhorns beneath him. But I think from the first he saw the ranch simply as a stepping stone to more power. He thought he could use it to impress Brett with his capabilities until Brett was ready to hand over the entire meat-packing empire to him."

"Is he, at least, capable?" Eden asked hopefully.

Garrett sighed. "It's hard to say. As I said, he's intelligent, and he could probably develop an ability in almost anything. But, he does so little at the ranch it's hard to really judge his worth."

Frowning, Eden said, "I'm almost afraid to ask, but what *does* he do there?"

"Mostly, he entertains himself with our young Mexican cook." As Eden's frown deepened, he hurriedly added, "That's nothing to upset yourself about. It's perfectly normal behavior for a young man."

"I suppose," she agreed halfheartedly.

Dry-eyed now, she eyed Garrett keenly. "You don't much like working with him, do you?"

Garrett grinned wryly. "I don't much work with him."

She sighed. "I'm sorry. I never should have begged you to get involved in the Double M. Maybe it would have been best for everyone if I'd just stood back and let Burton fail there."

"No mother wants to watch her son fail."

"No. But perhaps he would have been a better man for it." She shook her head ruefully. "What a lot of lives I've wrecked with my meddling—yours, Ben's, Burton's."

"Don't say that!" He caught her chin in his hand and gave her a piercing stare. "I'm sure neither Ben nor I feel you've ruined our lives. As for Burton—what he thinks is hardly worth worrying about."

"Oh, Garrett, what am I going to do?"

"I don't think there's a great deal you can do, at least for the moment. Burton's only twenty-six. Young and headstrong. Perhaps as he gets older he'll change. Maybe then he'll realize that no one's trying to cheat him, and he'll appreciate the advantage of working with his brothers."

Eden stared at him pensively. "But you don't really expect that to happen, do you?"

"No, I don't. I'm not trying to turn you against your own son. I just think you ought to understand the situation."

She nodded. "I appreciate your honesty, and I value your judgment." For an instant, she hesitated. Then she asked, "Garrett, you don't think Burton is jealous enough of Ben to—I mean, he wouldn't actually do anything to threaten Ben's life?"

Garrett shook his head. "No. Burton talks and even thinks with a swagger. But, I don't think he's really inherently evil."

Forcing a smile, Eden said, "I'm glad to hear that. After all you've told me, I'm convinced I don't know him at all. But, after all, he's been away from home now for half his life. As soon as this war is over, I intend to go down to Texas to see him."

"And me?"

"Do you plan to go back there, even with the way you feel about working with Burton?"

"I certainly do! I've given that ranch six years of my life, and I'm not going to let it fail now. After all, I'm half owner of it."

Eden frowned. "But, how can you be sure it isn't falling apart right now, while you're away?"

"Because I left my old foreman, Charley Streeter, in charge."

Brightening, she asked, "Then you can still stay awhile?"

"As long as you want me," Garrett murmured as his hand caressed her cheek.

26
October–December 1863

Although they both knew that in time he would return to Texas, Eden and Garrett lived without thought of his ever leaving Chicago. They treasured each moment together, whether at the plant or at home.

Even while they continued to impose a vow of chastity upon themselves, they felt closer than many married couples ever felt in a lifetime. They were spiritual partners, sharing a joy so intense it demanded no physical demonstration.

Yet there always existed between them that flaming tension of suppressed desire. The memories of past lovemaking always lingered near the surface of their consciousness.

They felt, without discussing it, the certainty of their eventual separation, and that heightened the ecstasy of every shared moment.

The months flowed into one another, blurred by exhausting work, but sweetened by their closeness, until December, when the letter arrived from Clinton.

Eden entered the house alone that night. In the crush of preparing a shipment to the Army, she had not had time to stop for lunch, and she had nearly fainted when, at nine P.M., she and Garrett had been supervising the loading of the meat.

Insisting he could finish the work himself, Garrett had put her in a carriage, with orders to go home, eat, and rest.

Now, as she let herself into the foyer, Eden called to Louise, their aging cook. The old woman hurried from the kitchen, shaking her head reprovingly.

"I've had your dinner ready since six," Louise grumbled. "I'd begun to think you were never coming home."

"I'm sorry, Louise. There just wasn't even a moment to send a message."

"Hmph! Well, I can't guarantee as it won't all be dried out by now, but I'll get you something immediately. Is Mr. Martin home, too?"

233

"No. I'm afraid he won't be arriving 'til later. Could you be
an angel and fix me a tray and bring it up to my room?"

"All right." Louise turned back to the kitchen, muttering,
"And I suppose when Mr. Martin gets home I'll have to go
through the same thing all over again!"

A quarter of an hour later, when Louise brought her dinner tray, Eden had changed into a nightdress and wrapper,
and was sitting up in bed.

"My goodness!" Louise fussed, "you do look peaked! Not
getting sick, are you?"

Eden smiled weakly. "No, it's just my usual exhaustion—a
bit stronger than usual."

"Well, I don't see why you have to work so hard, especially
now that Mr. Martin's here."

Grimacing, Eden changed the subject. "Is Paige in her
room?"

"No. She sent word she's spending the night at her friend
Jessica Ford's. I hope she really is—that she's not out with
that gambler."

Eden frowned. "I don't think she's even seen Jefferson in
weeks."

"Oh, no?" Louise raised her brows skeptically. "Well, I
hope you're right." She set the tray across Eden's legs, smiling as her hand brushed an envelope lying beside the dinner
plate. "Anyway, here's something to cheer you up. A letter
from Clinton, I believe."

"Wonderful!" Eden excitedly snatched up the envelope as
Louise started for the door.

"Now, don't let your dinner get cold while you're reading,"
the old woman chided.

Smiling, Eden took a bite of roast beef, and waved her fork
at the cook. As soon as the door closed, she dropped the fork
and tore open the letter.

Dearest Mama,
I'm sure by now you've heard about the great success of our campaign at Chattanooga. We've really
driven the Confederates from Tennessee, and I'm
certain it will represent a turning point in the war.

After the bitter defeat I witnessed at Chickamauga,
victory indeed tasted sweet!

I had the honor of serving under General Philip
Sheridan in one of the most awe-inspiring charges of

this war. No doubt you've read something in the *Tribune* by now about the assault on Missionary Ridge. By rights, General Bragg and his rebels should have crushed us. We were, every man of us, a perfect target for the Confederates at the top of the ridge.

That we won the battle can only be credited to General Sheridan's daring leadership and the unwavering spirit of our troops.

You should have heard us going up that mountain— singing all kinds of songs, screaming like madmen, whooping like kids on a picnic, with rebel rifle fire and cannonballs whizzing around us all the while! I saw a Union bugler who just typified the spirit of the day. One of his legs had been shot off, but he just sat up on a rock outcrop and kept blowing "Charge!" until he fainted!

You know I've never been a war-hungry, bloodthirsty soldier, but the whole experience really sent chills down my spine. I think our spirit simply overwhelmed the rebels. What could they do but run when they saw these twenty thousand madmen rushing at them!

Of course, the losses were terrible, though nothing as compared to Chickamauga. Our side lost over seven hundred men. Nearly five thousand more were wounded.

That brings me to some rather unpleasant news. I was lucky enough to escape injury at Chickamauga, so I suppose it was too much to expect the same luck here.

Let me begin by assuring you I am perfectly all right now. Of course, I will have to remain hospitalized for some time, but the doctors say I am out of danger and I thank God I am alive.

About three quarters of the way up Missionary Ridge, I took a rifle ball in the stomach. I could not be rescued until some time later, and I have no idea how long I lay there. I lost a great deal of blood and fainted.

The doctors were able to remove the ball and "put me back together," but it seems I developed peritonitis as a result of the wound. I had a few

touchy days, but there is definitely nothing to worry
about now.

I hope that you and Paige are fine, and that
you've heard good news from Benjamin.

I'll close now, as I'm still a bit weak, and the
doctors say I ought not to overtax myself.

Please don't worry about me. Have as fine a Christmas as you can without your sons and husband. I
miss you all, but, for this year, I consider my life
enough of a Christmas gift. Next year, God willing,
we can all be together again.

> Your loving son,
> Clinton

Squeezing her eyes tightly shut, Eden sobbed softly as she
dropped the letter. She pushed away the dinner tray, her
hunger drowned by her concern for her son.

She pictured him lying in some overcrowded, understaffed
military hospital, his blue-gray eyes veiled with pain, his
middle bound by a tight bandage, gray and dirty, no doubt,
from infrequent changing.

Was he really all right? Or was he, with characteristic
concern for her, simply minimizing his problems?

If only she could see him! If only she could rumple his
sandy hair, as she had so often when he was a little boy!

She thought of him as a toddler, upsetting the honey crock.
As a young boy, comforting her after Burton had run off to
California. As a young man, going to Kansas to fight for his
principles, then returning, disillusioned, but not embittered.

Suddenly seized by the fear she would never see her
beloved son again, Eden gave in to sobs and tears that
seemed to well up from her very soul.

She didn't know how long she sobbed before she heard
someone at the door. Looking up, through her haze of tears,
she saw Garrett's creased brow.

"Eden? When you didn't answer my knock, I thought
perhaps you were asleep. But then I heard—"

A sob catching in her throat, she looked away from him.
She heard him striding across the room to her bedside.

"Eden, darling, what is it?" His eyes took in the letter, and
a sudden pain stabbed his heart. "Not—not Benjamin?"

"No." Picking up the letter, she pushed it toward him.
"Clinton!"

Garrett quickly scanned the letter. "But, darling, he says he's all right!"

"I know. But I'm afraid to believe it. He's so far away, and—oh, Garrett, what a terrible, terrible thing this war is!"

He sat down on the bed and cradled her against his chest, stroking her back, murmuring, "I know, darling. It is terrible. But, you've got to be glad he came through it all right. You've got to believe it will all be over soon, and you'll have your family home with you again."

"But when? Will it be over soon enough? Even if Clinton is all right, what will happen when he's well and they let him out of the hospital? Won't they just send him off to another battlefield so the rebels can have another shot at him? Have you any idea how many tens of thousands of young men have already died in this war? I'm sick of it!"

"We all are. But, we have to hold on to whatever hope and joy we can grasp each day. We have to rejoice in whatever small scraps of happiness fall our way."

"I try! Really I do! Oh, God, Garrett, what would I do if I didn't have you here?"

He answered in the only way that seemed right at the moment. His hand caressed her cheek, slid beneath her chin, and turned her mouth up to meet his.

Their lips lingered against each other for a long, questioning moment. Shivering, she pressed herself closer to his warmth.

"I need you so much," she whispered. "Everyone thinks I'm so strong, so independent. But, I need you so much."

Tears flooded her eyes again, spilling over to stream down her cheeks. He bent to kiss each tiny rivulet, tasting the warm saltiness as his lips moved up to caress her swollen eyes.

The dinner tray slid away, falling to the floor with a clatter that neither seemed to hear.

He eased her down on the bed, pressing his lean, hard form against her. He had intended merely to hold her, to comfort her. But, within moments, he was comforting her in the same way he had twenty years earlier.

His lips wandered down her body, teasing, caressing, inflaming the passions she had so long held in check. An involuntary moan escaped her throat as she pressed him to her. His mouth moved back to hers as he slid into her welcoming warmth.

At last, they were one again, filling each other's needs and basking in the blissful forgetfulness of passion. Her sobs faded, replaced by moans of fulfillment.

For a while, nothing mattered except their pulsing, inter-twined flesh. And, when at last they floated in exhausted satisfaction, they fell asleep without further talk or thought.

The bedroom was still blanketed with predawn grayness when Eden awoke and saw Garrett standing by the window.

As if sensing her eyes upon him, he turned and sighed heavily. "I'll be leaving soon," he said softly.

She frowned, trying to comprehend. "For the plant? Was there some problem last night?"

He shook his head. "For the ranch. For Texas."

Eden gasped, and he walked slowly toward her, his blue eyes swimming with misery.

"I have to go, Eden. Can't you see that? After last night, it's no good trying to pretend any longer. I can't go back to sleeping in the room down the hall, as if nothing ever happened."

She sighed, her blue-green eyes caressing his features. "No, I don't suppose you could. I don't suppose I would even want you to."

"I'm sorry. After all these months, I thought it wouldn't happen."

"Don't blame yourself. I wanted you. Even now, I'm not sure I regret that it happened. Only, I don't want you to go away."

"And I don't want to leave you. Now, more than ever, I want to stay. But, you do see that I must go, don't you?"

She nodded, forcing herself to think of Benjamin, to feel his pain at her betrayal. If Garrett did not go now, they would never be able to separate, and they would destroy Benjamin.

Grimacing, Garrett sat down on the edge of the bed and took her hand. "I feel like such a cad, leaving you alone."

"I won't be alone. I have Paige. And the plant will keep me too busy to think."

He picked up Clinton's letter from the floor beside the bed, and stared at it pensively before raising his eyes to hers. "You will be all right, won't you?" It was as much a plea as a question.

"Yes. Last night I was just overwrought. Exhausted. War-weary. And then when I read about Clinton—" She shook her head briskly, blinking the tears from her eyes. "Really, I'll be fine. I know I'm a good deal more fortunate than most women who have family in the war."

Pulling her into a tight embrace, he hid his glassy eyes in her chestnut hair. "Oh, Eden," he murmured, "if only we'd met at the right time, perhaps we wouldn't always be saying good-bye."

They were silent for several minutes, clinging to each other one last time. Then the clock in the hall struck seven, and he reluctantly pulled away."

"I'd better be going."

"Won't you at least stay for breakfast?"

He shook his head. "I think it would be better not to draw out our good-byes. Don't come down with me. I'll ask Louise to pack me some food to take along."

Eden nodded, the lump in her throat making it impossible to speak.

His lips brushed hers, and then he got up and walked to the bedroom door.

His hand on the knob, he turned back to her. "Eden, if anything happens—I mean if Ben—" He choked on the words.

"Yes, Garrett," she whispered before turning to bury her face in the pillow.

An hour and a half later, bathed, dressed, and dry-eyed, Eden sat alone at breakfast, determined to go to the plant and make the best of the day. As she lingered over a last cup of coffee, Paige came in from the foyer.

Forcing a smile, Eden said, "Good morning, darling. Did you have a pleasant evening at your friend Jessica's?"

Paige nodded distractedly. "Yes—we had a very nice time."

"I must say I didn't expect you home this early. With the Christmas holiday from school, I thought you would be sleeping later."

"Oh. Well, Jessica wanted to be up early to get ready to do some Christmas shopping. And I thought I'd just come on home to see if you and Mr. Martin needed me at the plant."

"How very thoughtful of you, Paige! I must say I'll be happy for your help. Mr. Martin's left for Texas, you see."

Paige gasped. "Today? Already?"

Eden nodded.

"But why didn't anyone warn me?"

Frowning at her daughter's distress, Eden said, "I didn't know myself until—last night. Apparently he'd been thinking of returning to the ranch for some time, and finally decided he couldn't put it off any longer."

"Well, I would have at least liked to have said good-bye."

Eden shrugged. "Well, it can't be helped. You were away, and he wished to leave quite early. At any rate, I'm sure he appreciates all the kindness you showed him while he was staying here."

"But why in the world did he decide to leave today? Surely he can't expect to ride all the way to Texas through the snow!"

"I think he intended to take the train as far as Kansas City. He was asking Louise about the schedule this morning. Anyway, I'm certain he knows what he's doing. Mr. Martin traveled in worse weather when he lived in Iowa and Illinois."

Eden paused, studying her daughter carefully. "What's wrong, Paige?"

The girl jumped. "What? Oh, nothing. I'm just surprised, that's all. When someone's lived in your home almost three months, it's just odd to suddenly find him gone."

"You're sure that's all?"

Paige flushed. "Of course, Mama!"

Draining her coffee, Eden nodded. "Do you feel like going to the plant with me right away?"

"I—I haven't had breakfast yet. Why don't you go ahead, and I'll meet you there in a bit."

"Fine. I don't want you missing any meals. I tried that yesterday, with disastrous results." Eden got up and went for her cloak. "Oh, by the way, there's a letter from Clinton on my bureau. He was wounded at Chattanooga, but he's fine now."

Surprised that Paige did not react to the news, Eden hesitated in the doorway. Then she shrugged to herself and turned away. "Take your time with breakfast, darling. I'll see you at the plant."

After her mother let herself out, Paige sat down at the table and buried her face in her hands. What was she going to do? She had hoped to find her mother and Mr. Martin both at breakfast, and somehow to detain Mr. Martin while her mother went on to the plant. Now it seemed she wasn't going to be able to talk to him at all.

But she had to talk with him! She absolutely couldn't

discuss her problem with her mother. Mama was always so understanding, but she couldn't bear to think of how Mama would react to her news.

It would be hard enough to tell Mr. Martin—Garrett as she always thought of him privately. She was sure he'd be shocked. But, perhaps he'd also see that there was a way he could help her. He could take her to the ranch in Texas, at least until it was all over. And, maybe, if they had some time alone, he might even fall in love with her and make everything all right.

Of course, that was too much to hope for. Besides, how could he take her with him when he'd already gone?

Unless his train hadn't left yet. Sometimes the trains were delayed by weather, or by troop movements somewhere along the line.

Jumping up from the table, Paige rushed out to the stable. She quickly saddled a horse, mounted, and sent it galloping toward the Chicago, Burlington, and Quincy train station, at Sixteenth Street and Michigan Avenue.

At the sooty, crowded station, Paige pushed her way to a clerk's window and demanded whether the train west to Quincy had departed yet.

The clerk scratched his head with infuriating nonchalance and mumbled, "Well, I don't know, for sure. She's supposed to pull out of here at eight o'clock every morning. But, ever since the war started, these here military transports and supply trains get precedence on the tracks. If I was you, I'd just mosey on over to the tracks and—"

Without waiting for him to finish, Paige turned and pushed toward the tracks. A passenger train was waiting, its locomotive belching smoke as it prepared to leave.

Just as she turned to ask the man beside her the train's destination, a conductor leaned out of a car and yelled, "All aboard for Aurora, Galesburg, Quincy, and points west!"

For a moment, Paige stood frozen, watching the passengers scrambling aboard, searching for a familiar blond head among them. Then, running along the side of the train, she looked frantically for the tall, rugged form of Garrett Martin.

The train clicked rhythmically as it began to crawl out of the station. Still, she did not see him.

The train whistle hooted, and Paige knew that in a moment the train would pick up speed and her chance would be lost. There was no time now to weigh the alternatives.

As she reached the entrance to one of the passenger cars, she grasped the railing beside the door and flung herself onto the steps leading to the car.

Panting from the exertion, she hauled herself up to the top step and sat down to catch her breath. She was sitting with her face in her hands when the conductor found her.

"You sick, miss?" he asked, touching her shoulder.

Paige shook her head and pulled herself to her feet. "No. I—I became separated from my—my guardian in the crowd. I just have to find him. He has our tickets."

The conductor frowned. "Where are you heading?"

"Kansas City, by way of Quincy."

He nodded. "Well, you've got the right train, all right. And it's a long way to Quincy. I suspect you'll find him by then."

"Yes. I'm sure I will. You needn't trouble yourself about me."

Shrugging, the conductor entered the car to begin taking tickets, while Paige turned to the connecting car to begin her search.

What in the world am I doing here? she wondered. I must be mad! Even when I find Garrett, what can I say to him? Whatever made me think I could talk to him more easily than to Mama?

She considered throwing herself back off the train. But it was now moving far too rapidly, and upset though she was, she had no desire to kill herself. Squaring her shoulders, she began her search.

Paige found Garrett in the third car she entered. He was sitting alone, lost in thought, his hat brim pulled low over his eyes. For a long moment, she hesitated, aware that she could easily walk by without him noticing her.

Timidly clearing her throat, she whispered, "Excuse me, Mr. Martin. Could I share your seat?"

He pushed back his hat, and his blue eyes flew open. "Paige, what in the world are you doing—" He broke off as his eyes widened in fear. "Eden—your mother—something's happened?"

Forcing a smile, she shook her head. "No. Nothing's happened. At least not to Mama."

"Then who? One of your brothers? Ben? Was there a telegram?"

"No."

"Then what the devil are you doing here?"

"I—I have a problem. I want to talk to you."

Garrett rolled his eyes. "And you couldn't talk to me while we were still in Chicago? You couldn't talk to your mother? Does she even know you're here?"

"No."

He sighed in exasperation.

"I'll send her a wire when we get to Texas."

"Texas! You're not going to Texas! You're going to get off at the first stop and ride right back to Chicago!"

With a stubborn shake of her auburn curls, Paige declared, "No! I'm not!"

"Your mother will be frantic!"

"If I stayed in Chicago, my mother would be frantic very soon, anyway."

Garrett drew a long, deliberate breath. "Paige, I'm sure you're underestimating your mother. Whatever your problem, I'm certain she'll be glad to help you handle it."

"I don't think so. You see," she paused and dropped her eyes, "I'm going to have a baby."

Stifling a gasp, Garrett took her hand. "Paige, are you sure?"

She nodded.

"You know, sometimes young, innocent girls imagine all kinds of things will make them have babies, when, really—"

"I'm not that innocent," she cut him off quietly.

"I see. The gambler?"

She nodded.

"Does he know?"

"It doesn't matter."

"What do you mean, it doesn't matter? If he's any kind of a man, he'll marry you! If it will help any, I'll go back with you and have a talk with him."

"It wouldn't help. He left Chicago early this morning. Anyway, Mama wouldn't want me to marry him. She never liked him."

"No. But under the circumstances—" He sighed. "She really thought you weren't seeing him anymore."

"I wasn't. At least, hardly ever. But—" She broke off. How could she tell Garrett she'd begun seeing Jeff again when she realized Garrett would never think of her as anything but her mother's daughter? It would be too humiliating!

This whole conversation was already too humiliating! Why had she ever followed him?

"Just why did you ever conceive of going to Texas?" Garrett asked gently.

"I just thought it would be better than staying in Chicago. At least I wouldn't be embarrassing Mama. She could just say I went to visit my brother."

"In the middle of a war?"

"Well, maybe she could say I went away on business for her. Surely she could find some reasonable explanation."

Garrett was silent, staring out at the passing countryside. His heart went out to this girl. But, what could he do? Surely she wouldn't be better off at the ranch. Burton would probably relish having something to hold over her and Eden.

He turned his gaze back to Paige, intending to tell her they would both get off at Aurora and he would take her back to her mother.

But he caught his breath at her flushed cheeks, her high-chiseled cheekbones, her gleaming auburn hair. Even with her gold-flecked green eyes, she looked so like Eden when he'd first met her.

Perhaps it was the obstinate tilt of her jaw. Or the strong, yet vulnerable, curve of her lips. At any rate, the words that came out of Garrett's mouth were not at all what he'd intended.

"Paige," he said gently, "will you marry me?"

27
December 1863–April 1864

In Quincy, Illinois, while they waited for a connecting train, Garrett and Paige were married by a local judge. They had just enough time to send a wire to Eden before boarding the Hannibal and St. Joseph Railroad train that linked Quincy with Kansas City.

Three weeks later, they were riding into the Double M ranch, and Garrett was still asking himself why he had married her.

Paige had been surprisingly little trouble on the rugged journey south from Kansas City, where the rail lines ended. The war had suspended stagecoach service between Missouri and Texas, so they had been forced to purchase horses for the journey. She had never complained, even on the nights when, far from a farm or ranch house, they had spread their bedrolls beneath the stars.

Still, Garrett could not quite believe that he had married Eden's daughter, a mere girl twenty-seven years younger than he. Thinking back, he could not even understand the noble impulse that had forced him to propose to her. He wondered how he could ever be a husband to the daughter of the one woman he would always love.

So far, he had avoided the physical intimacy due him by marriage, explaining that he did not want to hurt Paige or the child she was carrying. But how would he explain himself after the child was born, when, he knew, he would still shrink from touching her?

As they dismounted before the ranch house, Burton came out from the kitchen, smiling sardonically.

"Well, well, Garrett," he said, "I'd begun to think you'd forsaken the rugged ranch life for the comforts of Chicago." His gaze moved lazily to Paige, and he pursed his lips as he eyed her. "But I see that you at least made the trip worthwhile. Is she going to be a permanent resident of the Double M?"

"I should think so," Garrett replied coolly. "She's my wife."

"Your wife?" Burton choked back a laugh. "My God, man, she's young enough to be your daughter! I swear, the whole world's gone crazy! My mother marries a boy who could practically have been her son, and now you—"

"I'll thank you to show her a little respect."

Sobering, Burton swept into an exaggerated bow. "Your pardon, ma'am. Pleased to meet you, Mrs. Martin."

Paige, who had so far regarded the exchange uneasily, giggled nervously. "You really don't know me, do you Burton?"

He frowned. "Should I?"

"I suppose not, since I was only three when you left Chicago. I'm Paige, your sister, Paige!"

"Paige?" Burton looked incredulously from her to Garrett. "What kind of joke is this, Martin? Who is she, really? My sister? Your wife? Or neither?"

"Both," Garrett said curtly.

For a moment, Burton was speechless. Then he demanded,

"What the hell is this? Another plot to cheat me out of my inheritance?"

Paige gasped. "Burton, what are you talking about?"

"Never mind. It doesn't concern you. I suppose you're too young to really be involved. It was probably all Mama and Benjamin's idea—to have you inherit Martin's share, so I can never even get the ranch to myself!"

Garrett shook his head irritably. "You're even crazier than I thought, Burt! For one thing, I haven't even got one foot in the grave yet, so no one's going to inherit anything for a good long time. For another, despite what you might think, your mother has no intention of cheating you out of anything. And finally, Paige and I decided to marry without any interference from your mother."

Burton raised his brows. "Does Mama approve?"

"She didn't—" Paige began, but Garrett cut her off.

"She didn't disapprove. I'm sure she was surprised, but she didn't question our decision."

"I see." Burton shrugged. "Well, it's probably just as well we'll have another woman around here anyway. We might need her in a couple of months. Conchita's expecting a baby in April."

Garrett frowned. "You've married her?"

"Hell no!" Burton scowled. "And don't start lecturing me about my moral obligations!"

"I wasn't about to. But, you might want to think about saving your own skin. Does her brother, Rafael, know?"

"Rafael," Burton replied with a wry smile, "is no longer with us. His horse was frightened by a rattler last month, and Rafael had the misfortune of being half asleep upon him at the time."

Garrett grimaced. "He was thrown?"

Nodding, Burton said, "His neck was broken. There was nothing anyone could do."

Garrett clenched his fists, glancing at Paige, who was studying her brother with horrified fascination. He had hoped, for her sake at least, that Burton would have mellowed during the months he had been away.

Forcing himself to speak deliberately, Garrett said, "I trust there were no other catastrophes while I was away?"

"Nothing to speak of. You can ask your old friend, Charley, for a full accounting."

"I'll do just that as soon as I get Paige settled. It's been a grueling trip for her, and I'm sure she'd like to rest and refresh herself."

"Don't worry about my little sister," Burton said with sudden amiability. "Conchita and I will take care of her." Looking around in surprise, he asked, "She doesn't have any trunks?"

"We thought it would be easier to have her things sent later."

"I suppose so. Well, welcome to the Double M, little sister." Burton stepped up to Paige and hugged her tightly. "I'm sure we'll do all we can to make you happy here."

Garrett's eyes narrowed as he gazed at the embracing brother and sister. It was the reception he would have hoped for when they first arrived, the reception he would have expected from any other brother.

But, he didn't for a moment believe the relationship between the three of them would be smooth from then on. And the challenging glint in Burton's eye as he looked over Paige's shoulder only confirmed his dread of the future.

An uneasy truce existed on the Double M ranch for the next several months. Paige, who had so hoped to love her older brother, found herself despising his selfishness and insensitivity. Though he treated her more kindly than he did anyone else on the ranch, she was appalled by his mistreatment of the sweet Conchita. The fact that Conchita's situation so closely resembled her own with Jefferson Montgomery made Paige doubly sympathetic to the Mexican woman.

Feeling even less able to tolerate Burton than in the past, Garrett spent most of his time out on the range. He felt guilty leaving Paige at the ranch house for days on end, but consoled himself that there was little he could do for her.

At any rate, he preferred to suffer the guilt than to endure the discomfort of being with her. He was unfailingly kind to her, and even consented when she begged him to show her more of the ranch. But he could not reconcile himself to the fact she was his wife, tied to him until death.

Several times, he began letters to Eden, explaining why he had married her daughter. But, apart from the fact he could not articulate the reasons, even to himself, he could not betray Paige by revealing her secret.

Paige was his wife, for better or for worse. If he could give her nothing else, he at least owed her loyalty and discretion.

Not even Eden would ever know Paige had been carrying another man's child when they married.

Besides, what good would it really do to tell Eden? If she understood the marriage more, if she thought him more noble, if she loved him more than ever, what difference could it make? Perhaps it would be better, in the end, if she loved him less, if she felt that he had betrayed her. Now that they both were married, it should be clear at last their own love could have no future.

Eden's first letter after Garrett and Paige arrived in Texas was filled with restrained congratulations. She was glad, she wrote, that Garrett and Paige were happy together, and she assured Paige she could not have chosen a finer husband. She was only sorry they had kept their plans secret from her, since every mother dreams of attending her daughter's wedding. However, she wished them well, and looked forward to visiting them after the war.

Ignorant of her mother's true feelings, Paige was relieved by the letter. Garrett, however, imagined Eden's pain, and cursed himself again for marrying her daughter.

In April, Conchita gave birth to a dark-haired baby boy, whom she named Miguel. It was a long, difficult birth, during which Conchita screamed and writhed in pain and Burton left the ranch house in disgust.

While Garrett rode to Fort Belknap for a doctor, Paige, pale and frightened, tried to assist Conchita. She had no idea what to do, and was terrified by this first view of childbirth.

When the doctor finally arrived, Paige left Garrett to assist him, while she ran to her room, vomited uncontrollably, and collapsed on the bed, drenched in sweat.

Hours later, when she heard the child's first lusty scream, Paige summoned the strength to creep down the hallway. She waited anxiously outside Conchita's room until the doctor and Garrett emerged.

"Is she—are they—all right?" she whispered.

The doctor smiled with the condescension of one who has seen scores of births. "Of course! She has a fine, big boy. A cowboy no doubt. He put up quite a struggle coming out."

Frowning at his young wife's pale face and quivering lips, Garrett asked gently, "Are *you* all right, Paige?"

Unconvinced by her nod, he turned to the doctor. "She's expecting our first child in a few months."

"Is she?" The doctor's brows rose as his eyes traveled over

her trim figure. There could be a pregnancy concealed beneath those stiff crinolines, but she could not be very far along and still have a waist so tiny.

His eyes traveled back to her pale face, noting the fine line of sweat beaded on her brow and upper lip. "She does look a bit peaked. Maybe it's just the excitement and exertion of the Mexican woman's labor, but I'll have a look at her if you'd like."

Garrett nodded. "I'd appreciate that, doctor."

After examining Paige, the doctor called Garrett into the bedroom. Smiling, he announced, "Well, Mr. Martin, you'll be glad to know there's nothing to worry about. No doubt your wife needs a bit of rest, but, after that, she should be just fine."

"And the baby?"

The doctor hesitated. "I don't want to disappoint either of you, but she isn't carrying a baby."

Paige gasped. "But I am! I know I am!"

Shaking his head, the doctor asked, "How long have you suspected it?"

"Since December," she whispered.

"Why?"

"Well, because—" She flushed. Not being intimate with Garrett, she felt embarrassed discussing the situation in front of him. "Because of the usual signs," she whispered.

Sensing her discomfort, the doctor did not press her for specifics. "I see. And you've had no hemorrhaging since then? No sharp pains?"

She shook her head.

After several minutes silence, the doctor said slowly, "Well, sometimes when a woman wants a child very badly, she experiences the usual symptoms of pregnancy when she is not actually carrying a child. I've heard of it happening, occasionally, to women of ill-repute, too, when they begin worrying that they might be with child." Catching sight of Garrett's scowl, he said quickly, "Of course, that wouldn't concern you."

He patted Paige's shoulder patronizingly. "My advice to you, young lady, is simply to relax and get some rest. You're very young, reasonably healthy, and you've plenty of time to bear all the children you and your husband could want."

Turning, he nodded to Garrett, who showed him out of the ranch house.

Alone in the bedroom, all Paige could feel was profound relief that she would not have Jefferson's child, and would not soon have to bear the same suffering as Conchita. But, when Garrett returned to the room, still scowling, she felt suddenly fearful.

Her green and gold eyes widened and she whispered, "You don't—you can't think I tricked you?"

He shrugged carelessly. "Why should I think that?"

"I didn't! I swear I didn't! I really thought I was carrying a child!"

"I suppose you did think so. You heard what the doctor said—that worrying about it can make a woman have all the symptoms."

Paige flinched. He had never made her feel guilty for the circumstances of their marriage. But now she knew he was thinking of the doctor's allusion to whores. Unaware of his true feelings, she supposed he was blaming her for cheating him of months of marital intimacy.

"Oh, God, Garrett!" she sobbed. "How can I make it up to you?"

"There's nothing to make up. I don't suppose it's really your fault. I just think it's a shame that—"

She caught her breath. "That you married me? You're sorry now, aren't you?"

"I didn't say that! It's just a shame you had to leave your mother so abruptly, so young. A shame you have to waste what should be your young, carefree years on an isolated ranch."

"I don't mind, Garrett," she insisted. "I didn't plot it! Honestly, I didn't! But, I don't mind anything, as long as I'm your wife!"

He looked at her, her auburn hair falling haphazardly from its pins, her green and gold eyes streaming with tears, and he could not say anything more. Sitting down on the edge of the bed, he took her in his arms for the first time in their marriage.

She clung to him with youthful devotion, while he stroked her hair. But he did not feel the stirrings of passion that had always overcome him when he comforted Eden.

With a wry smile, he thought of the final irony possible in the situation. What if Benjamin did not come home from the war? What if Eden was finally free, while he was married to a mere child he would never have had to marry?

28
September 1864

"Ah, Sherman should have taken us with him," a young soldier muttered impatiently. "What's the point of our sitting here, watching Atlanta, when all the action's down south at Jonesboro?"

"You don't hear me complaining!" an older sergeant retorted. "Who wants to march another fifteen miles, anyway? I've marched enough since Chattanooga to last me the rest of my life!"

"Yeah, but I hear it's harvest time further south," another man in blue chimed in. "They're probably all eating that succulent sweet corn, while we're here rotting in these trenches, eating stale Army rations!"

"Well, the old one-armed rebel Hood's still in Atlanta, you know," said the old sergeant. "We may see some action yet."

Clinton McKinnon smiled to himself as he listened to the banter of the Union's Army of the West, entrenched outside Atlanta.

It was September 1. The Union had been driving toward this goal since May, when Clinton had been released from the hospital in Chattanooga and assigned as an adjutant on the staff of Major General Henry W. Slocum.

Under the command of General William Tecumseh Sherman, one hundred thousand men in blue had set out from Chattanooga, Tennessee. They had defeated the rebels at Resaca, Georgia, suffered a setback at Kennesaw Mountain, then triumphantly crossed the Chattahoochee River, the last great barrier before Atlanta.

By mid-July, the rebel leaders were saying there was no way to stop Sherman short of Atlanta. By the end of that month, the Union had proved them right, defeating General Hood in the Battle of Atlanta, north of the city. Now it was only a matter of time before the city itself fell.

Leaving Slocum's forces to guard the city, Sherman had

taken the rest of his army southwest, to cut off the rail lines
to Atlanta. Hood had sent forces under General Hardee to
meet them at Jonesboro. The word coming north tonight was
that Hardee had been defeated.

Perhaps, Clinton thought hopefully, it would all be over
soon. General Grant was making progress north of them, in
Virginia. Perhaps by Christmas he would be back home in
Chicago.

Suddenly, the sky over Atlanta was ablaze with bright
lights. The ground quivered under the feet of the entrenched
army.

"What the devil!" someone cried. "Is Hood attacking?"

"He can't be! He hasn't got the forces left in Atlanta to beat
us!"

"Then, what's going on?"

The questions and exclamations rushed up and down the
trenches. Clinton went to find General Slocum, who sent him
to the picket lines for an explanation.

The explosions continued, reverberating through the
trenches. Still, it seemed there was no fire directed at the
Union forces. As Clinton reached the pickets, a tremendous
cheer rose from the lookouts, carrying back to their entrenched comrades.

"What is it?" Clinton demanded. "What's happening?"

Turning to him with a gleeful smile, a picket exclaimed,
"Hood's finally admitted defeat! He's pulling out of Atlanta!"

Looking toward the city, Clinton finally understood the
explosions. General Hood's rear guard was blowing up the
carloads of ammunition they could not take with them!

The next morning, General Slocum led his troops into the
defeated city. For the most part, the men were in high
spirits, joking among themselves, anticipating the comforts of
a city after months in the trenches.

Clinton, however, was silent and thoughtful, wondering
how anyone could find comfort in this broken city, which had
once been the queen of the South. He swallowed the bile
that surged up his throat as he looked around at the ragged
shells of buildings, wrecked by the long bombardments.

Who had lived in those houses? Who had shopped in those
stores? How many lavish dinner parties had taken place in that
dining room, where a half-destroyed wall revealed brocaded
wallpaper, blackened by gunpowder? Where were the inhabi-

tants now? What if this had happened in Chicago? What would have become of Mama?

Along the parade route, women were hurrying out to set buckets of drinking water, appeasement offerings to their conquerors, at the curb. Many of the men, stopping to drink, grabbed at the frightened women, lewdly inquiring what other gifts they might offer.

Sickened and embarrassed by his comrades, Clinton turned away. But, it was a hot day, and he could not resist stopping for water a few blocks later. Stepping to the curb, he took a long drink from a pail that had just been set down by an attractive young blonde girl.

"Thank you," he said quietly, as he set the bucket down. "It must be hard to be so kind after what we've done to your city."

The girl stared at him with hard, unflinching blue eyes. "It's not kindness," she said coldly and deliberately. "And don't think for a minute that it's love for you Yankees. Call it self-preservation. It's nothing more." Turning stiffly, she walked away.

The troops marched to City Hall, where Slocum raised the Stars and Stripes. Then he sent Clinton to the telegraph office with a message for Secretary of War Stanton: "General Sherman Has Taken Atlanta."

When Clinton rejoined his general, he was setting up headquarters in a modest, undamaged home. As adjutant, Clinton was given a small room to share with two other junior staff members. Then, he set to work preparing dispatches to Sherman and Grant.

At noon, the officers assembled in the dining room for a meal prepared and served by several local women who had reluctantly agreed to do so. To Clinton's mixed pleasure and discomfort, one of the women was the blonde he had spoken to that morning.

She was younger and prettier than the other women, and most of the men eyed her with interest. Still, there was something cold and forbidding about her, leading most of the officers to the conclusion they could find easier conquests elsewhere in the city.

As she moved stiffly and haughtily around the table, the girl's cornflower-blue eyes caught Clinton's. He felt a sharp stab of pleasure as he saw their momentary flash of recognition.

Then she turned away angrily, her long, slender neck rigidly proud.

After dinner, while the other officers lingered over cigars, Clinton slipped out the front of the house, then went around the back to find the kitchen.

He found the blonde struggling with a heavy tray of dishes, which he hurried to take from her. "I was glad to see you again at dinner," he said. "Will you continue working here?"

Ignoring both his question and his chivalry, the girl said, "I'm not here by choice!"

Clinton smiled faintly. "That goes without saying. Neither am I."

"Ha! you Yankees are the ones who started this war! All we wanted to do was secede in peace!"

"I'm sure no one really wanted a war," Clinton replied quietly. "But, now that we've been fighting for well over three years, let's hope at least some good comes of it."

"That's a foolish thing even to hope!"

He shrugged. "Maybe. But, if nothing else, at least the slaves will be free."

"What do you know about that? All you Yankees are always spouting self-righteousness about slavery, when you don't know a thing about it."

"I worked on the Underground Railroad for three years. I saw how desperately some of them wanted to be freed."

"And I've seen how devoted slaves can be to a good master. They're like children. They don't want freedom. They just want someone to take care of them."

"Jocelyn!" one of the older women called from the wash basin, "are you going to bring those dishes over here, or is that Yankee going to requisition them before they're even washed?"

Clinton carried the dishes over to the basin, then turned back to the blonde. "Jocelyn," he repeated. "What a lovely name!"

Without answering, the girl picked up a linen towel and began drying the dishes the other woman was washing. Not to be put off, Clinton grabbed another towel and joined her.

"Since I know your name, or at least part of it," he said, "allow me to introduce myself. I'm Lieutenant Clinton McKinnon."

Jocelyn stared at him stonily and did not reply.

When they had finished the dishes and were preparing to

leave, one of the women turned to Jocelyn. "You're sure you won't come home with me? There's plenty of room."

Jocelyn shook her head. "I've already abandoned one home to the Yankees. I won't do it again."

The woman's forehead puckered in concern. "Well, it just doesn't seem right, you staying here with a house full of strange men. Perhaps I'd better stay with you."

"Thank you. But you belong with your husband. Besides, there's hardly enough room left here for me. I don't know where I'd put another woman."

"All right," the older woman agreed dubiously as she moved toward the door. "But, both offers stand if you change your mind."

When they were alone in the kitchen, Clinton turned to Jocelyn with sympathetic eyes. "This is your home?"

"My grandmother's."

"Where is she?"

"Dead," she replied bitterly. "You Yankees killed her! Oh, not directly. But all the life went out of her when she got the telegrams—first that Papa had been killed, then my brother Andrew." Choking back a sudden rush of tears, she turned away.

"I'm sorry," Clinton said softly. "Haven't you anyone? Your mother?"

"Mama died of a fever in 1860. It's just as well, I suppose. She couldn't have borne all this. When Papa and Andrew enlisted, they sent me here, to Grandmother. Last month, I got word the plantation had been burned." She stopped abruptly. "Oh, why am I telling you any of this? What do you care?"

"I do care. I'd like to help you."

Whirling on him, her eyes snapping with rage, she demanded, "Do you think for one moment I'd accept your help? I've heard how you Yankees help women—the things you demand in return."

Clinton stared at her in exasperation. "We're not all alike, you know—any more than all you rebels are alike."

"All right, just suppose I accept that thought. How can you possibly propose to help me?"

He hesitated. "I'm not sure yet. Perhaps, for a start, I could just be your friend."

"I don't want a Yankee for a friend!"

"Then don't think of me as a Yankee. Can't you just think of me as a man?"

For a long moment, Jocelyn stared at him. Clinton thought he saw the beginnings of fresh tears in her cornflower-blue eyes before she turned away from him again. "Just leave me alone!" she pleaded.

For the next several days, while the rest of Sherman's army marched into Atlanta to rest and refit, Clinton had few military responsibilities. His comrades urged him to join them in their explorations of the city, but he had little taste for carousing.

Wherever he went, whatever he did, he felt haunted by the cornflower-blue eyes of the girl whose full name he had now learned was Jocelyn Megan O'Connor. In them, he read all the tragedy, all the pathos of that terrible war that was leaving thousands homeless and without families. Now he had a new reason to wish a swift end to the war—to bring some relief to those troubled, bitter eyes.

Far from discouraging him, Jocelyn's tart words and embittered attitude almost forced Clinton to seek her out. Recognizing the legitimacy of much of her anger, he allowed her to vent it on him, hoping that in time it would be exhausted and she would at last accept his friendship.

As the days passed, he was relieved to see she turned away from him less often. Sometimes they talked for an hour or more in the evenings, though she still pretended his very presence annoyed her.

On the evening of September 8, six days after Slocum's troops marched into Atlanta, Clinton went to the kitchen with a heavy heart. He had spent the entire day in staff meetings at Sherman's headquarters, and the news he brought was far from pleasant.

Finding the kitchen empty, he went to Jocelyn's room, adjoining the kitchen. Hesitating before he knocked, he thought how bitter it must be for her to live in a cramped space once assigned to her grandmother's servants.

Although he heard her stirring in the room, Clinton had to knock several times before Jocelyn answered.

"Who is it?" she called warily.

"It's Clinton, Jocelyn. I've got to talk to you."

"Go away. I have a headache."

"I'm sorry. But it's really urgent. We must talk!"

"Tomorrow."

"No! Now!" Assuming the door to a servant's room could not be locked, Clinton turned the knob. The door opened, and he stepped through the doorway.

Jocelyn stood staring at him, her wavy hair flowing loose around her shoulders, her blue eyes crackling with anger, her chin lifted defiantly.

"I knew it would come to this!" she sputtered. "I knew it would be just a matter of time before you'd think you had the right to barge into my bedroom! But, I'm warning you, Mr. Clinton McKinnon, you have no rights to me, and you'll have to kill me to get any!"

Grimacing, Clinton slammed the door behind him. "Calm down, Jocelyn. I have no intention of even touching you. As I said, we have to talk."

"I told you, we can talk tomorrow."

"Tomorrow might be too late. We've got to make some plans. Now."

Frowning, she sank down on the edge of her bed, spreading her skirts carefully around her. "What do you mean? Are you trying to scare me?"

"No. I'm trying to make you face the truth while we can still do something about it." Pausing, he drew a deep breath. "Sherman's ordered Atlanta evacuated."

Jocelyn stiffened, raising her chin a notch higher. He could see her lips quivering, but her voice was steady when she spoke. "Has he, indeed? Well, you can tell your General Sherman that the citizens of Atlanta are not members of his army, to be ordered about at his will! We will not desert our homes!"

Clinton sighed. "Look, I know how hard this is for you. But the general's not going to give you a choice."

"What will he do if I refuse to go? Order me shot?"

"Probably not. But he wouldn't hesitate to have you carried off bodily."

"No. I can't believe that."

"Well, you'd better start believing it, and start thinking about what you're going to do. Your General Hood's already agreed to a ten-day truce to facilitate the evacuation."

Paling slightly, Jocelyn repeated, "Ten days? They expect us all to move that quickly?"

"I'm afraid so. Generals in war have been known to expect

far more impossible things. What I'm concerned about is, where will you go?"

Drawing herself up proudly again, she said, "I've already told you, I won't go!"

"And I've already told you there's no question of your staying. Now, have you any relatives, anywhere?"

She shook her head. "None that I know of."

"Are there friends who would take you in? One of the women who work in the kitchen, perhaps?"

"I hardly think I could ask. They'll have enough trouble, losing their own homes. Even if they have family to take them in, they can hardly arrive with an extra mouth to feed."

"Then, have you any idea where you could go, what you could do?"

Jocelyn shrugged. "The plantation's gone. But, I have some money. If your General Sherman absolutely drives me from my home, I suppose I could go to another city until the war is over and I can come back to restore Grandmother's house."

Clinton hesitated, grappling with the grim horror of reality. Sighing heavily, he whispered, "There might not be anything to come back to."

Her blue eyes widened in disbelief. "You can't mean that? After that demon Sherman forces us all out of our homes, he couldn't—he wouldn't—would he actually destroy the city?"

Shrugging, Clinton replied, "I can't say. Really, I haven't heard it discussed yet. But, it's always a possibility in war. The British burned Washington in 1814, you know."

"Yes, and maybe they should have burned the rest of the Northern cities along with it! Then maybe we wouldn't be in this predicament right now! Oh, what do you care? Why did you come here tonight, anyway? To see a poor Southern woman suffer?"

"No. To help you, if you'll let me."

"No, you didn't! Why should you want to help me?"

"Because I love you."

He hadn't meant to say that, hadn't even thought it yet. Still, he supposed it was true.

They stared at each other for a long, uncomfortable moment, and finally Clinton said, "I'd like you to go somewhere I can be sure you'll be safe. I want you to go to Chicago, to stay with my mother."

Touched, despite herself, Jocelyn dropped her eyes. "I

don't know what to say. That's very kind of you. But, I can't leave the South."

He sighed. "You won't be doing anyone a bit of good by staying here. And you could just get yourself killed."

She shrugged. "So what if I do? It hardly matters to me anymore."

"It matters to me."

Jocelyn stared at her hands, trying to sort out her thoughts and emotions. "I'm not sure—I don't know what sort of relationship you're suggesting."

Clinton smiled. "I'm not sure I know, either. An honorable one, I assure you. If there were time, I could court you, and ask you to marry me. But there is no time. And I don't think it would be fair to force you into a marriage right now, when you hardly know me. I'd be taking unfair advantage of a tragic situation."

"Then, what are you suggesting?"

"Just what I've said—that you go north and stay with my mother, at least until the war is over. Then, perhaps we can sort out our own feelings for each other."

Frowning, she asked, "Wouldn't your mother mind my intrusion? Wouldn't she resent having a Southerner in her home?"

He shook his head. "I'm sure she wouldn't. My mother is the most unprejudiced woman you'd ever care to meet. She's married to a half-breed Indian. She loved the Indians, even though they killed her father. She's—well, you'll see."

"I haven't yet said that I'll go."

"You're afraid, aren't you? You're afraid I'll play on your gratitude after the war to get you to marry me."

She was silent.

"Jocelyn, I promise you, no matter what you finally decide about us, if you want to come back here, I'll bring you. I'll do everything I can to get your property back for you."

Smiling sadly, she nodded. "All right, Clinton, I'll think about your offer. I can't decide in a moment's time to leave my home. But I understand the need for haste, and I'll let you know tomorrow."

Nodding, he started for the door.

"Clinton?" He turned to face her again, and he saw her cornflower-blue eyes were brimming with tears.

"Thank you," she whispered. "I guess you're different from most Yankees, after all."

29
October–November 1864

Jocelyn looked around uneasily as the Illinois Central train puffed into Chicago. After her trip north, through the ravaged South, the streets and buildings of Chicago looked far too perfect, far too unscarred.

Here, there were no crumbling walls, half-destroyed by bombardments. There were no parlors here with smoke-blackened wallpaper bared to the view of any passerby. In fact, Chicago looked not only unscarred, but remarkably prosperous.

As she had throughout all of the long, wearisome journey, at every station in every war-torn town, and over all of the hundreds of miles between Atlanta and Chicago, Jocelyn wondered again why she had come.

Why had she let Clinton convince her? Was it because, beneath her cool exterior, she was in such despair she did not know where else to turn? Was it because he had touched her so with his concern? Because she doubted that anyone else still cared for her? Because she trusted him when she felt she could trust no one else? Or because she actually returned his affection?

Now, with six hundred miles separating them, Jocelyn could admit that she did care for Clinton. But did she love him? Perhaps in another time, under other circumstances, she might have. But how could she ever love a man who had been part of the conquering army that destroyed her beloved Atlanta? Could she forget that? Could she lose her bitterness in Clinton's goodness after the war was over?

The train stopped at the Randolph Street station, and Jocelyn sighed as she got to her feet. Now to face Clinton's mother. Perhaps it would be easier simply to disappear in the crowd and pretend no one was waiting to meet her.

She was still considering that possibility as she stepped

down from the train and a tall, slender, middle-aged woman hurried toward her.

"You must be Jocelyn," the woman said, smiling. "Clinton wrote to me about your beautiful hair and eyes! I'm Eden McKinnon, Clinton's mother. Welcome to Chicago!"

Jocelyn stared a moment, her eyes moving over Eden's figure, almost too trim for a woman her age, her perfectly coiffed chestnut hair, barely touched with gray, the high-chiseled cheekbones that made her face seem younger than her fifty-two years. In that glance, it seemed to her that Eden McKinnon was more beautiful than any Northern woman of her age had any right to be.

With a forced smile, Jocelyn nodded. "Yes, I'm Jocelyn O'Connor. It's very kind of you to meet me, Mrs. McKinnon."

Though somewhat dismayed by Jocelyn's cool tone, Eden warmly took her hand and pulled her toward the street. "Please, call me Eden," she said. "I know Chicago will seem strange, perhaps even a bit barbaric after the Southern gentility you've been accustomed to. But, we're all good-hearted people here, and we'll do our best to make you comfortable."

Hesitating, Jocelyn looked away. "Perhaps it would be best if I didn't stay with you, Mrs. McKinnon. Certainly there must be hotels in town where I could—"

"I wouldn't hear of that!" Eden cut her off. "It's sweet of you not to want to impose on me—I felt the same way when I first came to Chicago and lived with my friends the Kinzies. But, really, I have more room than I know what to do with. At one time, there were six of us, plus the servants, living in my house. Now there's just me and our dear old cook, Louise. So, you see, I could do with a bit of company."

"But, Clinton mentioned that you're very busy with your work. I wouldn't want to interfere."

"There's little chance of that, since my work is all done at the plant. Of course, you understand, being at the plant every day, I won't really be able to entertain you. But, Louise will see to your needs, and I'll be glad to do whatever I can when I'm home. No, Clinton would never forgive me if I let you go to a hotel."

Jocelyn eyed her keenly. "Clinton and I—we're not promised to each other, you know."

Smiling, Eden nodded. "Oh, yes. Clinton's last letter made that very clear—though I'm certain you must know he'd like nothing better. But, I think you're both being wise in putting off a decision. War can so easily distort our emotions and our ability to reason. It would be a shame to marry too quickly and regret it for the rest of your lives."

With a nod of agreement, Jocelyn climbed into a carriage beside Eden. But, she could not help wondering, as they rode toward the McKinnon home, whether Eden's words were meant to be more than a harmless offering of good sense. Was the older woman warning her she did not like her? Was Eden saying she was not suited to Clinton?

At the house, after showing Jocelyn to Paige's old room, Eden excused herself, saying she had to return to the plant.

Jocelyn began unpacking the few gowns in her valise. In the hurry to leave Atlanta, there had been no time to pack more. Clinton had been anxious for her to go at once, while another adjutant could accompany her as far as Nashville, and had promised to send her trunks as soon as possible.

As she hung the last of her gowns, she heard the clatter of china behind her, and turned to see Louise in the doorway, carrying a tea tray.

"I thought perhaps you could do with a little refreshment," the old woman said. "It's a beastly long trip up from Georgia, isn't it?"

"Yes, it is," Jocelyn answered as she sat down on the bed. "Have you ever been there?"

"I was born there! But it's nearly forty years since I left."

"I'm surprised Clinton didn't mention that to me."

Louise smiled as she set the tray on the night stand. "I doubt that he knows. Most folks say I don't even have an accent anymore. And, of course, I didn't come from the fine class, like you."

Smiling grimly, Jocelyn said, "There won't be much of a fine class left when the Yankees get through with us." She paused, looking intently at the cook. "Do you ever regret leaving?"

Louise shrugged. "Oh, I did at first. It was a terrible trip up here, and we didn't have trains in those days, you know. But, I was dirt poor in Georgia, while here I've never had to worry about having a roof over my head. So, I guess things have worked out for the best."

"But, when the war started, didn't you ever feel you didn't belong here?"

Sighing, Louise shook her head. "No. After all, I've lived most of my life up here. Anyway, I don't take sides in this war. I don't understand it. I think it's just a terrible waste of young lives."

Jocelyn frowned. "I shouldn't think you see much of that up here. From what little I've seen, Chicago seems to have fared quite well in this war."

"Well, sure, it hasn't been burned, and there aren't any cannonballs exploding in the streets. But there's hardly a family here, rich or poor, that hasn't lost at least one son or a husband to the war. And now there's the prisoners at Camp Douglas to show us how bad things are in the South."

"You mean there are Confederate prisoners in Chicago?"

Louise nodded. "Thousands of them. They started bringing them in two years ago. And even the staunchest Yankee has to feel sympathy for the poor, bedraggled souls."

At dinner that night, Jocelyn asked Eden about the prisoner-of-war camp, and Eden reluctantly confirmed Louise's story.

"Yes. I understand there are nearly eight thousand of them here now."

"Really? And where is this camp located?"

"A few miles south of here, on Cottage Grove Avenue, between Thirty-first and Thirty-fourth streets. It was an induction center for Union troops at the start of the war. Then, after the siege of Fort Donelson in Tennessee, the army converted it into a prisoner-of-war camp."

"I see." Jocelyn was silent for several minutes, her eyes taking on a faraway look. "Tell me, would it be possible to visit the prisoners?"

Eden hesitated. "Yes, it's possible. But"—she paused again—"it's not really advisable."

"Oh? Why not? Surely you Northerners are not so hard-hearted as to object to showing compassion for some poor, harmless prisoners?"

"Of course not. But, there's a feeling in Chicago that the prisoners may not be so harmless. Last year, they attempted a mass breakout. Then, only a few months ago, when the Democrats held their Presidential Convention here, there was talk of another break—a conspiracy between the prisoners and Southern sympathizers in the area."

Jocelyn smiled condescendingly. "Surely the good citizens of Chicago were imagining that. Was there ever proof of such a conspiracy?"

"No. Only rumors. And then the camp commandant sent for one thousand reinforcements, so any break would have been impossible." Laughing nervously, Eden admitted, "It's quite possible the whole conspiracy was imagined. The southern portion of the city, near Camp Douglas, has a large number of residents who originally came from the South. I think Chicago's politicians, and the Board of Trade, which has always been ardently patriotic, are still afraid some of them might sympathize with the Confederacy and might make the prisoners into heroes."

"What do you think?" Jocelyn asked pointedly.

"I think they are heroes, in their own way. They were captured fighting for what they believed in. Whether or not I agree with them, I must admire their courage."

"And, would you object to my visiting them?"

Eden sighed. "I don't think the fact you are living in my house gives me any right to dictate your behavior. I wouldn't encourage such a visit, but—" she paused, surveying Jocelyn's earnest cornflower-blue eyes. "You're already homesick, aren't you?"

Jocelyn nodded. "Terribly. But, it's more than that, I guess. I feel sort of—guilty, for leaving the South. I know Clinton was right when he said I couldn't do any good there. But, maybe here I could. At least, I could ease the prisoners' suffering a bit. And talking to some Southerners might make me feel less homesick."

"I suppose it might," Eden agreed. "No matter what the Board of Trade might say, I really can't find fault with your suggestion. If Clinton, or my husband, Benjamin, were being held prisoner, I would hope for someone to be as kind to them."

"After all Clinton's already done, you don't think it's ungrateful of me?"

"Of course not. I'm sure he wouldn't, either." Eden hesitated. "If you really want to visit the camp, there's a woman who works at the plant who goes there every Sunday. She's Irish by birth, but she lived in Georgia several years before moving to Chicago. I believe she has a nephew among the prisoners. I'll introduce you if you'd like."

"Yes," Jocelyn agreed quickly. "I'd appreciate that."

The following Sunday, while Eden worked over the books of McKinnon Meats, Jocelyn O'Connor accompanied Mollie

Flanagan, a short, plump, middle-aged Irishwoman, to Camp Douglas. What she saw sickened her almost as much as the wrecking of Atlanta.

Men of all ages, some hardly more than boys, others old enough to be her grandfather, were crammed into the camp. Dressed in tattered butternut pants, many hadn't even a decent shirt to cover their backs. They wrapped themselves in ragged bits of bed quilts and filthy scraps of carpet that substituted for blankets.

Overall, the prisoners seemed healthy enough. The seriously wounded or ill had all been transferred to St. Luke's Hospital, where both Confederate and Union soldiers were cared for. But, they suffered the common prison problems of lice infestations, meager though nourishing food, and the misery of isolation from the outside world.

Every man, young or old, with whom Jocelyn spoke, had dull, sunken eyes that seemed to have lost all hope months before. They all stared at her as a vision from another world, and kissed her hand in touching remembrance of a dying era.

As she sat beside Mollie on the horse-drawn streetcar rolling north on Cottage Grove, away from the camp, Jocelyn turned to the older woman with stricken eyes. "How horrible!" she whispered. "For men to have to live that way, while Chicago feeds off the war and firms like McKinnon Meats grow fat on profits!"

Mollie shrugged. "It could be worse. It's a war, after all. My nephew tells me they are not mistreated."

"Not mistreated! Didn't you see them! Think of the homes some of those men must have come from—and now, to bear the humiliation of living like that!"

"They're alive, aren't they? In war, no one can ask for more."

"Oh yes, one can! Seeing that, I'm almost glad Papa and Andrew were killed, instead of being taken prisoner!"

"Ah, child, you don't know what you're saying."

"Yes, I do! I wish I could free them all, right now, and get them into decent clothes and homes!" Jocelyn stopped abruptly, staring at the older woman intently. "Mollie, is it true what Eden told me? Was there a conspiracy to free them?"

Paling slightly, Mollie looked away. "Hush, child, that's not a thing to be discussing in public."

"Mollie, I want to know! I want to know if there's still a conspiracy. I want to help. I've got money. The Yankees didn't leave me much else, but I'll give all I have."

Mollie frowned. "You're talking nonsense. What would Mrs. McKinnon say, after she's opened her home to you? What about her son?"

"What about those men in Camp Douglas?"

Her face hardening, Mollie insisted, "There's little we can do for them. All we can do is visit, take them whatever food or clothing we can, try to cheer them. There is no conspiracy. There never was."

For the next three weeks, Jocelyn accompanied Mollie on her visits to Camp Douglas. They regularly rode the horse-drawn streetcars, starting south from Randolph and State streets. The trip took an hour each way. She never got over her horror at the camp, and yet she felt forced to return, time after time.

During the week, while Eden was at work, Jocelyn spent most of her time in the shops along Lake Street, purchasing clothing, blankets, and other essentials for the prisoners. Often, she included tobacco, candy, or books among her purchases, as added gifts to cheer the men.

Seeing nothing actually wrong with Jocelyn's preoccupation with Camp Douglas, Eden felt glad her young guest had something to occupy her time. Away at the plant from ten to twelve hours a day, Eden had neither the time nor the energy for entertaining, and was relieved to see Jocelyn did not expect it.

Eden would have been less pleased had she realized how greatly Jocelyn's involvement with Camp Douglas was intensifying her resentment of Northern prosperity. Every visit to the camp seemed to underscore the stark contrast between Chicago's thriving populace and the suffering prisoners. Each time she saw a Southern gentleman, reduced to ruin by his months as a prisoner, Jocelyn thought of her family's burned plantation, and of her grandmother's home, occupied by arrogant Yankee soldiers.

Although she tried to appreciate the kindness of her hostess, Jocelyn could not help seeing Eden as a prime example of the ruthless Yankee profiteer. The mere fact that Eden devoted so much time to McKinnon Meats seemed proof enough that she was dedicated to making as much money as possible from the war and the suffering of the South.

Even when Eden sent several large donations of meat to Camp Douglas, Jocelyn was not impressed. The businesswoman was simply trying to salve her conscience, Jocelyn insisted to herself, for all the harm her firm had done to the South.

To Jocelyn, Eden's part in the war seemed more evil than that of any Union soldier. Her time with Clinton had taught her that at least some Union soldiers were principled men, risking their lives for a cause they believed in. But, to her eyes, Eden McKinnon, and other business leaders like her, risked nothing while they grew rich on the profits of war.

Still, she cared for Clinton, she was grateful for his kindness and understanding. Someday, she might even consider marrying him. But, how could she become part of a family that had fed off the devastation of the South? What could she do to prove, to herself and to her Southern compatriots, that she had not forgotten where her loyalty should lie?

After Jocelyn's fourth visit to Camp Douglas, as she and Mollie were beginning to ride north, the older woman turned to her with a serious look. "You'll stop at my house for tea?" Mollie asked.

Sure she was being invited for more than tea, Jocelyn quickly nodded. "Yes, of course. I've told you I'll do anything—"

"Hush!" Mollie frowned, her brow creasing. "It's for tea I'm inviting you, nothing more."

"Of course, I understand." But, Jocelyn's blue eyes sparkled with excitement for the rest of the ride. At last, she would have the chance to do her part!

As Jocelyn had suspected, when they stepped into Mollie Flanagan's modest home on East Twenty-Third Street, the parlor was already crowded with men and women, many of whom spoke with a distinct Southern drawl.

As Mollie introduced her, an elderly gentleman with a snowy beard caught Jocelyn's hand. "Ah, Miss O'Connor," he said softly, "I understand you are lately from Atlanta. How was that fair city when you left?"

"Suffering!" Jocelyn replied. "Half the buildings were shot to bits, and the remaining ones were overrun with Yankees."

"Tch!" The man shook his head. "I understand that Sherman is a devil! No telling what he's doing, now that he's shipped all the good Southerners out of there!"

"That's so," put in another man. "They say he might even torch it, just for pure spitefulness!"

Her eyes filling with tears, Jocelyn nodded. "I've heard the same. Lord knows, I'd never have left if I could have avoided it."

"And, would you be willing to do something to help avenge Atlanta, and all our other fair Southern cities?" asked the elderly man.

"Of course! Mollie knows that. I've been begging to do something for weeks."

The men exchanged glances, nodding to one another before the elderly one continued. "Well, now you have your chance. We need money. A great deal of it. And very quickly."

"Are you going to liberate Camp Douglas?" Jocelyn asked eagerly.

The man hesitated. "Perhaps. We need the money to outfit a force of several thousand—before the November elections."

Jocelyn nodded. "I can give you at least nine hundred dollars. Possibly a bit more. But, can't you tell me what you're planning?"

The elderly man pursed his lips in consideration, but the younger man quickly cut in. "It would be safer if you didn't know—if you would just trust us. Since you're living with Mrs. McKinnon—"

"You don't trust me?" Jocelyn demanded. "You think I'll tell her?"

"Of course not. But, with her position on the Board of Trade—well, it's just safer if as few people as possible know the details."

"One thing we can tell you," the elderly man assured her, "is that the money will not be wasted. Missouri, Indiana, Ohio, and Kentucky are all cooperating with us on this plan. We cannot fail, and we will not!"

They talked a bit longer, instructing Jocelyn about how and when she might pass the money to their organization, the Sons of Illinois. Then one of the men accompanied her home to Eden's, with a firm warning to keep her excitement under control.

The next afternoon, Jocelyn took a break from her shopping to meet another woman for tea in the Sherman House, at Randolph and Clark. There, she discreetly passed the woman a purse containing almost eleven hundred dollars.

One week later, on November 7, the morning before the national Presidential elections, Eden was preparing to leave for the plant when she heard the front doorbell. Hurrying from the breakfast table, she opened the door to four officers of the Union Army.

"Mrs. McKinnon?" one of the men asked politely.

Paling, Eden felt her heart twist in fear. Which of her men had been killed? Benjamin? Or Clinton?

She relaxed slightly as the man continued, "Is there a Jocelyn O'Connor staying with you, ma'am?"

"Why, yes. But I'm not certain she's risen yet. It is very early, you know. Did my son, Clinton, send you?"

The soldier frowned. "No, ma'am. We've been sent by Colonel Benjamin J. Sweet, commanding officer of Camp Douglas. I'm afraid you and Miss O'Connor will have to come with us."

Wrinkling her brow, Eden replied, "I'm sure I don't understand."

"You and Miss O'Connor are wanted for questioning for your parts in the Chicago Conspiracy."

30
November 1864–March 1865

"Have you any idea what this is all about?" Eden whispered to Jocelyn as the soldiers escorted them to the Union encampment, just outside the walls of Camp Douglas.

Jocelyn nodded smugly. "Yes, I'm quite sure I do."

"Well, then, for heaven's sakes, tell me, so I can figure out how to get us out of this!"

"But I don't want to get out of it," Jocelyn replied calmly. "I'm proud to be doing my part for the Confederacy. I am sorry if I've involved you, but I'm quite sure you'll be released once they realize you know nothing of the plan."

"Jocelyn, for heaven's sake, I want to help you!"

"But I've told you, I don't want to be helped!"

Resolutely tossing her blonde curls, Jocelyn stared straight ahead and refused to speak for the rest of the ride. In fact, she would be embarrassed to admit how little she had done, how little she even knew about the conspiracy. But, she would never tell Eden, nor even the Union Army investigators. Let them all think she was a trusted confidante of all the conspirators.

Colonel Sweet stared at Eden and Jocelyn sternly as the soldiers ushered them into his office. Shaking his head, he said quietly, "Mrs. McKinnon, I am utterly shocked that a woman of your standing would involve herself in such a plot! After all Chicago has given you, over so many years, how could you, in good conscience, conspire for the downfall of your native city, and of the United States of America?"

"Colonel Sweet," Eden replied clearly, "I assure you, I have no idea what you are talking about."

The commandant shuffled through some papers on his desk. "Do you have any dealings with the prisoners of Camp Douglas?"

Eden hesitated. "I've had no direct dealings with them."

"But you have sent them several shipments of meat, is that correct?"

"Yes, I have. But I've never been told that mere kindness constitutes a breach of law. The records show that my firm has sent thousands of times more meat to the Union troops over the years."

"Quite so. Quite so. But that's not the issue at the moment."

"Colonel Sweet," Eden cut in coldly, "if you don't explain yourself and release me immediately, that *will* be the issue. My plant is shorthanded enough, and if I'm not there this morning to supervise operations, there will be no more shipments to Union troops."

The colonel frowned, his face flushing. "Are you threatening me, Mrs. McKinnon?"

"Not at all. I am simply trying to make you understand a basic fact."

Jocelyn, who, to that point had been ignored, looked from Eden to the commandant. She was not particularly concerned with helping Eden, but she saw no reason why the older woman should receive any undue credit for the conspiracy.

"Mrs. McKinnon is telling the truth!" Jocelyn blurted. "She wasn't involved in the conspiracy. You couldn't find a more staunch supporter of the Union."

For the first time, Colonel Sweet stared intently at Jocelyn. "And why," he asked, "should I believe you?"

"Because I *am* a part of the conspiracy. And we don't want any Union sympathizers besmirching our cause!"

Eden gasped. "Jocelyn, be careful what you say!" Turning to the colonel, she explained quickly, "Miss O'Connor is recently from Atlanta, and I'm afraid she's been most deeply scarred by the fighting down there. I'm sure you can understand, she's young, and she's disillusioned, and sometimes she says things without realizing—"

"I know exactly what I'm saying," Jocelyn cut in. "And I don't wish to retract a single word of it!"

"Hmm." The commandant stared at the two women as he stroked his chin in thought. "You realize, Miss O'Connor, that your confession forces me to detain you, at least until this entire conspiracy matter has been resolved?"

Jocelyn nodded, proud to be jailed for the Confederacy.

"Mrs. McKinnon," the colonel continued, "I'm going to release you, under the custody of two of my officers, so there will be no interruption in the shipment of provisions to our troops. Being ninety percent certain of your innocence, I apologize for the inconvenience caused you by the officers' presence. However, in a case as serious as this, I can afford to take no chances."

"I understand," Eden said. "I would only ask, sir, since I am to be under custody, that you also release Miss O'Connor."

"Eden, I told you," Jocelyn burst out angrily, "I don't want your help!"

Frowning, Colonel Sweet said, "At any rate, I'm afraid I couldn't grant your request, Mrs. McKinnon. Captains Hardy and Wilson will see you home, and remain with you until I issue further orders."

As the two officers escorted her from the camp, Eden asked, "Can't someone please tell me what this is all about?"

The captains exchanged a significant glance before one of them asked, "You really don't know?"

"Of course not! I thought the conspiracy, if there ever was one, was put down this summer."

The captain sighed, "Everyone thought so. It's just lucky we found out in time. By tomorrow night, Chicago could have been no more than a flaming inferno."

"I still don't understand," Eden said.

"According to our reports," the other captain, Wilson, began, "the conspiracy intended to send a thousand men to Camp Douglas tonight to free the prisoners. Then, they were all going to march to Courthouse Square and join forces with five thousand Sons of Illinois."

"Sons of Satan would be more appropriate," Captain Hardy muttered. "The scheming Southern supporters!"

"Anyway," Captain Wilson continued, "their aim was to seize the polls tomorrow, stuff the ballot boxes, and only accept votes for George McClellan—which, you know as well as I, would be about the same as electing Jefferson Davis President of the United States."

Eden smiled ruefully. "Not quite, you know. McClellan was a rather effective Union general for the first years of the war."

"Yes, well, anyway, after securing the city for McClellan, the conspirators planned to sack it and burn everything they couldn't carry off for themselves or their Southern brothers."

Eden stared at the two captains incredulously. "Why, that plot is really just too fantastic to be believed! Do you really think it could have been carried out? Or, that that innocent young girl you brought here with me tonight could in any way be involved?"

Both officers shrugged.

"Well, time and a more thorough investigation will tell," said Captain Wilson. "But today there was no time. If the army hadn't acted immediately, it might have been the end of Chicago."

His eyes and throat burning from the dark smoke clouds billowing around him, Clinton turned for a last look at Atlanta. The flames licked angrily over the ruined city, and he muttered a quick prayer of thanks that Jocelyn was not there to witness the final destruction of her grandmother's home.

It was November 15, 1864. After two and one-half months, General Sherman was finally leading the Union Army out of Atlanta—or what had been Atlanta. By the time the flames died down, there would be little left.

Now, sixty-thousand strong, the Union troops were headed southeast, through three hundred miles of enemy territory. If they were successful, they would march all the way to the Atlantic Ocean, and take Savannah, Georgia.

If they failed, it could be weeks before anyone knew. For, Sherman had conceived of a bold, unheard of, military maneuver. For three hundred miles, his troops would be beyond the reach of telegraph wires, newspaper correspondents, or even Union railroad supply lines. They were cutting themselves off from communications and would live off the enemy's land.

As adjutant to General Slocum, Clinton had sat in on most of the meetings planning the march to the sea, and he knew the maneuver was not as risky as it might at first appear. The troops would not starve in Georgia's rich farm country. And Hood's Confederate forces were too far west, all the way in northern Alabama, to cause much worry.

But, the thought of being cut off from correspondence worried Clinton, especially when he thought of Jocelyn. By tomorrow, at the latest, she would know that Atlanta had been burned. How would she feel when she heard nothing from him for weeks, or even months afterward?

If only he could be with her, to share her grief! If only he could communicate to her how terrible he felt at this moment. He knew the news would renew her bitterness, would confirm her earlier judgment that all Yankees were fiends. And he wished that he could prove to her that he, at least, was different.

But, he hadn't even had time in the last few days to send a letter. Perhaps by the time he could write to her, her heart would be too hardened even to accept his condolences. He could only hope his mother could comfort her and keep her from becoming too embittered.

"Hey, Lieutenant, what's the matter, you forget the words?"

Startled, Clinton looked at the grinning young soldier marching beside him. For the first time, he realized the men were singing "John's Brown Body." Smiling grimly, he thought of Old Brown, the fanatic abolitionist, and of that day in Kansas when his half brother, Swift Elk, had died.

Did any of these men, singing so lustily, have any idea what John Brown, hanged five years earlier, had really stood for? Could they even imagine the ruthlessness of the man, or the crazed look in his eyes as he executed proslavers?

Perhaps they could. Perhaps John Brown's soul really was marching on, in the merciless burning of Atlanta. Perhaps "John Brown's Body" was an appropriate theme song for this day.

By the end of the first week, Clinton realized with horror that the song was an appropriate theme for the entire march. Sweeping through Georgia, the army cut a path of destruction forty miles wide.

The men lived well, on food taken from smokehouses, pantries, and plantation barns. Well-fed, vigorous, and with no Confederate Army to oppose them, they took what they wanted and destroyed the rest. They left a flaming trail of homes, stores, cotton and cottin gins.

The Confederacy sent General Joe Wheeler and his cavalry to stop the march. But Wheeler's meager force of six thousand was no match for a Union Army ten times that size. There were skirmishes along the edges of Sherman's columns. But, for the most part, the Union soldiers simply shot the cavalrymen from their saddles and continued on the march.

When they crossed rail lines, connecting Georgia with the Confederate capital, Richmond, Virginia, the troops paused to tear the rails out of the ground. They heated the rails red-hot and twisted them around trees, calling their handiwork "Sherman's hairpins."

The campaign made Clinton heartsick, doubly so when he thought of how Jocelyn would hate him for even being a part of this army of destruction.

Sometimes, as he rode between the columns, carrying messages between General Slocum and the other generals, he became physically ill as well. The army had slaughtered so many mules, horses, cattle, and hogs, that decaying carcasses lay everywhere, permeating the air with their sickening stench.

At night, sitting around the campfires, Clinton joined the other officers arguing the morality of the campaign.

"Well," a captain said, "you can't blame Sherman. He didn't actually order all this destruction. But, after all, the men have to eat. And it seems fitting that the South should feed them. After all, the rebels started the war."

"Sure," Clinton agreed. "And I wouldn't have any qualms if all we took was the food and supplies we need. But, what's the sense of all this killing and burning? Sherman himself says only about a fifth of all the destruction is to our advantage. The rest is just pure and simple waste."

"That's true," a colonel admitted with a shrug. "But this is war. And when a war's been going on this long, it's just as important to break the spirit of the whole enemy population as it is to beat their army. In the long run, all the looting and burning will be worth it. It'll bring the war to a quicker close."

Still, Clinton could not reconcile himself to the wanton destruction, even when, the following day, he heard Sherman himself justify it.

"I've got Southern friends I cherish as my own family,"
said the lean, red-haired general. "I would not, for the world,
make them suffer. And yet, when someone accuses me of
making war vindictively, I must reply he's damned right! War
is war, and there's no other way to make war!"

In mid-December, after a month of destruction, Sherman's
forces stormed Fort McAllister on the Ogeechee River. On
December 22, they marched triumphantly into Savannah,
which Confederate troops had abandoned two days earlier.

They had reached their goal, and the nation resounded
with the news that General Sherman had presented President Lincoln with a rare Christmas gift—the city of Savannah.

For Clinton, the victory represented a more personal gift.
At last, they had reestablished communications with the North.
At last he could write to Jocelyn.

Jocelyn O'Connor held her head high as she walked down
the steps of the Chicago courthouse at LaSalle and Randolph
streets. It was December 23, and she was going back to
Eden's for the holidays.

She supposed she should consider it a welcome Christmas
present, to be free after nearly seven weeks in jail. But, what
did it matter? Atlanta had been burned. The Chicago Conspiracy had failed. And she had not even had the satisfaction of
being named a principal in the plot.

The conspiracy leaders had been transferred to Cincinnati,
for trial by a military commission. Most of the other partici-
pants in the plot remained under guard at Camp Douglas.
However, the few women involved, including Jocelyn, had
been transferred to more comfortable accommodations in the
courthouse.

Now, after thorough investigation, the authorities had determined that, despite her claims, Jocelyn knew almost nothing about the conspiracy.

In the end, the army would release all but four men, whom
they convicted of conspiring to free the inmates of Camp
Douglas and destroy Chicago. Three were sentenced to prison
terms, while their leader, Colonel G. St. Leger Grenfell, was
sentenced to be hanged.

At the foot of the courthouse steps, Jocelyn stopped beside
Eden to listen as Frank and Jules Lumbard, brothers and
Chicago's favorite singers, began teaching a new song to a
gathering crowd.

Frank shouted that it was a new composition, written by fellow-Chicagoan Henry C. Work, to honor General Sherman. Then, as the crowd hushed, the brothers launched into the stirring marching song, "Marching Through Georgia."

Within minutes, the excited crowd had taken up the chorus:

> Hurrah! Hurrah! we bring the Jubilee!
> Hurrah! Hurrah! the flag that makes you free!
> So we sang the chorus from Atlanta to the sea
> While we were marching through Georgia.

Turning to Jocelyn with sparkling eyes, Eden said, "I didn't have a chance to tell you yet. The newspapers are full of the story. Sherman got through! Clinton must be safe in Savannah!"

Jocelyn paled slightly, unsure how to react. For the last month, the Confederate press had been sending north rumors of Sherman's demise. They had said Sherman's men were starving, that the citizens of Georgia were shooting them down along the road, that thousands had been taken prisoner. And Jocelyn had wanted to believe the rumors.

Still, she hadn't wished any harm to Clinton. He had been good enough to send north almost all her belongings that could be shipped before Atlanta was burned. She would always be grateful to him. But surely Eden couldn't expect her gratitude would make her rejoice over a Northern victory.

Watching Jocelyn's face, Eden sobered. "I'm sorry. That was insensitive of me. I didn't mean to indicate I was glad for anything Sherman might have done to your native state. I've just been so frantic about Clinton these last weeks, and I thought you would feel—"

"Of course," Jocelyn cut her off. "I'm very glad to know Clinton is probably all right. Really, I am."

She stiffened slightly as the crowd continued the song: "Sing it as we used to sing it, fifty thousand strong. While we were marching through Georgia. Hurrah! Hurrah!—"

Eden lay a hand on her arm. "I think we'd best go on home. After all that time in jail, I suspect a hot bath and a clean bed will be a welcome change."

"Yes, well, I can get both of those things at a hotel. Perhaps it would be better if I—"

"I think we already had this discussion when you first came to Chicago," Eden cut her off.

"Yes, but at that point, I had not yet been part of a conspiracy to destroy the city."

Eden smiled ruefully. "At your age, in your position, I'm not sure I wouldn't have done the same thing. Besides, the army has acquitted you, so who am I to censure you?"

Jocelyn gritted her teeth. She supposed she should feel humbled and grateful for Eden's magnanimity. Instead, it infuriated her. Of course, Eden could afford to be understanding while her own home was untouched by war, her business continued to thrive, and now even her son appeared to be safe.

"No," Eden continued briskly, "I simply could not think of letting you spend Christmas in a hotel. With my own daughter and sons so far away, I'll be pleased to have your company. Besides," she added pointedly, "after the amount you donated to the conspiracy, I don't imagine you could afford to support yourself in a hotel for too long."

That much was truer than Jocelyn cared to admit. With a forced smile, she accepted Eden's hospitality. But she promised herself her stay would last only until she could reorganize her life and decide what to do about Clinton.

In February, Sherman's army turned north from Savannah and marched into the flooded, swampy low country of South Carolina. In Savannah, the army had given up pillaging and behaved like gentlemen. But now they were entering the state that had started the war, the first state to secede, and it seemed that almost every soldier had a personal vendetta against that state.

Again, they left a fire-blackened trail. On February 17, they occupied the state capital, Columbia. When they marched out, the city was in flames. Sherman had not ordered the fire, and some said the rebels had set it themselves. But Clinton had the sickening conviction that it was the work of the men marching beside him.

Clinton hardly felt a part of this crazed army anymore. He could not understand the hatred that motivated his comrades. They marched almost unopposed, and yet they destroyed more than they had in any of their worst battles. By March, they had burned their way into North Carolina.

The one thought that kept Clinton going was that it would all be over soon. The South had been broken. Surrender was imminent. General Grant was holding Lee in Virginia. Mobile was under siege and facing collapse. The Confederates could scarcely rally a force against any Union general.

At night, Clinton wrote long letters to Jocelyn, begging her to forgive him for the position he found himself in. The destruction of the South made her seem somehow more precious to him. If he had fantasized about her love before, he now found himself craving it.

The few replies he received seemed cool and distant. He tried to console himself that some people could not express themselves in letters. But there was an apparent strain in his mother's letters, too, and he wondered what the two women were hiding from him.

The plundering army swept on. On the thirteenth of March, Fayetteville fell, and the last Confederate arsenal in the East was obliterated. The officers learned that General Schofield and his regiments, fresh from a Union victory at Nashville, would be joining them soon. Schofield's forces had been shipped to the Carolina coast from Washington, D.C. Their addition would make Sherman's army invincible.

To Clinton, the news seemed particularly cheering, since he knew that Benjamin was with Schofield's forces. After three years, the thought of a reunion with his brother filled him with joy. Perhaps they could witness the end of this conflict together, and return home together to the women they loved.

The Confederate General Joe Johnston had heard of Schofield's advance too, and everyone knew if he was going to strike, he must do it now, before the two armies were united. Still, after months of lighthearted marching, Sherman's men did not really expect much of a battle. They underestimated Joe Johnston.

On the nineteenth of March, Sherman's forces were marching through rain, rain which had been almost constant since they left Savannah in February, but which had never slowed their pace.

Clinton, still attached to General Slocum, was in the lead corps. Eight miles separated them from the second Union corps, which had been held up by accidents along the road. At noon, when Slocum's corps reached a clearing and rebel artillery fire began to rain around them, they had no choice but to enter battle.

Slocum split his corps into three divisions, and for a while they held the enemy. Then, suddenly, a bloodcurdling rebel yell resounded through the woods, and half of Johnston's force came rushing at the Union's vulnerable left flank.

The Confederates fought like madmen, inspired by the knowledge this might be their last stand. They surrounded an entire division of Slocum's corps, cutting them off from the other two divisions, and forcing them to the very edge of a swamp.

Still, the Union troops rallied. Part of Slocum's other divisions charged the rebels with bayonets. As the Confederates turned to meet the charge, the second Union corps, which had been delayed on the road, reached the clearing and joined the battle.

Slocum watched the rally with a grimly determined smile. He motioned to Clinton and pulled him aside.

"Ride back and tell General Sherman that Joe Johnston's finally sent out his welcoming party," Slocum said. "Tell him we ought to have the rebels back in their trenches by nightfall, but any reinforcements he could send up would be greatly appreciated."

Clinton ran for his horse and started off at a gallop southwest, toward Averasboro. He hunched low over the horse's neck, avoiding the shots whizzing around him. Within minutes, he was out of range of Confederate artillery and rifle fire. Sitting up a bit, he urged his mount on.

The road ran through rolling, thickly wooded upland country. From the top of a hill, he could dimly make out marching men in blue a few miles distant.

The sounds of battle became fainter, replaced by the wind rushing in his ears. The wind rocked the woods lining the road, and a few branches crashed to the ground around him.

Stroking his horse's neck, Clinton kneed him to a faster gallop. He heard a sudden crack of thunder, but there was no accompanying lightning flash.

Suddenly, his horse stumbled, and he saw a red splotch spreading across its shoulder. Stunned, he turned partway in the saddle as the horse screamed in pain and lurched to the ground.

It all happened so quickly he had no time to think. The horse rolled to one side, pinning his leg beneath it. He heard another crack, this time sickeningly close. White-hot pain surged through his crushed leg, and he realized his thigh bone had snapped.

A gleeful cackle assailed his ears. Looking up, he saw a

gray-bearded old man limping out of the woods. As the man came closer, he raised a rifle to his shoulder and took careful aim at Clinton's chest.

The man stopped a few feet away, cocked the rifle and grinned in satisfaction.

Nearly unconscious with pain, Clinton bit back an agonized scream as he waited for the shot.

31
May–August 1865

Eden paused on the front stoop, inhaling the clean, spring air before climbing into her carriage to go to McKinnon Meats. For the first time in four years, spring really did seem to be bringing a promise of renewal. The war was over at last.

Any day now, Clinton and Benjamin would be coming home. They would be stepping off a train full of living, joyous men, unlike the funeral train that had stopped in Chicago last week with the remains of President Lincoln. Remembering that somber occasion, Eden shuddered and thanked God her husband and son had survived the war.

At least, she assumed they had survived. She had not received letters from either in the last month. But, no doubt the mails were swamped with notes from soldiers eager to return home. If they had written at all, Ben and Clint would probably arrive before their messages.

They must be coming home. The War Department had not sent her any telegrams to the contrary.

Squinting into the early morning brightness, Eden looked south on Wabash Avenue. In the distance, she could see a tall, slender, dark-haired man hurrying north, his soldier's kit slung over one shoulder.

For a moment, she studied his smooth, familiar walk, her breath catching in her throat. She saw him stop and stare at her, one hand shielding his eyes against the early morning glare. Then he broke into a run, and she felt herself trembling all over.

Lifting her skirts above her ankles, she ran down the steps and rushed to meet him.

"Benjamin!" she screamed. "Oh, Benjamin!"

They met in the middle of Wabash Avenue, oblivious to the few passersby, as Benjamin dropped his bag and pulled her into a powerful embrace.

She was laughing and crying, clinging to him as she covered his face with kisses. She leaned back in his embrace to study his beloved face, caressing his cheek with her fingertips, noting with tenderness the tears of joy in his gray-green eyes.

"Ah, how good it is to have you home!" she exclaimed. "At last, I can begin to live again!"

"So can I," Benjamin murmured as he hugged her again. "So can I."

Kissing her forehead, he looked down at her with smiling, loving eyes. Shifting his eyes to the carriage still waiting at the door, he asked, "You're going to the plant?"

"I *was*," Eden corrected. "But, not now. I'll send a message later that the workers can take a holiday."

"Good," he said with a sad smile. "I've seen enough slaughter for a long, long time."

Eden sobered. "It was terrible, wasn't it?"

Benjamin looked away. "Worse. To have countrymen killing one another—" He sighed. "It's something I suppose I'll never understand. Many's the time I wished I'd never enlisted. But," he forced a smile, "we'll have the rest of our lives to talk about that. For today, let's just be happy together."

Her arm around his waist, Eden pulled him toward the house. "With you here, I can't be anything but happy!"

The house was quiet inside, as Jocelyn had not yet arisen, and Louise was napping after having made Eden's breakfast.

"What would you like first?" Eden asked her husband. "Coffee? Breakfast? A hot bath?"

Benjamin surveyed her with glowing eyes. "You," he said simply.

Flushing, Eden laughed. "Darling, you already have me!"

"But I haven't had you in nearly three years," he said quietly. "And it's the one thing I've dreamed of more than anything."

Smiling radiantly, Eden took his hand and led him upstairs to their bedroom. He lay on the bed, watching her undress, a smile of rapture never leaving his face.

"You're more beautiful than ever," he murmured.

Eden laughed. "You don't have to flatter your own wife, Ben! This war has made an old woman of me!"

"No, it hasn't. If anything, it's made you stronger and more attractive." He stretched his arms out to her. "Come here."

She sat down beside him and helped him undress, feeling his readiness long before they dropped his trousers to the floor. For a moment, she could not help thinking of the last time she had lain with a man in this bed—a man who was now married to her daughter.

She thought of the pain of the morning after, of all the empty, agonizing nights and mornings after Garrett had left. And she knew, as she and Benjamin became one, that she and Garrett had been right to separate.

"Ben," she whispered afterward, as they lay together and she stroked his firm, smooth muscles, "when you saw all those beautiful young Southern belles, didn't you ever regret tying yourself to such an old woman?"

Benjamin frowned. "Eden, I told you you're not old!"

"I'm fifty-three, and you're not even forty yet."

"You're the woman I love," he insisted firmly. "The only one I ever have loved, and the only one I ever will love. But, all this talk is making me think *you* regret our marriage. Maybe you're not so happy to have me home, after all."

"Oh, Ben! How could you even say that? You know I'm happy!"

"Then let's not hear any more foolishness about you being too old for me."

"All right." She smiled. "The only thing that could make me happier at this moment would be to have Clinton home, too."

Benjamin hesitated. "You haven't heard anything from him?"

"No. But I hadn't heard from you, either. I assumed you'd both get here before any messages could."

Nodding, he sat up and swung his feet to the floor. "You're probably right. I'm getting hungry now. Do you suppose we could go down and find me some breakfast?"

"Of course. Louise is probably fixing something for Jocelyn by now."

"Jocelyn? The girl Clinton sent up from Atlanta?"

"Yes. But, if you don't feel up to meeting someone new right now, I can just bring up a tray for you."

"No. I'm sure Louise would feel hurt if I didn't come down and greet her and personally compliment her on her cooking.

Anyway, I'll enjoy eating at a table with real linens and china and silver again."

After Benjamin had quickly washed up and dressed in fresh civilian clothes, he and Eden went downstairs hand in hand. Jocelyn was sitting at the dining room table, reading the May issue of *Godey's Ladies Book* while she waited for Louise to bring in her breakfast.

Eden was about to introduce Jocelyn when Louise bustled in from the kitchen and let out a yelp of joy. "Oh, Lord! Mr. McKinnon! What a sight for sore eyes! If I'd have known you'd be here, I'd have stayed up all night baking your favorite sweet rolls."

Smiling, Benjamin bent to kiss the cook's cheek. "Hello, Louise. It's good to see you. And don't worry about the sweet rolls. Whatever you serve is bound to be a thousand times better than what I ate in camp."

"Why, Benjamin," Eden scolded in mock outrage, "you're not disparaging our own product, are you? I seem to remember shipping quite a lot of McKinnon Meats to the Union camps."

"And they were gladly received—when they got through. But no army cook could do justice to them like Louise here."

Louise flushed happily. "Oh, Mr. McKinnon, you always were a diplomat, just like your father! Well, I'll just give this plate to Miss Jocelyn here, and I'll—"

"Please," Jocelyn cut in a bit coolly, "give the plate to Mr. McKinnon. I can wait. After all, the conquering hero deserves some special treatment."

Benjamin threw Eden an apprehensive glance before turning to Jocelyn. "Miss O'Connor, in all the excitement, I'm afraid Eden hasn't had the chance to introduce us. Please, call me Benjamin. And, I insist that you take your plate. I'm not in the habit of taking food away from my guests."

Shrugging, Jocelyn accepted the plate, and Eden asked Louise to bring them coffee while they waited.

Jocelyn flipped through a few more pages of the magazine before looking up with a forced smile. "I didn't mean to be rude. I'm sure you must be very happy to be home, Benjamin, and it can't be any treat to find a stranger sitting at your breakfast table."

"On the contrary, it's always a pleasure to entertain an attractive woman. Besides, you're not exactly a stranger. Eden has written me quite a lot about you."

"Oh." Jocelyn glanced at Eden, wondering how much Benjamin knew. "Well, I shouldn't be imposing on you much longer. Just until Clinton comes home, which I suspect will be very soon."

Benjamin looked down at his coffee. "Yes, I suspect so."

"You wouldn't know when I could expect him, would you?"

"I'm afraid not. We were in different corps, you know."

"Yes, but I understood your commander joined Sherman at the end, so I thought perhaps—"

"No. The combined armies had ninety thousand troops, so it's not surprising Clinton and I never ran into one another."

At that moment, Louise bustled in again, and Benjamin was able to escape further inquiry.

After breakfast, Jocelyn went out for a walk, and Eden went to prepare a bath for her husband. As he sank into the steaming tub and she handed him the soap, she demanded, "All right, Ben, what do you really know about Clinton?"

Benjamin's brow wrinkled. "What do you mean?"

"You never were very good at hiding things from me, you know."

"As I told Jocelyn, I really don't know anything."

"But—?"

He sighed. "All right, I did try to find him several times between when we joined Sherman at Goldsboro and when Johnston finally surrendered to Sherman a month later. But, I didn't have any luck, which isn't all that surprising in a body of ninety thousand men."

"Isn't it? You knew, didn't you, that Clinton was attached to General Slocum's staff?"

Benjamin hesitated. Perhaps he should just say he hadn't known, that knowing Clinton's position would have made him much easier to find.

"Ben!" Eden's voice was becoming agitated. "What are you keeping from me?"

"Nothing, really. I don't know anything."

"Yes, you do!"

For a long moment, he stared into his bathwater. Then he took her hand and gazed sympathetically into her eyes. "Eden, I went to General Slocum's headquarters and—they couldn't tell me where Clinton was."

Paling, she whispered, "What do you mean?"

"He's—he's missing. Slocum sent him to Sherman with a message one day and—he hasn't been heard from since."

"Oh, my God! When?"

Unable to bear her tortured gaze, Benjamin dropped his eyes. "The nineteenth of March. The day of the last battle with Johnston's forces."

"Two months ago! Then he's—"

"Eden, he's missing," Benjamin cut her off. "That's all anyone knows. He might have been wounded. He might be in some camp hospital and the report just never reached Slocum. He could have been taken prisoner, which means by now he would have been released. He's probably on his way to Chicago right now."

"Do you really think so, Ben?"

"Of course." Inwardly, he cringed at the lack of conviction in his tone. "In fact, that's why I decided to come ahead home. I thought about staying in North Carolina longer, to look for him. But in all the confusion there, I figured I'd miss him and he'd be home with you, while I'd still be wandering around Raleigh."

"Of course." Eden nodded. "I'm glad you didn't delay coming home. At least," she added, blinking back tears, "I'll have one of you with me."

Hoping to save her needless worry, Eden and Benjamin agreed not to tell Jocelyn that Clinton was missing. But, by the end of May, as more and more soldiers streamed home to Chicago, the girl was becoming restless and apprehensive.

"The least he could do is write and explain this delay," she burst out one evening as they sat in the parlor after dinner.

Eden and Benjamin exchanged a significant glance before Benjamin said softly, "Perhaps he can't, Jocelyn."

"What do you mean?"

"Perhaps he was injured. He might be in a hospital."

"Then, wouldn't the army send Eden a message to that effect?"

Benjamin sighed. "There may not have been time yet. At the moment, the army is swamped with paperwork—mustering out men, notifying the families of the deceased. Simply accounting for everyone is a mammoth task that's bound to take months."

Jocelyn frowned. "You got home rather quickly."

"I was fortunate."

"Well, I can't wait here forever. I appreciate what Clinton—what your whole family—has done for me. But I want to go home!"

"Jocelyn, be sensible," Eden put in quietly. "I know this waiting is hard for you. It's hard for me, too, and for Ben. But there's no sense in your running off to Atlanta just yet. I'm afraid you won't find much of a home there, and, from all reports, the South today is not a very safe place for a woman alone."

Sighing petulantly, Jocelyn asked, "So what would you suggest I do?"

"Wait at least a bit longer, for Clinton's sake. Imagine how he would feel if he came home now and found you were gone."

"All right," Jocelyn relented. "I'll wait. But it can't be forever. Chicago's not my home, and it never can be. Clinton understood that. He promised to take me back to the South."

But, I really don't think Clinton's coming home anymore, she added silently.

By July, they still had heard nothing. Benjamin contacted the army, only to be informed Clinton McKinnon was missing and unaccounted for. He wrote to every hospital, military or civilian, in the area of Bentonville, North Carolina, where Clinton had been riding when he disappeared. The letters proved fruitless.

Knowing how Eden was suffering, Benjamin announced if there was still no news by the end of August, he would personally return to North Carolina to search for his brother. In the meantime, he kept Eden as busy as possible at McKinnon Meats.

With the phenomenal growth of Chicago's meat-packing industry during the Civil War, both the packers and the rail lines which served them realized they needed a new, more efficient stockyards system. Instead of several stockyards, owned and operated by various packers throughout the city, they could all profit from one, large, unified yard.

It was a project Eden and other packing executives had discussed even before the end of the war. Nine railroads, all of which made a large profit from carrying livestock, agreed to put up most of the money to build a Union Stockyards, to serve all the packers.

They chose a three hundred-twenty-acre site near the South

Branch of the Chicago River, at the intersection of Halsted Street and Egan Avenue. On June 1, 1865, when construction began, it was a marshy tract that most Chicagoans considered worthless. But the packers were determined to drain the marsh and create a miniature city there by Christmas Day.

Together with the other packers and rail executives, Eden and Benjamin planned pens for twenty thousand cattle, twenty thousand sheep, and seventy-five thousand hogs. They designed hotels, restaurants, a stock exchange building, connections for all nine railroads, and a small canal to link the yards with the Chicago River.

Since the new stockyards were located four miles southwest of downtown Chicago, Eden and Benjamin decided it would be impractical to keep their own plant at its present location at Twelfth and State. Besides, they would no longer need their extensive stockpens, though they could use more space for actual meat packing.

So, they began building a new plant, just west of the Union Stockyards site. The new headquarters of McKinnon Meats, at Packers and Exchange avenues, was scheduled to open by the end of the year.

Planning and supervising the new plant construction was a blessing to both Eden and Benjamin. The work kept them occupied, even on weekends, crowding worries about Clinton to the backs of their minds.

The construction projects, coupled with her concern for her younger son, also enabled Eden to put off her proposed trip to Texas. Though she had been serious when she told Garrett she would visit the ranch, her enthusiasm for the journey had waned since Garrett and Paige married. Renewing her own devotion to Benjamin, she had been fully prepared to greet Garrett as only a dear friend. But, she still could not imagine embracing him as her son-in-law.

Unlike her host and hostess, Jocelyn found little to occupy her time. Still resentful of Northern prosperity, she could not take an interest in McKinnon Meats. Nor could she feel much warmth toward the young women to whom Eden introduced her. She spent most of her time in the McKinnon house, reading or brooding over her unhappiness.

More and more, Jocelyn was becoming convinced she owed nothing at all to Clinton McKinnon. If he had been killed, she was sorry. Clinton had been a good man, but surely no better than her own brother and father and countless neighbors who had perished in the war.

If he was alive, no matter what his situation, he ought at least to have sent her a message by now. Even if he could not himself write, surely he could find someone to do so for him.

Except for the several servants Eden had hired since the end of the war, Jocelyn was alone in the house one afternoon early in August when she heard the front door open. Looking up from her seat in the parlor, she frowned to herself. It was too early for Eden and Benjamin to be home.

For a moment, her heart beat faster. Perhaps Clinton had come home at last! Well, if he had, she decided, lifting her chin stubbornly, she would just tell him a thing or two about the way he had neglected her!

Rising stiffly, she started toward the foyer. But the man who stepped into the parlor doorway and surveyed her with dancing eyes was neither Clinton nor anyone else she had ever met.

"Pardon me, ma'am," he said sweeping into an exaggerated bow. "This is still the McKinnon residence, is it not?"

Jocelyn nodded, studying the man haughtily. He was broader than Clinton, and his hair was redder. But there did seem to be a family resemblance.

Grinning, he said, "Then I suspect you must be Miss Jocelyn O'Connor. My little brother seems to have developed excellent taste! I'm Burton McKinnon, Clinton's brother."

Forcing a smile, Jocelyn extended her hand. "I'm pleased to meet you, Mr. McKinnon. Eden did not mention that you were coming up from Texas."

"I'm not surprised, since she didn't know! But things were getting rather dull down there, so I thought I'd come north for a spell. I assume my mother and stepfather"— he paused and smiled wryly at that word—"are at the plant?"

"Either there or at the site of their new plant. They rarely come home before dark."

Burton snorted. "Still as dedicated as ever, I see!"

"You don't approve?"

He shrugged. "I've got nothing against success, but I can't see the point of a proprietor working harder than his employees. Where's Clinton? Did he desert you for the plant, too?"

"No," Jocelyn answered slowly. "Clinton hasn't come home from the war yet."

"He hasn't?" Burton's eyes widened, and for a moment Jocelyn thought she saw them flash in pleasure. Then his tone softened, and he patted her arm apologetically. "I'm sorry to hear that. I'm sure it must be very hard on you."

She nodded. "They say he's missing, that he may still turn up. But sometimes I think it would be easier if they just said he was dead."

"What will you do if—if he doesn't come back at all?" Burton asked solicitously.

"I—I'm not sure. Right now, I'm not even sure what I'd do if he came home. We aren't officially engaged, you know."

"You mean, you might not marry him?"

"I don't know. I just don't know! All I really know is that I want to go back home. I want to go back to the South!"

Burton nodded, leading her to a settee and sitting with her. "I can understand that. After all my years in Texas, I feel like something of a Southerner myself. Of course, I don't suppose Texas is as genteel as your Georgia. But, there are those who say our ranches compare to your plantations. And, of course, we were a part of the Confederacy."

Jocelyn looked at him with new respect. "Did you support the Confederate cause?"

"It would be hard to be a citizen of the South and not support it."

"But you weren't in the Confederate Army?"

"I—I was in the Texas militia," Burton lied. "As it happened, our state saw only a few small skirmishes. Nevertheless, we had to be ready to defend it."

"Did your mother approve of your enlistment?"

"She didn't know," he replied quickly. "I'm not certain she would have understood, when her husband and other son were fighting for the Union. Of course, I didn't want to hurt her. But I felt compelled to fight for the state I had come to love."

Inwardly, he smiled. How sickeningly noble he sounded! Still, this girl of Clinton's seemed to accept his words without question and with open admiration.

Where was Clinton, anyway? They had never been particularly close, but if someone had to perish in this war, Burton would have preferred it to be Benjamin, or even Garrett. He had never considered Clinton much of a threat to his future. Clinton was too soft, too concerned with pleasing everyone. Besides, Clinton had never even been very interested in meat packing.

Burton's eyes moved lazily over Jocelyn. A pretty girl. A pleasant contrast after the darker, more mature beauty of Conchita. Conchita had begun to bore him lately. She and Paige were always fussing over that brat, Miguel, reproaching him because he didn't act like a father to the child. Well, why should he? He hadn't asked for a baby. It had just been Conchita's plot to trap him into marrying her, and it hadn't worked.

Yes, this Jocelyn O'Connor might be a pleasant diversion. Perhaps her presence would even warrant extending his stay in Chicago for several months. And if Clinton never returned —or even if he did—who knew what might happen?

32
September–October 1865

"I tell you man, the war is over. It must be by now. It was practically over back in March, when you shot my horse out from under me!"

Clinton sighed and closed his eyes. He had argued with the old man so many times now he ought to know it was futile. The old man had no intention of releasing him. Perhaps he never would.

Perhaps the old man would just die, and he, Clinton, would be left to starve, chained to the wall in this rude cabin in the backwoods of North Carolina.

The old man chuckled, shifting his rifle across his knees. "I don't know why you don't just save your breath, sonny. I done told you a hundred times, this war ain't over 'til the last Confederate surrenders. And I ain't about to surrender!

"Somebody's got to pay for my six sons and four of my grandsons bein' killed by you Yankees. Somebody's got to pay for the way my Sally died of a broken heart. So it might as well be you, and you might as well get any notion of leavin' here right out of your head!"

The glint of the old man's eyes as he spoke reminded Clinton of the fanatical fire in John Brown's eyes during the days of Bleeding Kansas. Instinctively, he knew it was as futile to argue with this man as it had been to try to alter Old Brown's crazed sense of justice and retribution.

Sighing, he said, "Well, you ought to at least let me write to my family. I'm sure all the other prisoner-of-war camps allow that much."

"You can go ahead and write anything you want, but there ain't no letters goin' out of this house. I don't fancy havin' the whole Union Army swooping down on me to deliver you."

Clinton shifted slightly on his cot, gritting his teeth at the pain he still felt in his right thigh. At least his captor had had the decency to set his leg, though the results had been less than professional. The break had not healed cleanly, and now his leg was always stiff. Stiff and slightly shortened, so he could not walk without limping.

As the old man chuckled again, Clinton closed his eyes wearily. He wondered just how long he had been a prisoner in this cabin. At least five months. Probably longer.

The old man had not shot him on the road from Bentonville. But Clinton had passed out from the intense pain in his thigh, where his horse had fallen on him. He had some dim, pain-shrouded memories of being dragged away, and a few recollections of the first delirious days in this cabin.

For the first few months, the old man had not had to worry his prisoner would escape, since Clinton could scarcely move. Even now, Clinton doubted he could outstrip his captor in a race. Still, just to be certain, the old man kept him chained to an iron ring attached to the wall beside his cot. He was allowed out once a day, to fetch wood for the cooking fire, always with a rifle trained on his heart.

The days passed in infinite boredom. There were no books in the cabin. Clinton doubted that his captor had ever learned to read.

They never had any visitors, though the old man sometimes went away for nearly a whole day. During those hours, Clinton chafed his ankles and hands trying to break free of his bonds. Upon returning, the old man always examined his prisoner, chuckling gleefully over his obviously futile efforts.

For recreation, the old man occasionally pressed Clinton into a game of checkers, using hand-carved pieces on a home-made board. He refused to tell Clinton his name, insisting the prisoner could simply call him "sir."

After the first month, despite his own mental and physical

misery, Clinton realized with shock that he actually felt sorry for the old man. His mind obviously had snapped under the strain of losing his loved ones. It might have been better for the old man to die from the heartbreak, as his wife had.

Feeling the rifle barrel prodding his ribs, Clinton opened his eyes.

"Wake up, sonny," the old man chortled, "we got company coming!"

Clinton blinked. "Company? Here? After all these months?"

"Yep! And it's time you made yourself presentable." The man shoved a basin at him. "Better sit up and give yourself a little bath. And I got a clean shirt over here I been saving for this occasion."

"A bath and a clean shirt, eh? Well, thank God for company!"

"Don't get smart, sonny. Just do as you're told."

After Clinton had washed and changed his shirt, the old man went outside to dump the basin and wait for his guests. A few minutes later, Clinton heard horses approaching. Then a young man's voice said, "Well, here she is, Gramps. I brung Cousin Peggy Jean, just like you said."

"That's fine, boy," the old man said, surprising Clinton with the unfamiliar gentleness of his tone. "Now, you better turn around home, so you can get there before dark."

A young woman spoke softly. Clinton could not make out her words. Then a baby began to bawl lustily, and the old man cleared his throat uneasily.

"I hope she ain't goin' to be crying like that all the time."

"She'll be all right, Gramps. She's just not used to bein' around menfolk."

"Well, she'd better get used to it right quick! C'mon, I'll take you inside."

As they entered the cabin, Clinton saw a petite girl of no more than fifteen, carrying a baby only a few months old.

"This here's my granddaughter, Peggy Jean," the old man said. "The baby's Priscilla. You damned Yankees killed her father. So, we're going to even the score a little bit. You and Peggy Jean are going to get married!"

Benjamin ran a hand haphazardly through his hair as he stepped off the train at Randolph Street. Eden was not waiting on the platform. She was not expecting him. He hadn't had the heart to telegraph that his search had been in vain. It would be better to tell her in person. At least then he could try to comfort her.

After more than a month in North Carolina, he had not even found a trace of Clinton. He had searched the area around Averasboro and Bentonville, where Clinton had disappeared, with no luck. No one recalled seeing a man of Clinton's description, alive, dead, or wounded.

He had even ventured a bit west of the towns, into the sparsely settled rolling hill country. There, the residents had received him warily, insisting they knew nothing of the man he was seeking. Assuming that in this time of reconstruction they would accord any Northerner the same wary reception, Benjamin had accepted their stories and turned back to the coast.

Before going home, Benjamin had gone to Washington, to inquire at army headquarters. Officially, he was told, Clinton McKinnon of the 42nd Infantry was listed as "missing." There was nothing more to report.

Assuming Eden was at the plant, Benjamin hired a carriage and directed the driver to Twelfth and State. As expected, he found her in her office, poring over estimates for canning machinery for the new plant.

Benjamin hesitated in the doorway, gazing tenderly at her bent, auburn-haired head. Why must he always be the one to bring her sad news? How he hated to hurt her again!

He cleared his throat softly, and her head jerked up. With a gasp of surprise, she jumped from her chair and rushed to embrace him.

For several moments, they held each other silently. Then she asked, with remarkable composure, "You didn't find him, did you?"

"No."

She lifted her head to gaze into his gray-green eyes. "Did you find anything—anything at all?"

He shook his head.

Stifling a cry of pain, Eden nodded. "You were gone so long without even a message that I'd begun to suspect as much. It's strange, but I'm almost accustomed to the idea now that Clinton simply isn't coming home."

"Eden, the army still considers him 'missing.' There's still a chance—"

"No, Ben," she cut him off quietly. "I don't want to keep

my hopes alive, just to have them smashed weeks, or months from now. It's better to accept the obvious, don't you think?"

"I don't know. I suppose it's best to do whatever causes you the least pain. But, remember when Burton first went away—how long it was before—"

"Burton wasn't in a war." She sighed. "Well, I always knew it could happen. Every day of that damned war I worried about both of you. Thank God at least I still have you!"

They held each other again, drawing strength from each other.

"What shall we tell Jocelyn?" Benjamin asked.

Eden shrugged. "The truth. That you didn't find him. I have a feeling she won't take it too hard. Burton's been providing her with a good deal of diversion and consolation."

"I know. To be honest, I don't think Jocelyn and Clinton were very well suited."

"What do you mean?"

"Just that she seems very comfortable with Burton. And Burton is not really much like Clinton."

Eden smiled wryly. "No, he's not, is he? If Jocelyn is comfortable with him, she may be the only one in our house who is. He's such a stranger to me—my own son, and I don't understand him at all! He says he came to visit because he feels out of touch with the business. But he has yet to spend one full day at McKinnon Meats. He's always too occupied with Jocelyn."

"Perhaps he just feels sorry for her."

"Much as I hate to admit it, I don't think my son is capable of feeling sorry for anyone, unless he sees some profit in it for himself."

"Well, after all that time cooped up on the Double M, you can't really blame him for taking advantage of the company of a young, attractive woman. Anyway, after all his years away, he probably feels a bit awkward at the plant. Besides," Benjamin added softly, "I don't think Burton likes me much."

"Ben!" Eden tried to sound surprised, but her eyes dropped away from her husband's probing gaze.

He lifted her chin to look her in the eye. "Do you think I'm wrong to say that?"

"Well, I—of course I'm sure Burton doesn't dislike you. You're brothers! Oh, maybe he misunderstands a few things— Garrett Martin mentioned something like that when he was here during the war. But, time and being together will smooth out any problems."

Benjamin smiled, his lips lightly brushing hers. "Whatever you say, my love. I certainly want to be friends with Burton again, as we were when we were boys. Only, sometimes I feel as if that will never again be possible."

Sitting beside Jocelyn in the parlor, Burton casually slid an arm around her shoulders. Eden and Benjamin had just retired, and now they were alone to discuss the news Benjamin had brought from North Carolina.

"I'm sorry," Burton said. "I wish I knew how to comfort you."

Jocelyn sighed. "After all this time, I can't really say I'm shocked. I'd hoped Benjamin would find something, but I really didn't expect it. I'm sad, of course. Clinton was one of the best men I've ever known. But, well, there's nothing more to say."

"If one of them had to die, I wish it could have been Benjamin."

"Burton! That's a terrible thing to say!"

"But, be honest, haven't you thought the same?"

"Well—I—of course I'm looking at things from a different perspective. Benjamin is a very kind, thoughtful person. I would never wish him any harm. Still, it seems rather unfair that Eden should get him back safe and sound—especially at her age, when she's already enjoyed one husband—while I—"

"You don't really like my mother, do you?" Burton asked pointedly.

"Of course I do! She's been very generous with me!"

"You can be frank with me. I'm not fool enough to believe she's a saint, just because she's my mother."

Jocelyn's cornflower-blue eyes narrowed. "Well, I can't honestly say I dislike her. It's just that I—I guess I sort of resent all the money she made from the war. I mean, people in Atlanta are just trying to scrape together the funds to build themselves some kind of simple homes, and she's building a gigantic new meat-packing plant with her wartime profits."

Burton smiled. "It does seem rather unfair, doesn't it?"

"Of course it's unfair! It's easy enough for her to play Lady Bountiful with a poor little Southern girl like me when the misfortune of the South has practically made her a millionaire!"

She stopped abruptly, flushing as Burton grinned. "I'm sorry. I'm afraid I got a bit carried away. You're so easy to talk to, you make me say things that would be better left unsaid."

"Not at all. I'm glad you feel you can tell me such things. It may surprise you, but I'm inclined to agree with you about my mother. However, I ought to tell you that Benjamin is not the kind, thoughtful person you think."

"Oh?"

"Between them, he and my mother are plotting to take away my inheritance."

"Why would Benjamin want to do that? I thought Clinton told me he was your half brother."

"He is. And it seems he couldn't be content with what he'd inherit through my father, so he married my mother to close me out of the business."

Jocelyn shook her head. "I don't know. It just doesn't make sense. Why should Benjamin even want your share? I'm sure his own inheritance is more than enough to keep him rich for the rest of his life."

"Some men will do anything for more power, Jocelyn."

She frowned. "Perhaps. But, even if I accept that analysis, and even if I admit I'm not terribly fond of your mother, I can't believe she would plot against her own son."

"Well, I was never her favorite. I was never as compliant as Clinton, nor as sweet as my little sister, Paige. And, I think Mother still wants to punish me for running off to California when I was thirteen."

"But that was fifteen years ago."

"Well, there's no point in discussing it further," Burton said briskly. "What do you plan to do now?"

"Your mother mentioned something about a memorial service for Clinton. I'll stay for that, of course. But then there's really no reason why I shouldn't go back to Atlanta."

"Isn't there?" His arm tightened around her shoulders.

"Of course not."

"Jocelyn, I wish you wouldn't go."

"Why?"

"It's not likely to be a pleasant homecoming. I doubt there's really anything there for you to go back to."

"But I can't stay up here. I hate the North! The South is my home."

"I understand. But you could go somewhere else in the South. Texas, for instance."

"Why would I want to go there?"

"Because I'm asking you to—as my wife."

Her eyes widened. "Burton, I—I don't know what to say."

"I'm not really a Northerner, you know. I haven't lived in Chicago for fifteen years. You and I could make a good pair, Jocelyn. We see people the same. We agree on things."

She bit her lip. What would she find in Atlanta, anyway? What was the point of going back to a burned home?

Surely she would not find a husband there. Whatever young, unattached men had survived the war would be looking for women with some means to help them rebuild their homes. Having given most of her inheritance to the Chicago Conspiracy, Jocelyn would have nothing to offer them.

Why not marry Burton? Why not profit from the McKinnon wealth? Surely she deserved it more than Eden.

She didn't love Burton. But he hadn't mentioned love, so why should she? In the aftermath of war, it was enough to find a pleasant companion who could take care of her and take her back to the South.

Burton touched her cheek, turning her face to his. "You're not going to refuse me, are you?"

"No, Burton," she whispered. "I won't refuse you. I'll marry you just as soon as we can arrange it."

33
January–July 1866

Clinton sat on his cot, idly massaging his aching thigh as he watched Peggy Jean rolling biscuits. It was the first time in the three months since she had come to the cabin that they were alone together. The baby was asleep, and the old man had gone off in search of the circuit preacher.

So far, Clinton supposed he had been lucky. There had been no circuit preachers in the area, and the old man would not consider taking them in to Bentonville, where Clinton might somehow manage to escape. So, he and Peggy Jean still were not married.

Watching the girl, Clinton felt sorry for her. She was too young to be a widow. But, dammit, he was not the man to take her husband's place! He had a girl waiting for him in Chicago.

At least, he hoped he did. After all this time, he could hardly blame Jocelyn if she'd gone back to Atlanta. But, even if she had, he'd follow her there. If he could just get away from this crazy cabin!

"Peggy Jean," Clinton said softly.

The girl looked up with inquisitive brown eyes, the back of her hand brushing a strand of brown hair off her forehead.

Clinton rattled his chain. "Can't you unlock this thing, just until your grandfather gets back?"

She shook her head. "I can't hardly do that. You know Gramps has the only key. And he was wearin' it around his neck when he left this morning. I'm right sorry to see you chained up like that all the time, but there don't seem to be nothin' I can do about it."

Clinton sighed. "You could tell your grandfather you don't like to see your betrothed in chains. Maybe he'd release me then."

She laughed. "Nobody tells Gramps nothin'! I don't reckon he'll unlock that chain 'til after the weddin'. Maybe not even then."

"You really think he'll still make us go through with this wedding?"

"Oh, sure. Just as soon as he finds a preacher. I heard tell the last circuit rider got killed or quit or something during the war. I guess maybe there just ain't been a new one assigned yet."

"Peggy Jean, you don't really want to marry me, do you?"

The girl shrugged. "It don't really matter much what I want. If Gramps has got it in his head we're gonna be married, then I guess we're gonna be married."

"But, just between you and me, what do *you* want?"

"Why you askin' me that? I told you it don't make no difference. But, I guess you don't much want to marry a scrawny little girl with a baby."

"It's not that at all, Peggy Jean," Clinton said carefully. "You're a pretty girl, and don't you ever forget it. But, the fact is, I've got a woman waiting for me at home."

Peggy Jean frowned. "You're married?"

"Engaged."

"Oh, that poor girl! Waitin' and waitin' for you when you ain't never comin' home. Just about like Richie Andrews is waitin' for me, I guess."

"What?" Clinton jumped at her last, mumbled words.

"Nothin!" she flushed.

"What about this Richie Andrews?" Clinton pressed. "If I'm to be your husband, I think I ought to know."

"It don't matter," Peggy Jean insisted.

"Yes, it does!"

"All right!" She turned away to hide her red face. "I'll tell you, though there's nothin' anyone can do about it now. I met Richie in 1864. He was a sergeant in the Confederate Army. Oh, he was a fine figure of a man! I used to go to Averasboro to sell my mama's eggs, and that's where I met him. He was from Mobile, but he was stationed here for a while.

"Anyway, we fell in love. And I—I let him love me. It just seemed so right. We was gonna get married as soon as the war was over anyway. Then he got sent down toward Atlanta, and after he was gone, I found out I was gonna have a baby.

"Well, I couldn't tell my mama I was havin' a baby when I wasn't even married, so I told her we was married in secret, and Richie was comin' back for me after the war.

"I thought everything would be fine. He kept writin' me these love letters—Mama had a friend in Averasboro who'd taught me to read and write, you know—and sayin' how much he was gonna love our little baby. Then, just before Priscilla was born, I stopped gettin' those letters.

"Mama started gettin' real suspicious, and sayin' maybe we wasn't married after all. Then I started gettin' real worried that maybe he wasn't comin' back. Finally, I told Mama I got a letter from his general, and that he'd been killed."

"But he hadn't?" Clinton asked quietly.

Peggy Jean shook her head. "Just before my Cousin Alex brought me up here, I got another letter. He'd been wounded real bad, and when he finally got sent home to Mobile, he had to try to help his family out of the mess after the war. But he promised he'd still come for me."

"Then, why in the devil didn't you tell someone?"

"I did! But when Mama found out I'd been lyin' all along, she walloped the livin' daylights out of me! Then she said she'd never let me marry Richie, and she sent me up here, just like she and Gramps had planned."

Peggy Jean started to sob. Her shoulders heaved pitifully, and Clinton's heart went out to her. "Come here," he whispered, opening his arms.

She ran to him and buried her head against his chest. Stroking her hair, Clinton murmured, "We'll think of something. We'll find a way out of this, Peggy Jean."

At that moment, the old man burst into the cabin, followed by a black-suited circuit preacher. "Well, ain't this nice!" the old man sneered. "The sinners in each other's arms. Probably just got through fornicating!"

"Don't be absurd," Clinton barked. "I can hardly even move with this damned chain on my leg."

Ignoring him, the old man pointed to Priscilla, who was now awake and crying fearfully. "You see that baby, rev'rend? She's the product of their sinning! Now, I know you can't do much to save their evil souls. But, for that innocent baby's sake, I hope you'll hurry up and marry them, before they poison her life anymore."

"The man's lying, reverend!" Clinton cried. "Just take a good look at him, and you can see he's out of his mind! There's no need for you to marry us. The fact is, Peggy Jean and I are already married—to other people. But, for some crazy reason, he's gotten it in his head to hold us prisoners here. Isn't that right, Peggy Jean?"

The girl hesitated, looking fearfully at her grandfather. Then she nodded slowly. "Yes, Clinton here is tellin' the truth, rev'rend. Ever since the war, Gramps—"

"I'll give you 'ever since the war'!" the old man yelled.

The preacher frowned. "I'm sure you can all understand I hardly know whom to believe. Now, if we could all just sit down and talk peacefully—"

"I'll show you what to believe," the old man snarled, pushing his rifle barrel into the preacher's face. "I guarantee you, you can believe this! Now, you start sayin' them marriage vows, before I send you for an early trip to Saint Peter!"

Glancing apprehensively at the cocked rifle, the preacher pulled a small black book from his coat and began reading the marriage vows.

Burton smiled across the breakfast table at his wife. They had married in December, a month after the memorial service for Clinton, and had stayed on in Chicago for Christmas and the grand opening of the Union Stockyards.

By January, Jocelyn had been suffering her first bouts of morning sickness, and had agreed it would be best to put off traveling. But now it was April, she was feeling healthier with her advancing pregnancy, and she had begun to nag him about his promise to take her to Texas.

Of course, he could not take her to the Double M ranch. He had no intention of having Jocelyn meet Conchita and his two-year-old bastard. Even if he somehow managed to get Conchita and the brat off the ranch before he and Jocelyn arrived, his dear sister Paige would probably mention them.

Anyway, Burton was not anxious to return to the Double M at all. As long as Garrett Martin was there, he would never have the power he wanted. Nor could he expect a top position here in Chicago, where his mother and Benjamin ruled the packinghouse. But, a letter from Garrett yesterday had given him a new idea, one he was certain Eden and Benjamin would approve.

Garrett had written that several ranchers near him were planning a cattle drive to Sedalia, Missouri. He was not enthusiastic about the venture, since it would follow nearly the same treacherous route he had taken on his drive to Jefferson City, three years earlier. That drive had been difficult enough with a small herd. With several thousand longhorns, it could be nearly impossible.

Still, Garrett had written, he was willing to send a small herd north. But he advised waiting until the following year, when the railroads should have extended further west, for a more extensive drive.

As Eden and Benjamin sat down to breakfast, Burton asked, "How are you going to reply to Garrett's letter?"

Eden shrugged. "I think he knows better than I what the best course would be. I'll leave it up to him. Don't you agree?"

Burton nodded. "He may as well send a few hundred head north this year, but I do think it would be prudent to save the big drive 'til next year. And, speaking of next year, I've another suggestion to make."

Pleased that her son finally seemed to be renewing his interest in the firm, Eden smiled. "What do you suggest?"

"I think we ought to consider building another plant, at Kansas City."

"Oh?"

"It's just good business sense," Burton went on enthusiastically. "If the Texas ranchers are going to be driving their cattle to Missouri and Kansas, we can profit by having a plant as close to the end of the trail as possible. Then we won't have to transport the Double M steers, or any longhorns we buy from other ranchers, so far. We'll be able to offer a higher price for cattle we buy, since we won't have to pay rail freight charges all the way to Chicago."

"It's a sensible plan," Benjamin agreed. "But you can't be suggesting we close down the plant we just built."

"Of course not! Chicago is the meat-packing capital of America. With the new stockyards, it's bound to remain the leader for some time. I just think we'd be smart to expand our interests, especially now, when we can afford it."

Eden frowned. "I can certainly see the merits of your plan, Burton. And I think Kansas City is large enough now to support a packing plant. Surely there must be a lot of men home from the war looking for work. But, I can't say I'd be pleased to leave our new Chicago plant just now to go there and start another plant."

"I wasn't suggesting that," Burton grinned. "I'd like to take responsibility for the Kansas City plant myself!"

Ignoring Jocelyn's surprised gasp, he went on. "Garrett doesn't really need me in Texas, and to be honest, I've always been more interested in packing than in ranching. Of course, you and Ben don't need me here, either. So, I just thought it would make sense—"

"But you promised to take me to Texas!" Jocelyn interrupted.

Burton shot her an annoyed glance, then spoke with exaggerated patience. "What difference does it make, Jocelyn? Kansas City, Missouri, is practically a part of the South. Missouri was a slaveholding state before the war."

"But it wasn't even a part of the Confederacy!"

"It practically was. It was full of Confederate sympathizers. I can assure you, Kansas City is nothing like Chicago." Turning away from his wife, Burton looked to his mother. "Well, what do you think?"

Eden hesitated. "I like your plan, Burton. But I can't, in good conscience, give my approval if it will make Jocelyn unhappy. You ought to know I've never believed a man should do whatever he wants, without regard for his wife."

Burton sighed irritably. "She's just surprised by the proposal, that's all, Mama. She's never been to Kansas City, so she can't possibly know how happy she'll be there. The fact is, I was thinking of Jocelyn when I formulated my idea. I don't think she'd enjoy the isolation of ranch life very much. She'd be happier in a city, where she could have some close women friends."

Pursing her lips, Eden looked to Benjamin for his opinion. They would both be more comfortable with Burton out of Chicago, and she would be doing Garrett a favor by not sending him back to the Double M.

Besides, Burton's plan really did make good business sense. Perhaps, as the head of his own plant, he would feel he had the power he craved, and would become less hostile toward Ben.

Benjamin looked from Eden to Jocelyn. "I'm inclined to endorse Burton's plan," he said carefully. "But I don't want to see anyone hurt by it. It's certainly not worth it to expand the business if you, Jocelyn, are going to be unhappy.

"However, I think you ought to think about all Burton's said, and consider the alternatives. If he does take you back to Texas, I believe he'll be unhappy. He has a good idea, and he deserves the chance to try it out. Furthermore, he may be right in feeling you'll be happier in Kansas City than on an isolated ranch.

"Of course, if you do find the city is not to your liking, I think Burton should agree to move, once he's had his chance. What do you say, Jocelyn? Will you give your husband that chance?"

Jocelyn sighed petulantly. "With all of you against me, I don't really think I have much choice."

For a few minutes after the marriage ceremony, Clinton had dared to hope he would be freed from the cabin very soon. Surely the preacher could not condone that travesty of a wedding. When he rode away from the cabin, the preacher would get help. By the next morning, at the latest, he and Peggy Jean would be free.

However, after the wedding, the old man had ridden away with the preacher. Clinton and Peggy Jean had heard a shot, and the old man had returned to the cabin, grinning in satisfaction. Clinton had known then that no help would be coming. He had also realized the war had demented the man even more than he had suspected. God only knew what else his crazed mind was planning.

Still, when he was still alive six months after the wedding, and more than a year after his capture, Clinton refused to give up hope. The old man had begun to wonder out loud why he had no great-grandchildren on the way, hinting broadly that Yankess simply were not adequate in bed. But, when Clinton had pointed out that he might be more successful if his leg were unchained, his captor had turned away with a bitter laugh.

In actual fact, Peggy Jean could not become pregnant, because she and Clinton had never consummated their marriage. Knowing their union could be annulled if it was never consummated, Clinton had whispered that fact to Peggy Jean the first night they lay together on his cot. Though still doubtful they could ever escape, Peggy Jean had been relieved she would not have to submit to Clinton.

Of course, Clinton supposed they could also obtain an annulment based on the fact they had been forced into the marriage. But, it would be easier if Peggy Jean did not bear him any children.

As if sensing the new rapport between Clinton and Peggy Jean, the old man watched them suspiciously, never leaving them alone together for more than a few minutes. But, in July, reassured that Clinton could not possibly escape, and that Peggy Jean was too afraid to try, he rode away early one morning.

Now as desperate as Clinton to escape, Peggy Jean immediately began searching the cabin for something with which to break Clinton's chain. Clinton told her to look for a file, but the best she could find was the whetstone the old man used to sharpen his knives.

The whetstone was a poor substitute for a metal file, but Clinton set to work with it, drawing it back and forth over a link of the chain near his ankle. By midday, he had worn a small groove in the link, but he had begun to despair that he could ever wear it completely through.

By evening, the old man still had not returned, and Clinton began to suspect that something had happened to him. Still, fearful that he might yet return, Clinton and Peggy Jean sat up all night, taking turns with the whetstone.

It was midafternoon of the second day before Clinton finally broke free. Anticipating his success, Peggy Jean had packed a small bundle of food and had ransacked the cabin for the few coins her grandfather owned. Clinton picked up Priscilla, now nearly a year old, and Peggy Jean, carrying the bundle of food, followed him to the door.

"Do you know the way to the nearest town?" Clinton asked.

The girl nodded, biting her lower lip. "Bentonville's closer than Averasboro, but we'll never make it there on foot before dark."

Clinton shrugged. "Would you rather wait here 'till tomorrow and chance your grandfather coming back?"

She shook her head. "Not as long as we ain't got a gun. I just wish Cousin Alex hadn't taken my horse back with him. Oh, well," she sighed, "we might as well git goin'. We ain't gonna get to Bentonville standin' here!"

About two miles from the cabin, they found the old man lying on the ground, his horse grazing peacefully nearby. His rifle was lying a few feet away, where he had dropped it when he fell.

Picking up the rifle, Clinton prodded cautiously at the old man's body.

"Is he—dead?" Peggy Jean whispered.

Nodding, Clinton knelt beside the corpse. "I think maybe his old heart just finally gave out—if he ever had a heart. Well, at least we've got the rifle and the horse now, to get us into town. It's a good thing, too. I've been chained up so long I'm not used to walking, and my thigh was beginning to give me hell. Come on, I'll help you onto the horse."

Peggy Jean stared in horror. "Ain't we even goin' to bury him?"

"With what? Do you happen to be carrying a shovel?"

"No. But, maybe back at the cabin—"

Clinton sighed irritably. "Peggy Jean, I wasted more than a year of my life in that damned cabin, and I'm not going back there now, for anything or anyone. I'm sorry if that strikes you as hardhearted, but your grandfather sure didn't do much to make these last months pleasant. Now, are you coming?"

She nodded, and they rode the rest of the way to Bentonville in strained silence.

Sitting behind her in the saddle, Clinton held his arms protectively around Peggy Jean and her baby. But his thoughts were on a pair of cornflower-blue eyes, a long, slender, white neck, and a head of golden blonde hair.

In Bentonville, they would have the marriage annulled. Then, if they sold the horse, and possibly the rifle, they ought to have plenty of money to send Peggy Jean to her beloved in Mobile, and pay his own train fare to Chicago.

By tomorrow morning, he would be on a train headed west, back to the cornflower-blue eyes he had been dreaming of all these months!

34
August 1866

Bent over a report from the Double M, Eden did not lift her head when she heard her office door opening. "How does the stock from Sedalia look, Ben?" she asked, still looking at the report on her desk.

"Ben?" she repeated when no one answered.

She looked up then, freezing in openmouthed surprise at the sight of the young man walking toward her. He looked thinner, more gaunt, with a touch of bitterness in his blue-gray eyes. But, oh God, he was alive! Alive!

"Clinton," she whispered disbelievingly, pushing herself away from her desk. Then, louder, affirmatively, "Clinton!"

He embraced her tightly. "Hello, Mama. When no one was home, I thought I might find you here." He laughed shortly. "Actually, I thought I'd find you at Twelfth and State. I had to stop in at the Board of Trade on South Water Street to find out what had become of McKinnon Meats!"

"Oh, it's Wednesday," Eden said distractedly. "Most of the servants are off, and Louise probably went out for a visit before making dinner. But, Clinton, how did you get here? Where have you been? It's almost like you've come back from the dead! Oh, my dear, dear son!"

She embraced him again until Clinton gently pulled away. "It's a long story, Mama. Incredible, really. I'll tell you everything later. Right now, it's just so good to be home, and I'm sure you can understand I'm anxious to see Jocelyn."

Eden's shining eyes clouded. "Jocelyn's not here, Clinton."

He frowned. "She's gone back to Atlanta? I was afraid she might. I can't really blame her. Well, I'll send her a telegram at once and go down after her."

Shaking her head, Eden said softly, "She's not in Atlanta, Clinton. She's in Kansas City."

"Missouri? But why? Never mind, it's closer than Atlanta. I can probably get there in a day."

Turning away from him, Eden whispered, "It might be better if you didn't go."

"Mama, that's impossible! Do you know how many nights I lay awake, thinking of her beautiful eyes, her—" He broke off abruptly as a horrible thought struck him. "Oh, my God, don't tell me she's married!"

Eden nodded. "Clinton, darling, we all thought you were dead! She waited a long time. Benjamin had even gone to North Carolina to look for you."

"When did she marry?"

"In December."

"To someone she met here?"

"Yes."

"Anyone I know?"

She nodded, unable to look at him.

"For God's sake, who?"

"To—Burton." Eden barely whispered the answer.

"Burton! He's away from Chicago for fifteen years, and when he comes back, he steals my intended!"

"Clinton, it's no one's fault! None of us knew—"

"Maybe it's my fault! I should have made her marry me in Atlanta! At least, I should have made her promise to wait. But no, I had to be so fair—so fair that I cheated myself out of the one girl I've ever wanted!"

"Clinton, it might not have made any difference if you had married her. After all those months, how could we help but think—Jocelyn was young. No one could expect—"

"I don't blame her!" Clinton cut her off. "But I can't quite believe—never mind. I'll stay with you and Ben a few days. After that, the least I can do is go to Kansas City to congratulate my brother and his bride."

Sighing irritably, Jocelyn shifted in her armchair and leafed through the latest issue of *Harper's Monthly Magazine*. The trouble with being eight months pregnant was one couldn't do anything. Certainly, she could not go out in society in this grotesque, graceless condition.

It would help a bit if her husband at least showed her some consideration. But, since their move to Kansas City, Burton had thrown himself into meat packing with exactly the zeal he had claimed to despise in Eden and Benjamin. He was rarely home, and when he was, he treated her with a bored condescension that infuriated her.

Too late, Jocelyn had realized that Burton was nothing like his late brother, Clinton. Burton was too preoccupied with his own schemes even to think of her feelings. Just because she had been unhappy in Chicago, he seemed to think she should be eternally grateful to him for taking her away from that city.

Well, she wasn't grateful! Kansas City was hopelessly provincial, and she hadn't made a single friend since their arrival in May.

Worst of all, she now realized that she and Burton could never share the quiet affection she had hoped for when they married. She had been prepared to live without love. Still, she had expected some warmth between them.

If only Clinton had come back from the war! She had not loved him, either. But she had been fond of him, and he had claimed to love her. In hindsight, she thought that would have been enough.

"Madam, you have a visitor," Jocelyn's maid said from the door of her sitting room.

Jocelyn grimaced. "I thought I made it clear I did not want to receive guests until after the baby is born."

"Yes, madam, but he says he's a member of the family."

She frowned. It must be Benjamin, the only male member of the family. But why was he in Kansas City? Why hadn't he wired that he was coming? Why couldn't he have left her alone and gone directly to Burton, at the plant site?

"All right," she sighed irritably. "I'll see him in the parlor, downstairs."

Angry at Benjamin for appearing unannounced, Jocelyn took her time about going to the parlor. But as she stepped through the door and saw the visitor, all color drained from her face. Weak-kneed, she stumbled to a chair.

Watching her, Clinton felt suddenly sorry he had not sent a wire announcing his arrival, as Eden had advised. He had not wanted to give Jocelyn time to censor her reactions and compose herself. He had wanted to see exactly how she felt when she learned he was alive. After all his months of waiting, hoping, and dreaming, he had felt he deserved that much.

When Eden had pressed him about sending a telegram, he had for the first time in his life lied to her. He had pretended to agree.

Now, as he watched Jocelyn's trembling hands clutching at

her distended stomach, Clinton wished he had listened to his mother. Perhaps he should not have come at all.

"Jocelyn," he asked urgently, "are you all right? Is there anything I can do for you?"

"Oh, my God," she murmured. "Oh, my God! It's you! It's really you! You're alive! Oh, my God!"

She began to sob, great, wracking, pain-filled gasps tearing from her chest. She covered her face with her hands.

"If only I'd waited! But, how long could I wait? How was I supposed to know? How long could I wait?"

Clinton stared at her uneasily, tears filling his own eyes. He had learned what he wanted to know. But, was it worth it?

Kneeling beside her chair, he took her hands gently in his. "Jocelyn, Jocelyn, please calm yourself. I didn't mean to upset you. I thought you'd just be glad I'm alive."

"Yes," she sobbed. "Yes, of course I'm glad! Only, it's too late! I waited all that time for you, but I didn't wait long enough."

Clinton drew a long breath. "It's all right, Jocelyn. I don't blame you. You hadn't made me any promises. And, what else could you think when I didn't come home for so long?"

"Where *were* you?" she demanded as she dried her eyes.

"I was wounded and captured by a crazy old man near Bentonville, North Carolina. He kept me chained up in his cabin. I couldn't escape, couldn't even send a message."

"Oh, God, how I wish you could have at least done that!"

"So do I. It could have saved you and Mama and Benjamin a great deal of pain." He hesitated, considering her last remark. "But, you're happy with Burton, aren't you?"

Jocelyn dabbed at her eyes and blew her nose, stalling as she composed herself. "Of course we're happy. Especially with the baby coming. Don't I look the glowing picture of impending motherhood?"

He forced a laugh. "At the moment, with those bloodshot eyes, I can't say you look very glowing! But, that's my fault. I shouldn't have surprised you."

"No. It's the best surprise I've had in months. Really. I hope you will stay with us a long, long time."

"I'd like that. It's been a long time since I've seen my brother. I assume he's at the new plant?"

"Yes. He's always—he works very hard."

"If you'll give me directions, I'll go on over there now. Anyway, in your condition, you must need your rest."

"No! Please, stay with me. All I ever do is rest! Burton can see you later. Anyway, he'll be too busy at the plant to greet you properly."

Clinton eyed her closely. Had she mellowed so much in the two years they'd been apart? He could not remember any time in Atlanta when she had spoken to him so affectionately.

"All right," he agreed. "I guess I can see Burton later. You don't think he'll be jealous if I spend the afternoon with you?"

"Jealous?" Jocelyn's laugh was brittle. "No. I don't think he'll be jealous of his own brother."

"Need I be?" a voice asked from the parlor doorway.

Jocelyn and Clinton looked up to see Burton watching them with a sardonic smile.

"Hello, Burt," Clinton said, rising and extending his hand.

Ignoring him, Burton addressed his wife. "Since you're always whining about being neglected, I thought I'd come home for tea with you. But, I see I needn't have bothered. Quite a touching scene, you and the returning hero."

Turning to Clinton, he sneered, "What were you doing down on your knees, little brother? Not proposing, I hope. In case you haven't noticed," he cast a sidelong glance at Jocelyn's middle, "this woman is already taken!"

Though his eyes snapped and he was clenching his fists so hard his nails dug into his palms, Clinton said evenly, "It's been much too long, Burton. It's good to see you."

"Is it? I don't suppose you expected to see me under quite these circumstances. Should I apologize for stealing your intended?"

Clinton winced. "Not if you've given her a happy, loving home," he replied.

Burton snorted. "Still suffering from an incurable urge to be noble, aren't you, little brother? I would have thought the war would have taken the edge off your idealism."

His blue-gray eyes hardening, Clintron retorted, "And you're still as selfish as ever, aren't you, Burton? I'd have thought, in all your years of ranching, that you would have grown up!"

"Aha! So you've finally gotten some spunk, after all. Tell me, did Mama send you down to spy on my new plant?"

"Hardly," Clinton said coldly. "Mama did not even want me to come."

Burton raised his brows quizzically. "Then I guess you have changed, after all."

Turning to Jocelyn, he explained, "My brother devoted his young years to pleasing our mother. So you see, the two of you would not have been very well matched."

Addressing Clinton again, he said, "Jocelyn was not too fond of Mama."

Jocelyn paled as Clinton looked at her questioningly. "That's not quite true," she whispered. "Eden was extremely kind to me, and I was very grateful. It's just that I felt uncomfortable living in the North, depending on Yankee charity."

Clinton nodded. "Perhaps I was wrong to send you there. I didn't want you to be uncomfortable. But, you couldn't have stayed in Atlanta, and I'm afraid you would have been unhappy anywhere else in Georgia."

"Don't apologize," Burton cut in. "If you hadn't sent Jocelyn to Chicago, I wouldn't have met her, and we wouldn't be married now. So, you see, things worked out for the best—at least for some of us."

"I'd like to think so," Clinton said, eyeing the pale, uncomfortable Jocelyn.

Burton scowled. "I came home for tea. Are we going to have it, or shall I just go back to the plant?"

Nervously wetting her lips, Jocelyn said, "You and Clinton have something. I'm afraid my stomach doesn't feel quite up to any food or drink right now." Rising, she hurried out of the parlor and up the stairs.

Watching her, Burton smiled wryly. "I'm afraid my wife is prone to be a bit dramatic about this pregnancy. That's one thing I'll say for Mama, as I recall, she managed quite nicely caring for us and the inn while she was carrying Paige—and with none of these theatrics."

He shrugged and walked to a cabinet, where he took out a bottle and glasses. "Since Jocelyn won't be joining us, I think we can indulge in something a bit stronger than tea. A friend just brought me this Jim Beam from Kentucky. You're not a teetotaler, are you?"

Shaking his head, Clinton took the glass offered him. He sipped in silence for a few moments, then said, "I apologize if I upset Jocelyn. I suppose I shouldn't have come unannounced."

"You didn't upset her," Burton replied offhandedly. "As I said, she's fond of these little theatrics. Sometimes I think she plans them to make me feel guilty for impregnating her." He paused, holding his bourbon glass up to the light and squinting at the amber liquid. "You know, even if you'd come back sooner, she wouldn't have married you."

With an effort, Clinton kept his voice level. "Oh?"

"She told me herself, she was just waiting for you to come back, so she could break the news in person. Anyway, you ought to thank me for taking her off your hands. To tell the truth, she's quite the little bitch."

Clinton's tone became sharper. "It's obvious you don't love her, so why did you marry her?"

Burton shrugged, grinning sardonically. "Only callow youths marry for love. It was time I had a wife. Jocelyn was reasonably attractive. And we had some important things in common—our dislike for Mama, for example. Anyway, you needn't worry yourself about her. She's not suffering, and I'll always take good care of her." He laughed shortly. "I don't beat her, you know."

"Not physically, perhaps."

Burton stared intently at his brother, as if considering a retort. Then he downed his drink and started for the door. "I've been away from the plant too long. I'll see you at dinner."

Almost an hour later, Clinton was pacing irritably in the bedroom assigned to him when he heard a muffled cry from another room. Stepping into the hallway, he heard the cry again, more clearly. It was Jocelyn.

"Clinton! Clinton!" she sobbed. "Help me! Please! Clinton!"

Following the cry, he rushed to her bedroom. He opened the door and found her collapsed on the floor, weakly calling his name.

"Jocelyn! For God's sake, what happened?"

"I—I don't know," she murmured. "I—I felt something—down there. And then, all of a sudden, there was something wet on my legs—and blood—and—ooh!—the pain!"

Clinton trembled as he looked at her. "I'll go for a doctor immediately."

"No! Don't leave me. Send—send Josie—my maid. Tell her—Doctor Hillman."

"All right." He turned and saw that Josie was already hovering in the hallway, her eyes round with fright. As the girl hurried off on her errand, Clinton knelt beside Jocelyn and took her hand. Her pulse felt strangely weak.

Pale with worry, he lifted her gently and carried her to her bed, wincing as he felt the wet spots on the back of her gown.

"I'll send for Burton," he suggested.

"No!" Jocelyn almost screamed her protest. "He'll—he'll just accuse me of being foolish. Please, don't leave. Stay with me!"

He stayed, though tears stung his eyes and he felt her pain almost as keenly as she. Finally, he heard running footsteps on the stairway, and Josie led the doctor into the room.

Barely glancing at Clinton, the doctor ordered, "Kindly step outside, so I can examine Mrs. McKinnon."

"No!" Jocelyn insisted. "I want him here!"

The doctor frowned. "You're the husband?"

"No. The brother-in-law." Christ, Clinton thought, hadn't Burton even taken the time to meet his wife's doctor?

"I think you'd better leave."

"No!" Jocelyn clung to Clinton's hand.

Gently peeling away her fingers, Clinton whispered, "It's all right, Jocelyn. I'll be right outside the door. If you need anything, I'll be right here."

He fled the room and paced the hallway until the doctor came out, half an hour later.

"She's started labor," the doctor said briskly, "she'll have the child."

"How soon?"

"You might as well ask Mother Nature. Find that girl and tell her to get me some clean linens."

When Burton arrived home at seven o'clock, Clinton was sitting at the top of the stairs. Weak with worry, he had collapsed there, hiding his head in his arms to muffle Jocelyn's pain-wracked screams.

"What's going on?" Burton demanded, running up the stairs to confront his brother.

"Your wife is giving birth."

"Christ! Why didn't anyone let me know?"

"I didn't think you'd care. Besides, I assumed you'd be home before the actual birth. The doctor assured me it would take hours."

"That's just what I mean! If I'd known this would be going on, I'd have stayed at the plant. Do you think I want to listen to her scream all night? Well," he shrugged, "we might as well go down and have dinner."

Clinton stared at him. "You can't be serious! How can you even think of eating now?"

"Because I'm hungry, and there's no point in my sitting here twisting my hands. From the looks of you, you've already done enough of that for both of us."

"Aren't you at least going to go in and see her?"

"Whatever for? I assume Josie and the doctor are taking care of her. If the doctor should need me, God forbid, he'll call for me."

"Maybe Jocelyn needs you. Maybe it would help her to see you."

Burton rolled his eyes. "I seriously doubt that. Are you coming to dinner?"

"No. I don't think I'll have any appetite until this is all over."

Sighing in exasperation, Burton turned and galloped down the stairs.

After dinner, Burton closed himself in his downstairs study, with a bottle of Jim Beam to keep him company. Clinton remained in the upstairs hallway, shivering at the sounds coming from Jocelyn's room.

Her screams intensified. Then, shortly after the parlor clock struck ten, Clinton froze at the sound of a baby's cry. A few moments later, Josie bustled out of the room, carrying a whimpering bundle. She hurried past Clinton, into another bedroom, before he could even ask the child's sex.

Still, he was relieved the ordeal was over and Jocelyn was no longer screaming. By the time the doctor emerged, twenty minutes later, Clinton was smiling.

"May I see her now, doctor?"

"The baby? Of course. She's a fine, healthy girl."

"No, I mean Jocelyn. I'd like to see her for just a moment. Or, is she sleeping?"

"She's—"

For the first time, Clinton realized how somber the doctor looked. "For God's sake, don't tell me something's happened to her?"

The doctor hesitated. "I think I'd better talk to the husband. Is he home now?"

"Yes, in his study. But—tell me!"

"Please, show me to your brother."

Clinton, followed by the doctor, burst into Burton's study

without knocking. Looking up from his half-empty glass of bourbon, Burton smiled dourly. "So it's over, is it? What do we have?"

"A daughter, Mr. McKinnon. A fine, healthy girl. A bit large for a premature birth. Perhaps that's why—"

"A girl, eh?" Burton cut him off. "I don't suppose she'll be much use to me in the business. But, then again, look at my mother."

He stared into his bourbon for a moment. "I suppose you wanted to see me about your fee, doctor? Would you care for a drink first?"

"No. Mr. McKinnon, it's about your wife—"

"For God's sake, doctor," Clinton cut in in an anguished tone, "out with it! What happened to Jocelyn?"

"Well, she—she hemorrhaged rather extensively. You know she was bleeding before you even called me. And then, when the baby was born—well, as I said, the child was quite large—and—I just couldn't stop the blood. She—"

Unable to bear the suspense, Clinton demanded, "Is she alive?"

"I—she's—" The doctor sighed. "No."

There was a horrible silence in the room. Even Burton looked stunned. Slowly, he pulled himself from his chair and took a step toward the doctor.

"Get out!" he shouted. "Get out of my house, you god-damned butcher!"

"Mr. McKinnon, I assure you, I did everything possible. It's one of the unfortunate risks of bearing children that—Mrs. McKinnon was, as I'm sure you know, quite frail, and—"

"Out!" Burton roared.

The doctor glanced apprehensively at Clinton as he backed toward the door. "Of course. I understand. The shock. Perhaps tomorrow, or the day after—"

"Out!"

The door slammed and Burton turned on his brother. "You, too, you idealistic son of a bitch! Get the hell out of my house and don't come back!"

"Take it easy, Burt. I must feel as bad as you."

"She wasn't your wife!"

"Well, for the last three hours, you've acted as if she weren't yours! You couldn't even stop in to squeeze her hand or kiss her forehead, for Christ's sake!"

"I mean it, Clinton. Get out! I'm not going to listen to you preach to me! If you hadn't shown up, this never would have happened."

Clinton paled. All evening, he had worried that he had somehow caused the premature birth. "I don't believe that," he said shakily.

"Well, I do, and that's all that matters! So, get out! And take that goddamned brat with you!"

Now Clinton's blue-gray eyes flashed fire. "I ought to take her, because I imagine you'll be one hell of a rotten father! But she's your flesh and blood. She belongs here."

"I don't want her! I never wanted a daughter. I wanted a wife. Now, thanks to you and that baby, I don't have a wife. I won't tolerate that brat in this house! Take her back to Chicago. Give her to someone on the train. I don't care what you do with her! But, I warn you, if you leave her here, I won't be responsible for what happens to her!"

35
December 1867–May 1868

"Pretty! Pretty!" The tiny child stared at the Christmas tree in delight, her blonde curls bobbing as she nodded excitedly.

Clinton smiled down at her tenderly, lifting her into his arms and hugging her tightly. Her cornflower-blue eyes glowed as she returned his hug, and he had to blink back the tears from his own eyes.

It was hard to believe she was already sixteen months old, hard to believe something so precious and beautiful had come from that terrible day in Kansas City. Clinton had named her Mara, and he loved her as his own daughter.

Indeed, the child called him "Daddy." It was easier that way, and by now Clinton had accepted the fact that Burton would never claim her.

At first, expecting his brother to soften with time, Clinton had sent him numerous letters and telegrams, begging him to visit the child. He had described Mara's infant progress in minute detail, hoping to spark her father's pride. None of his messages had even received a response.

Now it was Christmas again, and Mara would have no gifts from her real father. Perhaps it didn't matter. She wouldn't know. And she was happy with Clinton, with Eden, or "Gamma," as she called her, and with Benjamin, whom she called "Gampa," since she was far too young to understand he was really her uncle.

Eden entered the parlor, carrying a stack of brightly wrapped Christmas gifts. She stopped to kiss her granddaughter's cheek before kneeling to place the packages beneath the tree.

"These arrived today from Texas—Paige and Garrett," she told Clinton. "Something for you, for Benjamin and me, and three packages for Mara."

Clinton smiled cynically. "It's too bad all my siblings can't be so thoughtful."

Sighing, Eden averted her eyes. "He can't help it, Clint. He's suffering. It takes a long time to overcome the death of a spouse."

"Mama, you know that's not it! I loved Jocelyn ten times more than he ever did! Besides, Burton doesn't know how to mourn. From the time we were boys, he could never think of anyone but himself."

Eden eyed him disapprovingly. "You used to be more compassionate, Clinton."

"I still am compassionate—to those who deserve it."

She sighed, turning to stare at the gifts for a long, wistful moment. "Wouldn't it be wonderful if we could all be together again for Christmas? Do you know how long it's been since I had all my children home at once? Seventeen years! Now Paige is in Texas, Burton's in Missouri. Well, at least I have you and Ben, and my darling little grandchild."

Clinton smiled. "No doubt Paige will be back here someday, at least to visit—probably with several more grandchildren in tow."

"I wonder. They've already been married four years, and Garrett's so much older than she. Not that I could have chosen a finer man for her. But, I still can't understand why they ran away together so suddenly."

"A lot of people did surprising things during the war."

"I suppose. I just hope neither of them has been disappointed. They both deserve so much."

                              *   *   *

At the Double M ranch, Paige stared moodily out her
bedroom window. She frowned as three-year-old Miguel's
laughter and his mother Conchita's happy chatter drifted to
her from downstairs.

Paige adored her little nephew and treasured the friendship of his mother. But, lately, whenever she saw Miguel,
she felt a pang of jealousy that he was not her own.

How she craved a child of her own! At twenty, she felt
more than ready to endure all the pain of childbearing, which
had so terrified her when Miguel was born. Sometimes, she
almost wished she had borne Jefferson Montgomery's child.
At least then she would have one child.

As it was, she had begun to despair of ever conceiving.
How could she when Garrett rarely made love to her?

She had always assumed that her husband would be passionate and demanding in bed. But, to her profound shock,
she found herself ardently desiring Garrett while he approached lovemaking with indifference, or, worse, as if he
felt resigned to a duty.

On the rare occasions when he did make love to her, he
was tender and considerate of her needs. But, afterward, she
often felt as if he had not really wanted to do it, and was not
really satisfied.

Paige had begun to feel she lacked some important attribute.
However, she was too embarrassed to question her husband,
and so she suffered in silence, never confiding her feelings in
anyone.

On reflection, she felt she had very little to complain
about. Garrett was kind and indulgent to a fault, and all of
the cowboys and vaqueros were unfailingly polite. It was true
the isolation of ranch life allowed her few close women friends.
But she was very close to Conchita, and saw other ranchers'
wives at occasional parties.

Over the Christmas holidays, just past, Garrett had stayed
home more than usual, to escort her to several parties and
host their own open house at the Double M. He always
complimented her on her appearance, and always seemed proud
to present her to other people.

Now, however, the holidays had been over for a month,
and Garrett was back on the range, where he seemed most
relaxed. Paige could not fault him for his thorough personal

involvement in the business, though she sometimes felt he was avoiding her.

Oh, stop it! she admonished herself as she threw off the covers and got out of bed. What did you expect when you chased after him in Illinois? You wanted him to marry you. Well, he did. You succeeded. You got the man you'd fallen in love with. It's no one's fault if everything hasn't turned out like a dream. But, is this really all there is to love?

Squinting into the sunlight, Garrett watched his foreman, Charley Streeter, riding toward him. In another two years, Charley would be seventy. But he still looked every inch the cowboy, ready to live and die on the range, with neither possessions nor emotional involvements to tie him down.

Watching Charley, Garrett felt a twinge of envy and wondered if he wouldn't have been happier if he hadn't been born on the owner side of the ranching hierarchy. In a lot of ways, his life might have been much easier.

Oh hell, Garrett thought, I guess I've got too much ambition just to be a cowboy. It's not the ranching that bothers me, it's some of the trappings that go with it—like a wife.

He smiled grimly. That's not being fair to Paige. She's a decent girl, and she'd make an excellent wife for some man half my age. Even with all the differences between ranch life and the way she grew up in Chicago, she's never been one to whine or complain.

In fact, there's only one thing wrong with her, and that's more my fault than hers. She's not Eden. She's Eden's daughter. And every time I go to bed with her I feel like I'm committing some kind of incest.

God, what an idiot I was to ask her to marry me! Even under the circumstances, thinking she was pregnant, I should have been able to think of a better solution. I guess my mind was just too messed up from the night before, with Eden.

Paige deserves a better marriage. She deserves a husband who'd give her more companionship. But, if I spent more time with her, I'd go mad, thinking about her mother. It wouldn't work, and we'd end up despising each other. At least that hasn't happened yet. I am fond of Paige, and I think she's actually in love with me.

"Trying to solve the problems of the world?" Charley asked as he rode up to Garrett.

The rancher forced a smile. "No. Just thinking about our cattle drive later this year."

"Hell, that's nothing to frown about! We ought to be able to send a couple thousand head. And, now that the railroad's made it all the way to Abilene, the drive won't be half bad. No mountains or forests to spook the damned longhorns."

Garrett nodded. "Yes, it should be a relatively easy drive. And things ought to be pretty comfortable at the end of the trail. I hear Joe McCoy is building all kinds of barns, stables, stockpens, and loading chutes, so they can herd the cattle right onto trains and ship 'em east. He's even putting up a hotel for the packers and ranchers to meet in. He'll make a fortune from his investments. I'm surprised Eden and her boys didn't think of doing it."

Charley grunted agreement. McCoy was an Illinois meat dealer who had just been starting when Garrett and Charley left Iowa for Texas. Recently, he had approached the Kansas Pacific Railroad and arranged special low rates on cattle shipped east from Abilene, Kansas. The Hannibal and St. Joseph Railroad, running from Kansas City to Chicago, had agreed to similar concessions. Now, McCoy was preparing for the first meeting of drovers, cattle, and buyers at Abilene.

"So," Charley pressed, "what's the problem? I could see your frown a mile away."

"No problem," Garrett insisted. "But, since it will be the first of its type, I think I'll head up this drive."

Charley stared at him. "You ain't figuring on taking your wife along, are you?"

"On a cattle drive? You ought to know better, Charley."

"Well, I don't think she'll like staying behind too much, and I can't say as I'd blame her. I mean, you could be gone a good three months."

Garrett shrugged. "Paige grew up in the meat business. She understands. Her own mother was tied up in the business most of the time."

"That was different. For one thing, it was during the war. For another, Mrs. McKinnon went home nights. She didn't have to stay away completely for weeks or months at a time. Anyway, there's no reason you have to go. You didn't go up to Sedalia the last two years. You got plenty of men on this ranch you can depend on to manage this drive."

"Whose side are you on, anyway, Charley?"

The old man gave him a hard look. "I didn't know there

was sides to be taken. I didn't know you and the wife was at war."

"We're not!" Garrett snapped. "I've just been talking about business. You're the one who's trying to make a problem where there isn't one."

"Okay." Charley shrugged. "What does an old bachelor like me know about wives, anyway? I was just tryin' to give you some advice, but I guess maybe you don't need it."

Softening, Garrett clapped his old friend on the shoulder. "It's all right, Charley. But you just don't understand how things are between Paige and me. Believe me, I know what's best, and it's best that I go on that drive."

"Maybe it would've been better if you'd never married the girl!" Charley mumbled.

For the next several months, Garrett kept thinking of that conversation with Charley Streeter. He put off telling Paige that he intended to go on the drive. Still, he felt convinced he should go.

It wouldn't be right, he told himself, to let any of the vaqueros handle the sales in Abilene. This would be the Double M's first major drive, meeting more important packers than ever before. It was only right that he should lead it.

Finally, in May, Garrett decided he could no longer put off telling Paige his plans. Coming in one afternoon after several days on the range, he announced, "I've decided to head up our drive to Abilene next month. It's an important step in the cattle business, and it wouldn't be fair to entrust all the responsibility to one of our employees."

To his surprise, Paige clapped her hands and exclaimed, "Wonderful!"

Garrett's blue eyes narrowed. "You don't mind?"

"Of course not! In fact, I was hoping you'd want to go! You see, just yesterday, I received a letter from Mama. She and Benjamin have decided to go down to Abilene to meet the drive."

Closing his eyes, Garrett sighed. Why hadn't he asked Paige if there was any news before he told her his plans? If Eden and Benjamin were going to be there, Abilene was the last place he wanted to go. He didn't think he could bear to see them together as husband and wife.

"Well then," he said quickly, "if your mother and her husband are going to be in Abilene, I guess there's really no reason why I'd have to go. They can take care of any negotiations themselves. Actually, everything will work out better that way. I'll admit I was rather concerned about leaving you here with just Conchita and Miguel and a handful of cowboys for the three months or so I'd have to be gone."

"But I didn't intend to stay here," Paige said. "I thought if you went on the drive, I could accompany you."

Garrett stared at her. Of course. That was why she was so excited. She thought she would have a reunion with her family. If he hadn't been so wound up in his own feelings, he would have realized that at once.

Still, her proposal was out of the question. Women simply did not go on cattle drives.

"Paige, dear," he said evenly, "I'm afraid you have no idea what you're suggesting. I'd be a very poor excuse for a husband if I agreed to take you on this cattle drive."

"Why? I've heard you discussing it with the other ranchers, and you all seem to agree it will be much easier than previous drives."

"Easier, yes. But that doesn't mean it will be easy."

She sighed. "Garrett, I'm not expecting luxury. In case you've forgotten, I managed quite well when we came down from Kansas City on horseback. And Abilene is closer than Kansas City."

"Paige, a cattle drive is hardly the same as a horseback ride. When you travel with a couple thousand longhorns, even on the edge of the herd, you've got to eat the dust they kick up every day of the drive. You never feel clean. Even the food in the chuck wagon gets coated with dust. You taste it at every meal."

"Do you think I'm too fragile to withstand a little hardship?"

"No, dammit! But there's no reason to subject you to it. Besides, it's more than hardship. A cattle drive can be downright dangerous, even to someone who knows longhorns. You never know what might cause a steer to roll his tail and start a stampede. A flash of lightning in the middle of the night could do it. You could be killed, crushed to death in the middle of it. It happens—even to experienced cowboys."

"You just don't want me with you, do you? You want to get away from me, like you always do, even when we're home."

"Don't be absurd! I've already told you, since your mother and Benjamin will be in Abilene, there's no reason for either of us to go. We'll both stay home."

"But I don't want to stay home! I'm sick and tired of sitting in this ranch house, doing nothing. I haven't even got any babies to take care of! I want to be a part of the business. If my mother is, why can't I be?"

"You're not your mother!" Garrett exploded.

Immediately, he was sorry. He felt the color drain from his face as Paige's mouth dropped open. Did she realize the full meaning of those words? No, of course not. She couldn't.

Averting his eyes, he cleared his throat uneasily. The silence in the room felt oppressive. "Paige, be sensible," he said quietly. "Your mother works in a plant office. Before that, she managed an inn. She works very hard, I know, but what she does is not comparable to riding the range or herding cattle. If you want to be more active in the business, I'll teach you to do the ranch bookkeeping. In fact, I'd greatly appreciate your taking that responsibility off my shoulders."

Paige stared at him for a long moment before nodding. "Fine. I'll be glad to keep the books. In fact, I was very good with figures when I was in school. But, I still want to go to Abilene this summer. After four and one-half years, I think I've a right to want to see my family."

36
August 1868

Standing between Benjamin and Burton, Eden surveyed the stockpens of the Kansas City plant of McKinnon Meats. Within the month, they would be filled with cattle shipped east from Abilene.

"You've really done an admirable job here, Burton," she said sincerely. "The plant is running so smoothly, it's hard to believe you only started building it a little over two years ago."

Burton smiled sardonically. "You sound surprised. You really didn't think I'd be successful, did you?"

"Of course I did! We all did. You were always so interested in meat packing, even as a little boy."

"Unlike my little brother, Clinton. I'm surprised to hear

he's thrown himself into the business so thoroughly. But then, he always would do anything to please you!"

Eden winced, knowing Clinton's sudden interest in McKinnon Meats was not to please her. Ever since he had returned from Kansas City, with the infant Mara, he had seemed driven. In contrast to his infinite tenderness with the child, he had a bitter edge now.

More than anything else, Clinton wanted to stake his claim in McKinnon Meats to keep Burton from becoming too powerful. Several times, he had told Eden and Benjamin it was a disgrace to let a man of Burton's character run the Kansas City plant.

Still, despite all her disappointment in him, Eden could not cut Burton off. He was her son. Her firstborn. She still hoped that time would heal all the wounds within the family. In the meantime, Burton was doing a good job in Kansas City. No one could deny that.

Suddenly aware of the uneasy silence, Eden said quickly, "You're sure you don't want to come on to Abilene with us, Burton? Paige and Garrett will be there. I'm sure they'd be glad to see you."

"Are you really? I'm not so sure! Anyway, I trust you and Ben to pick out the stock. It shouldn't be too difficult, since you can start with a few thousand prime head from the Double M."

"Yes. Well then, I'll just give Paige and Garrett your greetings. It's a pity you and your sister have never had much chance to get to know each other."

"Oh, we had enough time at the end of the war, when I was still living on the ranch. Can't say I ever did really understand why she married Garrett Martin, though. Of course," Burton added slyly, "there was the baby."

"Baby?" Eden stared at him in surprise.

"You didn't know? I just assumed they would have written you about it. For the longest time, they thought Paige was carrying a baby. Must have been conceived right about the time they got married. Then, all of a sudden, the doctor examined her and said she wasn't expecting at all."

"I—I never knew," Eden stammered. "Of course, maybe with the war, the letter might have been lost. And, since then, I suppose they haven't even wanted to think about it. Especially now that they've been married close to five years and they still haven't any children."

My God! she thought to herself. Is that why Garrett married her? It's not possible, is it? He couldn't have been making love to my daughter in my own house! And then, that last night, with me—but, why else didn't they tell me about the baby?

"Eden, are you all right?" Benjamin asked urgently. "All of a sudden, you're looking very pale."

"I—no, I'm fine. It's just the sun out here. It's hotter than in Chicago."

"Of course," Burton smiled condescendingly. "We're further south. And of course, you're not as young as you used to be, Mama. We'd better go in."

Flashing Burton an angry glance as they turned and walked into the plant, Benjamin said, "Speaking of babies, you might be interested in knowing Mara is doing very well."

Burton remained impassive. "With a fine father like my brother, I'm sure she must be."

"Don't you ever wonder about her?" Benjamin pressed.

"Why should I? I know she's in good hands. Besides, as I told Clinton, I never wanted a daughter. Anyway," he went on with a wry smile, "I figure I'm doing all of you a favor, letting you keep her. You'll certainly never have any children of your own. Unless, of course, you're planning to marry some young girl, once Mama passes on. I suppose you wouldn't have much trouble finding someone, with the McKinnon money to back you up!"

Benjamin's gray-green eyes narrowed, flashing fire as he stared at his half brother. Then his fist shot out, meeting Burton's jaw and sending him crashing against the corridor wall.

As Eden gasped and the stunned Burton rubbed his jaw, Benjamin spoke softly. "That was for your mother's sake, Burt. You know I'm not the fighting kind, but maybe the pain can get a few things through your thick head. Number one, I love your mother. That's the one and only reason I married her. Number two, I'm not a fortune hunter. I happen to feel a certain pride in building the business my father founded, and I simply like the challenge of meat packing. I'm not out to take anything away from you, or Clinton, or anyone else—"

"Get out!" Burton muttered through clenched teeth. "If Mama weren't here, I'd beat you to within an inch of your life! So, get out, before I have second thoughts and do it anyway!"

Taking Eden's arm, Benjamin led her toward the plant exit. He stopped in the doorway and turned back toward his half brother. "I don't believe you for a moment," he said. "You don't care any more for your mother than for anyone else—and you never have!"

Outside, he turned to Eden apologetically. "I'm sorry. I shouldn't have put you through that. But it's time someone told Burton off, for everyone's sake."

She nodded, squeezing his arm. "I know. And I'm not sorry for anything you said—or did. I just hope it's not too late to do some good."

Garrett shifted uneasily as he and Paige waited at the Abilene station of the Kansas Pacific Railroad. He wished for the hundredth time that he had stayed at the Double M. Now it was too late. Eden and Benjamin's train would be in at any minute.

He had managed to convince Paige she could not participate in the cattle drive. But her disappointment had so touched him that he had relented and agreed to accompany her to Abilene by stagecoach.

For a while, he actually had considered sending her alone while he stayed behind at the ranch. But that would have been cowardly. Eden would have understood why he was not there. But he could not expect Paige to understand, especially since he had at first wanted to make the trip.

Well, the situation couldn't be helped. Paige deserved the reunion with her mother and half brother. It was the least he could do for her.

As soon as Eden and Benjamin arrived, Garrett intended to leave Paige with them and ride south to join the cattle drive, still on its way to Abilene. With any luck, he could be gone three or four days. And by the time he got back, he'd be too involved in cattle sales to spend much time with them.

A train whistle caught his attention, and Paige tugged at his arm excitedly. "I never thought I'd be this anxious to see Mama," she exclaimed. "I mean, I always loved her, but we did have our disagreements at times."

Garrett forced a smile. "All mothers and daughters do, I suppose. No doubt she's every bit as anxious to see you as you are to see her. I'm glad you talked me into bringing you."

"Oh, so am I!" Impulsively, Paige stood on tiptoe to kiss her husband's cheek as the train slowed at the station.

Looking down from the train window, Benjamin patted Eden's shoulder and pointed. "There's Paige and Garrett. They certainly look happy together."

Despite her best intentions, Eden winced slightly at the sight of her daughter kissing her own former lover. "Yes," she replied dully, "they do look happy, don't they?"

Benjamin frowned. "What's the matter? You're not still brooding about that story Burton told us about Paige carrying a child? I wouldn't believe anything he says. But, even if he wasn't lying, what difference does it make? As long as Paige and Garrett are married and love each other, that's all that matters, isn't it?"

Eden nodded. "Yes. Of course. I guess it's just kind of a shock to actually see my youngest with a husband almost as old as me."

"Well, you'll get used to it. After all, their age difference is less of an oddity than yours and mine."

By that time, Paige had caught sight of them, and was waving furiously. Infected by her daughter's enthusiasm, Eden rushed off the train to embrace her. Then, while Paige hugged Benjamin, Eden extended a hand to Garrett and spoke quietly.

"Hello, Garrett. You're looking as fine as ever. Thank you for taking such good care of my little girl."

His eyes searched hers as he took her hand. She looked older this time, as if her fifty-six years had finally begun to catch up with her. Still, he could see the same resilient spirit that had charmed him since their first meeting in the Bull and Boar Inn.

"Hello, Eden," he answered. "It's always good to see you."

She trembled slightly at the touch of his hand and averted her eyes. "You remember my husband, Benjamin, don't you?"

"Of course, though the last time I met him, he wasn't your husband." Garrett offered his hand to Benjamin, who shook it warmly. "Good to see you again, Ben. I'm glad you and Clinton both got home safely from the war."

I really am glad, he insisted to himself. *If you hadn't come home, I'd never forgive myself for marrying Paige.*

Benjamin smiled. "From what I hear, you were something of a war hero yourself. That must have been some cattle drive through the Ozarks! I guess my little sister's gotten herself quite a husband."

"I just hope I'm good enough for her," Garrett replied. "Speaking of cattle drives, our current one hasn't quite made it up to Abilene yet. Now that I know Paige is in safe hands, I thought I'd ride down and meet it."

"Yes, Garrett never quite gets enough of being a cowboy," Paige teased. "Maybe you'd like to go with him, Ben. It surely would give you a different view of meat packing than what you see in Chicago."

Garrett glanced uneasily at Eden. "I can't say I'd recommend the trip. If you're not used to cow punching, it could even be a bit dangerous. Of course, it's not up to me to tell you what to do."

Benjamin nodded. "I'd like to come along, and I think I can stay out of your way. It's true I've lived in the city nearly thirty years, but I had a taste of roughing it in the army, and my Indian upbringing ought to count for something."

"Do you really think you ought to go, Ben?" Eden asked.

"Well, I won't if you don't want me to. But we are half owners of the Double M, so we ought to be aware of what's involved in a cattle drive."

"I suppose. Go, if you want."

Why shouldn't he go? she thought. What does it matter if Ben and Garrett spend a few days together? Garrett's too discreet to reveal anything of our past. Benjamin's too trusting to suspect anything.

And, why should Garrett care if Ben rides with him? He's been married to my daughter nearly five years. Obviously, he no longer cares that I'm married to Benjamin.

Sitting in Eden's hotel room, Paige eyed her mother closely. "Mama," she said carefully, "you're not still angry, are you, that Garrett and I eloped?"

"Angry? I was never angry. Surprised, yes. Disappointed that I couldn't attend my only daughter's wedding. But not angry."

"That's what I'd always thought. But, at the station today, when you greeted Garrett, you seemed rather—cool. I'd thought you would kiss him or something. After all, he is your son-in-law now, a member of the family."

"Well, Paige, it's hard to stop seeing people the way we always have. You must understand, I'd known Garrett Martin for over twenty years—since before you were born—as a—a friend and later a business partner."

"But, you don't object to our marriage?"

"Not if it makes you happy. I trust it does?"

"Of course," Paige replied a bit too quickly. "I couldn't ask for anyone better than Garrett. He's at least twice the man Jefferson Montgomery was." She sighed. "What a naive child I was about Jeff."

Eden smiled. "I'd almost forgotten about him. But, I suppose your experience with the young gambler was all part of growing up. At least it didn't hurt you any."

"No." Paige averted her eyes. Anxious to change the subject, she asked, "You stopped in Kansas City on the way down, didn't you?"

"Yes. The new plant is really splendid. I wish your father could have lived to see it."

"And how's Burton?"

Eden sighed. "Burton is—Burton. I still don't know what to make of him. I guess I'll never understand his giving up Mara. At the time, I thought it was just the intensity of his grief. But, even now, two years later, he's not at all interested in the child."

"I don't understand, either," Paige said. "If Garrett and I had a baby—" She broke off, flushing. "Well, I suppose I shouldn't be too shocked at Burton's behavior. After all, he abandoned Miguel, too."

Seeing her mother's frown of confusion, Paige felt instantly sorry she had spoken without thinking. If only her mind hadn't been on the babies she and Garrett didn't have!

"Who is Miguel?" Eden asked quietly.

"Oh, I should have known Burton wouldn't tell you! I almost wrote you about him dozens of times, but Garrett said it wasn't our place to interfere. Miguel is Burton's son. He's four now. An adorable boy."

"He—he lives at the ranch?"

"Yes, with his mother, Conchita. She's my best friend on the Double M."

Dimly, Eden recalled a conversation with Garrett, years earlier. "Mostly," Garrett had said, "Burton entertains himself with our young Mexican cook."

"Burton never married the girl?" Eden asked Paige.

"No. He seemed to think it was beneath him to marry a Mexican. And he said he didn't want a baby."

"And all that time, when he was courting Jocelyn in Chicago, he had a son in Texas!"

"I'll be honest with you, Mama. None of us were sorry he didn't come back. Even Conchita realizes she's better off without him. And I think Miguel was too young to remember him."

Eden shook her head. "I don't know how Burton turned out as he did. He doesn't seem to care about anyone, and I'm afraid very few people like him. Benjamin punched him in the jaw when we were in Kansas City."

Paige giggled. "Good for Ben! That's something I think Garrett would have loved to do, many times. Actually, I'm surprised Burton's made a go of the Kansas City plant. He never did much of anything on the ranch."

"Well, maybe he's more interested in packing than ranching. I don't know," Eden shrugged. "I can't go on making excuses for him. It was despicable of him to abandon Mara. And now, to learn he has another child—"

"Would you like to meet Miguel?"

"Yes. And his mother. Perhaps you and Garrett could think about coming up for Christmas and bringing them with you. In the meantime, as soon as Ben and I get back to Chicago, I'll see about making some continuous financial arrangements for both of them. Surely that's the very least we can do."

Benjamin stretched his pleasantly aching muscles and smiled as he rode beside Garrett and the three thousand lowing longhorns. "I'm glad Paige suggested I come out with you," he said. "When we're working at the plant, I don't get much chance to ride. It's been a pleasant, and instructive, change of pace."

Garrett nodded. "You ride very well for someone unaccustomed to it."

Grinning, Benjamin replied, "I'm an Indian, remember. It's in our blood! Seriously though, I've enjoyed this chance to get to know you, Garrett. I can understand now why my father respected you so much, why he trusted you to build up the Double M. Eden and I are grateful for what you've done there—especially since Burton must have been more hindrance than help."

Dismissing the compliment with a shrug, Garrett said, "The ranch is half mine. I'd have been a fool to do less than my best with it."

"Burton didn't seem to feel that way."

"If you'll excuse my saying so, Burton isn't much of a man.

I've never been able to figure out how he could be Brett and Eden's son."

Benjamin laughed shortly. "Nor have I! He's showing good business sense with the Kansas City plant. But, most of the time, I'd rather not even admit we're related!" After a pause, he added, "I don't feel the same about you, Garrett. I'm proud to have you as a brother-in law."

Now it was Garrett's turn to laugh. "For a moment there, I thought you were going to call me your son-in-law!"

Smiling wryly, Benjamin said, "Our family does have a rather confusing set of relationships, doesn't it?"

They rode in silence for several minutes. Then Benjamin said, "I haven't had the chance yet to thank you for all you did for Eden during the war."

Garrett shifted in his saddle, leaning forward to pretend to adjust the bridle. "I didn't do much of anything."

"Don't be so modest! She's told me what a great help you were at the Chicago plant. Eden's an extraordinarily strong woman. But we all need someone to lean on from time to time. I'm glad you were there when I couldn't be."

With an effort, Garrett looked Benjamin in the eye. "Well, I'm glad I could be there to help, though I'm sure she could have managed without me. Anyway, I reaped my own reward. I met Paige there."

Nodding, Benjamin stared at him intently. "You love her, don't you?" he asked quietly.

"Of course. Why else would I have married her?"

"I don't mean Paige. I mean Eden. You love her." It was a statement, not a question, now.

After a brief hesitation, Garrett replied, "Eden and I have been friends for years. From the time you were only a youth at the Bull and Boar. I suppose friendship is a type of love."

"But I think you always felt more than mere friendship. I may only have been a youth when you started coming to the Bull and Boar, but I wasn't blind. That was a time when things weren't good between Eden and my father, partly because of me. It wasn't a happy household to live in. Yet, I noticed that Eden always seemed a bit cheerier when you were staying at the inn."

"I told you, we were friends. When she had problems with Brett, I suppose my friendship seemed more valuable to her. What's the point of all this, Benjamin? You're talking about things that happened over twenty-five years ago."

"No point, really. I'm certainly not blaming you for loving my wife. I don't really see how anyone who knows Eden could help loving her. But, I'm curious. Eden's said herself that she's never really figured out why you married Paige. Was it because you were in love with Eden?"

Slowly, Garrett shook his head. "No. In their own ways, your wife and your sister are both remarkable women. They're both beautiful, and they both have very strong characters. But, they are individuals. They're not alike. A man would be a fool to marry one because of the other."

37
September–December 1868

Garrett slid his stetson over his eyes and feigned sleep as the stagecoach swayed south, toward Texas. Thank God it was all over and he could finally relax! He had been on edge ever since that conversation with Benjamin on the last day of the cattle drive.

One thing he had to say for Benjamin—he was a hell of a lot more perceptive than Brett had ever been. Just how much did he really know, or at least suspect? Had Benjamin sensed that he and Eden were sleeping together back in the forties? Did he suspect that they had shared a bed, even as recently as the war?

Outwardly, Benjamin showed no bitterness or resentment. He seemed as quiet, self-contained, and friendly as he had always been in his brief encounters with Garrett at the Bull and Boar or at the Chicago plant. But, Garrett could never shake the feeling that Ben was watching him. And he couldn't blame the younger man. In Benjamin's position, he would have been consumed by jealousy.

As expected, Eden had seemed reserved and somewhat cool. They had had no opportunity to talk privately, but Garrett was thankful for that. No doubt she would have asked him why he married Paige, and he would have felt forced to lie. He could never betray Paige's trust by revealing she had thought herself pregnant.

Paige had been the only one who seemed blessedly ignorant of the tension among them. If she noticed it at all, she probably attributed it to continued strained feelings over their elopement. Thank God she had not even been born yet when he and Eden began their affair! At least she could not have any memories such as Benjamin's.

The coach jolted to a stop in Wichita, and the door opened to admit new passengers. Opening his eyes, Garrett smiled at his young wife. "Glad to be going home?"

She pursed her lips. "Yes and no. I did miss Miguel and Conchita, and even your friend Charley Streeter. But I was sorry to leave Mama and Ben so soon. I'm already looking forward to Christmas and another reunion."

Garrett sighed. "Remember, Paige, we haven't yet decided for sure that we'll go up for Christmas. It depends on how things go on the ranch."

"But December and January are never busy times at the Double M. And Mama will be so disappointed if she doesn't get to meet her grandson."

"She'll meet him sooner or later. We'll just see what happens."

Arriving at the Double M, they found the ranch in an uproar. Miguel rushed out of the ranch house and into Paige's arms, sobbing, "Mama's gone. Mama's not coming back!"

Frowning, Garrett looked to Charley Streeter, who had been left in charge. "What's the boy talking about? Where's Conchita?"

"She's—" Charley swallowed and jerked his chin toward a tree some distance from the ranch house kitchen. "She's buried," he whispered.

Looking up with horrified eyes, Paige demanded, "What do you mean? What happened?"

"She—it was a fever. Very sudden. Terrible. Miguel was sick, too—only he got over it."

Garrett rubbed his jaw thoughtfully. "Were Miguel and Conchita the only ones sick?"

Charley nodded. "They were the only ones on the ranch drinking milk."

"Milk fever?"

"It looked like it. After they took ill, I found out one of the milk cows had the trembles. I've gotten rid of her now."

Garrett nodded. "When did Conchita pass away?"

"Almost a week ago."

"And you're sure the boy is all right now?"

Charley sighed, shifting his eyes to Miguel, quiet now as he clung to Paige. "He ain't sick anymore, if that's what you mean. But I wouldn't exactly call him 'all right.' Most every night, he wakes up screaming for his mama. And lately he got it in his head that you two weren't comin' back neither. The little mite's scared to death of bein' left alone."

Bending, Garrett took the boy from Paige and hugged him tightly. "Miguel," he asked quietly, "how would you like to go on a nice, long trip? You could ride in a stagecoach, and on a train, and meet some nice new people—even a little girl for you to play with."

Miguel regarded him with dark, serious eyes. "Will you come with me?"

"No. But Aunt Paige will."

"Will Mama be there when I get there?"

Garrett sighed. "No, Miguel, I'm afraid she won't. But your grandmama will be there, and some more uncles, and a —a cousin."

The little boy frowned. "But, what if Mama comes back here, while I'm gone?"

"She won't, Miguel. I'm sure of that."

"Well, then," Miguel said slowly, "maybe I will go." He turned his gaze to Paige. "Do you want to go with me, Aunt Paige?"

Paige nodded, her eyes shining with unshed tears. "Yes, darling, you and I will go, just as soon as we can get ready." To Garrett, she said, "It's a very good idea. I'm sure all the excitement will help him forget. But, I wish you were coming, too."

Garrett shook his head. "You know it wouldn't be wise for me to leave again so soon. I'll have Charley accompany you as far as Abilene and put you on the train. If I find I can get away for Christmas, I'll join you in Chicago then."

Sitting in her mother's parlor, watching the first snow of the season build up on Wabash Avenue, Paige sighed dejectedly. Garrett's latest letter lay crumpled in her lap.

From the side of the house, she could hear Miguel and

Mara laughing as Clinton taught them to build a snowman. At least Miguel was happy. It had been right to bring him to Chicago. He and two-year-old Mara adored one another.

Eden stepped into the parlor doorway, frowning at her daughter's sad expression. "I thought I'd go over to Field and Leiter's to do a bit of Christmas shopping," she said brightly. "Would you care to come along?"

Paige shook her head.

"We could stop for tea at the Tremont House."

"Thank you, Mama, but I just don't feel like it."

Eden's eyes fell to the letter on Paige's lap. "Bad news from Texas?" she asked gently.

"You might say so. Garrett's not coming up for Christmas."

"Oh, Paige, I'm so sorry! I hope nothing's wrong?"

"No. He just doesn't feel he should leave the ranch right now. 'The usual crush of work,' he says. And some of the vaqueros want to go down to Mexico for the holidays."

"Well," Eden shrugged, hoping to hide her own relief at the news, "Garrett's been ranching long enough to know what's best. Does he want you to return to Texas for Christmas?"

"Oh, no. He says it's best for Miguel and me to stay here—that it would be too hard for Miguel to face Christmas on the ranch, without his mother."

Eden nodded. "That makes sense. Certainly the snow and all the new people here will be a good diversion for the boy. And, I'll admit, I'd be very disappointed to have you leave. I've been looking forward to your being here for the holidays."

"So have I! But I wanted Garrett here, too! Next week is our fifth wedding anniversary, and we won't even be together! Not that Garrett will mind. I think he's actually enjoying this separation. He never wants to be with me, even when I'm home on the ranch."

"Now, Paige, I'm sure you're exaggerating. You're upset that Garrett's not coming up, and you're reading all kinds of meanings into his actions. He's probably just as sorry about the separation as you are. But, men just don't express those feelings very well."

"No, Mama. You don't know Garrett the way I do. Ever since we got married, he's avoided me. I might as well admit to myself that he just doesn't love me."

"Of course he does, darling! I don't know how you could

think that. Certainly he wouldn't have married you if he didn't love you."

"No. You don't understand, Mama. Garrett married me because I threw myself at him. Because he felt sorry for me. At sixteen, I was naive enough to think everything would work out for the best. But, it hasn't."

Sinking into a chair, Eden gazed at her daughter intently. "You're right, darling. I don't understand. In September, in Abilene, you gave me the impression you and Garrett were very happy. What's happened?"

"Nothing. The marriage was just wrong from the start." She sighed. "You might as well know that I did everything but propose to Garrett myself. I didn't know where else to turn. I—I thought I was carrying a child."

Eden gasped, the color draining from her face. "Then, Burton wasn't lying."

"*He* told you?"

"He said you were pregnant when you came to the ranch. That you must have conceived right after your marriage. Actually, he insinuated—"

Paige cut her off with a bitter laugh. "That Garrett had seduced me before we were married? Hardly! Even as my husband, he's never been too anxious to share my bed."

Eden felt a twinge of guilt as relief washed over her. How could she feel glad Garrett didn't desire Paige when she truly wanted both Garrett and Paige to be happy? Surely, she assured herself, she was simply relieved to know Garrett had not seduced her daughter. But then, who had?

"It was Jefferson Montgomery," Paige said simply. "You were right about him, Mama. He was too suave, and I was too willing."

"But, I thought you had stopped seeing him soon after Garrett arrived in Chicago that fall."

"I had, for a time. But—oh, I don't know—I thought I'd fallen in love with Garrett, but he was so busy helping you at the plant all the time. I mean, he was always very kind to me, but he didn't seem to see me the way I wanted him to—as a woman. And then Jeff was still here, and he was always telling me how much he loved me—always, that is, until I told him I was carrying his child. Then—well, you can guess the rest.

"The worst part is," Paige finished in a whisper, "sometimes

I actually wish I'd borne the child. At least then I'd have someone."

"I'm sure you and Garrett will still have children of your own," Eden said quickly. "You're young and healthy. Sometimes it just takes time, especially after the strain you must have felt at the beginning of your marriage."

Paige shook her head. "How can we have children when we're never even together?" She looked away, rubbing her eyes. "I'm sorry, Mama. I shouldn't have told you all of that. I don't want you worrying about me. Only, maybe it's better you know, so you'll understand if Garrett and I should decide to part."

"Paige! You can't be serious! You haven't actually been considering leaving Garrett?"

Paige shrugged. "No. But perhaps I should. Why keep him tied to a woman he doesn't want?"

Eden swallowed nervously. "He hasn't—he's never given you any indication he'd be happier with someone else?"

"No. But that doesn't change the fact he's not happy with me."

"Has he ever told you that?"

"Mama, he doesn't have to! I'm not a naive little child anymore. I can tell that my husband is avoiding being with me!"

Eden looked away, wondering, would it help any to tell Paige that Garrett might actually be avoiding her, Eden? No, surely it would only make everyone more uncomfortable.

With forced calm, she said, "You haven't said, yet, how you feel about Garrett. Have you stopped loving him?"

"Of course not! I still care for him. I still want to bear his children. I know he's a fine man. But, our marriage isn't working out as I'd expected."

"Few things in life do," Eden said quietly. "In some ways, Paige, you *are* still a child. You expect love and marriage to be like a fairy tale, but you forget that fairy tales aren't real. Your father and I had our share of difficulties in our marriage, too. Once, we even spoke of separating. But, neither of us ever seriously considered it."

"But, at least you always knew you had Papa's love. At least he never avoided you."

"No?" Eden raised her brows. "You've shocked me a bit today. Now, I'll shock you. Do you know how your father died?"

"In a fire in the dry goods district."

"Yes. But he wasn't in any of the dry goods establishments. He was in another business on that same block. A house of ill repute."

Paige's eyes widened in horror. "Oh, Mama! How could he have done such a thing? I always thought Papa was so—so above reproach!"

"And I always wanted you to think of him that way. Even now, I'm not trying to destroy your image of your father. He was a good man, an exceptional man. But he was a man. And no man—or woman—is perfect.

"As far as why he went to that house, I suppose I was as much to blame as he. If I had given him all he needed, he would never have felt compelled to look elsewhere. He was a troubled man in his last months, and I was never able to give him all the solace he required."

Paige was silent for several moments, fingering the letter in her lap. "You're telling me that I ought not to give up on my marriage to Garrett? That I owe him something?"

"I'm reminding you that we all have our failings. We all have our secrets from the past."

Paige frowned. "And you think there's something about Garrett's past that's keeping us apart?"

"It's possible. I can't say for certain. But, one thing I can say—if there is something, if you ever find out, you mustn't hold it against him. That's a lesson I learned too late with your father."

38
1869

Paige stared out at Nebraska's endless wheat fields as the Union Pacific train rattled west, toward Wyoming Territory. After almost a year's separation, she was finally going to meet her husband at the Wyoming cow town of Cheyenne.

Early in the year, Garrett had written from Texas that he had heard about good grazing land in Wyoming and the surrounding territories. Since the westward push of settlers and the building of the transcontinental railroads had obliterated most of the buffalo herds on the northern plains, the lush grass was just waiting for longhorns.

Garrett had proposed driving a young herd north in the spring and establishing a ranch somewhere near Cheyenne. The young steers could fatten on the northern range for the next few years, then be shipped directly east from the Wyoming Territory. The meat, he pointed out, would be of better quality, since the fattened steers would be near a rail line and would not have to undergo the five-hundred-mile drive from Texas to Abilene just prior to marketing.

In the meantime, while the Wyoming herd fattened, the Texas branch of the Double M could continue supplying the market at Abilene, and continue breeding young steers to be sent north to fatten.

Eden, Benjamin, and Clinton had quickly seen the merits of Garrett's plan, and urged him to put it into effect. The only problem had been Paige.

She had wanted to return to Texas immediately, to help Garrett arrange the trip to Wyoming Territory. However, he had insisted it would be foolish for her to leave Chicago yet.

It would be unthinkable, Garrett had written, for Paige to accompany him on the cattle drive from Texas to Wyoming. The trip would be nearly twice as long as the drive from Texas to Abilene, and far too dangerous and rigorous for a woman.

Since there were no railroads connecting Texas and Cheyenne, and stage routes had yet to be established, it would be much more sensible for Paige to remain with her family until Garrett had arrived in Cheyenne and built them a house. Then, she could travel west on the new Union Pacific Railroad, in comfort and safety.

Under pressure from her mother and brothers, Paige had been forced to admit that Garrett's plan did make the most sense. So, she had waited, telling herself a few more months' separation was nothing compared to what women had suffered during the war.

Finally, in August, Garrett had wired that he was safely in Wyoming Territory and would have a ranch house waiting for her. By then, Miguel had become so attached to Mara he had not wanted to leave Chicago. Paige had reluctantly agreed to leave her nephew with her family, with the understanding that he would come to visit her at the new ranch very soon.

Now, as the train jostled over the plains, Paige thought of the man awaiting her in Wyoming. Garrett Martin. Her husband. A stranger.

After all these months, would he be glad to see her? Or only kind, indulgent, tolerant, as always? Would he treat her as a wife this time? Or, only as a pleasant companion who sometimes shared his bed?

As she had for months now, Paige wondered, was there a secret from Garrett's past that kept them apart? What could it be? How could she convince him to confide in her?

At the station in Chicago, when her mother had said goodbye, Paige had felt a sudden, fleeting sense of understanding.

"Take care of yourself, darling," Eden had said. "And of Garrett, too. You both deserve so very much."

Sitting on the train, Paige recalled her mother's words, the tender inflection of her voice. And, she wondered, was her own mother part of Garrett's secret?

Of course not! Mama and Garrett simply shared the tenderness of friends who had known each other for years. Still, they had been together almost constantly when Garrett had been in Chicago during the war. Benjamin had been away a long time then. It wasn't impossible—

No! It *was* impossible! Mama was too devoted to Ben, and Garrett was too honorable to have that kind of relationship with another man's wife. To say nothing of the fact Garrett was not particularly passionate—at least not with her.

Besides, if Garrett had been in love with Mama, he would never have married her, Paige. Or would he? Would he have married her simply to spare Mama the pain and embarrassment of having an unmarried, pregnant daughter?

Paige closed her eyes, shaking her head. She really was being foolish. She was on her way to start a new life with her husband in a new place. She must not let any ridiculous doubts ruin this chance for a better marriage.

Eden lay her head on Benjamin's shoulder as their carriage rolled north from the plant at Packers and Exchange avenues. It had been a busy, enlightening day, beginning with a visit from an inventor from Detroit.

The man, George W. Hammond, proposed building ice-refrigerated railcars for shipping fresh meat across the continent.

His idea could revolutionize meat packing, just as the intro-
duction of icehouses had twelve years earlier. If Hammond's
design worked, packers could ship fresh meat at any time of
the year, with little risk of spoilage.

Later that afternoon, Philip D. Armour, who had opened a
meat-packing plant in Chicago two years earlier, had visited
McKinnon Meats.

"I'm afraid this visit is long overdue, Mrs. McKinnon,"
Armour said as he settled his hefty frame into a chair in
Eden's office. "I've been meaning to come over and intro-
duce myself for some time. But, as you know, Armour and
Company's main plant is still in Milwaukee, so I don't get to
Chicago all that often."

Eden smiled. "I'm glad you finally did drop in, Mr. Armour.
I've been wanting to meet you. When your Chicago plant
first opened, I thought the name Armour sounded familiar.
Then I heard that you'd begun to make your fortune during
the California gold rush, and I realized where I'd heard of
you. You traveled with my elder son, Burton, didn't you?"

Armour smiled. "Yes, I did. We had a sort of partnership
for a while. I was always sorry that Burt decided to end it so
quickly."

"Well, you and Burton were among the lucky ones. From
what I've heard, scores of men never found even a handful of
gold dust."

Laughing genially, Armour said, "You don't think I financed Armour and Company on my gold stake, do you? If
I'd had to depend on that, I'm afraid I wouldn't even have
had the money to pay my way back East. I'm sure Burt must
have told you how little we found.

"Still, I made out all right digging ditches and selling water
rights to other prospectors. Guess that road to fortune was
just a little too slow for Burt. Can't say that I blame him,
though. After all, he was younger than me, and more impatient.
What ever happened to Burt? The last I heard, he was
working on the Cabrillo ranch in the San Joaquin Valley."

Eden hesitated. "He managed our ranch in Texas for a
number of years, but now he's established a McKinnon plant
in Kansas City."

Armour nodded. "Oh, yes. I'd heard you'd expanded there.
Smart move. We'll probably do the same quite soon. Tell me,
what do you think of this refrigerated railcar idea?"

They spent the next half hour discussing the future of meat

packing. Then Armour excused himself and asked Eden to remember him to her son.

Alone in her office, Eden brooded about her older son. So, everything she had imagined about his time in California had been right. Not only had he never owned a ranch, but he had never even had any success in the gold fields. Of course, what did any of that matter anymore? A few lies from California were nothing compared to what he'd done since.

How had Burton turned out to be so deceitful? Where had she failed in his upbringing?

She asked Benjamin the same questions later that afternoon, when she recounted her conversation with Armour.

Benjamin smiled and shrugged. "What makes you think you failed? Parents aren't totally responsible for the way their children turn out, you know. If they were, there would be no way of accounting for all the fine sons and daughters of thoroughly disreputable parents! Anyway," he added with a mischievous twinkle, "no one can doubt you're an excellent mother. Look what a fine job you did raising me!"

"Benjamin, be serious!"

"All right, I will. It's time you stopped worrying about Burton. He's thirty-two years old, and there's not much you can do to change him anymore. I'm not sure there ever was. Anyway, Armour didn't tell you anything today you didn't already know."

"No. He just confirmed my suspicions—the ones Garrett hadn't already confirmed." She sighed. "You're right, I shouldn't worry about Burt anymore."

"Of course I'm right," Benjamin quipped. "Aren't husbands always right?"

Now, as their carriage rolled home, Benjamin slid an arm around Eden's shoulders and lightly kissed her brow. "Not still brooding about Burton, are you?" he asked quietly.

Eden shook her head. "No. Actually, I was thinking of Paige. She ought to be about to Cheyenne by now. I hope things work out for her and Garrett."

"Umm." Benjamin's fingers caressed her shoulder. "It's got to be an awkward situation, at best. Garrett's a good man, and I don't doubt he wants to do what's best for Paige. But, how can he be the husband she wants when he's in love with you?"

Eden tensed, glad for the twilight that shadowed her

expression. She shivered and Benjamin pulled her closer to his side.

"You do know he's in love with you, don't you?"

"Of course not! Ben, that's absurd!"

"Not at all. Garrett Martin's always been in love with you. From way back in the days at the Bull and Boar."

"You're imagining things, Ben! Garrett and I have been friends for a long time. He was Brett's friend, too—and he's yours."

"None of that would keep him from falling in love with you. I did, even when you were married to my father."

"No. It's just not possible."

Benjamin laughed, brushing her cheek with his lips. "Dear, dear Eden! Always so sensitive. And yet, so remarkably naive about the way men see you! You never realized it when Father wanted to reconcile with you. You never knew I was falling in love with you. Isn't it possible Garrett Martin fell in love with you without your realizing that, either?"

"I suppose, but—"

He frowned. "Why are you so set on denying it? You ought to be flattered. I am. Knowing you're my wife, when another man, especially a man of Garrett's caliber, wants you, makes me feel very proud."

"But, what about Paige?"

"Ah," Benjamin nodded. "That is what really complicates the situation. Maybe he actually loves her, too. Maybe they'll work things out. To tell the truth, I never have been able to figure out why he married her. When we were on the cattle drive, going into Abilene, I asked Garrett point-blank if he'd married Paige because he was in love with you. He assured me that wasn't his reason."

Eden hesitated. "Did you—did you actually ask him if he was in love with me?"

"Yes. He didn't deny it."

For a long moment, Eden was silent, wondering how much more Benjamin knew, or at least suspected. He was remarkable, really, for his insight and understanding. She would always love Garrett, but she could never really be sorry she had chosen Benjamin.

She could only hope Ben would never know the full story of her relationship with Garrett. She could not bear to hurt him.

"Ben?" she whispered, snuggling closer to him.

"Hmm?"

"I love you."

He smiled. "That's the best bit of news I've heard all day! Even though I already know it, it's always good to hear."

Smiling as his wife refilled his coffee cup, Garrett said, "For a girl who never did much cooking, you're getting to be quite a chef! Those flapjacks were just about the best I've ever eaten!"

Paige returned his smile. "Why, thank you, sir," she replied with forced lightness. "Were they good enough to make you want to come home for dinner?"

Garrett's smile faded. "I would if I could, Paige. You know that. But I've got to spend a couple of days out on the range, getting the cattle rounded up before the winter sets in. They say the Wyoming winters can be pretty brutal, and I don't want to lose any head if we don't have to."

She nodded, biting back a plea to accompany him. She knew what the answer would be. Just as in Texas, there was no place for a woman among the cowboys on the range. Only here it was even more apparent than in Texas, for Wyoming Territory had far fewer women.

Sighing, Garrett gazed at her with his penetrating blue eyes. This couldn't be an easy life for her, so isolated, often without even her husband for company.

In the two months since she'd come to Wyoming, he hadn't spent much time with her. Even when he could have left more of the work to the cowboys, he'd made excuses, saying he'd wanted to make sure everything about the ranch got off to a good start. Too bad he'd never been able to do the same with this marriage.

Not that Paige was complaining. Since their reunion, she'd gone out of her way to please him. The cooking, for instance. He'd offered to hire a cook, or to have the bunkhouse cook prepare their meals, but Paige had insisted on doing it herself.

"I haven't anything else to do with my time," she'd said. "The bookkeeping doesn't take much, and I'd like to be of more use around here. Maybe later, when we have children, I'll need some help in the kitchen."

But, there were still no children on the way. Although they never discussed the fact, Garrett knew it was a constant disappointment to Paige. He wished Miguel would have come

West with her. At least the boy could have helped divert her thoughts.

Scraping his chair away from the table, he said, "Well, maybe I'll be lucky and this roundup won't take as long as I expected. Anyway," he added with a dimpled smile, "you'd better enjoy your solitude while you can. We'll probably be snowed in here so long you'll get sick of my company!"

Paige smiled ruefully. "I'd like to have that chance."

He looked away, guilty at the mild rebuke in her tone. "I'd better be off. The shotgun's there, loaded, if you need it. But I doubt that you will. One thing you can say for the West, men out here have more respect for women than the so-called civilized city folk."

Nodding, Paige thought, maybe it would be better for me if they didn't. Then maybe you wouldn't feel you could leave me alone so often.

Her face masked her thoughts as he brushed his lips across hers. "Take care of yourself, darling," she said with false cheeriness. "I'll have a nice roast ham and cornbread waiting for your return."

She leaned against the door frame, watching him ride away with the cowboys. Sighing, she turned back to the kitchen. What would she do for the next few days and nights? Reread the few books she'd brought from Chicago, all of which she'd finished weeks ago? Cross-stitch a new quilt for their bed? Write another long letter to Mama, and another to Clinton, and one to Miguel?

Stop being such a spoiled child, Paige McKinnon Martin! she told herself sternly. What do you want, anyway, a husband who'll entertain you every minute of your life?

No, just one who doesn't avoid me. One who wants my company as much as I want his. One who finds me fascinating enough to spend some time with.

Well, maybe I'm not fascinating enough. Maybe I'm just too young and inexperienced to interest a man as worldly as Garrett. Of course, a lot of older men marry girls my age. But, most of them just want a showpiece wife. Garrett's not that kind of man.

But, what *does* he want? How can I give it to him?

Oh, I wish I had a baby! Then I could worry about it, and I wouldn't be worrying about Garrett so much.

Paige sat in the small parlor, darning socks and fretting all morning. When noon came, she did not bother to make lunch. She wasn't hungry.

Toward midafternoon, she heard a wagon in the yard, and went to the kitchen to look out. A plump, middle-aged woman was climbing down and hurrying toward the door.

"Mrs. Martin?" the woman called cheerily as Paige stepped onto the porch. "I'm Carrie Phillips. My husband owns the saloon and hotel in town."

Paige smiled as she ushered the woman into the kitchen. "I'm pleased to meet you, Mrs. Phillips. It's not often I have the pleasure of entertaining guests. In fact, I'm afraid I haven't even any cake or pie to offer you. My husband's going to be gone a few days, so I didn't bother to bake anything today."

The older woman chuckled, patting her ample middle. "Oh, that's all right, honey. One thing Mr. Phillips is always saying is that I don't need anything more to eat. Guess he's right, too. But, by the time a woman's borne and raised five children and helped to run a business, I guess she deserves to stop worrying about her figure. Do you have any little ones?"

"No. I'm afraid not yet."

"Well, you're plenty young. I suspect they'll be coming along any time now."

"Yes." Paige flushed, anxious to change the subject. "Would you care for some tea, Mrs. Phillips?"

"Yes, thank you. And call me Carrie."

As Paige busied herself at the stove, the woman said, "I suppose it gets kind of lonely being a rancher's wife. Your husband must be out on the range quite a bit."

"Yes. But I'm getting used to it."

"Well, believe me, it's probably better having him out, rather than home all the time, like mine. You know the saying, 'Absence makes the heart grow fonder.' But then, I suppose a young woman like you does find herself itching for things to do."

"Oh, I manage to occupy my time."

"Do you really? Are you so busy you wouldn't care to take on another project?"

Paige hesitated, wishing the woman would come to the point. "That would depend upon the project, I suppose."

"Of course." Carrie eyed Paige thoughtfully. "You're very young. What do you know about the fifteenth amendment to the Constitution?"

"I know that Congress passed it just this year, and that it ensures voting rights for all Negro men."

Carrie nodded. "And, do you approve?"

"Of course. Why should a man be denied the right to vote, simply because of his color?"

"Exactly. By the same token, why should a woman be denied the right to vote, simply because she's not a man?"

"I—I'll admit I hadn't considered that."

"Well, you ought to! We women give a great deal to this country. Think of the sacrifices and contributions we all made during the war just past! Think of the women who kept businesses going—"

"You needn't remind me, Carrie," Paige cut in. "My own mother runs a prosperous meat-packing firm, and I spent more hours than I care to think about working there during the war."

"Then, you see what I'm talking about! Women in the United States do too much to be treated as second-class citizens. It's time we demanded our rights!"

Paige smiled as she poured two cups of tea. "What do you suggest we do, Carrie?"

"Right now, there's a movement afoot to get women their voting rights. There's a good chance that Wyoming's territorial legislature will pass a bill, even before the end of the year, giving women the right to vote within the territory. If that happens, it will help the movement in all the other states and territories across the nation. Already, we have a National Woman's Suffrage Association, campaigning for our rights."

Carrie paused, eyeing Paige as she sipped her tea. "By now, I'm sure you've guessed the reason for my visit. We'd like you to join our movement. Every woman who gives her energies to the fight brings us closer to our goal. You'd be doing something for yourself, your mother, your children, your grandchildren."

Paige thought of Garrett. No doubt he'd be glad to see her involved in something. Perhaps he'd even be proud of her. Involvement in the suffrage movement would make her more independent, more like her mother.

"Of course," Carrie Phillips added, "if you're not interested, I wouldn't want to press you. The movement is too important to include anyone who doesn't feel truly dedicated to it."

"You're quite right, Carrie," Paige said briskly. "But, your enthusiasm has infected me. I'm anxious to do whatever I can for the movement."

39
October 1871

Chuckling, Clinton looked up at his mother as he finished reading Paige's latest letter.

"My little sister has certainly turned into a whirlwind orator, hasn't she?" he said.

Eden sighed. "Sometimes I almost wish she'd never heard of the suffrage movement! Flitting to Washington for national conventions, going to Utah Territory to campaign for the vote. Where will she turn up next?"

"Well, it's good to see her committed to a worthy cause, isn't it? At least she had something to keep her occupied last year when Garrett was tied up with that outbreak of hoof-and-mouth disease."

"Oh, it's not that I disapprove of the cause, or of her involvement in it. If I had more time, I'd do more for the suffrage movement myself. But, I worry that she's neglecting Garrett. She has a commitment to him and their marriage, too, you know."

Clinton shrugged. "Well, as long as Garrett's not complaining, what can I say? The way they choose to live is between them. You'll have to admit they have kind of a strange marriage, anyway." He paused, shrugging again. "By the way, you and Ben are still planning to attend the grand reopening of Crosby's Opera House with me tomorrow night, aren't you?"

"Yes, we've been looking forward to it. But, I must say for a while today I thought they'd be forced to put it off. It seemed the fire department would never manage to get that fire just west of the river under control."

"From the newspapers today, I understand it pretty well demolished four square blocks. But, I suppose we have to expect such tragedies in a city the size of Chicago. The fact is, the city's just grown too fast, and most of the buildings are just too flimsy to withstand a fire."

348

Eden shuddered. "I know. And everything's so dry! Here it is the beginning of October and most of the trees have already lost their leaves. They say we've only had an inch and a half of rain since the Fourth of July. Even the wood block pavement and plank sidewalks are dry as tinder."

"Well," Clinton said, "we probably shouldn't worry too much. It's true any place in the city could go up in flames at any moment. But, we do have a fine new waterworks to supply the firemen. They've got all the water in Lake Michigan at their command. That ought to be enough to keep *any* fire under control."

At that moment, Benjamin came in, and Eden rose to greet him. "How were things at the Chicago Club tonight, darling?"

Benjamin grimaced. "A bunch of self-satisfied, stodgy, old businessmen! I don't know why I bother going there."

"No interesting news?"

"Not from the club. But, it looks like the firemen have another blaze on their hands. West of the river again, a little further south than the one that started last night. You can see the flames all the way over on Michigan Avenue."

"Oh, dear!"

"Well," Benjamin yawned, "I'm sure they'll get it under control, same as they always do. Anyway, there's no sense our worrying about it. It's on the other side of the river. The river should act as a pretty good firebreak." He yawned again. "Are the children in bed?"

Clinton nodded. "They've been asleep a couple of hours." He thought of both Mara and Miguel as his own now. Miguel had even begun to call him "Papa," though the boy knew Clinton was not his real father.

"Well, after a night at the club, I'm about ready to turn in, too. Nothing makes me more tired than a bunch of old men. Are you coming up, Eden?"

She nodded. "Yes. Will you take care of the lights, Clint?"

"Sure. I'm about ready to turn in, myself."

The house had been dark and quiet for nearly two hours when Eden awoke to the sound of breaking glass. She tensed, listening. Then she heard it again, a low, ominous rumble, and more glass breaking.

Benjamin stirred beside her, and she whispered, "What in the world is that noise?"

He sat up, listening more closely. "I don't know. It reminds me of the artillery fire during the war."

Going to the window, he pulled aside the curtain. The
room was immediately flooded with dancing light, and Eden
gasped in horror. A bell began to clang as she leaped out of
bed to join Benjamin at the window.

"That sounds like the Courthouse bell!" she said.

Benjamin nodded, scanning the skyline. "It is. The Courthouse is on fire!"

She swayed against him gazing at the burning bell tower,
only three blocks west of their house. "My God, the children!
We've got to get them out of here! I'll get dressed."

"No! There isn't time!" He had opened the window now,
and was leaning out, looking to the south and west. A wave of
hot air poured into the bedroom.

Benjamin jammed his legs into a pair of trousers and ordered,
"Just slip into a dressing gown, and hurry! It looks like the
entire downtown area's ablaze. With that southwest wind,
the fire could be here in no time!"

The bedroom door banged open, and Clinton rushed in,
his nightshirt hastily tucked into a pair of trousers. "Mama!
Ben! Have you seen—"

Benjamin pulled them both into the hall. "Let's get the
children and get out!"

They found five-year-old Mara in Miguel's room, whimpering with fear as she clung to her seven-year-old half brother.

"Where are we going, Daddy?" she asked as Clinton lifted
her into his arms and tucked a quilt around her.

"Out. For a walk. To the lake," Clinton answered sharply.

"Is the house going to burn down?" Miguel demanded.

"Of course not," Eden said quickly. "We just want to—to
be sure."

"We're going to burn!" Mara wailed.

"Hush, Mara. We are not," Miguel insisted. "Grandpa and
Grandma and Papa won't let us burn!"

Bravely, the little boy took Eden's hand as she and Benjamin hurried down the stairs behind Clinton. Downstairs, the
servants were rushing about in panic. Benjamin urged them
to get out of the house as quickly as possible.

Wabash Avenue was mobbed with people, most dressed
only in their night clothes, fleeing the flames. The air felt
stifling as a wave of heat preceded the fire.

Benjamin scooped up Miguel, who protested he could walk by himself.

"We'll go faster this way," Benjamin said. "Just be a man and don't complain."

The Courthouse bell continued to peal ominously over the noise of the crowd. Glass windows shattered from the intense heat long before the flames ever reached them. The dull booming Eden had heard when she first awakened continued.

"They must be blowing up buildings for a fireblock," Benjamin mused.

The wind intensified, raining down a torrent of hot cinders that had been swirled up from the burning buildings. It was impossible to sidestep the glowing red and black rain. Little Mara screamed in terror as it stung her skin.

"Where should we go?" Eden yelled over the noise of the crowd as she held onto Benjamin's arm.

"We'll try the baseball park at the foot of Washington Street," he replied. "At least it will provide some sort of temporary refuge."

Clinton nodded agreement, and they struggled east. It was impossible to see more than a few feet ahead through the intense rain of red-hot cinders and searing black ashes.

Cows, dogs, and horses, crazed by the heat and the pain of blistering cinders, bolted through the streets, knocking pedestrians to the ground, trampling the unwary underfoot.

Some of the crowd clutched bedspreads or pillowcases, filled with their most cherished possessions. Others carried armloads of fine clothing and bolts of silk, their bleeding hands testifying to the shop windows they had smashed to obtain their booty.

For an instant, Eden wished she had thought to save the portrait of her father that had once hung in her grandparents' house. At least her best portrait of Brett was hanging safely in her office at McKinnon Meats.

Or was it safe? Were the stockyards, and everything around them, burning too?

The baseball park was already crowded with refugees. Some, who had been alerted sooner, sat among piles of possessions. A few had even dragged mattresses to the park. Several women, laughing hysterically, were dragging in huge trunks, full of clothing and heirlooms. Another group was struggling to wheel in a piano, rescued from a burning house.

Benjamin set Miguel down and looked around with a sigh.

Already, the rain of ash and cinder was drifting into the park. Here and there, people were beating out small fires that had begun on their mattresses or piles of clothing.

"I'm afraid you won't be safe here for very long," Benjamin told Eden. "When it gets too hot, or if any of the small fires start to burn out of control, take the children out and stand in the lake with them. You should be safe there."

Eden stared at him. "We? What about you? You're not planning to leave us here?"

He nodded. "I wouldn't if I thought you needed me. But, I know you can manage without me. I'm going back downtown. The firemen and police must need every man they can get."

"No! It's too dangerous!"

Benjamin grinned. "Not really. I dodged rifles and artillery fire for three years during the war. This shouldn't be much different. I promise you I won't do anything foolish—like plunging into a burning house."

"Oh, Ben! I wish—" She gestured around her. "Look at all the other men here! They're not going—"

"Ben's right, Mama," Clinton cut in. "I'm going back with him." He handed her the still-whimpering Mara. "You look after the children and don't worry about us. We'll look after each other."

Before Eden could protest more, Benjamin quickly kissed her and turned away. Blinking back tears, Eden watched her husband and son leave the ballpark.

"Will they come back?" Mara asked tearfully.

"Of course they will," Eden soothed, reminding herself she must appear calm, for the children. "They're just very good, very brave men, and they want to help other people get away from the fire."

"They should have taken me with them!" Miguel announced petulantly. "I'm a man, too!"

"Of course you are," Eden said. "That's why they left you here. They trusted you to take care of me and Mara."

"Oh, all right," Miguel said, reaching up to slide a possessive arm around his grandmother's waist.

They sat on the ground, huddled together, with Mara's quilt wrapped around them. The air had become so hot they did not need the extra warmth of the quilt. But there was something comforting and homey about it. Eden realized that quilt might be the only material thing to survive from the house.

Thank goodness old Louise had left three days ago to visit her grandniece in Missouri. At least they did not have to worry about her. After all the years they had shared, it would be terrible to lose the old cook in this fire.

Stop it! Eden thought sharply. We're not going to lose anyone in this fire! A lot of property will be destroyed, but that can all be replaced or rebuilt—probably stronger and safer than before. But, if people just keep their heads, there's no reason for anyone to die, no matter how many homes and stores and offices are destroyed.

She sighed grimly, admitting that hundreds of people had already lost their heads. Scores had cut their hands and arms while looting through the broken windows of burning stores. On Wabash and Michigan avenues, she had seen several families with their valuables piled in their yards, furiously digging holes to bury the goods before they could be burned. One group of servants had even been trying to bury a piano.

Now, as the fire came closer, a group near Eden was trying to dig a hole in the ballpark turf, to bury their silver. Other groups were also digging with any available object, heedless of a lone policeman who ran around shouting frantically that they must not deface the ballpark.

An hour after he had left them, Benjamin stumbled up to Eden and the children, his face and clothing blackened by smoke.

"Oh, thank goodness you're back!" Eden exclaimed.

"Just for a moment." He turned away, coughing violently. "The city officials had forgotten about the prisoners in the ground floor jail of the Courthouse. Guilty or not, the poor devils would have burned! Clint and I finally got a policeman to release most of them. We helped bring the accused murderers down here in handcuffs."

"Where's Clinton now?"

"Over there," Benjamin gestured toward a section of bleachers, "helping the policeman chain them up 'til they can find somewhere else to move them." He paused again, bending double as his chest wracked with coughs.

"Ben, are you sure you're all right?"

He nodded, choking out between coughs, "All right—just the smoke—"

"You'd better stay with us now."

"No. There's—more—to—do." He gulped at the fresh air,

holding back a new spasm of coughs. "Really, I'm fine. I just
needed some air."

Clinton came up beside them and asked, "Ready?"

Benjamin nodded.

Reaching down to tousle Miguel's hair, Clinton said, "You
take care of Grandma and Mara, now."

As they turned away, a loud rumble filled the air, and the
Courthouse bell clanged one last time. Turning his head back
to Eden, Benjamin said, "That must have been the Courthouse cupola falling. We got those men out just in time. The
whole building will be crashing down any second."

A moment later, another crash confirmed his prediction.
Benjamin touched Eden's cheek, then strode back toward the
business district with Clinton.

The fire had so brightened the sky that it was difficult to
tell when dawn actually came. Eden knew only that they had
been sitting in the ball park for hours, and that Benjamin and
Clinton had not returned. Exhausted, Mara and Miguel had
finally fallen asleep with their heads in her lap.

Reports of the fire's progress circulated through the ballpark
continually. But it was impossible to guess what was true and
what was mere rumor. Some said the fire had leaped north,
across the river, and had already nearly destroyed the city's
north side.

The waterworks, the pride of Chicago, had caught fire,
rendering all its pumps useless. The water tower still stood,
but its reserve of water would soon be used up. All the water
in Lake Michigan offered Chicago no consolation now.

Toward midmorning, the giant lumberyards located along
the river caught fire. The air in the ballpark became suffocating,
and Eden knew she would have to take the children into the
lake.

Carrying Mara, and holding Miguel's hand, she waded out
until the water was past Miguel's waist. She stood there for
several minutes, scanning the crowded shoreline for Clinton
and Benjamin, wondering how long she could hold her little
granddaughter.

A high-wheeled wagon and team, part of A. T. Willett's
trolley system, splashed up alongside them and the driver
reached down a helping hand.

"Why don't you and the little ones get in, ma'am?" he

offered. "Mr. Willett says we're to stay out here as long as necessary, so you might as well keep dry in the wagon."

"Thank you." Eden handed up Mara, while Miguel clambered in. Then she climbed up beside them. Within minutes, the wagon was filled with other wet refugees.

Looking back, it seemed the entire city was ablaze. A curtain of red and orange flames licked up and down the shoreline, as if daring the lake to overcome it.

By noon, Mara was whimpering that she was hungry.

"So am I," Miguel told her. "But Grandma can't help it, so you'd better just be quiet." Turning to Eden, he asked, "Will Papa and Grandpa be able to find us out here?"

"I'm sure they will," Eden assured him. "They told us to come out here, remember?" Still, she stared anxiously toward the shore, wondering where they were.

Finally, she caught sight of Clinton's sandy hair. As he moved closer through the crowd, she saw that he seemed to be supporting someone. Someone with dark hair. Benjamin?"

Eden's heart wrenched as they reached the water's edge and she saw that it *was* Benjamin. Clinton was bent nearly double as he dragged his half brother along.

"Clint!" she shrieked, waving furiously. "Out here!"

She saw Clinton straighten slightly, scanning the lake. Benjamin raised his head at the sound of her voice, and stumbled forward.

Eden screamed again, and Ben took a few more steps before falling to his knees and crumpling to the sand. His body heaved violently as the waves rolled around him.

"Oh, my God!" Eden shrieked. "Oh, my God!"

She scrambled from the wagon and began fighting through the crowd to the shore. By the time she reached them, Clinton had managed to pull Benjamin from the water. Exhausted, he lay beside Ben.

Falling to her knees, Eden took Benjamin's head in her lap. He was coughing too violently to speak, but he weakly pressed her hand.

Clinton struggled up on an elbow and took her other hand. His eyes were red-rimmed, and his brows and hair were singed. But his expression of horror and misery was more upsetting than his physical appearance.

"My God, Clint," Eden whispered, "what happened?"

For a moment, Clinton looked away, unable to speak. Then he began, "We were at State and Quincy, at the Palmer

House. Somehow, the fire missed it last night, and a lot of the guests had stayed, thinking they might be safe. I don't know, maybe they just didn't know where else to go. Anyway, when the fire backtracked this morning, the hotel started to burn. We were helping evacuate it when Ben just—collapsed."

"The—smoke—" Benjamin choked out between coughs. "I'll be—all right."

Eden looked up at Clinton, who shook his head. "I thought if I could get him down to the lake, maybe he could get some fresh air. Anyway, there was nowhere else to go," he said.

She nodded, hugging her husband closer, willing her own strength into his body. "Clinton," she said in the steadiest voice she could manage, "the children are out in that Willett coach. Perhaps you'd better go out and see them. They've been very worried about you."

"You're sure you'll be all right?"

"Yes. Go on. I'll join you after—later."

As Clinton walked into the lake, Benjamin began to cough again. Eden rocked him tenderly in her lap, bending to kiss his brow. In two weeks, they were to celebrate their tenth wedding anniversary.

The coughs subsided again, and Benjamin gazed up at her, his gray-green eyes flooded with misery.

"Sorry," he murmured.

Eden forced a smile and smoothed his dark hair away from his forehead.

"So—sorry," he repeated.

"No," she whispered. "You've nothing to be sorry about."

He opened his mouth to say more, but the coughs began again, wracking his whole body even more violently than before. Then, suddenly, he was still, staring up at her with unseeing eyes.

For a long moment, Eden gazed at those beloved gray-green eyes. Slowly she reached down and closed them, then brushed her lips across his forehead.

"No, Benjamin," she whispered, "you never did anything, in all your life, to be sorry about."

40
November–January 1872

Eden sat at her desk at McKinnon Meats, watching the workmen hang the new portrait of Benjamin opposite the one of his father. The Great Chicago Fire had not touched the stockyards, McKinnon Meats, or any of the other meat-packers.

In its twenty-five-hour rampage, the fire had leveled more than two thousand acres, destroying seventeen thousand four hundred and fifty homes. It had killed more than three hundred people and left ninety thousand homeless. But it had not destroyed the one industry for which Chicago had become famous.

In some ways, Eden, Clinton, and the children had been more fortunate than most. They had been able to take shelter at the plant until they could find a new home. Eden had also opened the plant to any McKinnon workers left homeless, and to several friends and neighbors.

In the first month after the fire, McKinnon Meats had given away thousands of pounds of meat. Eden and Clinton had already arranged to give away much more. They felt it only right to give back whatever they could to the city that had given them so much.

Still, they could not deny that Chicago had also robbed them of a great deal. Eden, Clinton, and the children could adjust to living at the plant temporarily. But how could they ever become adjusted to life without Benjamin?

Clinton came into the office and slid an arm around his mother's shoulders as he stared up at the portrait. "It's a good likeness," he said. "The eyes have Ben's compassion." He sighed. "I still can't believe I've seen both of my brothers die. First, Swift Elk. Now, Ben."

"You still have one more brother," Eden said softly.

"No, I don't." Clinton's tone was bitter. "If I hadn't disowned him before, I would now. Kansas City isn't that far. He could have come up for the funeral. At least he could have

357

sent you a wire of sympathy. Paige at least had the decency
to offer to come."

"Clinton, please. For the second time in my life, I've lost
my husband. I don't want to talk about losing a son, too."

"You lost Burton a long time ago, Mama. Maybe it's time
you admitted as much. Surely you can see it. You've always
been so astute about everything else."

Eden averted her eyes. Of course, she knew Clinton was
right. She had always known. Even when Burton first ran off
to California, she had been the only one to see through his
lies. She and Benjamin—who had been too diplomatic to
admit Burton was lying.

Clearing her throat, she said, "I got another letter from
Paige today. She wants to visit during the Christmas season."

"Good." Clinton nodded. "We should have the house ade-
quately furnished by then."

They had recently purchased a house on South Michigan
Avenue, near Twenty-Second Street, in an area untouched
by the fire. The former owner, a widow, had accepted the
fire as an omen that she ought to move back East, to join her
aging parents.

Though Eden had not been especially charmed by the
house, she had agreed with Clinton that it was best to move
the children out of the packing plant as quickly as possible.
Soon afterward, she had purchased a tract at Prairie Avenue
and Eighteenth Street, and commissioned an architect to
begin plans for a house to be built during 1872. The location
seemed especially fitting, being just west of the site of the
Fort Dearborn massacre, where her own father had perished
in 1812, while Black Eagle had rescued her and her mother.

"Will Garrett be coming with Paige?" Clinton asked.

"I—I don't know. She didn't say. It seems to me that
perhaps he won't, since she mentioned something about stopping on her way from a suffrage meeting in Pennsylvania."

In truth, Eden hoped Garrett would not come. It would be
far too painful to see him now, when Benjamin was gone and
he was married to her daughter.

"It will be too bad if he can't come," Clinton mused. "It
would be nice to have the whole family, or what remains of
it, together for the holidays."

Eden sighed. "That's a dream I gave up long ago." She
paused. "Clint, have you ever thought of starting a family of
your own?"

"I have a family. You and Mara and Miguel."

"You know what I mean. I understand that when Mara was younger you wanted to give her all your time—to make up for what Burton did. Now, I hope you won't hesitate to take a wife because you feel you need to look after me."

He laughed. "Mama, I doubt that there's a woman in the world who needs looking after any less than you! I don't flatter myself that you need me."

"Everyone needs a bit of looking after, Clinton—the special kind that only a husband or wife can give."

Gazing at her earnestly, he replied, "The fact is, Mama, I'm very happy living the way I do. But, if I should choose to marry, I'll do so in my own time. After all, I'm only thirty-two. Papa was older when he married. So was Ben. I suspect it's too soon even to say this, but I could put the same suggestion to you. If ever you should wish to remarry, I hope you won't hesitate because of me and the children."

Eden shook her head. "No, Clinton, I'll never marry again. I'm quite certain of that."

Paige arrived alone, two days before Christmas. At twenty-four, she seemed more self-assured than ever before in her life. She had blossomed under her commitment to the suffrage movement, and she brimmed with enthusiasm as she recounted her experiences lecturing and meeting with other suffragettes.

Still, Eden detected a certain melancholy in her when she played with Mara and Miguel, and she noticed that Paige seemed evasive when Clinton asked about Garrett.

Late that night, when she and Paige were alone in her sitting room, Eden asked, "Garrett is well, I hope?"

Paige nodded, her green and gold eyes shifting away from her mother. "He was fine when I left Cheyenne for Philadelphia last month. Earlier in the fall, when I first planned the trip, he even talked about meeting me in Chicago for Christmas. But he changed his mind when your wire came about the fire and Benjamin. He said it might be better if he didn't infringe on the immediate family this Christmas."

Eden swallowed the sudden lump in her throat. "That was thoughtful of him. But, of course, he is family, too."

"That's what I told him. But he insisted it would be best if he didn't come." Paige's eyes moved back to Eden's, searching. "When the telegram came about Ben, I think Garrett hurt as much as I did. There were tears in his eyes when he read it, Mama! In eight years of marriage, I'd never seen Garrett so close to breaking down."

Averting her eyes, Eden said, "Well, he and Ben were very close in age. I suspect it's quite a blow to a man, especially a man who still considers himself young, when one of his contemporaries dies."

"No. It was more than that. It was something very personal."

"Benjamin was his brother-in-law, after all," Eden said quickly. "And I'm sure at least some of the pain Garrett felt was for you, knowing how upset you must have felt. It's only natural, when a husband cares for his wife, for him to share her grief."

"I suppose." Paige sounded unconvinced.

"I'm sorry, though, that you have to be apart at Christmas. If I'd realized that, I might have told you not to come."

Paige shrugged. "It doesn't matter. We're apart more than we're together, anyway. I suppose it's for the best."

Probing, Eden asked, "You don't fight? Garrett doesn't mistreat you?"

"Heavens, no! We just don't have much in common—including children," she added softly.

"Well, perhaps that's for the best. I don't suppose you could be much of a mother with the time you put into the suffrage movement."

"If I had children, I wouldn't be putting that time into the movement."

"Garrett doesn't object to the time, or to all your traveling?"

"Oh, no! I think he's delighted. And he heartily approves of the movement. In fact, I think he respects me more since I've gotten involved in it. I'm not such a silly little girl anymore."

She sighed. "Really, Mama, things aren't so bad. Garrett and I don't have the kind of marriage you and Papa or you and Ben had. But, we're friends. I suppose that's more than a lot of wives can say."

The next night, Christmas Eve, all serious discussions were put aside as Mara and Miguel squealed with delight over their Christmas gifts. As usual, Eden and Clinton had bought dozens of presents. Paige had brought a satchel full of gifts from her travels.

Five-year-old Mara was enchanted by an imported Swiss

music box Paige had found for her in New York. Miguel, at seven, was fascinated by a toy train and insisted that Clinton help him set up the track at once.

Watching her son and grandson on the floor, Eden smiled. "What a blessing to have little ones here," she said to Paige. "Without them, this first Christmas without Benjamin might have been unbearable." She paused, frowning slightly. "Did you just hear the doorbell?"

"Yes. Carolers, perhaps."

"Perhaps. Or maybe Garrett changed his mind after all."

Eden and Paige both rose and started for the parlor door. Both froze as a familiar voice greeted the maid, and then a familiar figure stood in the doorway.

"Merry Christmas!" he shouted, shaking fresh snow from his reddish hair.

Eden's knees felt weak. "Burton!" she whispered.

"I hope this is a happy surprise," he said, advancing to kiss and embrace her. "I certainly intended it to be."

Touched and confused by her son's uncharacteristic warmth, Eden blinked back tears. "Of couse it is! I'm just so surprised, I don't know what to say!"

"What's so unusual about a man wanting to spend Christmas with his family?"

"Nothing. I—I just didn't expect it, that's all."

Still smiling, Burton turned to embrace Paige. "Well, little sister, you're looking as beautiful as ever! But, you didn't bring your husband?"

"No, Garrett couldn't get away from the ranch just now."

"What a pity! I'm sure it would have meant a great deal to Mama to have the entire McKinnon-Martin clan together."

He stepped away and extended a hand to Clinton, who was still on the floor, pretending to be absorbed with connecting train tracks. "Clinton, good to see you again," Burton said jovially.

Clinton hesitated, debating whether to turn away. Then he saw the plea in Eden's eyes, and the question in Miguel's, and he reluctantly clasped his brother's hand.

"Mara, Miguel," Clinton said stiffly, "this is your Uncle Burton, Grandma's oldest son."

Miguel gravely shook Burton's hand, while Mara eyed him shyly.

"She tends to be rather suspicious of strangers," Clinton said, emphasizing the last word.

Ignoring the sarcasm in his brother's tone, Burton smiled.
"Well, perhaps I have a little something to melt her coolness."

He stepped into the hall and rummaged in his bags, then
returned with an armload of packages. For Mara, there was a
delicate bisque doll. Miguel received a mechanical penny
bank that fascinated him almost as much as his new train. It
was a bear, holding a crock of honey. When the boy placed a
penny in the bear's paw, it dropped it into the crock.

While the children played with their new toys, Burton
distributed gifts to the adults. He gave his mother a length of
aquamarine watered-silk, which she exclaimed would make a
lovely evening gown for the Potter Palmers' next dinner
party. Clinton received a copy of Mark Twain's recent work,
Innocents Abroad, and Paige received a new handbag. Burton also presented her with a package for Garrett, saying
again what a pity it was he could not be there.

Soon after the gifts were distributed, Clinton announced
that the children ought to go to bed, or Santa Claus would
not come. A few minutes later, Burton said he was tired from
traveling, and Eden showed him to a room.

When Clinton returned from tucking in the children, Paige
was alone in the parlor. Looking up at her brother, she
smiled. "Well, it certainly turned out to be a strange evening,
didn't it?"

Clinton nodded. "I don't like it. I wonder what he wants."

She shrugged. "Maybe the Christmas spirit just finally
overcame him."

"I doubt it. If he thinks he's going to come here and charm
Mara and Miguel away from me now, he'd better think
again."

"I don't think there's much chance of that, Clint. Those
children adore you. Besides, Burton didn't seem to object
when you introduced him as their uncle."

"No. But he may just be biding his time. He was al-
together too nice tonight—and Burton hasn't been nice since
he was twelve years old."

Paige sighed. "Well, maybe you're right. But, don't say
anything to Mama yet. Let her enjoy having all her children
together, at least for a little while."

As the holidays progressed, Clinton's uneasiness increased.
Burton was unfailingly charming to everyone. Even old Lou-

ise remarked on how the air in Kansas City must have
changed him.

The children enjoyed the novelty of a new "uncle," and he
was very kind and patient with them. Still, he did not seem
anxious to assume responsibility for them. In fact, when
Miguel asked if he might visit his uncle in Missouri, Burton
replied offhandedly that he was still a bit too young, but
someday he might ask his papa for permission.

So, Clinton wondered, if he doesn't want the children, just
what does Burton want?

Eden, too, was wondering at the change in her elder son.
Although she had always hoped he would reform, she could
not quite believe he actually had. There had to be some
explanation for his behavior. But, try as she might, she could
not find one.

The day after New Year's, the family took Paige to the
station for a train west to Cheyenne. After they returned to
the house, as she sat with her sons over mugs of mulled
cider, Eden said, "I suppose you'll have to be going home
soon, yourself, Burton."

Burton smiled wryly. "I thought this was my home."

She flushed. "Of course it is. But, you know what I mean.
You've built quite a business in Kansas City. I imagine you
must feel restless being away from it too long."

"Not really. After all, Kansas City is just a small branch of
the larger business. I could easily relegate the responsibility
there to someone else, if, for example, I was needed here."

Eden hesitated, glancing at Clinton, who was clenching his
hands around his cider mug. "I don't think that's necessary,
Burton. Your plant is doing so well, I'd hate to see you leave
it in someone else's hands."

"But I'd like to help you, Mama. Now that Benjamin's
gone, and with you getting on in years, I'm sure you must
need help in overseeing the business."

"I'm really not *that* old, dear. Only fifty-nine. Ben's death
does put more work on my shoulders, but I'm glad for the
work. I really believe that hard work saved my life when your
father was killed."

Burton's expression hardened. "In other words, you're still
determined to keep me out of my rightful place in the business!
I should be the head of McKinnon Meats, you know. It's my
right as heir!"

"No, Burton," Eden said quietly. "I should head the firm,

as I have since your father's death. When I choose to retire, and I don't expect that to be for some time, you can step in."

"Meanwhile, you'll be grooming Clinton to take your place! He always was your favorite, wasn't he? Too bad you can't marry him, too!"

"Oh, shut up, Burt!" Clinton exploded. "No one's ever tried to cheat you out of what you deserve. If anything, you've cheated yourself. Ben and Mama always intended McKinnon Meats to be a partnership one day. But, you had to lie and scheme and imagine all sorts of plots against you. Then, to top it off, you had the utter indecency to abandon your own children. You don't even deserve to bear the McKinnon name! If it were up to me, I'd have cut you out of the firm long ago!

"Now you come here pretending concern over Benjamin's death, when the truth is you don't give a damn! Where were you three months ago, when it happened? Down in Kansas City, rejoicing and planning how you could use the tragedy to your advantage!"

"Clinton, please—" Eden cried.

"No, Mama, don't stop him," Burton said with a sardonic smile. "It's interesting to see what kind of man my little brother's become. Someday, when you're not here to stand between us, I'm going to enjoy fighting him for control of McKinnon Meats. And, believe me, I will fight him. And I'll win!"

V

THE HARVEST

1878–1890

41
June 1878

Smiling slightly, Eden looked around her private railcar as the Union Pacific Railroad pulled it west, toward Cheyenne. At sixty-six, she felt entitled to feel pleased with her accomplishments.

In the years after the fire, while Chicago rebuilt and expanded, McKinnon Meats had continued to grow and modernize. Now the firm stood beside those of Philip Armour, Gustavus Swift, and Nelson Morris as one of the most successful packers in the nation. McKinnon Meats had markets all over the United States, and in every country of Europe.

There had, of course, been problems to overcome. The bank panic of 1873, and the subsequent depression, had limited business for a time. But, just as it had in 1837, and again in 1857, McKinnon Meats had weathered the panic. The McKinnon reputation for quality and integrity had kept the firm solvent while more than five thousand other businesses across the nation had failed.

Eden had overcome another problem in 1874, when she tried to implement the plans for refrigerated railcars that had so impressed her a few years earlier. Every railroad she approached had refused to build the cars to her specifications.

Finally, she had financed building the cars, sort of moving icehouses, herself. Their success had more than proven the soundness of her investment. With them, McKinnon Meats could ship fresh beef and pork almost anywhere in the nation, at any time of the year.

The firm had expanded in other directions, too. Meat canning, which Brett had experimented with in the 1850s, had now become a major division of the Chicago plant. McKinnon potted beef and tongue were favorites in England, and canned soup was becoming popular among all the McKinnon markets.

Although McKinnon and other packers had always found

367

uses for their waste products, their salvage processes had
become more refined than ever. Excess fats were sold to
oleomargarine manufacturers, or to soapmakers, or were used
to produce lard within the plant. Pig bristles were saved for
making paintbrushes. Bone was ground for use in fertilizers.
Glue, gelatine, and even beauty-products manufacturers bought
other parts of the butchered animals.

Hardly a month passed without someone stopping in Eden's
office to propose a new use for some nonmeat portion of a
carcass. Her rival, Gustavus Swift, often chuckled, "We
use every portion of a pig but its squeal!"

Looking over to the inlaid onyx and obsidian game table,
where fourteen-year-old Miguel and twelve-year-old Mara were
playing chess, Eden suddenly noticed her grandson smiling
back at her.

"Why the smile, Grandma?" he asked, his dark eyes dancing with love.

She shrugged. "Oh, I'm just counting my blessings, thinking how fortunate I've been."

Miguel laughed. "If I know you, you're dreaming up some
new business scheme! You'll probably want to wire instruc-
tions home to Papa at our next stop!"

"I'll do nothing of the kind! I promised Clinton this trip to
see Garrett and Paige would be a vacation, and I intend to
keep that promise."

"Well, I have a feeling you'll get some business in there,
somewhere. After all, the ranch *is* part of McKinnon Meats."

Eden laughed. "I had been counting you and Mara among
my blessings, but perhaps I'll have to revise my list. You're
getting a bit too smart for your own good, young man!"

Grinning, he got up to kiss her cheek. "It's only because I
love you! And I promised Papa I'd look after you, make sure
you really did get some rest."

She grimaced. "I've told you before, I won't have any of
you treating me like an old woman! It's not as if there's
anything wrong with me. To tell you the truth, I wouldn't
even be taking a vacation, except to placate Clinton."

"Well, one vacation in the twenty years since you took over
the firm hardly seems like too much. You ought to relax and
enjoy your success once in awhile, Grandma."

Mara nodded. "He's right. Look at this beautiful private
car the railroad gave you. It seems to me you should use it
every now and then."

Eden snorted. "They only gave it to me because McKinnon Meats practically supports them, paying their freight charges. But, I suppose it is nice. I'm glad you children can enjoy it."

Sighing, Miguel said, "It's too bad Grandpa can't be here to enjoy it, too."

"Yes," Mara agreed. "Both Grandpas."

A few years earlier, Eden and Clinton had explained to the children that Brett, whom they had never known, had been their real grandfather, while Benjamin had really been their uncle. They had not, however, told either child their true relationship to Burton. Though Miguel knew he had had a different father, he did not know his identity, and both children still thought of Clinton as their father.

With a slight frown, Miguel said, "Well, maybe it's just as well our real Grandpa can't be here. I'm sure he would be pleased at how successful his business has become. But, maybe he'd feel bad about the problems in the family."

He paused thoughtfully. "Grandma, what's wrong between Papa and Uncle Burton, anyway?"

Eden hesitated. She and Clinton had never discussed Burton in front of the children. Fearing Miguel and Mara might one day discover Burton was their father, Eden had not wanted to poison their minds against him, though she knew Burton's own actions had probably done so already.

Aware Miguel was waiting for an answer, she said, "What makes you think anything's wrong?"

"It's obvious. Mara and I aren't such little children anymore. We can figure things out. Papa never talks about Uncle Burton. And Uncle Burton hasn't been back for a visit since that Christmas after Grandpa Ben died. Even then, I don't think Papa was too pleased to see him."

"Well, men often have differences that prevent them from getting along with one another. Just because they're brothers doesn't mean they must be friends."

"No. But I'd expect them to make some effort, for your sake at least. I know Papa would do almost anything to please you. Only," Miguel hesitated, staring at Eden intently, "I don't suppose he'd compromise his principles for anyone. The problem between Papa and Uncle Burton—it's something serious, isn't it, Grandma?"

Eden sighed. "It's a personal thing between them. I don't think we ought to discuss it."

"Does it have something to do with Mara and me?" he pressed.

"Miguel, I said we would not discuss it!"

"It does have to do with us, doesn't it? That's why you don't want to tell us."

"No," Eden said firmly. "It has nothing to do with either of you. The misunderstanding between them is more closely connected with Benjamin. Your father was very upset that Uncle Burton didn't come to the funeral."

Miguel frowned. "There must be more to it than that. Even before the fire, Uncle Burton never visited, and Papa never spoke of him."

"Well, they've had their differences all through life. As I told you, some men just don't get along. The explanation is as simple as that."

But, she could see in Miguel's dark eyes and Mara's cornflower-blue ones, that neither child really believed her.

Paige, still looking girlish at thirty-one, met them at the crude wooden train station that served the Union Pacific in Cheyenne, Wyoming.

"Garrett's sorry he couldn't be here," she said. "But he had to make a sudden trip down to Texas. Charley Streeter died in the influenza epidemic."

"Oh, I'm so sorry!" Eden exclaimed. "I know how close Garrett felt to him."

"Yes, Charley was almost like a father to him, and a grandfather to me. Still, I suppose we had to expect it sometime. After all, Charley was seventy-eight." Turning to Miguel, she asked, "Do you remember Charley at all?"

Miguel nodded. "Vaguely. I remember he was there, staying at the ranch house when my mother died, when you and Uncle Garrett were away."

"Yes. He was such a good man. We were all lucky to have him there at that time, especially since Bur—" She broke off abruptly. "We were very lucky we could depend on Charley."

As anxious as Paige to cover her slip, Eden asked, "Will Garrett be gone long?"

"I expect him back at the end of the week. He rode down alone, so he ought to make good time. I might have gone with him, but I didn't want to miss seeing all of you."

"If you'd wired us, we could have put off our arrival for a week or two."

"Oh, I know you could have. But then I wouldn't have had the chance to see you at all. I'm leaving for Washington next weekend, and I can't be sure how long I'll be gone."

"Paige, you should have told me!"

"And let you cancel your whole vacation? Clinton would never have forgiven me! Besides, I wasn't sure I'd be going until about ten days ago. The suffrage amendment is up before Congress, you know, and we badly need lobbyists."

"Ten days ago! Then you did have time to wire us. We could have just put off the trip for a few months, as long as necessary."

Paige sighed. "Mama, you don't vacation in Wyoming in the middle of winter! There's nothing to do here then but watch the snow. Besides, in a few months, Mara and Miguel will be back in school, and I knew you wouldn't want to take them out to make the trip. Everything will work out fine, you'll see. By the time I leave, Garrett will be back here to entertain you. He's looking forward to it."

Ten days later, Eden and Garrett sat in the ranch house kitchen, drinking coffee after Mara and Miguel had gone to bed. At first, Eden had been determined to leave the ranch immediately after Paige. But the children so loved Wyoming that she hadn't the heart to cut their vacation short.

Garrett sighed heavily as his blue eyes roamed the kitchen. "Well, this is the way we might have ended up if you'd accepted my proposal thirty-odd years ago. I suppose we could still have ended up together if I hadn't been foolish enough to marry."

Eden swallowed. "Garrett, why did you agree to this arrangement with Paige? Why didn't you insist she wire me and tell me she wouldn't be home? Didn't you know I'd be uncomfortable? Aren't *you* uncomfortable?"

He shrugged. "I wanted to see you. It's been too long. Anyway, I'm more comfortable with Paige gone than I would be if she were here."

Eden reached across the table to touch his hand. "I'm sorry things didn't work out for you," she said softly.

"It's mostly my fault. I was old enough to know better. I shouldn't have expected a sixteen-year-old girl to be a replica of you, even if she was your daughter."

"It wasn't entirely your fault, Garrett. I know why you married Paige."

"No. You can't."

"She told me. I know about the baby she thought she was carrying. You were her knight in shining armor. I know she's always been grateful."

He smiled wryly. "Gratitude's not much of a cornerstone on which to build a marriage. Neither are memories of some-one else. As I said, I blame myself, not her. How could she ever hope to measure up to you?"

"It hasn't really been all that bad, has it? At least you don't fight. You respect one another. I know you've been very good to Paige. I hope she's been as good to you."

"Oh, yes. Under the circumstances, I couldn't have asked for more. She's turned into quite a woman. I'm proud of her. You should be, too. The only trouble is, we're not really a husband and wife. We're friends—friends who happen to live in the same house—at least for part of the year—and happen to share a name."

They were silent for several minutes. Then Garrett got up to refill their coffee mugs. As he turned to set the coffeepot back on the stove, he said quickly, "When Paige comes back from Washington, I'm going to ask her to divorce me."

Eden gasped. "Do you really think that will make things better? If you're thinking of us, don't! It's too late for us now."

He turned to face her, his penetrating blue eyes seeming to bore into hers. "No, it's not. It won't be too late until one of us is dead!"

"Garrett, it's an impossible situation! If you'd never been married to my daughter, it might be different. But now—"

"I'm not suggesting that we marry. I couldn't do that to Paige. It would be too humiliating for her. But, at least we could be together sometimes—discreetly—without any guilt to mar our happiness."

"No. I'd always feel guilty, thinking of Paige."

"Damn it, Eden! Can't you see it's the best solution for her, too? I wouldn't even suggest it if it weren't. Paige is still a young woman. She's only thirty-one. She's intelligent, attractive. She can remarry, maybe even have the children I was never able to give her."

"Maybe she won't want to remarry. Maybe she's in love with you."

"Eden, be serious! You've seen how Paige and I have avoided each other for years. At one time, I thought she was in love with me—though even that was probably no more than girlish infatuation. But, there hasn't been anything more than friendship between us for years." Lowering his eyes, he added, "I couldn't tell you the last time we shared a bed."

"Garrett, I don't want to hear about your intimate relations with my daughter!"

"Why not? At one time, you told me the most intimate details of your relationship with Brett!"

"That was different. I was so much younger. And you weren't related to Brett."

"All right, I guess it was different. But, Eden, I want you to understand! I want you to agree this is the best thing for Paige. I'll admit, there were times during our marriage when I probably didn't think of her enough. I tried, but I could never stop comparing her to you. But now, I'm convinced this is something I can do for her. I want to give her her freedom."

Eden was silent, wondering what it would mean to them if they were both free after all these years. After thirty-seven years, did she even dare to imagine?

Still, they could never marry. They could never really share a life. Outwardly, their relationship must remain the same. In all likelihood, Garrett would stay at the ranch, at least a few more years, while she would remain in Chicago. But, if nothing else, they could exchange letters without guilt.

"Eden, darling, say something! My suggestion can't come as much of a shock to Paige. I would imagine she's considered divorce herself from time to time. Only, she'd never suggest it because she feels responsible for our marrying in the first place."

Thinking of the time, almost ten years ago, when Paige had first confessed the problems of her marriage, Eden nodded. "Perhaps you're right. All right, discuss your proposition with Paige. It's between the two of you."

"Just promise me if Paige doesn't want the divorce, you won't force her. I can't build our future on my daughter's unhappiness, any more than I could have on Brett's or Benjamin's."

42
September 1879

"Really, Mama, it's all well and good to be amassing millions of dollars, but it's time we started doing something for the workers, too!"

Eden smiled across her desk at Paige. "I don't think we've neglected them, dear. We've always paid the highest wages in meat packing. And, I think the fact that few men voluntarily quit McKinnon Meats proves that we provide some of the best working conditions anywhere."

"Yes, of course. I don't mean to indicate you're a heartless businesswoman. I remember all you did for your workers during the war—paying their wages and supporting their families even when they were away in the army. But, I think it's time we did more, as an example to other packers and industrialists."

"And, you have a plan?" Eden smiled affectionately at her daughter. Since the defeat of the woman's suffrage amendment the previous year, Paige, like many suffragists, had turned her energies to other social reforms. Eden had known it would be only a matter of time before her reforming mind focused on McKinnon Meats.

"Yes!" Paige's green and gold eyes sparkled with enthusiasm. "You know, most of your workers are immigrants. They live in some of the tiniest, most dilapidated homes imaginable while they try to save money to better themselves in the land of their dreams."

"You're not going to suggest we build them all new homes?"

"Of course not! The beauty of America is that they can achieve their dreams, if they work hard. But, in the meantime, we can do something to alleviate the squalor of their lives."

"Go on."

"I'd like to set up some sort of meeting place for them, near the stockyards, in their own neighborhood. It would be a place where children could come, after school. You know, many of their mothers work in factories, or as domestics, so the children have no one waiting for them at home. Perhaps we could also set up an all-day nursery there, for children too young for school.

"My center would also be a place where women could meet, perhaps to learn about proper nutrition. And where men could meet, to discuss politics, or work, or whatever else interests them.

"It could be a place to hold dances, and parties, a forum for public speakers, a place to help immigrants who wish to become citizens.

"It seems to me any firm bearing the name McKinnon has a special obligation to help these people. So many of the workers in meat packing are Ulster-Scots. Papa's own ancestors may have known their families."

Eden smiled indulgently. "It's a fine idea. But—to do all that—you're asking quite a lot of yourself, Paige."

"You and Papa asked a lot yourselves when you set out to build a meat-packing empire."

"So we did. But—we always had each other to lean on."

Paige sighed. "If you think that I can't do it without a husband to help me, you're wrong Mama! Really, you ought to know better. How many years have you stood alone at the helm of McKinnon Meats?"

Eden shook her head. "I don't doubt that you can do anything you set your mind to, Paige. And, of course, you know Clinton and I will give you all the help we can. I just wonder if you're being fair to yourself."

Frowning, Paige said, "I don't understand."

"It's been nine months since you and Garrett parted, and you haven't given yourself much chance to meet anyone new."

Paige laughed lightly. "Oh, Mama! What would you have me do? Start attending debutante balls?"

"Of course not. But, perhaps you should give yourself the chance to be carefree and frivolous for a while. I'm afraid the war robbed you of that chance when you were a girl."

"And when were *you* ever carefree and frivolous?" Paige demanded in a gently accusing tone. "No, Mama, I'm too old for such nonsense. Besides, I don't want to meet any spoiled society men who are too wrapped up in their own lives to notice what's happening in the rest of the world. If I ever marry again, it will be to a man who shares my concerns."

"I hope you find such a man," Eden said quietly. "More than anything else, Paige, I hope you do."

That evening, as her carriage rolled toward her Prairie Avenue mansion, Eden reviewed her discussion with her daughter. She had agreed to give Paige several thousand dollars to implement her plan, and had promised whatever other support she might need.

Eden was proud of her daughter. Still, she had worried about her ever since Paige returned to Chicago last Christmas. She was pleased with Paige's commitment and independence, and the matter-of-fact way she had accepted her divorce. But she still wanted Paige to find personal happiness, the kind of deep happiness she had known in the first years with Brett, with Benjamin, and even in those rare, precious moments with Garrett.

Would none of her children ever know the joys of marriage? At forty, Clinton seemed the confirmed bachelor. But at least he had raised two children. Would Paige ever have that opportunity, which she had craved for so many years?

Sometimes it seemed to Eden that, in some strange way, Paige was paying for her own affair with Garrett. If her own life had not become entangled with Garrett's, almost forty years ago, he would not have been in Chicago, staying at their house, during the war. Paige would not have become infatuated with him, and would not have thrown herself into an ill-fated marriage.

Still, the marriage had not been totally disappointing. Paige had grown up through the experience. She and Garrett had remained friends and still exchanged occasional letters.

Perhaps, after all, Eden thought, I've suffered more than Paige—knowing Garrett and I are both free, but can never marry now. Perhaps that is my final punishment for being untrue to two husbands.

The carriage stopped before the mansion at Prairie Avenue and Eighteenth Street. Pushing her concerns to the back of her mind, Eden smiled. Tonight, she would be having dinner alone with her grandchildren, a treat she looked forward to. Clinton was dining at the Chicago Club, while Paige was meeting a friend from the National Woman's Suffrage Association.

As Annette, the downstairs maid, let her in the front door, Eden asked, "Are the children waiting in the parlor?"

"Yes, ma'am." Annette nodded, then added timidly, "There's a guest waiting with them."

"A guest? We didn't invite anyone for dinner tonight."

"No, ma'am." The maid shrugged as she retreated with Eden's cloak.

Eden stood at the foot of the stairs, debating whether she ought to go to her room to freshen up. No. Why should she trouble herself for an uninvited guest? The sooner she got rid of the person, the sooner she could enjoy her evening with Miguel and Mara.

Flushing suddenly, she wondered, could it be Garrett? Wasn't there some hint in his last letter that he might be coming east soon?

Overwhelmed with anticipation, she rushed to the parlor. In the doorway, she froze, as Burton rose with a smug smile.

"Why, Mother," he said, "how delightfully girlish you look! Something tells me I'm not the person you were expecting."

"I wasn't expecting anyone," Eden replied with forced calm. "But, I most especially was not expecting you."

Burton grinned. "I'm sure you weren't. But, after eight years, I thought I was due for a visit. You tell me so little about the family in your business communications."

"You never ask about anyone in yours," Eden countered.

"Hmm." Burton cocked an eyebrow. "Well, I've just been getting reacquainted with my *niece* and *nephew*." He placed a mocking emphasis on the terms.

"I see. Will you be staying for dinner?"

"If you'll be so kind as to invite me. I believe we all have a great deal to discuss. And, since Miguel tells me that Clinton is out for the evening, I think this would be the most opportune time to do so."

Eden stiffened. "If the conversation concerns Clinton, I'd prefer that we wait until he's here."

"Still protecting your little boy, aren't you, Mama? By the way, Mara tells me Paige is back in Chicago. Garrett Martin didn't quite measure up as a husband, eh?"

"Whatever happened is between Paige and Garrett. They parted amicably. That's all I know. Now, I believe dinner is probably ready."

All through dinner, Eden felt uncomfortable, wondering precisely what Burton wanted, what he had already said to Miguel and Mara. It wasn't until after dinner, when they were all seated again in the parlor, that Burton revealed his purpose.

"I suppose you know why I'm here, Mama."

"If it's about the business, I'm still not ready to retire. I know I'm sixty-seven, but I still enjoy the thrill of doing business, and I still feel I'm capable of keeping McKinnon Meats competitive with the other packers."

Burton nodded, smiling lazily. "I'm sure you are. You certainly appear as energetic as ever. The fact is, I didn't come to talk about the business. I came to talk about my son."

Eden glanced at her grandchildren. Mara's eyes were round with curiosity, but Miguel was staring at Burton with open hostility. In fact, she realized suddenly, Miguel had been unusually quiet throughout dinner.

Moving her eyes back to her son, Eden spoke crisply. "I hardly think this is the time for such discussion, Burton."

"I rather imagined you would think this is exactly the right time. After all, wasn't Benjamin exactly fifteen years old when Papa took him back into his home?"

"Burton, that's enough! This is my home. Either abide by my wishes, or leave!"

Burton's eyebrows rose mockingly. "I guess Clinton's finally succeeded in poisoning your mind against me. I never thought my own mother would threaten to turn me out of her home."

Staring at him intently, Eden replied, "You've done all the poisoning yourself, Burton. I've tried to resist it. At first, I made allowances, because of your youth and your desire to please your father. Later, when my disappointment in you began to grow, I consoled myself that at least you were a hardworking, sensible businessman. I let my pride in your success in Kansas City overshadow my disappointment in the person you'd become.

"But I can't make allowances for you forever. You're forty-two years old. It's time you grew up and considered the feelings of others."

Burton smiled condescendingly. "But, Mama, that's exactly what I'm trying to do! Have you no sympathy for the prodigal son? You can't hold me responsible for all my actions. At least where my children are concerned, I simply followed the example set by my father. You still loved him, despite whatever wrongs he'd committed."

Suddenly remembering the children were still there, silently listening, Eden turned to them. "Mara, Miguel, perhaps you'd better go upstairs."

Obediently, the children rose and started for the door.

"Afraid to let them know the truth about their family?" Burton taunted.

Miguel spun back toward Burton, his dark eyes flashing angrily. "If you mean the truth about you, I already know! I know that you're my so-called real father!"

Eden gasped, and Miguel went to lay a hand on her shoulder. "I'm sorry, Grandma. But it's better to get everything out in the open, isn't it?"

"I suppose my damn brother told you!" Burton snarled. "I suppose he told you all sorts of lies about me!"

"No. He never spoke of you at all. I figured it out for myself. It really wasn't so hard.

"Since I was a small boy, I wondered at the animosity between you and Papa. It didn't seem right to me, because Papa gets along so well with everyone. I asked Grandma, but she just said it was some personal disagreement between the two of you.

"Then, last summer, when we were out at the ranch in Wyoming, Aunt Paige accidentally mentioned your name when we were talking about when Mama had died. She tried to cover her mistake, but it made me think.

"I remembered then that you had once been connected with the Double M. Of course, I was too young to remember when you left. But when I was a little boy, Uncle Garrett and Aunt Paige and Mama mentioned your name from time to time. Sometimes Mama even cried out your name in her sleep."

There was a bitterness in his tone that made even Burton flinch. Still, Burton forced a smile. "So you know you're my son, eh? It's something I've wanted to tell you for a long time. I'd like you to come back to Kansas City with me. I could teach you about the plant there. Someday, you could expect to take it over."

Miguel stared at him impassively. "I wouldn't go anywhere with you! You abandoned me as a child, and now you expect me to leave my family and come with you!"

"Miguel, I *am* your family. I'm the closest family you'll ever have. I'm your father."

"No!" Miguel shook his head adamantly. "You're nothing to

me! Your brother is the only one I'll ever acknowledge as father. He was the one who comforted me and cared for me as a boy. He, and Uncle Garrett before him."

"Miguel," Eden cut in gently, "perhaps you'd better sit down and calm yourself."

"What should I do, Grandma? Embrace a man who hurt my mother? I'm old enough to figure out what must have happened between them! He never even had the decency to marry her, did he?"

"Men of means don't marry women of a different race," Burton said coldly. "Just ask your grandmother about your grandfather."

"What's he talking about?" Miguel demanded. "Did Grandpa wrong a woman?"

Eden sighed. "Some might say he did. You know Benjamin was part Indian. Your grandfather was married to Benjamin's mother, according to the Indian tradition. Later, they decided to part. Her people were being sent west, and she wanted to go with them. By Indian standards, they were divorced. Your grandfather remained in Chicago, where he later married me. In the end, Benjamin's mother, Morning Star, returned to spend the last years of her life in our home."

Miguel frowned. "That doesn't sound anything like what *he*," he paused to glare contemptuously at Burton, "did to my mother."

"Of course it doesn't!" Burton snapped. "She's glossed over the facts to protect the memory of my dear father! The truth is, he abandoned a wife and two sons!"

"I don't believe you," Miguel said quietly. "And, even if I did, it would make no difference in my judgment of you."

Turning back to Eden, he added, "I'm sorry, Grandma. I suppose you'd like to see the reconciliation of father and son. But, I can't hurt Papa that way. And I can't dishonor the memory of my mother."

"What about you?" Burton demanded, turning suddenly on thirteen-year-old Mara, who was still hovering in the doorway, embarrassed, but entranced by the conversation. "Are you as stubborn as your brother? Too pig-headed to accept your own father?"

The girl paled, her eyes widening. "You mean I—you—you're—?" she stammered.

"Yes. I'm your father," Burton said impatiently. "And you

needn't act as self-righteous as your brother. I was married to your mother. She died giving birth to you."

"And you didn't want me?" Mara whispered.

"Of course I did! But I was terribly grief-stricken when your mother died. And I thought you'd be better off living here, in a house with other women."

Slowly, Mara shook her head. "No. That can't be true. If you'd just wanted me to live here, you would have told me you were my father long ago. You would have come to visit me. But, you only came once. And you said you were my uncle."

"I had to say that. My brother had usurped my place as father, and I didn't want to confuse you. You were too young then to understand. But now that you're a young lady, I think you can see—"

"Oh, yes," Mara interrupted. "I can see everything quite clearly! You didn't want me or Miguel, and now, for some reason, you do. Why? So you can torment Papa by taking us away? Well, you won't do it!"

She paused, sniffling back the tears that had suddenly begun running down her cheeks. "It's too late for you to want us now, because we don't want you!"

Turning abruptly, Mara ran up the stairs, sobbing loudly.

Burton stared after her a moment. "Quite a dramatic exit," he said sarcastically. "Obviously, she inherited her mother's talent for theatrics." His eyes moved back to Miguel. "Aren't you going to follow your sister's example?"

Miguel stared at him coldly, clenching and unclenching his fists. "I'll go to comfort her. But, not until I'm satisfied that you've left this house. You've caused my grandmother enough agony for one night."

Cocking an eyebrow, Burton smirked at Eden. "Protective little man, isn't he?" Shrugging, he added, "For your sake, and Clinton's, that's just as well. Because, I guarantee, there will come a time when you'll all need protecting!"

43
1882–1886

Garrett smiled tenderly and kissed Eden's whitening hair as she lay in his arms. He was glad he had made this trip back to Chicago. To his delight, she was as tender and passionate at the age of seventy as she had been at the age of thirty.

Snuggling against him, she sighed. "I wish we could always be together like this."

"Why can't we?"

"You'll be going back to the ranch in another week or two."

"I don't have to go back, you know. I could retire."

She raised herself on an elbow and gazed at him lovingly. "You're too young to retire, Garrett Martin! If I can keep on working at the age of seventy, you certainly can't retire at sixty-two!"

Garrett grinned. "I may be forced to. Since you won't come out to the ranch to stay, it seems the only way we can be together is if I stay in Chicago."

Seeing her about to protest, he quickly added, "Oh, I don't mean living in your house—though it certainly is convenient just to creep down the hall to your room at night! I realize we'd have to be discreet. Society can accept my visiting here when I'm your out-of-town business associate and your son and daughter and grandchildren live here. But I couldn't very well just move in. As it is, I suppose some people can't accept my even visiting, in the same house as my former wife, though I don't think it upsets Paige at all—"

He paused, reading the anxiety in Eden's eyes. "Am I wrong? Does it upset her? Do you think she suspects anything about us?"

Eden shook her head. "I don't know. Sometimes she looks at me almost as if she knows everything. And yet, curiously, I don't think she'd mind. She's secure in her own life now. She realizes you and she never belonged together."

"I'm glad. I care about Paige, and, for her sake, I'd never

flaunt our relationship. But, I've been thinking a lot this last
year, Eden. We're getting too old to let the years slip by.
We've got to be together. We've got to make every day count
now. That's why I've decided to leave the ranch."

She looked away, hesitating. "I'd hoped you'd stay on in
Wyoming, just a few more years."

"What, wait until we're too old to fully enjoy being together?"

Eden winced at the impatience in his tone. "Of course not,
darling. But—well—now that he's finished school—Miguel's
expressed an interest in the ranching part of the business.
I—that is Clinton and I—hoped you'd take him back to
Cheyenne with you and teach him what he needs to know."

Garrett whistled softly. "This reminds me of a discussion
we had about twenty-seven years ago, in the Tremont Hotel."

"It's not the same, Garrett. Miguel's nothing like Burton. I
know him better than I ever knew Burton. He's lived with
me longer. I can guarantee he's a dedicated, hardworking
boy."

He sighed. "I believe you. But, when can we stop sacrific-
ing ourselves for your family?"

Eden shrugged, biting her lower lip. "It would just be for a
year or two, darling. Miguel's a quick learner."

"I know. He picked up a lot from me when you brought
him and Mara out four years ago. But, to tell you the truth,
he could probably learn as much from one of my foremen as
he could from me."

"You know that's not true, Garrett. No one out there has
the knowledge and years of experience you have. Besides,
you're family. We'd all feel better sending Miguel out there if
he was under your care."

"Family, huh?" Garrett muttered, grudgingly. "That's all
I've ever wanted to be to you, Eden. But it seems to me
you've spent the greater part of forty years pushing me away,
in the name of the family you already have."

She sighed. "When our lives touch others, we can't pretend they don't. You'll take Miguel, won't you? He's been
talking about the idea for weeks."

Garrett smiled reluctantly. "When have I ever been able to
refuse you anything?"

As Eden's private railcar, which she had insisted Garrett
and Miguel use, rolled west, Miguel smiled gratefully.

"I really appreciate this, Uncle Garrett," he said. "Grandma mentioned that you'd wanted to retire from ranching—that you're staying on as a special favor to me."

Garrett shrugged. "Well, I suppose I'm not really old enough to retire, anyway. It's just a silly notion I got when I tasted the easy life in Chicago again. I suppose I'd be bored if I was away from the range too long."

"Well, I'll try to learn as quickly as possible, so I won't interfere too much more with any plans you might have." The young man paused thoughtfully. "In a way, though, I feel kind of bad about leaving Grandma."

"That's only natural. You've lived with her most of your life. But you'll get over your homesickness."

Miguel shook his head. "That's not what I mean. Of course I miss her and Mara and Papa. But there's something else. I'm afraid for her."

Garrett frowned. "She's not ill, is she? She never said anything. Neither did Clinton."

"No. She's as strong as ever. At least as far as I know. Still, we can't deny she's getting old, and my father—my real father—" He broke off uncomfortably and Garrett's eyes probed his.

"What the hell is Burton up to now?"

"Nothing. I mean—I hope nothing. But I'm afraid to trust him. Three years ago, he came up to Chicago and tried to get Mara and me to go back to Kansas City with him. When neither of us would agree, he got pretty nasty. He threatened Grandma. He told her there would come a time when she and Papa would both need protecting. I don't know what he meant, exactly, but I still worry about it."

"And, in the last three years, he's never done anything to follow up his threat?"

"Not as far as I know. He just went back to managing the plant in Kansas City."

Garrett nodded thoughtfully, mumbling to himself, "I wonder why Eden never told me about that visit."

"She probably thought it was just a personal, family problem. I suppose she might have even been embarrassed about it. I know I am. I hate to even admit I'm related to him."

"Well, that was just an accident of birth. No one can blame you for who your father was."

"But some people say that sons turn out to be like their fathers." He hesitated. "Did you know my grandfather, Uncle Garrett?"

Garrett dropped his eyes. "Yes. I knew Brett McKinnon."

"Was he—is my father like him?" Miguel's voice sounded pained.

Raising his eyes again, Garrett shook his head. "No. Brett was a fine man—the only kind of man your grandmother would ever marry. More like Benjamin than your father, though not as soft-spoken as Ben."

He clapped a hand on Miguel's shoulder. "If I were you, I wouldn't worry much that you'll turn out like your father. You've neither the greed nor the jealousy that motivates him."

"And what about his threats to Grandma? Should I worry about them?"

Sighing, Garrett shook his head. "I don't think so. Especially not after three years. I've known your father ten times that long. He's always talked big. But he's never had either the inspiration or the initiative to carry out his threats.

"Burton's a hollow man. And hollow men don't give much cause for alarm."

In the next two years, while Miguel learned to manage the Wyoming ranch, the range industry expanded at an incredible rate. Between 1882 and 1884, as many steers were shipped north, to the rich grazing lands, as were shipped east, to market.

A steer worth five dollars at the start of its life increased its value to between forty-five and sixty dollars in only four years of grazing on the open plains. It was no wonder that new ranchers streamed west in numbers reminiscent of prospectors setting out for the gold fields thirty years earlier.

The rapid growth made Garrett uneasy. It was too fast. There was a limit to what the grazing lands could support. By the end of 1884, Miguel, at twenty, seemed capable of managing the ranch on his own. Still, Garrett stayed on, vaguely afraid he would be needed in the future.

The first problem to arise was rustling. Since the Double M North covered forty square miles, most of it unfenced, it was impossible to police all of the area efficiently. A determined rustler could easily make off with a few hundred head over a period of time, altering the brand markings.

By 1885, when the range had finally become overcrowded, rustling was a common problem suffered by all the ranchers. Still, it did not cut into profits enough to actually hurt the

Double M. That was left to the weather, coupled with the overcrowding.

The winter of 1885–1886 was the most brutal in anyone's memory. Along with the drought of the following blistering summer, it destroyed most of the free feed on the Great Plains. Overcrowded as they were, the cattle could not find enough food. Many dropped dead from starvation and thirst.

The Double M, like other major ranches, managed to send a small supply of beef to market. But its quality was far below what people had come to expect. Even with the intense shortage, the public was outraged, and beef prices crashed.

That same year, sheepherders began moving their flocks west across the plains. The sheep intensified the feed problems by eating not only the grass but the roots, leaving behind huge areas of barren range. The flocks also tainted the water, causing frequent battles between cattlemen and sheepmen.

Newly arriving homesteaders caused the ranchers even more problems. The homesteaders began establishing farms, fencing in large areas of the previously open range.

At that point, Garrett realized the range cattle industry, booming only two years earlier, was doomed. The Double M North could only survive if it made some drastic changes—and quickly.

Clinton agreed to come west during the fall of 1886 to help plan the future course of the Double M North.

Sitting at the ranch house kitchen table with Clinton and Miguel, Garrett sighed. "I suppose McKinnon Meats took quite a beating this last year. I'm sorry. Miguel can tell you we did all we could."

"It wasn't as bad as it might have been," Clinton assured him. "We had a good supply of pork to keep us going. That and a little bit of lamb and mutton."

"Sheep!" Garrett snorted. "I'm glad you got some worth out of them. They sure did whatever they could to wreck the range lands."

Miguel nodded. "The sheep destroyed a good part of the range, and whatever's left is getting fenced up by the nesters faster than we can brand a steer."

"Yeah," Garrett said, "I talked to a rancher the other day who had a few choice words for whoever invented barbed wire. Said the guy ought to have a ball of the stuff rolled all around him, and then all the cattlemen could give the ball a kick and watch it roll straight to hell!"

Clinton laughed. "I suppose you find the suggestion tempting?"

Shrugging, Garrett replied, "Oh, I don't know. It's progress of a sort, I suppose. Anyway, there's no way we can "uninvent" barbed wire, so we might as well start turning it to our own use."

"You want to fence in the ranch?"

He nodded. "I think it's the only way. The days of free-grazing cattle are over. If we fence in, we'll have better control of our cattle. We'll be able to control their breeding better, too—probably even develop some superior breeds for market."

"It could save us a lot of feed problems, too," Miguel put in. "If the other ranchers' cattle and sheep are fenced out, they won't be able to destroy our grazing land. And we can grow our own hay for supplemental feeding in the winter."

"It sounds sensible to me," Clinton said. "So, why are so many ranchers against the idea?"

Garrett shrugged. "Fencing in is a lot of work. Besides, most of these ranchers just don't take kindly to change."

"The cowboys don't either," Miguel said with a chuckle. "They're already grousing about having to do more work. Most of them are used to lying around for five or six months during the winter, doing nothing. They don't much like the idea of riding out to check and mend fences, haying, and feeding the cattle hay all winter."

"But they'll do it?" Clinton asked.

"Sure they will," Garrett said, "as long as we pay them enough."

"So, when do you want to start?"

"As soon as we can get the barbed wire shipped out from Joe Glidden's plant in DeKalb, Illinois. Anything to avoid another disaster like this year."

Ten days later, in late October, the Double M North began the mammoth task of fencing in. They all knew they weren't likely to finish the job before the winter snows stopped them. But Garrett and Miguel were determined to do as much as possible, to get a jump on the following spring.

Clinton stayed on to help in whatever way he could. He enjoyed riding out each day with Miguel, seeing the calm,

sure way his adopted son accepted responsibility, the respect
the other cattlemen accorded him.

Often, when the fence building took them far from the
ranch house, they stayed out overnight. They lay awake in
their bedrolls beside the campfire, staring at the stars and
talking of the new Double M North, which Miguel would one
day manage alone.

Since the job of fencing in was so large, Garrett and Miguel
had taken out separate crews of cowboys to work on different
areas of the ranch. As they started work one morning, Miguel
realized he had a question about the property line, and
Clinton offered to ride over and consult Garrett about the
problem.

"After all," Clinton said, "I'm probably the most expend-
able member of this crew. I might as well do something
useful."

"All right," Miguel agreed. "In the meantime, we'll just
work on the other end of this section. So, it might be easiest
if you just spent the night at Uncle Garrett's camp and rode
back in the morning."

By midafternoon, Miguel was glad he had made that
suggestion. The sky was blanketed in dark clouds, and he
hated to think of Clinton trying to ride back in a sudden
snowstorm.

An hour later, it began to snow, huge downy flakes that
coated the ground within a few minutes. Miguel and his crew
suspended work, built up the fire, and settled down for the
night.

"Looks like the last fencing we'll be doing this year," one of
the cowboys remarked. "This one looks like a real blizzard."

"I sure hope your old man ain't ridin' arond in this,"
another said to Miguel. "A man could get himself lost forever
in one of these storms."

"No, I'm sure he reached the other camp before noon,"
Miguel said. "He'll spend the night there. Even if he'd
started back here, he'd have turned back when he saw the
sky."

The next morning, the snow was still falling in a thick
curtain of white that made it impossible to see for more than
a few feet. About noon, the snow stopped, and the sun came
out, blinding the cattlemen with its brightness.

Agreeing that work must be suspended, Miguel directed
his crew to pack up and head back to the bunkhouse. He

assumed that Garrett was doing the same, and that Clinton would ride back with him. Still, he felt vaguely uneasy, and decided to ride out toward Garrett's camp before turning back toward the ranch house.

Two hours away from camp, he sighted a lone rider approaching him. He spurred his horse and saw the other horse increase its pace, too. Miguel's heart sank when he saw the other rider was Garrett.

Trying to ignore the worried frown on Garrett's face, Miguel asked, "Did Papa ride on in with your crew?"

Garrett's frown deepened. "No."

Miguel swallowed, feeling as if his heart was about to pound through his chest. "What do you mean? Where is he?"

"I'd hoped he was with you."

Miguel stared with wide, horrified eyes, and Garrett continued. "He left our camp almost two hours before the snow started. It was too late then to send anyone out after him. I thought he might be able to make it back to your camp. I hoped—"

He broke off abruptly as Miguel continued to stare. "You didn't see anyone—or anything—riding here?"

The young man shook his head.

Scanning the barren horizon, Garrett was silent, thinking the things they both knew, but dared not say.

A man, even a man who knew the area well, could easily become lost and disoriented in a blizzard. Last winter, one of the neighboring ranchers had lost his way from his own house to his barn and froze to death. There was no shelter on the open plains. There weren't even trees to provide a windbreak or firewood.

Looking up at the sun, Garrett sighed. "We'd better head in. As it is, we'll be lucky to reach the house before dark. The snow makes for slow going."

Miguel shook his head despairingly. "We can't just go in when Papa might be—"

"He might be home," Garrett cut him off gently. "And if he's not—well—" he paused and shrugged, his voice fading into a mumble, "we won't do him a bit of good by staying out here."

They rode silently, a little apart, each scanning the range for some hopeful sign. In his mind, Miguel berated himself for letting Clinton ride off alone.

I should have known how quickly a blizzard could start up, he thought. *I should have warned him. At the very least, I should have insisted he plan on spending the night at Uncle Garrett's camp, instead of just suggesting it.*

Garrett, too, was blaming himself. *Why in hell didn't I at least look at the sky before I let Clinton ride off again?* he thought. *He didn't know the weather out here the way I do, the sudden changes that could cost a man his life.*

What will this do to Eden? Hasn't she lost enough loved ones? If one of them had to go, why not that bastard, Burton?

He shook his head sharply, realizing he was already thinking of Clinton in the past tense. *Clinton might have survived. He must have!*

Half a mile from the ranch house, Miguel's horse stumbled over something hidden by the drifted snow.

Quickly dismounting, the young man reached into the drift and felt the edge of a cowhide jacket, stiff and frozen. Furiously, he began pushing away the snow. Roused from his own thoughts, Garrett dismounted and stumbled through the snow to join him.

Fear gripped Garrett's throat. Almost certain of what they would find, he lunged toward Miguel, hoping to pull him away.

It was too late. By the time Garrett reached him, Miguel had uncovered Clinton's face, futilely wrapped in a muffler, crusted with ice crystals.

For a long, horrified moment, Miguel stared at the white, frozen features. He cupped the face in his hands, shaking his head as tears coursed down his cheeks.

"No!" he shrieked suddenly. "No! Papa, it's not you! It can't be! No, Papa, no!"

The wind carried his screams away, across the eerie expanse of silent, darkening range. The white frozen face lay expressionless in his hands, until Garrett gently grasped his shoulders and pulled him away.

44
November 1886

Garrett rubbed his eyes as the maid, Annette, led him into the parlor of Eden's Prairie Avenue mansion. He had hardly slept in the three days since they had discovered Clinton's body, and he still did not know how he could possibly break the news to Eden.

He and Miguel had decided against wiring her. Garrett could not bear to think of her receiving the news without him there to comfort her. And Miguel was still so numbed by grief that he accepted any suggestion Garrett made.

Standing by the green-clothed center table of the parlor, toying absently with the plush family photograph album, Garrett tried to compose his thoughts. He heard a sound at the parlor door and looked up to see Eden, her cheeks flushed with pleasure.

"Garrett, darling! What a wonderful surprise! I never dreamed you would be coming back with Clinton! But then, I didn't really expect him yet, either. Did Miguel come, too?"

Wincing, Garrett replied, "Yes. He's—they're—down at the station yet—taking care of the—luggage."

"Oh, it will be just wonderful having you all here! How long can you stay? At least until Christmas, I hope!" She paused, at last taking in his haggard face. "Garrett, what's wrong? You look so tired. Was the trip so hard, or—surely you're not still upset about the losses the ranch suffered last year? No one blames you, of course."

Unable to speak, his eyes brimming with tears, Garrett crossed the room and enfolded her in his arms.

For several minutes, she clung to him, her head on his chest, feeling the frantic rhythm of his heart. Gripped by sudden fear, she pulled away and gazed up into his sorrowful blue eyes.

"Garrett, what *is* it? Tell me!"

His arm around her shoulders, he led her to a settee.

She stiffened slightly as they sat, preparing herself for a shock.

"Garrett, you have to tell me! You're all right, aren't you?"

Nodding, he mumbled, "I wish to God I weren't."

"What do you mean? Has something happened to one of the others? Miguel?"

He shook his head and whispered, "Clinton."

Eden paled, and she sank back against the settee cushions. "Clinton was hurt? How badly? You did say he was at the station, didn't you? Should we send a carriage for him?"

"No. Miguel will take care of things. They should be here very soon."

"And you came ahead to prepare me." Despite her fears, Eden tried to keep up a cheerful front. "How very thoughtful of you, darling. So, tell me quickly, what must I expect?"

He looked away, unable to bear the hope in her eyes. "Eden—" He took her hand, still keeping his eyes averted and began forcing out the words.

"There was a blizzard. We were all out on the range, trying to fence in as much of the ranch as we could before winter set in. We didn't really expect anything more than a few flurries this early in the year—which was foolish, I suppose. By now, I should have known no one can predict the weather out there."

Sighing, he dragged a hand haphazardly through his blond hair. "Anyway, Miguel and I were working with separate teams of cowboys, about fifteen miles apart. Clinton was riding between us with a message. The storm just came up out of nowhere."

He felt Eden's hand go cold in his.

"Garrett," she whispered, "look at me."

Reluctantly, he dragged his eyes to her tortured, blue-green gaze.

"Clinton's dead, isn't he?"

He nodded, tightening his arm around her shoulders. "Eden, I—"

"He—froze to death?" Her voice broke on the question.

Again, Garrett nodded, "We don't know exactly what happened. He must have got lost in the storm. And—there just isn't any shelter on the open range. Somehow, by instinct, I guess, the horse made its way back to the stable. But, Clint must have fallen off. Miguel and I found him about half a mile from the house."

Nodding, Eden stared ahead with unseeing eyes. "Forty-seven years," she mumbled. "Forty-seven years of a kind, caring life—snuffed out by a few flakes of snow. Life isn't fair, you know? Clinton never hurt anyone or anything in forty-seven years—and now—"

She laughed mirthlessly. "But, I should know by now that life and death are cheaters! Look what they did to Ben, and to Brett. Look how they took my mother before her time. And my father—"

"Eden, don't! It's pointless to rail against life. That won't bring Clinton back."

"But it's so unjust!"

"Of course it is. I've thought the same thing, at least a hundred times, between Cheyenne and here. I wish I could say something to make it all clear and easy to accept. But there's nothing to say."

"No, there's nothing to say." Eden sighed. "Poor Clinton! I wonder what he thought about when he was lost in the snow? Did he know he was going to die? I hope he didn't regret his life too much. He never really wanted to be a packer, you know."

"I'm sure he didn't regret it at all. He loved working with you. He was very proud of you. And he's raised two fine children."

"Yes. He had every reason to be proud of the way Miguel and Mara turned out. Clinton was a wonderful parent. Better than me, I suspect. He didn't have any failures."

"Miguel's pretty shaken up by the whole thing. He and Mara are going to need you to lean on."

Eden forced a rueful smile. "I don't know that I'm much support for anyone, anymore. I'm seventy-four years old, and I've suddenly begun to feel it. I think I need someone to lean on, myself."

"That's why I'm here. I'll always be here."

The same inner strength that had sustained Eden through the earlier tragedies of her life welled up again to help her through the following days. Still, she was grateful for Garrett's presence and the emotional support he provided.

Mara and Miguel were too overcome by their own grief to provide much comfort. Miguel was especially distraught, still blaming himself for Clinton's death. Paige tried to bury her own grief to comfort her niece and nephew. But no one could overcome the somber mood that had settled over the mansion.

Sitting at the funeral in the Plymouth Congregational Church, on Michigan Avenue, near Twenty-sixth Street, Eden thought back to a similar service twenty years earlier.

Then, she had sat in the Second Presbyterian Church, at Wabash and Washington, mourning for Clinton. But then there had been no body, and Clinton had returned the next year. Now, his body lay in the bronze casket before her, proof that he would never return.

Now, even the church where that first memorial service had been held no longer stood. The Second Presbyterian had been destroyed by the great fire. Its thrifty congregation had hauled the blackened stones north, to the new suburb of Lake Forest, to build a new church.

Eden frowned to herself, wondering how her thoughts could stray to facts so tenuously connected to her son's funeral. Perhaps she really was getting old.

Beside her, she heard Paige and Mara sobbing quietly. Miguel stared straight ahead, his features frozen in a pained grimace. On her other side, Garrett sat with one hand lightly touching her arm, as if to provide a constant flow of strength from his body to hers.

At the end of the service, as they stood to leave the church, Eden felt Garrett's hand tighten slightly on her elbow. She raised her eyes questioningly to his, then followed his gaze to the back of the church.

Burton stood in the last pew, his hands folded, his head bowed. As if sensing their gaze, he raised his head, inclining it slightly in greeting. Then he stepped into the aisle and walked out of the church.

As Eden and Garrett stepped out into the harsh November light, Burton was suddenly beside them.

He bent stiffly to kiss Eden's cheek, then said, "I'm sorry I wasn't here sooner, Mama. No one thought to notify me, and I had to get the news from the newspaper."

Eden bit her tongue, not wishing to argue on the church steps. There was still the burial to face, and she would need all her emotional strength for that.

To her surprise, she heard Garrett's voice apologizing. "It was my fault, Burt. I told your mother I'd wire you. Then I got wound up in some of the other arrangements and somehow forgot."

Eden felt a rush of tenderness. How kind of Garrett, who had never been one to mince words and could scarcely stand the sight of Burton, to lie for her! He knew she had decided against wiring Burton, rather than be hurt as she had been when he ignored Benjamin's death. Besides, she had known Miguel and Mara would be upset at his presence.

His eyes narrowing, Burton nodded. "No harm done, I suppose. I appreciate whatever you've done to help out here, Garrett—especially since you're not even a member of the family anymore. But, I can take over in consoling my mother, now."

Tensing, Eden said, "Perhaps you would be so kind as to escort your sister to the cemetery, Burton. I have Garrett to lean on, and Mara and Miguel have each other. I think Paige needs someone, too."

Burton's features hardened. "Wouldn't it be more appropriate for Paige's former husband to support her, and let me support you? As the oldest surviving male member of this family, I think my place is at your side."

Eden hesitated, then nodded. "I'll be all right," she whispered to Garrett. "Please, go with Paige."

Frowning, Garrett raised his eyebrows. But he nodded as Eden slid her arm into Burton's. "Of course," he muttered. "If you need me, we'll be right behind you."

Hours later, when all the mourners had finally left, and Eden, Paige, Mara, and Miguel had retired, exhausted by their grief, Garrett sat with Burton in the parlor.

The tension in the air was almost tangible as Garrett eyed the younger man. At forty-nine, Burton's reddish hair had begun to fade into brown, flecked with auburn and gray. But his eyes were as cold and bitter as Garrett remembered them.

Pouring himself a drink, Burton smiled broadly. "Well, I've waited a long time for this day! I guess it's true, after all, that all things come to him who waits!"

Garrett scowled. "What the hell are you talking about?"

"Come on, Garrett, you know! You couldn't have forgotten the things we talked about down on the old Double M."

"Yeah, but you were just a kid then. I thought by now you would have grown up."

Burton laughed shortly. "That sounds like something one

of my late brothers would have said! Not trying to take their places, are you?"

"Hardly."

"Then, why are you here?"

"Because I felt I was needed. Miguel was too torn apart to make the trip alone with Clint's body. And I thought Eden, for all her strength, might need someone to lean on."

"If she needed a man to console her, that should have been my job. Why didn't you contact me? Really?"

"I didn't think you'd give a damn about consoling anyone. From all accounts, you weren't too concerned when Ben died."

"That was different. Benjamin was only my half brother."

Garrett shrugged. "Anyway, I didn't want to give you the chance to upset your mother."

Burton's brows shot up. "Pretty protective of her, aren't you? You planning to marry her now? Since you couldn't hold on to Paige long enough to get the whole firm for yourself, maybe you can get it through my mother."

"God damn it, Burton! I don't want the damn firm! Whatever I do for your mother, or Paige, or Mara, or Miguel, I do out of concern for them. But, you wouldn't understand that, because you've never been concerned about anyone but yourself in your whole life!"

"On the contrary, if I weren't concerned about my mother, my sister, *and* my children, I wouldn't be here right now."

"Your children! How can you even call them that? I assure you, they don't think of you as their father."

"That's understandable, at the moment. But, they'll learn to change their views. After all, their shares in McKinnon Meats will pass to them through me."

"I wouldn't be so sure of that. Miguel's old enough now to take over the firm himself, if need be. He's capable, too. Mara will be twenty-one in another year, and she's been working in Eden's office for quite some time now. As for Eden herself, Clint's death was quite a blow to her. But, I don't think she's ready to give in yet."

Burton scowled. "Are you trying to tell me my mother's going to cut me out in favor of my kids?"

"I wouldn't presume to tell you anything. It's Eden's firm. She can do with it as she pleases."

"She won't cut me out. She hasn't all these years, even when her dear Benjamin and Clinton tried to turn her against me. No mother can turn her back on her firstborn. It's a crime against nature."

Pausing, Burton narrowed his eyes as he studied Garrett. "Still, I could do with fewer detractors around me. Might I suggest that you pack up and return to Cheyenne tomorrow? Now that I'm here, I don't think my family needs you to console them anymore."

Garrett stared at him coldly. "Now that you're here, I think they need me more than ever."

Stepping into his dark bedroom, still seething over his talk with Burton, Garrett sensed, without seeing, that someone else was there.

"Garrett?"

He closed the door quickly. "Eden! What are you doing here? I thought you were asleep hours ago!"

She sighed heavily. "How could I sleep tonight? I can't even bear to be alone."

"You should have come down and gotten me."

"No, I—I didn't want to see Burton. God, what a terrible thing to admit! I have one son surviving, and I can't even bear to be in the same house with him."

His eyes adjusting to the darkness, Garrett saw her sitting on his bed, her back propped against the pillows. He went to her and took her in his arms. His mouth sought hers, and he tasted the saltiness of tears on her cheeks.

He thought of a night more than twenty years ago, in the house on Wabash Avenue, when he had comforted her about Clinton. But then Clinton had only been injured in the war. Now, it seemed there was nothing comforting to say.

He felt her trembling against him as she drew a long, ragged breath. "So young," she murmured. "He was so young. They all were. Clinton at forty-seven. Ben, only forty-five. Even Brett was still a vigorous fifty-six. Not one of them lived to a natural death. All the men I loved. It makes me worry for you and Miguel."

"Don't be morbid, darling. It's not as if fate has marked you and all those you love."

"No. Not fate. God, perhaps."

"Eden!"

"Oh, I don't know what to think! At the cemetery today, when they lowered the casket, I kept wishing it were Burton instead of Clinton inside."

"Under the circumstances, I think that's only natural. I'll confess, the same thought crossed my mind."

"But, it's not natural! It's terrible! How could any decent mother wish one of her sons dead, even to spare her other son?"

"Eden, it's absolutely insane for you to feel guilty about that! Burton hasn't really been a son to you in a long time. Besides, we both know that you'd never actually wish anyone dead. It was just a passing thought, brought on by your grief."

She sighed. "Yes, I suppose so. It's true, I don't hate Burton. But I don't love him. I wasn't pleased to see him today. If anything, I felt apprehensive. I don't believe he came either to comfort me or to honor the memory of his brother."

Garrett nodded. "What *do* you think?"

"That he expected me to be so prostrated by grief that he could step right into my office, and never leave again. He thinks Miguel and Mara are too young. And he knows Paige isn't interested in the business, except as it affects her social work. So, I'm sure he thought that, given the slightest encouragement, I would turn to him."

"Will you?"

"Of course not! I intend to go on just as I have in the past. If Burton really does change, perhaps I will consider stepping down in his favor. But, I have to admit, I don't expect that to happen. And, right now, I think it would be an insult to the memories of Clinton and Benjamin even to consider such a course."

"Not to mention what it would do to your grandchildren. You may not hate Burton, but I sometimes think Miguel does. He doesn't have the driving ambition and greed that Burton has. I'm afraid if you turned McKinnon Meats over to Burt, Miguel might leave it completely."

"I know. I've thought of that, and it's another reason I can't give Burton what he wants. For almost forty years now, I've wanted to be reconciled with my son. But, I could never do it at the expense of my other son, and I won't do it at the expense of my grandchildren. Besides, even if I gave Burton everything, I'm not certain we could ever be reconciled now."

Sighing, Garrett gently kissed her eyelids. "Don't let it bother you too much," he whispered. "So many of us love you so much, you shouldn't even miss Burton's love."

"No. I shouldn't. But I do. I'm not the hardhearted, unfeeling businesswoman some people might think."

He pulled her closer, stroking her cheek as she lay against his chest. "I knew that the first time I saw you sitting behind the registry desk of the Bull and Boar."

The next morning, Paige left the house early, planning to drown her grief in her social work. Mara and Miguel asked for breakfast trays in their rooms. So, only Eden, Burton, and Garrett met at the breakfast table.

"I trust you slept well," Burton said as he eyed his mother. "You're looking a good deal less haggard than yesterday."

Eden smiled wryly. "Does that disturb you, Burton dear?"

"Of course not! How could I be anything but pleased to see my mother recovering so quickly from the tragedy you've just faced?"

She arched her brows. "I don't know. It just occurred to me you might prefer to see me remain a bit weaker."

Burton shot a scowl at Garrett before forcing a smile for his mother. "What nonsense, Mama! I don't know who could have given you such an idea!"

"You, perhaps." She gave him a long, piercing stare before continuing. "Burton there's no sense in our fencing with words. If you're truly here to honor Clinton's memory and to offer comfort to your family, I'm more than happy to have you. But, if you think that now you can simply step into the leadership of McKinnon Meats, I'm afraid I must disappoint you."

Burton's eyes darkened with suppressed anger. "I don't know what kind of lies Garrett's been feeding you, Mama! You should know I'm here to comfort you. Of course, if that comfort should include assuming any additional responsibility at McKinnon Meats, I'm more than willing to do whatever I can."

"I don't think that will be necessary, Burton. As you know, hard work has always been my best remedy for grief."

"But you're seventy-four now, Mama," Burton said with exaggerated patience. "It's conceivable you'll find the load too heavy."

"That's not likely. I have a number of very dependable assistants. And Mara has begun to show remarkable business talent."

"From my own daughter, I would expect no less. Still, she's just a girl. You must feel the need for a man's help."

"As I said, I have several capable assistants."

Burton's eyes narrowed. "Are you telling me you don't want me in McKinnon Meats?"

"Not at all. You've done an outstanding job with the Kansas City plant, and I'd be very happy and grateful to have you continue there."

"I've been there twenty years!" he exploded. "I'm nearly fifty years old! I think I deserve to know when I can step into the place my father intended for me!"

Eden remained impassive. "I don't know."

"What do you mean, you don't know? It's my right, and I demand an answer."

"I have to think of Mara and Miguel."

"What the hell does that mean? Are you planning to turn my own son and daughter against me?"

"No. You did that yourself, long ago. Personally, I would like nothing better than to see all of you reconciled."

"Well then, Mother dear, just exactly what do you intend?"

"To continue working at the plant. To let Miguel run the Cheyenne ranch. To continue training Mara. To depend on you in Kansas City. And then—we'll see."

"Oh, yes," Burton muttered. "We'll see. We certainly will see!"

45
September–October 1887

Inhaling the clear, country air, Eden smiled and took Garrett's arm as they strolled along the western boundary of the Double M North.

"I'm glad you convinced me to come out for the month," she said. "It's good to get away from the city now and then. Being out here, where there are so few people, reminds me of what Chicago was like when I was a girl."

"Umm," Garrett grunted, his blue eyes sparkling, "I wouldn't know. That was long before my time!"

She punched his arm affectionately, and lay her head against his shoulder as she gazed west, toward the Rocky Mountain foothills.

"No, I guess Chicago never was quite like this," she said. "Even in the beginning, Chicago never had the serenity I feel here. Chicago was always brawling and ambitious and determined to make something of herself. Here, one has the feeling there's no need for showiness, because nothing can compete with the magnificence of the view."

Garrett smiled. "Not thinking of retiring out here, are you?"

"Me? Retire?" She laughed. "No, Chicago and McKinnon Meats are a part of me. Much as I love it out here, I don't think I could ever leave Chicago permanently. I remember in the fifties how people whispered about me, a woman, taking over the firm. Now, I think very few people would be shocked if Mara should follow in my footsteps."

"She didn't mind staying behind in Chicago this trip?"

"Not at all. Actually, I think she was rather relieved I didn't ask her along. There's a young man, the head of our canning division, to whom she's become quite attached. It wouldn't surprise me at all if we have a wedding in the family soon."

"I wonder what Burton would think of that? Someone else to usurp his position in the firm?"

Eden shrugged. "Believe it or not, I've almost given up caring what Burton thinks. Anyway, his threats no longer bother me. It's almost a year now since the last one, and nothing's changed. The Kansas City plant is running as smoothly as ever, and I never hear from Burton, except in business reports.

"Maybe, underneath everything, he really does feel some affection and loyalty toward the family. Anyway, I don't think he'd do anything to destroy the firm he wants so desperately for his own."

"Will he ever have it?"

She sighed. "Probably not. Even Miguel and Mara don't know this, but as my will now stands, McKinnon Meats will pass to them. I've apportioned a certain percentage of the profits to Paige, and I've also stipulated that Burton shall remain in charge of the Kansas City plant as long as he wishes. I'm afraid if I didn't do that, Miguel might cut him out entirely."

Pausing, she laughed. "But, why even talk of this? I have absolutely no intention of dying!"

Garrett's laugh echoed hers. "I'm glad to hear that! Because I have a surprise for you. How would you feel about my coming back to Chicago with you?"

"For how long?"

"Forever."

"Garrett, that's wonderful! Do you mean it?"

He nodded, his brows raised in mock amazement. "I don't believe it! After forty-five years of begging you to let me spend my life with you, you're finally going to agree? You're not going to think of somewhere else you can send me, to keep us apart for another ten years or so?"

"Umm—well—let me think for a moment—"

He swept her into his arms, kissing her hard on the mouth. "No, I most certainly will not let you think for a moment! You're not getting rid of me this time, lady!"

"You're sure Miguel can manage without you?"

"Absolutely. That's why I stayed on with him this final year. Now that we're all fenced in, he shouldn't have any trouble at all."

"And you won't miss ranching too much?"

"Sure, I'll miss it. But, not even one-millionth as much as I've missed you all these years! Besides, it won't be the same anymore. It won't be like the open range days. In some ways, it will probably be better. But, I'm too old to change.

"More important, I'm too old to live without you anymore."

Paige met them at the Michigan Southern and Rock Island station on Van Buren Street. Her green and gold eyes were shining with an excitement that made her appear younger than her forty years.

She hugged Eden warmly and kissed Garrett's cheek. "Garrett! How nice to see you! Mama didn't tell us to expect you."

He smiled. "No. I'm afraid I caught her offguard. I've decided to retire to Chicago."

"You mean you'll be staying? Permanently?"

He nodded.

"You don't know how glad I am to hear that. I've been wondering whom I could depend upon to look after Mama."

Eden frowned. "Paige, whatever are you talking about? I'm not some doddering old woman who needs looking after."

"Oh, of course not. I've just been concerned that when I move out I might not always have the time. And, Mara being so young—"

"Move out! Paige, you're making less sense every minute! Why are you talking about moving out?"

"Because I'm getting married!"

"Married?" Eden repeated. "Now I *am* confused! I wasn't even aware you were seeing anyone."

"I wasn't until a week after you left. But then, I met a man. He's simply wonderful, Mama. I know you'll love him and the children as I do."

"The children?"

"Kenneth's a widower with eight children, Mama."

Eden sighed. "Paige, are you sure you know what you're getting into?"

"Quite sure. As I said, Kenneth's a wonderful person. And I'm not a naive, inexperienced child this time." Glancing at Garrett, she flushed, "I'm sorry, I didn't mean—"

Garrett smiled. "It's all right. If he's as fine a man as you say, I'm glad for you. It's what I wanted for you when I suggested we divorce."

Paige squeezed his arm gratefully. "You're still as understanding as ever, aren't you, Garrett? I'm sorry you couldn't find someone, too."

"Perhaps I have."

He glanced tenderly at Eden, and Paige felt a sudden flash of understanding. How long had she suspected this? How long had he been in love with her mother? Since before their own marriage? That could explain a great deal.

Still, she couldn't blame him for anything that had happened. She couldn't doubt that he had always tried to do what was best for all of them.

Eden's voice cut in on her thoughts. "Eight children, Paige! It's all so sudden! I hope you've allowed yourself time to really think this out."

"I've had enough time, Mama. Besides, for the children's sake, I can't take more. They need a mother. The youngest is only two years old."

"Oh, the poor thing! Still, you mustn't rush into marriage out of pity."

Seeing Paige's mouth set in a hard line, Garrett cut in

quickly. "Perhaps it would be better to continue this discussion at the house. It's been a long trip, and I, for one, could use some rest and refreshment."

In the Prairie Avenue parlor, after Eden had time to wash and change out of her traveling outfit, Paige faced her again.

"I hope, Mama, that you're not going to be difficult about my marriage."

Eden shook her head wearily. "That's not my intention, darling. Anyway, you're a bit old for me to tell you what to do. I just want you to be happy."

"I will be, Mama."

"Well then, tell me more about your intended. How did you meet him?"

"We met at the agency."

"The agency you started to help our workers?"

Paige nodded.

"Then, he must be a man with a social conscience to match your own. How did he hear about the agency? Did he come there to offer his help?"

Paige smiled. "Not exactly. He came to pick up his three youngest children. They stay at the nursery while he's at work and the older children are in school."

"You mean—"

She nodded. "Yes. Kenneth Harrigan works in our plant. He's a meatcutter, recently arrived from Ireland."

"And—his wife? I mean his late wife?"

"She died of consumption soon after their arrival. The children range from two to twelve. All very well behaved. I love them dearly. Having spent the last two Sundays with them, I think I can say they feel the same about me."

Eden was silent, and Paige stared at her calculatingly. "What's the matter, Mama? You don't disapprove of my marrying a man from a lower social class, do you?"

"No. I don't disapprove. I've never much believed in class distinctions. The only distinctions that mean anything are between hard workers and loafers, and between good, honest people and evil, devious ones. Still, I think you ought to consider that marriage to this man will mean a very different kind of life for you. Not that I wouldn't be willing to help out, of course—"

"Oh, no!" Paige cut her off. "Kenneth would never agree

to that! He's very proud, both of his family and his ability to support all of them."

The doorbell rang, and she hurried toward the parlor door. "I'm sure that's Kenneth now. I asked him to stop in after work."

In the hallway, Eden could hear Paige and Kenneth exchange affectionate greetings. Then a deep voice with a lilting Irish brogue said, "I hope I haven't kept you waiting too long. I had to stop home and change me clothes before meeting your mum."

"You're here in perfect time," Paige assured him. "It gave Mama a chance to rest a bit after her trip."

"You've told her already?"

"Yes, and she's anxious to meet you. Come in."

Eden rose as Paige led her intended into the parlor. He was a tall, brawny man in his early forties, with black hair and dark eyes that showed both kindness and suffering.

Extending her hand, Eden said, "I'm very pleased to meet you, Mr. Harrigan. Anyone who brings my daughter happiness is always welcome here."

He took her hand firmly, smiling rather shyly. "Thank you, Mrs. McKinnon. I've looked forward to meeting you."

She sat, nodding to him to do the same, and she felt a rush of sympathy for him as he lowered himself gingerly to the edge of a brocaded chair. "Would you like tea?" she asked.

"Normally, ma'am, I would be pleased to accept. But, I don't want to keep you more than a few minutes, since I know you must be tired from your trip. And, I must pick up my little ones very soon."

"Yes, Paige has been telling me about them. How sad for them all to be motherless."

He nodded. "For the older ones, especially. They'll remember their own dear mother, while the babies cannot." Taking Paige's hand, he added, "We're all very lucky your daughter has consented to take her place."

Eden nodded. "Having lost my own mother when I was only seven, and my father when I was a baby, I sympathize. I'll look forward to meeting the children, and hope they'll always feel at home in this house."

There was an uncomfortable silence, and then Kenneth blurted, "Mrs. McKinnon, I want to make sure you understand I'm not one of those fortune hunters, marrying your daughter just to get at her wealth. The truth is, I didn't even know she was a McKinnon when we met. I just knew she was a kindhearted lady that my little Lucy, my two-year-old, adored. And, before I knew it, I found I couldn't help adoring her myself.

"I also hope you won't think I'm trying to find an easy way to the top at McKinnon Meats. It's a good plant, and I'm proud to work there. But, I don't expect any special favors. You can ask anyone who works with me, and they'll tell you I'm a good hard worker. I'll take my promotions as they come, and when I deserve them.

"In fact, I've been doing a lot of thinking, and if you think it would be better, I'll go to work for a different firm, so none of the other workers will ever have reason to accuse anyone of favoritism."

Eden smiled. "I hardly think that's necessary, Mr. Harrigan. I'm glad you don't expect any rewards that aren't your due. But, I don't think I ought to punish you for marrying my daughter!"

Grinning, he stood up. "Well, I just wanted to make sure we understood each other, right from the start, ma'am. Now, if you'll excuse me, I have to run and get my little ones."

When Paige returned from seeing him out, Eden said, "He's a fine man. I'm sure your father would have approved." After a slight hesitation, she asked, "I trust he knows about Garrett?"

"He knows I've been married and divorced. He doesn't blame me."

"What about his church? I assume he's Roman Catholic?"

Paige nodded. "His church *would* blame me. That's why we've decided to be married in a civil ceremony."

"His church won't approve of that, either."

"No. But Kenneth feels that, for the children's sake, it's better to have a marriage of which the Church disapproves than to have no marriage at all."

"I'd say that's a sensible conclusion. But I understand the Irish are very close to their church. I hope that, later on, Kenneth won't regret his decision."

"He won't," Paige said confidently. "I'll never give him cause for regret. And, at my age, with my past, it's unlikely that we'll produce any more children between us, so we won't face any religion problems in that area."

Nodding, Eden asked quietly, "Is that why you're marrying him, Paige? To have the children you've always wanted?"

Paige shrugged. "It's a consideration. Part of loving Kenneth is loving his children. But I do love him, Mama. He's a decent man, and he'll make a good husband."

"What are your plans for your agency?"

"I'll cut back on my hours there. But I won't give it up entirely. We've discussed it, and Kenneth understands its importance. He wouldn't want to deny other families the comfort it's brought to his."

"Except," Eden said with a wry smile, "that I don't think he'd approve of any of the other workers marrying you!"

Paige laughed. "Oh, Mama! As a matter of fact, he said exactly the same thing!" Sobering, she asked, "Do you think you'll feel up to coming to the Courthouse to witness our wedding on Monday?"

"So soon?"

"Why wait? It will be better for the children if we all get settled as quickly as possible. Besides, at our age, there's no sense in long engagements."

Pausing, Paige studied her mother carefully. "What about you, Mama? Now that I'm finally settled, will you marry again?"

Eden flushed and forced a laugh. "At my age? I'm seventy-five! I've been widowed sixteen years now."

"Love knows no age. At least, that's what you told me when you married Benjamin."

"I still believe that. But I'm content with my life and my family. I don't plan to marry again. I had two good marriages. That's more than enough for any woman."

"Has Garrett ever asked you?"

Eden's flush deepened, and she dropped her eyes to her lap. "Somewhere, you've gotten some pretty silly notions, Paige McKinnon."

"Not really so silly. I probably know both of you better than anyone else alive. It's obvious to me you love each other. And there's no one now to keep you apart. So, why shouldn't you marry?"

Eden was silent, thinking of the scandal if she were to marry Garrett Martin, her daughter's former husband. As it was, the straitlaced society matrons could not understand how Garrett remained so close to the McKinnon family, nearly ten years after his divorce from Paige.

For herself, Eden could weather any snubs or criticism. She had lived with them when she took over the firm, and again when she married Benjamin. Whatever barbs society threw her way would be small payment for the joy and comfort of being married to Garrett at last.

But, she could not subject her loved ones to that criticism and ostracism. She couldn't bear to think of the matrons whispering behind their hands whenever Paige passed, speculating on how her mother had been carrying on with Garrett Martin, even while she, Paige, was married to him.

She couldn't, by her actions, encourage people to laugh at that fine, gentle man, Kenneth Harrigan, saying Paige had only turned to him to escape the scandal of her mother's house. Nor could she embroil Kenneth's eight innocent children, soon to be Paige's stepchildren, in the talk.

She could not risk causing a rift between Kenneth and Paige. It was entirely possible that, kind though he was, Kenneth would not understand the situation. And Paige, who was now closer to Eden than ever before in her life, would be forced to choose between defending her mother or honoring her husband.

Besides, at their age, what difference would it make if she and Garrett never married? They knew the love that existed between them. For more than forty-five years, they had loved each other, emotionally, spiritually, physically. Their love was richer now than ever. She had no doubt that, regardless of marriage vows, they would continue to share that love as long as they both lived.

Mistaking Eden's silence for annoyance, Paige said softly, "I'm sorry, Mama. I guess it's none of my business what you or Garrett do. I just wanted you to understand that I wouldn't be upset. I love you both. I want you to be happy."

Smiling, Eden rushed to embrace her daughter. "Your understanding is worth more than I could ever tell you," she whispered. "I am happy, darling. I'm very happy!"

46
1889

Smiling contentedly, Eden surveyed the guests crowding her Prairie Avenue ballroom as they whirled to the music of the Johnny Hand orchestra. Her eyes moved to Garrett, sitting beside her, trim and elegant in his white satin waistcoat and fashionably long-waisted English cut coat.

His face was leathery now, a legacy of his years on the range. But, even at sixty-nine, his cheeks still crinkled in boyish dimples as his eyes met hers.

"It's a lovely wedding, isn't it?" Eden whispered. "I'm so glad Mara chose you to give her away. Next to Clinton, you have always been the adult relative she loved best."

Garrett smiled wryly. "Even if I'm not, technically, a relative anymore! Still, I'm glad she still thinks of me as her 'Uncle Garrett.' I just hope Paige's husband wasn't offended by her choice."

"Kenneth? I'm sure he wasn't!" Eden looked across the room, to where Kenneth Harrigan stood. "He looks so ill-at-ease in that Ascot tie, I'm sure he would have been mortified to be at the center of attention, even for a moment, during the wedding ceremony."

"Maybe. But, it's still an awkward situation. I wouldn't blame him if he felt a bit miffed. After all, he's part of the family. My only connection with this family is through my former relationship with his wife."

"Oh, really?" Eden widened her blue-green eyes saucily, making Garrett chuckle and squeeze her hand.

"You know what I mean!" He paused, watching Mara glide by in the arms of James Merritt, her bridegroom. "It's just a shame things couldn't have been different—that she couldn't have had her real father give her away."

Eden sighed. "I know. But she wouldn't even hear of inviting Burton to the wedding. And, much as I'd like to see

409

them reconciled, I can't really blame her. I just hope he won't cause any trouble because of this."

"Why should he? He's never really cared what happened to either of his kids."

"No. But it's one thing for him to choose to reject them. It's quite another for them to reject him. I keep thinking of the time, when Mara was only thirteen, when she and Miguel both refused to accept Burton as their father. He was awfully angry then."

"Sure. But he's never done anything about it."

"Still, I keep thinking he might turn up at this wedding reception and he might—well, I honestly don't know what he might do, especially when he finds out James has become my chief assistant here at the Chicago plant."

Garrett smiled indulgently. "You've just planned so long and worked so hard for this wedding you're afraid something might spoil it. Don't worry, nothing will."

"I suppose not. I'm just acting like a foolish, fear-ridden old lady."

"That, my love, you'll never be! Believe me, I know. My mother was a prime example."

Looking up, they saw Philip Armour, approaching. Armour was talking with Miguel, who had come in from Wyoming for the wedding. When he reached them, Armour smiled genially as he took Eden's hand.

"It's a first-rate party, Mrs. McKinnon. But I'm afraid I'll have to be taking my leave now. Five o'clock in the morning comes early, you know."

Eden smiled. It was a well-known fact that Armour was always in bed at nine, up at five, and in his office by seven. "Tomorrow's Sunday, Phil," she said laughing. "Surely you don't have to be up *that* early. Both the yards and the grain exchange will be closed. And I'm sure Dr. Gunsaulus doesn't start church services at dawn. You'd be the only one to attend!"

Armour grinned and scratched his balding head. "Well, I'm just a poor creature of habit, Mrs. McKinnon. If I change my schedule tomorrow, I won't be able to get back on the track Monday, which *is* a workday."

"Well, you know what's best for you, Phil. Thank you for coming."

"I wouldn't have missed it. You know I think the world of

your grandchildren. Now," he rolled his eyes toward Miguel, "if you can just get this one married off—"

"It seems to me you still have an unmarried son, Mr. Armour," Miguel cut in good-naturedly.

"Sure. But P.D.'s still a few years younger than you, my boy. Oh, by the way," he said, turning his attention back to Eden and Garrett, "what did you think of the speech Secretary of Agriculture Rusk made last week?"

"About the need for federal meat inspection?" Eden shrugged. "I suppose it might be a good thing, though the Chicago city inspectors do a good enough job weeding out unfit animals at our stockyards and slaughterhouses. Anyway, respectable firms like yours and mine really don't need inspection. We'd be fools to sell tainted meat."

"Agreed," Armour nodded. "I can't see many packers trying to take advantage of the public that way. What would be the point? Someone would find out sooner or later, and no one would ever buy from them again."

"Still," Garrett put in, "I should think the proposal might have some merits, especially for a firm like Armour and Company, which built its fortune on pork. Federal inspection could help your foreign trade considerably."

"That's true. We've really suffered in the foreign markets in the last decade. Italy, Germany, France, Spain, Turkey, Greece, Rumania—none of them will even allow any American pork products past their borders, because of some crazy notion they might be infected with trichinae. If our government certified the meat, I suppose they'd all lift the restrictions."

"Well then," Eden said, "for your sake, Phil, I hope the government does decide to start inspections. Anyone they send is certainly welcome into McKinnon Meats at any time."

In the next few months, Eden rarely thought about the proposed inspections. She read with disbelief occasional newspaper reports of poor packing-plant sanitation and the selling of diseased meats. Surely none of her colleagues, Armour, Gustavus Swift, Nelson Morris, or the Libby brothers were party to such practices. Perhaps a few smaller packers were not as scrupulous. But she doubted that any would intentionally sell tainted meat.

To anyone who asked, Eden maintained that anyone, journalist, government official, or customer, was welcome to inspect the facilities and processes of McKinnon Meats at any time.

One morning in mid-September, Mara's husband, James, stepped into Eden's office with a worried frown.

"What is it, Jimmy?" Eden asked. "Mara's all right, isn't she?"

"Oh, yes, she's fine, Gram. But there's a man here from the U.S. Department of Agriculture. He says he wants to inspect our plant."

"Well then, I suspect we'd better let him. Actually, I'm glad to have him here. Perhaps his inspection will put to rest all those silly rumors about packers slaughtering diseased cattle and hogs."

Her grandson-in-law forced a smile. "I hope so."

"You seem rather hesitant. What's the problem?"

"This inspector, Mr. Grayton, says he's already had reports that we deal in tainted meat. He says he has signed affidavits from former McKinnon employees."

Eden frowned and drew herself up stiffly. "That's impossible! We've never bought, slaughtered, or sold any animal with the slightest suspicion of disease. This Mr. Grayton must have gotten his reports mixed up. Bring him in."

James stepped out of the office and, a moment later, ushered in a tall, stern-looking man of about forty-five.

"Mrs. McKinnon," the man said, nodding curtly to Eden, "I hope you are not going to try to bar our investigation."

Bristling slightly, Eden rose behind her desk. "I certainly am not, Mr. Grayton. I've always said that anyone is welcome to examine our plant, and I shall continue to stand by that statement. Now, what's this nonsense about affidavits?"

The man shrugged. "The department has in its possession several affidavits attesting to questionable practices of this plant. At this point, I'm not at liberty to tell you more."

"Surely you could at least tell me who is perpetrating these lies!"

"No, ma'am. I can't tell you anything, except that each of the statements was volunteered. We did not have to seek them out. Naturally, we feel compelled to investigate."

"I see." Eden lifted her chin proudly. "Well, Mr. Grayton, we at McKinnon Meats will be happy to cooperate with you. And, I can assure you, you will find all of these alleged affidavits to be quite false."

For the rest of the day, Eden and James accompanied the

inspector and his team of veterinary experts on a tour of the plant.

They inspected the stockpens, where newly purchased cattle, sheep, and hogs were kept. They checked the slaughtering areas and the fresh-meat-butchering operations, now headed by Paige's husband, Kenneth.

Next they investigated the canning plant, and the plant where hams and bacon were cured. They even inspected the rendering plant, where lard was processed.

At the end of the day, the inspector turned to Eden with a grim smile. "Well, Mrs. McKinnon, as you predicted, nothing seems to be amiss. In fact, your plant and operations appear to be a good deal more sanitary than anyone might expect."

"Of course," Eden replied with a complacent nod. "May I assume then, that you'll drop this absurd investigation?"

Grayton shook his head. "I'm afraid that's out of the question. There's still the matter of the affidavits. We can't discount all of them, simply on the basis of one inspection tour."

"You're welcome to make as many tours as you wish, but I'm confident you won't find anything different."

"I'm sure we wouldn't—especially now that you've been alerted." The inspector rubbed his chin thoughtfully. "I'm not certain what course the investigation will take now, Mrs. McKinnon. But, you may be sure the Department will remain in touch with you."

In her office, Eden tried to catch up on some of the paperwork that had piled up on her desk while she escorted the investigators. However, her mind kept straying back to the investigation and what had prompted it.

Who would have volunteered information, total fabrications, to the Agriculture Department? Why would any former worker make up the stories? How could he profit by the lies?

She tried in vain to think of any employee who had left McKinnon Meats unhappily in the last few years. She couldn't remember firing anyone, couldn't conceive of anyone having a grudge against her. Her own fair labor practices, coupled with the goodwill engendered by Paige's agency, made McKinnon Meats the most popular firm in Packingtown.

Perhaps another packer had paid men to lie about her firm. But who? Surely not Armour. Not Swift or Morris. Not

Arthur or Charles Libby. Despite their fierce competition, they were all too honest for such underhanded dealings.

There was one other possibility that kept nagging at Eden's mind. But she pushed the thought away, unwilling even to consider it. It wasn't possible, anyway. There was a limit to the vengefulness of any man.

Unable to concentrate, Eden finally gave in and left her office at seven P.M. She found Garrett waiting in her parlor on Prairie Avenue.

Closing the parlor doors, he took her in his arms and held her for several moments. "It's been a long day, hasn't it?" he whispered.

"How do you know?"

"First, because you're usually home at six. And, second, because I read the newspapers."

Gasping, Eden pulled away from him. "You mean it's in the papers already?"

"I'm afraid so." He nodded at a copy of the *Daily News* lying on a chair. A bold headline declared, "Packer Charged With Selling Bad Meat."

Snatching up the paper, Eden sank into a chair and scanned the article:

> Federal officials disclosed today that McKinnon Meats, one of Chicago's oldest and most prosperous meat-packers, is suspected of selling meat from diseased cattle and hogs.
>
> Although the U.S. Department of Agriculture will not yet reveal its sources, officials say they have in their possession several affidavits charging the firm with slaughtering and selling beef from lumpy-jawed cattle and pork from cholera-infested hogs. Both kinds of meat could cause serious health problems to persons eating them. The affidavits, according to officials, were supplied by a number of former employees of McKinnon Meats, who themselves witnessed the questionable slaughtering and butchering. City inspectors, who regularly inspect the livestock taken in at the McKinnon slaughterhouse, would not comment on the charges.
>
> McKinnon Meats was founded by Brett McKinnon, one of Chicago's early settlers, in 1835. Since his

death in 1857, the firm has been headed by his
widow, Mrs. Eden McKinnon.

The firm pioneered in the use of icehouses, and
later built and operated some of the first refrigerated railcars for the transport of fresh meat. During
the Civil War, McKinnon Meats was a primary supplier to Union troops. The firm also made sizable
donations of meat to Camp Douglas, the Confederate prisoner-of-war camp on the city's South Side.
Mrs. McKinnon's late daughter-in-law, Jocelyn
O'Connor McKinnon was implicated in the Chicago
Conspiracy involving the camp.

There is some speculation that the McKinnons
felt they could deal in diseased meats undetected,
since family members head almost all the firm's
departments. Mrs. McKinnon, 77, remains the sole
head of the firm. She has repeatedly spoken in favor
of regular federal inspections, inviting anyone to
inspect her plant at any time.

Her son-in-law, Kenneth Harrigan, oversees butchering operations, while her grandson-in-law, James
Merritt, heads the cattle and hog buying and super-
vises the canning plant. Her daughter, Paige Harrigan,
founded and runs a social service agency for plant
workers. Mara Merritt, Mrs. McKinnon's granddaughter, works in the main plant office.

Another McKinnon plant, in Kansas City, Missouri,
was founded by and is still headed by Mrs. Mc-
Kinnon's son, Burton. A grandson, Miguel, manages
the McKinnon cattle ranch in Wyoming, which supplies much of the firm's beef.

Asked what they intend to do about the charges,
Agriculture Department spokesmen said they will
thoroughly investigate, bringing formal charges if
necessary. "It is a serious matter to endanger the
public's health," one investigator said. "We cannot
let such actions go unpunished."

Looking up, Eden sighed. "It almost reads like an obituary
of the firm. Of course, they can investigate all they want.
They'll never find anything wrong with the McKinnon
operation. Still, until the charges are proved false, this kind
of article will really hurt our business."

After a slight pause, she added, "I just don't understand it all. Why would anyone do this to us? Who?"

Garrett stared at her intently. "Don't you really know?"

"No." She looked away, the color draining from her face. "You're wrong, Garrett. He wouldn't. It's his firm, his name, too. He wouldn't try to destroy it."

"But it's *not* his firm. At least not totally his, not the way he wants. Because of that, he might destroy it."

"No. I can't believe that."

"You'd better believe it. I think Burton has finally decided to make his move."

47
1889–1890

No matter how rationally Garrett, and later Mara and Miguel, argued, Eden could not bring herself to admit that Burton might be behind the federal investigation of McKinnon Meats.

Much as it grieved her, she had accepted years ago that her son was a bitter, greedy, power-hungry man. But, even when Benjamin and Clinton had been alive, when Burton had openly despised them both, he had never done anything to harm them or the firm.

Over the years, he had issued so many threats that they had begun to be meaningless. Never had he followed through. Why would he do so now?

Besides, he wouldn't do anything to harm the name of McKinnon Meats. Not when he believed he still stood some chance of inheriting the firm. And he must believe that. No one but Eden, Garrett, and Eden's personal lawyer knew the contents of her will.

Even if Burton suspected she had finally cut him out, he would have broken away and started his own firm by now. If he had done that, if his firm were already established and he didn't need the McKinnon name, she could understand him trying to destroy McKinnon Meats. But, as things stood, it made no sense.

The Agriculture Department set up a board of inquiry, and its investigation dragged on into 1890. The investigators found no concrete evidence with which to indict McKinnon Meats.

Still, as Eden had predicted, the continued publicity hurt the firm. Meat wholesalers throughout the country increasingly turned over their orders to McKinnon competitors. In England, where McKinnon's canned and dressed beef had sold nearly as well as domestic English meats, the firm's major customers suddenly stopped placing orders. One by one, buyers in other European countries followed suit.

With fewer orders to fill, McKinnon Meats began buying less livestock. Operations in every department of the firm slowed. It was pointless to produce more dressed beef or pork than could be sold, and it made no sense to build up large stocks of unsold canned goods.

Sitting in her parlor one evening with Garrett and Philip Armour, who had stopped in to offer whatever consolation he could, Eden sighed wearily.

"For myself, I hardly care what happens anymore. I'm nearly seventy-eight. If McKinnon Meats closed tomorrow and I lived another twenty years, I couldn't begin to spend half of the fortune I've accumulated. But it hurts to see everything Brett, Benjamin, Clinton, and I built up destroyed. And, when I think of how this could ruin Mara and Miguel and Jimmy's lives—"

"It won't ruin them," Armour cut in gently. "Everyone in the packing industry knows there's something trumped-up in these charges and this investigation. McKinnon Meats is one of the most respected names in packing. No one believes you've done anything wrong."

Eden smiled grimly. "The confidence of my peers is comforting. But, by the time the commission of inquiry admits you're right, we may not have a customer left, at home or abroad. The public's very fickle, it seems. Not that I blame them. One can't take chances with one's family's health."

"Well, if they're fickle, it means in a few years they will have forgotten all this. You'll get your customers back. Even if, for some reason, you don't, you'll never have to worry about your grandchildren. I'd be proud to hire them in a minute. So would Gus Swift, or Nels Morris, or Art Libby."

"That's a comfort, at least. I hope you can all do the same

for my workers. They've all been so loyal. With operations as slow as they are now, we ought to lay off about half of them. But I can't do that as long as I can afford to keep them on. After all, this whole mess isn't their fault."

Armour stared at her keenly. "No, it's not. But it's not your fault, either. Which brings us to the question, who do you think is to blame?"

Eden hesitated, dropping her gaze to her lap. "I—I wish I knew. I've asked myself the same question, hundreds of times."

Seeing Garrett scowl, Armour asked, "Has your son, Burton, had any thoughts on the matter?"

"No. At least, he hasn't made any suggestions."

Armour frowned. "That's strange, especially with him being the only surviving son and part of the firm. I know if Armour and Company were in trouble, my boys Ogden and P.D., Jr. would—"

"What she means," Garrett cut in, "is that she hasn't asked Burton's opinion. The truth is, she's afraid to! She doesn't want to find out what she already knows about him!"

"Garrett!" Eden's eyes darted between Garrett and Armour.

"Well, it's true, isn't it? Damn it, Eden, I'm not trying to embarrass you, but Phil here knows what kind of scoundrel Burton is. After all, they were business partners for a time during the Gold Rush, weren't they?"

Armour cleared his throat uneasily. "Yes, we were. But, of course, he was just a boy then."

"But, would you say," Garrett pressed, "that he seemed deceitful?"

"Well, I don't think I could really say. I think what struck me most about Burt was his driving ambition. Even at thirteen, he was determined to make something of himself. Only, he wasn't really willing to work for it the way I was. He wanted fortune and success handed to him. That's why we parted company soon after we arrived in California. We hadn't made a gold strike, and he thought my idea of digging trenches and selling water rights to other prospectors seemed too tedious."

"So, instead," Garrett said, "he got a job on a ranch and pretended to his parents that he actually owned it."

Forcing a smile, Armour said, "Well, he was a boy. He exaggerated. Still, it's not the sort of thing I'd have thought to write to my parents. I guess that's the other thing that always struck me about Burt. His lack of closeness with his family. I had a devil of a time convincing him to write home at all.

"At the time, I figured I had no right to judge him, that maybe his folks just weren't like mine. But then, when I finally met the rest of the McKinnons—well, I don't know. Last year, for example, I couldn't imagine him not coming up for Mara's wedding. And now, with all the trouble—"

He broke off abruptly, reddening as he realized Garrett's implications. Pulling out his pocket watch, he stared at it as he tried to compose himself. "Well, it's later than I thought. I'd better be going, Mrs. McKinnon. But please, if there's anything at all I can do, don't hesitate to ask."

As a maid let Armour out, Eden turned on Garrett with snapping eyes. "How could you have done that? You made us all very uncomfortable!"

"I did it," Garrett replied calmly, "because I had to make you see the truth already. I hope you noticed that, once Phil realized what I was driving at, he didn't say anything to refute my opinion. He knows the kind of man Burton is. You do, too. And I can't, for the life of me, understand why you keep rejecting the one course of action that can probably get to the bottom of this whole investigation quicker than anything. You say this commission of inquiry, and all the publicity around it, is hurting the firm and hurting your grandchildren's future. All right then, you'd better do what you can to get it over with as quickly as possible!"

Eden sighed wearily. "What would you have me do?"

"Go to Kansas City. I'll go with you. Go through the plant there. Confront Burton. Of course, he'll deny any involvement in the scheme, but we'll be able to tell if he's lying."

"What if he's not? What if he truly hasn't done anything wrong? How can I accuse my own son, without even a scrap of evidence?"

"Eden, you have evidence! Isn't it evidence enough that he hasn't even contacted you once since this investigation began?"

"No. He hasn't taken an active interest in the Chicago plant, or in any of his family, in years."

Sighing in exasperation, Garrett turned away from her. "I'm going home," he said curtly. "There's no sense talking to you when you won't listen to reason."

"All right," she whispered. "I'll go to Kansas City. We'll

go. Tomorrow afternoon. Lord knows there's not much to keep me in Chicago right now. With business as slow as it is, there's nothing to do at the plant."

At breakfast the following morning, the *Chicago Tribune* headlines glared up at Eden. "Meat Inquiry Moves to Kansas City." Scanning the article, she saw that investigations had begun at Burton's plant. Burton himself was quoted, saying McKinnon Meats had always been a reputable firm and had nothing to hide.

She had barely had time to digest the article when Garrett arrived, followed by a messenger from Western Union.

The telegram, from Burton, read, "Stunned by inquiry. On way to Chicago. Will arrive 7:30 P.M."

Passing the message to Garrett, Eden said, "I guess there's no point in going to Kansas City now."

Garrett frowned. "I suppose not, for the moment, at least." He hesitated. "It's a ruse, you know."

"What?"

"Burton's coming here. All of a sudden, he's decided to play the role of concerned son. Funny he didn't think to do that any time in the last five months."

"The problem didn't touch him as closely then. But, don't worry, I'll be wary. Besides, I'm sure I can trust you, Mara, and Jimmy to point out anything suspicious in his behavior or conversation. Kenneth, too, I think. His Irish temper is really flaring that anyone would dare question the integrity of his butchers or his family."

"Doesn't Paige feel the same?"

"In her own way, I suppose. She doesn't want to see anyone in the family hurt. But, I think she feels the meat-packing industry could do with some reforming. And, if it has to come at the expense of McKinnon Meats, well, so be it."

Garrett grinned wryly. "That's my Paige! Once she devotes herself to a principle, nothing stands in her way. Still, she's turned into a woman to be proud of. Two good children out of three isn't a bad percentage!"

Forcing a laugh, Eden replied, "If we were in the yards, discussing stock, we'd say it was a terrible percentage!"

Eden and Garrett were waiting at Union Station, on Canal Street, when the Chicago, Burlington and Quincy arrived that evening with Burton on board. Shaking Garrett's hand,

Burton smiled sardonically. "Old faithful Garrett Martin! I suppose you've been quite a comfort to the family these last months."

"Someone had to be," Garrett replied coldly.

Frowning, Burton turned to his mother, "I really would have come sooner, Mama, but I knew you've always been strong enough to do without me. Then too, it seemed wiser to maintain some distance between the two plants. If yours went down, I hoped mine could still survive and offer work to Mara and her husband, and to Paige's husband. Miguel, I imagine, should be quite secure with the ranch. He can always sell the stock to other packers."

Smiling slightly, Eden said, "Your concern for your daughter and sister and their families sounds quite noble. But, I'm sure you can see your reasoning makes absolutely no sense. If my plant falls, it will pull yours down with it. The name McKinnon will be ruined."

"Well," Burton said hastily, "my rationale makes little difference now, since my plant is under investigation, too. Which is precisely why I've come. We must work together and decide how to handle things in order for McKinnon Meats to survive."

"I don't see that there's anything at all for us to decide," Eden replied. "We've always run clean, law-abiding packing plants, and eventually the commission will have to admit as much."

"Well, of course we've always done everything in our power to make sure we produce wholesome meat. But, even the best-run plant can suffer an occasional accident. And, this commission of inquiry seems so anxious to prove their charges, I'm afraid they'd pounce on the slightest irregularity."

"No doubt you're right, Burton, but I still have every confidence they won't discover anything. Everyone connected with the plant has been more watchful than ever since the investigation began. Besides, business has slowed so much that none of our operations is ever rushed, so the workers aren't likely to make mistakes."

Burton shrugged. "Well, think what you wish. I don't know why I should care, anyway. The firm isn't mine, and it never will be."

Eden stared at him keenly. "What do you mean?"

"Oh, nothing." Quickly, he changed the subject. "Have you considered buying off any of the commission members?"

"I should say not! How could you even suggest such a thing?"

"Come now, Mama. You've been in business over thirty years. You can't be so naive you don't realize the power of the dollar."

"Yes, Burton's an expert on the subject," Garrett cut in sarcastically. "How do you think he avoided the draft during the war?"

"I don't want to hear another word on the subject," Eden said firmly. "The carriage is waiting, and there's a nice supper being prepared for us at home. We'll discuss the problems of the firm later."

Hours later, after Burton had retired and Garrett had discreetly left for his own home, a block west on Indiana Avenue, Eden lay awake, reviewing that conversation at the train station. What had Burton meant when he said the firm would never be his? Was he only speculating? Or did he really know?

He couldn't know for sure. She, Garrett, and Chad Ramsay, her lawyer, were the only people who knew the contents of her will. She hadn't even told Mara or Miguel.

Still, there had been a certain sureness, a certain finality to Burton's statement. Even more disturbing, Burton hadn't wanted to discuss the matter at all. He'd seemed almost embarrassed he'd mentioned it, as if he'd let something slip that he shouldn't have. In the past, he never would have steered the conversation away from his inheritance. He'd always badgered her to tell him when and how much he would inherit.

Chilled by the implications of that conversation, Eden lay awake until dawn. Then she dressed and hurriedly went downstairs.

She left a message on the breakfast table for Burton, saying she had left early for the stockyards, but he was welcome to join her at the plant later that morning. If she was not in her office, Mara's husband, James, would show him around.

Slipping out unnoticed by any of her servants, Eden quickly walked west on Eighteenth Street, turning south on Indiana Avenue to Garrett's mansion. Garrett himself, still wearing a satin dressing gown, opened the door when she rang.

His eyes widening in surprise, he reached out and drew

her gently into the house. "You're up very early, darling. Have you even had breakfast yet?"

She shook her head.

"You walked over?"

"Yes."

"Well, come in and have something to eat and tell me what's bothering you."

"I've been awake all night. I don't think I can eat."

Garrett cocked an eyebrow. "You'd better eat. With your beloved son in town, you're going to have to keep up your strength and stay on your toes."

He led her into the dining room, calling to his cook, "Kathleen, you'll have to set another place. Mrs. McKinnon's come to breakfast."

He poured her a glass of orange juice, then heaped a plate with eggs and sausage and pushed it toward her. "Eat!" he commanded. "The sausage is especially good—McKinnon's finest."

Forcing a smile, Eden asked, "You mean you still buy their products, after all the papers have said about them?"

"No," he quipped, "I get them for free. I've got something going with the old lady who runs the firm!"

"You don't say?" She sipped her orange juice and took a few bites of eggs before sighing and putting down her fork.

"All right," Garrett said softly, "what's Burton done?"

Eden shook her head. "Nothing, yet. But I can't get something he said at the station out of my mind."

Frowning, Garrett waited.

"Garrett, you never told him, did you, about my will—about my cutting him out in favor of Miguel and Mara?"

"Eden, I haven't even seen Burton since Clint's funeral. And you didn't tell me about the will until the next year."

"That's what I thought. But, Garrett, he knows! I'm sure of it!"

His frown deepening, Garrett reviewed the conversation at the train station. "He did seem rather sure he'd never get the firm," Garrett agreed. "But he might have just finally realized what your actions have been telling him all along. I mean, I've always said Burt's not stupid."

"No. But he's always had a certain blindness about McKinnon Meats. He's always thought the firm would have to come to him, eventually."

Garrett nodded thoughtfully. "Besides me, who else have you told about your will?"

"No one. The only other person who knows anything about it is my lawyer, Chad Ramsay."

"Then, I think as soon as I'm dressed, we'd better pay a visit to Chad Ramsay."

Eden and Garrett were seated in Chad Ramsay's waiting room in the Drover's Bank Building of the Union Stockyards when the lawyer arrived.

Smiling and extending his hand, the lawyer said, "Mrs. McKinnon, Mr. Martin. I can't really say I'm surprised to see you. With the stories that have been appearing in the papers, I've wondered when you'd decide to sue for defamation."

"The idea's crossed my mind a few times, Chad," Eden said. "But, I'm here on quite a different matter."

"Oh?" He ushered them into his office and closed the door.

"I'd like to speak to you about my will," Eden continued.

The lawyer's eyes flicked from Eden to Garrett and back again. "Thinking of making some changes?"

"Not at all. I simply wondered, have you disclosed its contents to anyone?"

Ramsay looked shocked. "Eden! I've been your lawyer and friend for nearly thirty years. You ought to know me better than that."

"I thought I did, Chad. But I'm wondering how it happens that my son, Burton, knows the contents of my will."

The lawyer blinked uneasily. "Well—Eden, my good friend, I'd be the last person to imply that you're getting old. I mean, we all tend to forget things now and then. And, right about that time, I suppose you were still all wound up over your granddaughter just getting married." He paused delicately. "Anyway, *you* told him."

"*I* told him?" Eden repeated incredulously.

"Well, that's what Burt said when he came to see me! He said the two of you had had a fight, and you'd told him he'd never get McKinnon Meats, and he just wanted to see if you meant it or if it was just an idle threat."

"So you told him?"

"Well, there didn't seem to be much harm in it, seeing as how he already knew. I mean, as long as you'd told him yourself, it wasn't exactly a secret."

"Chad, why in God's name didn't you contact me before giving out that information?"

"I told you, he already knew! You'd told him. I wasn't really giving out any information."

"Come on, Ramsay," Garrett cut in. "No decent lawyer reveals his client's confidential business to anyone else."

"Well, I did hesitate at first. But, all things considered, it seemed—"

"How much did Burton offer you?" Garrett pressed.

The lawyer looked away. When he spoke, his voice was barely audible. "Six thousand."

Eden gasped. "You sold my confidence for six thousand dollars!"

"Eden, please! It wasn't like that! I never would have told Burton a thing if he hadn't convinced me he already knew! But, under the circumstances, I just couldn't see that it made any difference. And"—his voice dropped to a whisper, and he shrugged piteously—"I needed the money."

"If you needed money, why didn't you ask me? You know I would have helped you out, Chad."

"I couldn't. It was too embarrassing. I—well—after my wife died last year, I started going to Washington Park, to the races, a lot. It was a way to pass the time. Anyway, somehow, I just got in over my head. When Burt came to me, I really needed money bad. So—I told him what he wanted to know."

Eden shook her head reprovingly. "You could have at least told me about the incident, Chad."

"I didn't see any point in it. You'd just had Mara's wedding. You were happy. Why discuss the hard feelings between you and Burton?"

Looking from Garrett's stern, calculating expression to Eden's hurt, resigned eyes, the lawyer asked weakly, "Does it really make so much difference, Burton knowing about the will?"

Sighing, Eden shrugged. "Perhaps not. He would have found out sooner or later. At least this way, I'm here to help my grandchildren through the battle."

"You mean, you think Burton's going to cause trouble about it?"

"Oh, he already has," Eden replied confidently.

Her gaze shifted to Garrett, and she added. "I just wonder what he's planning next."

48
May 1890

Burton did not keep them in suspense for long. Arriving at the plant later that morning, Eden found that he had already been there and left.

"I showed him around, as you asked," James said. "Though I can't say it was a pleasure. I can see why Mara doesn't like him."

Eden nodded. "How is Mara? Not getting herself upset about Burt being in town?" Mara was seven months pregnant, so she rarely came in to the plant now.

"No, she's fine," James assured Eden. "For the most part, she just pretends Burton doesn't exist."

"Hmm. It might be pleasant if we could all do the same. Unfortunately, I've just received evidence that Mara, Miguel, and Garrett were right about Burton all along."

"You mean he's responsible for starting the investigation?"

"It looks as though he is. He probably thought that in an operation of our size the investigators were bound to find something amiss. Since they haven't in all these months, I'm afraid Burton is going to manufacture a problem."

Staring at her incredulously, James whispered, "Do you really think he'd go that far? I mean, now with the Kansas City plant involved, it's his problem, too. Anyway, he's got as much stake in McKinnon Meats as anyone, hasn't he?"

"Never mind why. Did Burton show any special interest in any part of the plant when you showed him around this morning?"

"Well, he did ask an awful lot of questions in the dressed-beef department. About where the shipments go, when they're sent out, who buys from us locally. Kenneth finally got exasperated with all the questions. Said he couldn't stand around talking all day when there was work to be done."

"I suppose Burton was offended?"

"Oh, no. He was very cordial the whole time. Only, it was

kind of a fake cordiality, if you know what I mean." James flushed. "Well, I guess I shouldn't say that. I keep forgetting that he *is* your son."

Smiling wryly, Eden said, "Sometimes I think people have been apologizing to me for not liking Burton all his life. But, I can't very well expect people to like him. To be honest, I don't like him, myself."

She paused, thinking. "Did he say where he was going, or when he'd be back?"

"Not really. He said he wanted to look around the yards a bit, and then he wanted to call on some old friends."

"That's an interesting thought. I wonder if Burton even has any friends." Eden sighed. "I wish Mara's mother had lived. She and I failed to see eye to eye on quite a number of things. But, at least she was a decent woman. Perhaps she could have checked Burton's scheming."

"I rather doubt that," James said. "After all, all your influence doesn't seem to have done much for him."

"Perhaps you're right." Changing the subject, she asked briskly, "Is there any pressing business I have to take care of this afternoon?"

"No. I think everything's under control."

"Then, I think I'll ride over to the Pinkerton Agency and hire some of their men to keep an eye on the plant, particularly the dressed-beef department."

Burton did not return to the plant that day, and did not come back to the Prairie Avenue mansion until near dawn. Letting himself in, he was surprised to find Eden and Garrett waiting for him in the parlor.

"Well," Eden said, "I'd begun to think you'd gone back to Kansas City without even saying good-bye."

"Forgive me, Mama. I really didn't even think of sending a message. But, I didn't expect you to wait up for me. Of course," Burton sneered, "I see you have your faithful friend to keep you company. You *do* have a home of your own, don't you, Garrett?"

"Certainly," Garrett said coolly. "You're welcome to visit it any time you're not too busy worrying about McKinnon Meats or visiting your old friends."

"As a matter of fact," Burton retorted defensively, "I did exchange several telegrams with the Kansas City plant today. Then, when I was poking around the stockyards, I ran into

Phil Armour. He took me home with him, and we got to reminiscing about old times and the Gold Rush days, and we both just lost all track of time."

Eden quirked her brows. "That must have been some discussion! Phil is a stickler for getting to bed by nine every night."

"Well, apparently he found my company stimulating enough to break his rules! Anyway, Mama, I didn't completely forget about the firm's problems. It occurred to me that it might be a good idea for me to call on all of your competitors here in Chicago."

"Oh?"

"It may be that, coming from out of town, with a fresh viewpoint, I might notice something in their attitude that you and the rest of the family might have missed."

Frowning, Eden asked, "Are you suggesting that another packer might be responsible for our being investigated?"

Burton shrugged. "We certainly can't overlook the possibility. It does seem strange, doesn't it, that McKinnon Meats is the only firm being investigated? And, we have to consider the fact that meat packing is a highly competitive business."

He paused, yawning and stretching. "Well, I don't know about you, but I'm exhausted. Don't wake me for breakfast. I think I'll just sleep in. But, I would appreciate the use of one of your carriages later on. I have an appointment to meet Nels Morris for lunch at Chapin & Gore's, on Monroe near State."

As Burton clomped upstairs, Garrett smiled wryly. "He certainly is putting on an outstanding performance, isn't he?"

Eden nodded. "Not that I believe a word of it. I'm sure he wasn't at the Armours' tonight."

"No. At least not until this hour. But, something tells me he will be at Chapin & Gore's. I'll check with Nels when his office opens. If they are meeting for lunch, I'm going to be there. It's a pity the restaurant doesn't admit women, or you could join us."

"Garrett, you don't really think Nels is involved in Burton's scheme?"

Shaking his head, Garrett replied, "No. At least not knowingly. But I've a feeling that lunch might be a turning point in this whole investigation. What better place to indict a meat-packer than at lunchtime at the most popular restaurant in Chicago?"

* * *

Despite her sleepless night, Eden had no trouble keeping awake in her office at McKinnon Meats. Upon her arrival, the Pinkerton guards hired the previous afternoon informed her that Burton had tried to enter the plant during the night, under the pretext of getting some papers for his mother. However, when his entry had been barred, he had not argued, and had left the grounds immediately.

About ten o'clock in the morning, Garrett stopped in to tell her Nelson Morris had confirmed his luncheon date with Burton and agreed to have Garrett join them.

Now, it was eleven-thirty, and Eden waited impatiently for afternoon and the possible answer to all the questions plaguing her mind.

James stuck his head in the office door and said, "Gram, there's a woman here to see you. Says she used to work for you. I didn't want to disturb you, but she insists it's important, and she can only talk to you."

Eden sighed. "Well then, I suppose you'd better bring her in. She can keep my mind off other problems, anyway."

A small, stooped woman with frightened eyes shuffled into the office. It was a moment before Eden recognized Mollie Flanagan, the Irishwoman who had befriended Jocelyn during the Civil War.

"Why, Mollie!" she exclaimed, rising to clasp the woman's hand. "It's been years! When did you leave our plant? About 1875?"

"Seventy-six," the old woman replied. "But my youngest boy, Danny, worked for you till just a few years ago."

"Ah, yes, Danny. He was in our slaughterhouse, wasn't he?"

Mollie nodded. "Until he started to weaken with the consumption."

"How is he now? Stronger?"

"He's dead," Mollie said flatly. "He died two weeks ago. A month after his little daughter, Bernadette."

"Oh, Mollie. I'm so sorry."

"Yes, it was a terrible thing. But, maybe it was the good Lord paying him back for his sins."

Eden frowned. "I remember Danny as a fine boy."

"He was, Mrs. McKinnon. Up until the last year. But then, he was so twisted by hurt and worry for his little Bernie that he kind of lost his mind. He did you a terrible wrong, Mrs. McKinnon."

Eden waited, beginning to suspect what was coming.

"After he left McKinnon Meats, he couldn't find another job to pay near as good. And, he was so weak, he had trouble keeping any job. Then, when little Bernie got sick, he was always struggling to pay for her care.

"Just when he didn't know where else to turn, your son came to him. I don't know where he got Danny's name. Anyway, he told Danny if he'd sign a paper, he'd give him five hundred dollars. Then he said if Danny could get more people to sign more papers like it, he'd give him fifty dollars for each one that signed."

Eden's mouth set in a grim line. Even when she had finally accepted that Burton was at the bottom of the investigation, she had never understood where the affidavits held by the Agriculture Department could have come from. Now she knew.

Perhaps she should have known all along. After all, how often had Burton expounded on the power of the dollar? Clearly, he had spoken from experience.

"Danny didn't do it to hurt you, Mrs. McKinnon," Mollie said hurriedly. "Truly, he didn't. He always had the greatest respect for you. He just needed the money so bad. Then, when things started turning up in the newspapers, he felt terrible. But, he didn't know what to do."

Eden was silent a moment, thinking. She glanced at her office clock. It was a quarter to noon.

"Mollie," she said, "can you take a ride downtown with me? To Chapin & Gore's on Monroe Street?"

"Chapin & Gore's? Isn't that a gentleman's restaurant? I thought they didn't allow ladies in."

"They don't. But, there are some people there I'd like you to talk to."

Mollie hesitated. "About Danny?"

"Yes. I'd like you to tell them what you told me." Seeing that Mollie was still hesitant, Eden pressed. "It can't hurt Danny now, Mollie. And, I promise you, nothing will be held against you or anyone in your family. But, what you've told me could save my firm, and the future of my own grandchildren."

"Well, Mrs. McKinnon, that's why I came to you. So, I guess I'll do whatever you ask."

*   *   *

Entering Chapin & Gore's, Burton masked his surprise and annoyance as he saw Garrett chatting with Nelson Morris.

A year younger than Burton, Morris, a native of the Black Forest in Germany, was one of the most respected meat-packers in Chicago. It was said that "Little Nels," as he was known in the Stockyards, could tell which part of the country a steer was raised in simply by tasting a steak. With packing plants in Chicago, Kansas City, and St. Joseph, Missouri, and ranches in Indiana, Texas, Nebraska, and South Dakota, Nelson Morris and Company was a major McKinnon competitor.

Looking up, Morris smiled, "Ah, Burt! I hope you don't mind some extra company. I ran into Garrett at the yards this morning and asked him to join us."

"Umm," Burton grunted. "I suppose that must have been around four o'clock, when you do your usual cattle buying. Mr. Martin was just leaving my mother's house about then."

Coughing discreetly, Morris glanced toward the dining room entrance. "Shall we go in before it gets too crowded?"

"If you wish." Burton nodded. "Louis has a table reserved for us. I've asked someone else to join us, too. I trust you both know Joe Medill of the *Chicago Tribune*?"

Both men nodded, exchanging a wondering glance as they followed Burton through the Chapin & Gore liquor store, into the connecting restaurant. As they stepped into the restaurant, they passed the series of ranges behind the lunch counter, where steaks roasted over the coals in plain view of restaurant patrons.

"Do you see anything tempting, Nels?" Burton asked. "If not, I've heard Louis will send a hack over to the stockyards to have your selection cut to order."

Morris smiled. "I don't think that will be necessary. I've never had a bad steak here. Still," he paused and sniffed, "there is a bit of an unusual odor in the restaurant today."

"Oh?" Burton's eyes widened. "I can't smell anything. Your nose must be as sensitive as your palate, Nels."

"Well, maybe it's just me I'm smelling! I spent the morning handling cattle and hogs. Sometimes that odor just doesn't wash off too easily. If I'm not careful, Chapin and Gore will be throwing me out on my ear for driving away their patrons!"

"Nonsense. The place is as crowded as I remember it! Ah,

here's Medill now!" Burton stood and waved the newspaper editor over to their table.

After they had ordered, Medill, a tall, stately man of sixty-seven, turned to Morris, "Tell me, Mr. Morris, is it true you can tell where a steer was bred by the taste of its steak?"

"Yes, it's an ability I've developed over the years. But, of course, meat is my business, Mr. Medill. I pride myself on knowing it well, just as you, I suspect, as a journalist, must pride yourself on recognizing the difference between fact and fiction."

Medill nodded. "Well said, Mr. Morris."

"Do you suppose," Burton asked, "that you could carry your ability one step further? Could you identify what packer a steak came from, simply by taste?"

Morris smiled and shook his head. "That's asking a bit much, Burt! For cured meats, perhaps. We all have our special recipes and processes. But, I doubt I could do it for fresh-dressed beef. Your mother and I, for example, both have ranches in Texas. We both buy only prime grade steers. How could I taste the difference?"

"You don't believe the charges then, that McKinnon's sells inferior or diseased meats?" Medill asked.

"Absolutely not! If I did, I wouldn't even be seen lunching with a McKinnon! Do you believe the stories, Mr. Medill?"

Medill shrugged. "I must reserve judgment. It seems the investigators have found no proof. Yet, there are scores of affidavits."

Frowning, Burton nodded, "I must say, the affidavits bother me immensely. I would never believe anything but good about my mother's firm, but why would anyone sign a false affidavit? What do you think, Garrett?"

Garrett stared at him coldly. "I think someone engineered the entire investigation with the hope of personal gain."

"That's an interesting opinion," Medill said. "Who would gain by such a plot?"

"Actually, no one," Garrett replied. "Revenge doesn't represent much of a material gain."

"Revenge?" Medill's eyes widened with interest. "Are you suggesting—"

His question was cut short by a discussion at the next table. "I tell you, there's something wrong with this steak! It tastes—it tastes positively putrid!"

The waiter looked around anxiously as heads turned toward

the complainer. "I'm very sorry you're not satisfied, sir. I'm
sure our manager, Mr. Pease, will be happy to have another
steak prepared for you."

"I don't want another steak! This thing's turned my stomach so I can't even think of eating! What about you, Ambrose,
are you going to stay and eat this garbage?"

"Well," the man's companion said timidly, "mine does
taste a bit strange."

"Please, sirs," the waiter whispered urgently, "there's no
need to cause a disturbance. I'm sure Mr. Pease will be glad
to authorize a free meal for you anytime, at your convenience."

"Hmph! I never intend to set foot in this establishment
again!"

The man stomped out, followed by his friend, leaving a
wake of raised eyebrows and whispered comments.

"Well," Burton said with a smile, "I suppose in a restaurant this busy someone is bound to be dissatisfied now and
then."

Before any of his companions could reply, the waiter brought
their meals.

"All right, Mr. Morris," Medill challenged, "tell us where
this steak spent its grazing years."

Morris cut into his steak and took a bite. Almost instantly,
he frowned, his frown deepening as he chewed thoughtfully.

"Something wrong, Nels?" Burton asked.

Morris nodded, continuing to chew. He cut another bite
and lifted it to his nose.

"I don't think this beef is fresh," he said finally. "It's been
adulterated with something—boric acid, salicylic acid, I'm
not sure."

"A preservative?" Burton frowned. "That seems rather
unlikely. With the quantity of business Chapin & Gore's
handles, I'm sure they don't need to keep their beef from one
day to the next. They must buy fresh daily."

Medill had begun to sniff suspiciously around his steak.
"This acid," he asked, "is it poisonous?"

"In large enough quantities it could be," Morris said. "There
are some experiments going on with boric and salicylic acid as
preservatives right now. Nothing conclusive yet. Certainly no
one has yet proven them safe."

"But what would even be the purpose of using them?"
Medill pressed. "Surely Chapin & Gore's has an icehouse or
iceboxes to keep their daily shipments fresh."

"I'm sure they do," Morris agreed. "Which is why this seems especially strange."

He waved to their waiter, who hurried over to their table. "Would you happen to know," Morris asked, "when this meat was delivered to the restaurant?"

"This morning, sir."

"You're certain of that?"

"Yes, sir. All our meats are cooked and served the same day they are delivered."

"Are they ever treated with anything?" Burton asked.

The waiter frowned. "I don't understand, sir. The steaks are seasoned, of course, but treated?"

"You've never heard of anyone injecting them with boric or salicylic acid?" Burton pressed.

Horrified, the waiter shook his head. "No, of course not, sir! I don't know why—would you like to speak to Mr. Pease?"

"Yes, I think we should."

When the manager came to their table, Burton said, "Louis, Mr. Morris here seems to think his steak was injected with something. Boric acid or some such thing. Could that be possible?"

The manager looked affronted. "I assure you, sir, none of our meats are ever adulterated in any way."

Rubbing his chin thoughtfully, Burton asked, "Then, you're saying that Mr. Morris is wrong?"

Flustered, Pease shrugged. "I hardly know what to say, sir! I know Mr. Morris's reputation. But I can state positively that no one in this restaurant would ever inject anything into our steaks."

"What about someone from outside the restaurant?" Medill asked. "Would a packer adulterate the meat, to preserve it, perhaps?"

"I shouldn't think there would be any reason to, sir. We buy all our meats from packers right here in Chicago. It's not as if they have to transport them any distance."

"Of course, if your supplier's stock hasn't been moving, he might have been tempted to use a preservative," Burton mused.

Garrett, who had been sampling his own steak, dropped his fork and scowled at Burton. "What the hell are you driving at, Burt?"

Burton shrugged. "Nothing, really. Is your steak all right?"

"No, as a matter of fact, it's not. And something tells me

you know why!" Looking up at the manager, he asked, "Louis, where did your meat order come from today?"

The manager glanced around the table apprehensively. "I couldn't say, without checking. We deal with all the major Chicago packers."

"McKinnon's?" Garrett demanded.

"Yes, we buy from them. They've always given us good quality, so we've never believed the publicity against them."

"And today? Did McKinnon's deliver here today?"

"Wait a minute!" Burton broke in hotly. "Are you accusing my mother's plant—"

"No," Garrett cut him off calmly, "I'm accusing you!" Rising from the table, he continued, "Louis, I suggest that you close down the restaurant for the rest of the day and dispose of the meat that was delivered here this morning. McKinnon Meats will reimburse you for the meat and for the loss of revenue for the day."

"You aren't authorized to make that kind of offer!" Burton snapped.

Garrett cocked an eyebrow. "I think I am. I'm quite certain Eden will back me up." Starting for the door, he nodded to Morris. "Sorry your lunch was ruined, Nels. Stop by my place on Indiana any time, and I'll try to make it up to you."

Shifting his eyes to Medill, Garrett went on, "Joe, you might want to come with us, to get the rest of your story. But, I'm afraid it won't be quite the story Burton here had in mind when he invited you to lunch."

Following Garrett through the liquor store and onto Monroe Street, Burton spluttered, "You don't know what you're talking about, Martin! You've always had it in for me! You and all the other power-hungry, money-hungry men who've wanted McKinnon Meats! I guess my mother fooled you all, staying alive so long, staying in command of the firm."

Garrett smiled grimly as he stepped onto the sidewalk and recognized Eden's carriage. "Speaking of your mother, here she is now!"

Eden poked her head from the carriage, smiling brightly at her scowling son. "Oh, Burton, I'm so glad I was able to catch you! I hated to think of waiting till dinner, or whenever you might decide to come home, to give you my news. Mrs. Flanagan here has solved the mystery about the affidavits!"

Paling slightly, Burton turned back to face the curious gaze of Joseph Medill. "It was good lunching with you, Joe," he said hurriedly. "I'll be in touch with you again very soon."

"Oh, no," Garrett said, taking Medill's arm and pulling him toward the carriage. "I think Joe and the readers of the *Tribune* will be every bit as interested in this story as you and I."

49
August 1890

Eden smiled radiantly as she stood in the first pew of Plymouth Congregational Church, watching Dr. Frank Gunsaulus baptize her great-grandchildren.

In July, Mara had given birth to twins, a boy and a girl. She and James had named them Edward Halsey Merritt and Jennifer McKinnon Merritt.

Miguel, still unmarried but thriving at the Double M North, had come to Chicago for the baptism. He and Paige were godparents for little Jennifer. Philip Armour's younger son, P.D., Jr. and his wife May, were Edward's godparents.

Kenneth Harrigan and his eight children, Paige's stepchildren, filled the pew on the other side of the aisle. He gazed at his wife with such tenderness that it warmed Eden, and she said a silent prayer of thanks for her daughter's happiness.

Feeling another pair of eyes on her, she looked up at Garrett, standing beside her, his blue eyes filled with the same love that had strengthened her through forty-eight years. She reached out and squeezed his hand, her eyes sparkling with the secrets they would always share.

At the end of the service, as they stepped outside, Garrett took her arm. "It's a beautiful day, isn't it?" he whispered.

"Yes. Beautiful in every way. It's hard to believe anything could seem so perfect after what we went through a few months ago."

"Did Burton even know his grandchildren were being baptized today?"

Eden shrugged. "I'm not sure. You know, Mara still refuses to think of him as her father or the grandfather of her children. But, I think Paige wrote to him at the prison."

She paused, her expression becoming serious. "I wonder if he's repenting for what he did?"

"I wouldn't count on it. No doubt he's very sorry he's in prison. But, if he were out, he'd still be doing all he could to get the firm for himself or destroy it for anyone else."

Sighing, Eden nodded. "I'm afraid you're right. Never, in my worst nightmares, did I imagine he would do anything so terrible as to poison our meats—to put innocent people's lives in danger!"

She shivered at the memory. "I should have hired someone from Pinkerton's to follow him instead of just guarding the plant. Then maybe he would have been seen around the beef when it was delivered to Chapin & Gore's. And we would have suspected he'd done something to harm it."

"Well, there's no point in berating yourself about it now. Everything turned out all right. He didn't kill anyone. He didn't even manage to make anyone sick. The most he was responsible for was a few lost appetites—and getting caught in his own scheme."

"It's a good thing you were there to do the catching."

"Oh, Nels or Medill would have figured it out eventually. Now, enough of this discussion. This is supposed to be a celebration, remember?"

Eden smiled. "Yes, and what a celebration! Seventy-eight years ago this month, my mother was carrying me, a squalling baby, away from the tiny settlement of Chicago. Now, here I am, mistress of a fortune, in the Chicago metropolis of one million people, celebrating the baptism of my great-grandchildren!"

Turning, she saw Mara and James approaching, each holding a baby. "They behaved like little angels, didn't they?" Eden said. "Not even a whimper when Dr. Gunsaulus sprinkled the water on them!"

Mara laughed. "Yes, but even angels need their diapers changed now and then! We'll see you back at your house, Gram."

Eden watched, still smiling as Miguel helped Mara and James into their carriage and climbed in after them. Then Garrett helped her into her own carriage and settled himself beside her.

"I've been thinking," she said as they started north, toward Prairie and Eighteenth. "Perhaps we ought to consider changing the firm's name."

"Oh?" Garrett looked amused. "Can't you ever stop working, even for a family celebration?"

"I'm serious, Garrett! After all the bad publicity McKinnon Meats got in the last year, it might be wise to get a fresh start in the public's eyes."

"I don't think that's really necessary. Your sales are getting back to normal now that everyone's convinced McKinnon Meats never did anything wrong."

"I know. But it will be easier for everyone to forget the whole scandal if we have a new name. Besides, it will be a good way to greet the coming new century."

"What name were you thinking of?"

"How does M & M Provisions sound? It seems appropriate. It could stand for Mara and Miguel, or McKinnon and Merritt—"

"Or McKinnon and Martin," Garrett inserted laughingly.

She smiled. "That, too, of course!" Her smile broadening, she burst out, "You know, all of a sudden, I feel more like seventeen than seventy-eight! Even with all the heartache Burton's caused me, all the uncertainty I'll always feel about how much I was responsible for the man he became, I still have a really wonderful life!

"Oh, I've lost enough loved ones and shed enough tears along the way, but I still have so much. Paige and her family. Miguel. Mara and Jimmy and the twins."

"And me!" Garrett finished.

Her blue-green eyes sparkling, she squeezed his hand. "Oh, yes! Thank God I've always had you!"

Pausing reflectively, she added, "I guess that you and I are something like the starflower."

He frowned slightly. "The starflower?"

"Yes. Black Eagle and I used to find them along the woodland streams when I was just a little girl. Beautiful little white star-shaped flowers. I haven't even thought about them in years."

Garrett slid an arm around her shoulders. "And how, may I ask, are we like starflowers?"

"It's the way they grow. Every stem is divided into two thin stalks, each of which is crowned by a star-shaped flower."

"So, they're two separate flowers, but they're always connected?"

Eden nodded. "All their lives."

"Then I think, my love, that your comparison is more than fitting. We grew pretty far apart in some years, but I'm sure I never could imagine a life that was not connected to yours in some way."

"Nor could I," she whispered, brushing his cheek with her lips. "Lord knows I tried enough times. But there was always that thin, strong stem holding us together."

Cupping her chin in his hand, he gazed at her with his penetrating blue eyes. "Aren't you glad that bond was always there?"

Eden's eyes shone with all the eager love of a young girl. "Very glad. I'll always be very glad."

ABOUT THE AUTHOR

LYNN LOWERY was born and raised in Cleveland, Ohio, but
has lived in the Chicago area since 1967. Her fascination
with Chicago's early history led her to write *Starflower*.
Chicago history also plays a major role in her most recent
novel, *Moonflower*. Her first two romantic historical novels,
Sweet Rush of Passion and *Loveswept*, had nineteenth-
century Russian backgrounds, the result of her college
Russian major and travels in Russia. She is also the author
of *Larissa* and *Lorelei*. Lynn Lowery is married to James
Hahn, who is also a writer.

The captivating new bestseller by the author of
A WOMAN OF SUBSTANCE

VOICE
OF THE
HEART

by Barbara Taylor Bradford

Katherine Tempest, actress, star, ravishing paradox. Her greatest role was her own life, supported by the best of friends and lovers—until she betrayed them all.

Victor Mason, film idol and producer, gambled his career and fortune on the unknown actress who would soon make his nightmares come true.

Lady Francesca Cunningham, English aristocrat and biographer, gave her trust and loyalty unwisely, and far too soon.

Nicholas Latimer, bestselling novelist, was immune to Katherine's dangerous allure—until he fell passionately in love. . . .

Four destinies inextricably intertwined; twenty-three years of blind ambition, incestuous friendship and reckless love that swept them from the playgrounds and palaces of Europe to New York's glittering towers, from the hectic crossroads of Hollywood and Vine to the silent VOICE OF THE HEART.

Buy VOICE OF THE HEART, on sale March 1, 1984, wherever Bantam paperbacks are sold, or use this handy coupon below for ordering:

Bantam Books, Inc., Dept. BTB, 414 East Golf Road, Des Plaines, Ill. 60016

Please send me _____ copies of VOICE OF THE HEART (23920-1 • $4.50). I am enclosing $_____ (please add $1.25 to cover postage and handling, send check or money order—no cash or C.O.D.'s please).

Mr/Ms _____

Address_____

City/State _____ Zip _____

Please allow four to six weeks for delivery. This offer expires 7/84. Price and availability subject to change without notice.

VVG+H

HISTORICAL ROMANCES

Read some of Bantam's Best in Historical Romances!

☐ 23798	**Star Flower**—Lynn Lowery	$3.50
☐ 22927	**Daughters of New Orleans**— Emily Jane Toth	$3.50
☐ 14628	**White Trash**—George McNeill	$3.50
☐ 23056	**Jenetta**—Audrey Ellis	$3.50
☐ 20183	**Cayo**—Saliee O'Brien	$3.50
☐ 22933	**Ever After**—Elswyth Thane	$3.50
☐ 23581	**Carolina Woman**— Justin Channing	$3.95
☐ 23058	**Yankee Stranger**—Elswyth Thane	$2.95
☐ 22581	**Dawn's Early Light**— Elswyth Thane	$2.95

<u>Prices and availability subject to change without notice.</u>